# Law
## of the
# Land

## Forge Books by Elmer Kelton

# ELMER KELTON

# Law of the Land

## Stories of the Old West

A TOM DOHERTY ASSOCIATES BOOK
NEW YORK

This is a work of fiction. All of the characters, organizations, and events portrayed in these stories are either products of the author's imagination or are used fictitiously.

LAW OF THE LAND

A Forge Book
Published by Tom Doherty Associates
120 Broadway
New York, NY 10271

www.tor-forge.com

Forge® is a registered trademark of Macmillan Publishing Group, LLC.

ISBN 978-1-250-77516-0

Our books may be purchased in bulk for promotional, educational, or business use. Please contact your local bookseller or the Macmillan Corporate and Premium Sales Department at 1-800-221-7945, extension 5442, or by email at MacmillanSpecialMarkets@macmillan.com.

First Edition: November 2021
First Mass Market Edition: November 2022

Printed in the United States of America

0  9  8  7  6  5  4  3  2  1

# Copyright Acknowledgments

"North of the Big River" originally published in *Ranch Romances,* September 29, 1950, Vol. 161, No. 1. Also published in *There's Always Another Chance and Other Stories,* Fort Concho Museum Press, 1986.

"The Ghost of Two Forks" originally published in *Ghost Towns,* edited by Martin H. Greenberg and Russell Davis, Pinnacle Books, Kensington Publishing Corp., 2010.

"Lonesome Ride to Pecos" originally published as "Lonesome Ride" in *Ranch Romances,* April 29, 1949, Vol. 151, No. 4. Also published in *The Big Brand,* Bantam Books, 1986 and 1990.

"Apache Patrol" originally published in *Ranch Romances,* March 14, 1952, Vol. 170, No. 4. Also published in *There's Always Another Chance and Other Stories,* Fort Concho Museum Press, 1986.

"The Last Indian Fight in Kerr County" originally published in *Roundup,* edited by Stephen Overholser, Doubleday, 1982. Also published in *ReadWest,* Goldminds Publishing, 2011.

"Uncle Jeff and the Gunfighter" originally published in *The Pick of the Roundup,* edited by Stephen Payne, Avon Books, 1963. Also published in *The Big Brand,* Bantam Books, 1986 and 1990.

"Sellout" originally published in *Ranch Romances,* May 26, 1950, Vol. 158, No. 4. Also published in *There's Always Another Chance and Other Stories,* Fort Concho Museum Press, 1986.

"Die by the Gun" originally published in *Ranch Romances,* January 15, 1954, Vol. 183, No. 1. Also published in *Ranch Romances,* August 1967, Vol. 219, No. 3; *There's Always Another Chance and Other Stories,* Fort Concho Museum Press, 1986.

# CONTENTS

# Law
## of the
# Land

# THE FUGITIVE BOOK

**F**itzhugh Battles realized there were many things in the world he did not know for certain, but of one thing he was sure: outlaws were no damned good and ought to be ridden down like rabid coyotes. One item always with him, besides his Texas Ranger badge, bowie knife and six-shooter, was a handwritten notebook listing names and descriptions of wanted men. The fugitive book was part of every Ranger's equipment, to be consulted frequently and added to as necessary.

Few things gave him more inner satisfaction than to scratch through a name and write either apprehended or executed. It did not matter whether he or some other Ranger had done the apprehending or killing. What mattered was that one more miscreant had been locked away or buried, out of everyone's misery. The world would be better off when the last member of that lawless breed had been marked off the list. He did not expect to see it happen during his lifetime, unless that life was much longer than he felt he had any right to expect.

Now Battles was on his way to find and arrest—or if the situation warranted, kill—one Giles Pritchard, wanted in Waco for robbery and murder. The authorities had determined that Pritchard owned a ranch in Comanche County. It seemed plausible he had fled in that direction.

Battles had taken on this job with pleasure. He looked forward to working with the county sheriff, John Durham. They had served together as Rangers a couple of years until Durham had tired of the long horseback trips the Ranger service often required. He was a stay-close-to-home type. He also hated the frequent confrontations with fugitives, sometimes necessitating that they be made to bleed a little, and occasionally a lot. He had decided to run for local office, where such confrontations were likely to be less frequent.

Battles, by contrast, enjoyed the traveling, seeing different country, never remaining in one place long enough to become bored with it. The more he saw of horse thieves and robbers and murderers, the more his contempt grew, the more he was gratified when he saw them brought to ground. If that required spilling blood, well . . . they should have invested their efforts in whatever honest occupation the Lord had fitted them for.

He rode past several sandy-land farms. Most of them appeared to have yielded up good summer crops. He thought if he ever wearied of Ranger life he might enjoy settling down on such a place. Even more, he might enjoy ranching, raising cattle on the rolling grasslands which still dominated this part of the state a hundred miles beyond Fort Worth. But that was a long time in the future, if it was to be at all. In Battles's chosen line of work, he had no assurance that there would be a future.

The courthouse was no challenge to find; it was the tallest building in town, though that was hardly enough to brag about. Battles had been there before. He tied his horse and rifled through his saddlebags, sorting out the papers he would need.

Sheriff John Durham met him in the hallway, his hand outstretched, a broad grin lighting the place like sunshine. "Fitz Battles! Saw you through the window. I've been afraid some sneakin' hog thief killed you and it never made the newspapers this far out."

Durham was about thirty. At forty, Battles had had an extra ten years of sun, wind and strife to carve the lines deeper into his face. Durham's strong hand gripped like a vise. Battles tried to squeeze even harder and see if he could make Durham wince. "It'll take somebody with a lot more ambition than a hog thief has got. Glad to see the voters haven't kicked you out of office yet."

"I'd invite you down the street for a drink, but it wouldn't do for the public to see two officers of the law drinkin' whiskey in the light of the day. Come on in. I've got a bottle of contraband in my desk. It ain't prime, but it's cheap."

Battles was impatient to get at the task he had been sent for, but he enjoyed visiting with an old friend, reliving shared experiences, hot trails and cold camps. At length, when they had momentarily run out of talk, Battles laid the papers in front of the sheriff. "Do you know a man named Giles Pritchard?"

Durham looked surprised. "Sure. Got him a little ranch over west of town. Buys and sells horses, peddles them all over the country. Him and me punched cattle together once down on the Pecan Bayou. You got business with him?"

Battles pointed to the arrest warrant. "Seems like he created himself some trouble over in Waco. Best anybody could figure, he and a kid helper took a little string of horses over on the Bosque River and sold them to a trader. Must not have got as much as he wanted, because he stopped off at a bank in Waco that was flush with fresh cotton-crop money. He made a six-shooter withdrawal. Shot a teller dead. Him and his helper got away in a high lope."

"How do you know it was him?"

"Pritchard had a stroke of bad luck. The trader who bought the horses happened to be in the bank too, ducked down where Pritchard wouldn't see him. Pritchard may not know he's been identified."

Durham frowned. "Shootin' a banker could be considered a service. The country would be better off without so many of them high-interest highbinders."

"Same as it could do without so many lawyers, but the law calls for due process. Pritchard's method was undue process."

Reluctance was strong in Durham's eyes. "I always knew Giles was a shade too wild for his own good, but I never would've pictured him doin' such a thing as this. You sure there ain't been some mistake?"

"There was, and he made it."

The sheriff's face pinched hard. "What do you want of me?"

"You know it's Ranger policy to involve local peace officers whenever we can. I'd like you to take me out to Pritchard's place and assist me in the arrest."

Battles could see that Durham was wrestling hard with his doubts. Durham said, "I don't guess you know that Giles got married a year or so ago? I was at the weddin'. Alicia's about as pretty a girl as I ever met."

"I'm sorry Pritchard's a friend of yours. It doesn't change what he's done."

"His old daddy was one of the finest men I ever knew. I was a pallbearer at his funeral."

"It wasn't his daddy who killed the teller."

"The old man worried a right smart about Giles's streak of wildness. I'm glad he's not here to see this."

Slowly and with reluctance, Durham retrieved his hat from a rack in the corner. "It's ten miles out there. We'd better go down the street and get us some dinner before we start."

Durham had little to say on the long ride to the Pritchard place. He would begin to relate a story about something he and Pritchard had done together, or something about Pritchard's kindly old father. He would break off the stories before they were finished.

Battles said, "There must be a side to him that you never wanted to recognize. Flaws in him that you never saw."

"I always believed in givin' a man the benefit of the doubt."

"Give it to the wrong man and he's apt to kill you. At the least he'll leave you hurtin'."

"I've never known anybody who took as much pleasure in runnin' down outlaws as you do. I've seen you get damned near drunk on it."

"Bury enough friends and you'll get to where you hate them like strychnine. A couple of them snakes came in off of the railroad one time and killed my old daddy. Killed him for two dollars and a pocket watch. I tracked them down and shot them both like hydrophoby dogs. After that, I joined the Rangers." Battles scowled. "If it was up to me I'd stomp every last one of them like I'd stomp a scorpion."

He saw a small frame house ahead. By the dread in Durham's face, he surmised that this was Pritchard's home.

The sheriff said, "Knowin' your feelin's, I'd like to be the one serves the papers. I'd hate to have you shoot Giles when it's not necessary."

Battles was dubious about turning the responsibility over to a lawman so personally involved. "He's apt to be desperate, knowin' what he faces. You sure you want to do it?"

"He's my friend."

He's a murderer, Battles thought. This is where friendship ought to end. But his own liking for Durham caused him to waver. "All right, but watch him. He may not be as friendly as you think."

They rode up to a rough picket fence in front of the house. Durham dismounted. "You stay here, Fitz. I'll go talk to him."

Battles began having serious second thoughts as he watched Durham step up onto the narrow porch and knock on the door facing. "Giles, this is John Durham. I need to talk to you."

After a long minute that seemed like five, a young woman came to the door. She looked anxiously at the sheriff, then past him to Battles, who remained on his horse. "What do you want with him?"

"There's been some trouble over at Waco. I need to talk to him."

The woman's voice was shaky. "He's not here. He's out helpin' a neighbor work cattle."

Even at a distance, Battles knew she was lying. He had seen through far better liars than this woman would ever be. He could tell by the sheriff's uncertain manner that Durham sensed it too.

Durham said, "I hate to do this, Alicia, but I need to look through the house."

"No, John, please." The woman turned quickly and shouted, "Run, Giles! Run!"

Almost before the words were out of her mouth, Battles was spurring his horse around the side of the house. He saw a man bolt from the back door and sprint toward the barn, rifle in his hand. Pritchard was feverishly trying to work the lever, but it appeared jammed. Battles overran him and leveled his pistol. He fired it into the ground in front of the fugitive. The bullet raised a puff of dust.

Battles said, "The next one goes in your ear." Pritchard stopped and turned to face the Ranger. Eyes wide with fear, he dropped the rifle. "Don't shoot me. For God's sake, don't."

"I expect there was a teller in Waco said the same thing to you, or tried to. You shot him anyway."

Pritchard seemed so frightened he could barely control his voice. "Waco? Ain't never been in Waco."

"There's a witness back there who says different."

"What're you goin' to do with me?"

"Take you to Waco. Let you stand before your accusers."

Pritchard's eyes darted wildly back and forth. Battles thought he was probably already imagining that thick, slick rope around his neck, choking, strangling.

Durham hurried out the back door. He anxiously looked Pritchard over, his anxiety giving way to relief. "I thought Fitz had shot you. Damn it, why did you run?"

"I was scared. When Alicia hollered, all I could think of was to light out."

Battles observed, "If you were innocent, you had no reason to be afraid of us. You could've figured we stopped in for coffee."

"I'm afraid when I see a Ranger. They been known to shoot a man for no reason."

Battles said, "You took time to grab a rifle."

"Instinct. I never had no intention of usin' it."

That was a lie, Battles thought. In his panic Pritchard had somehow jammed it. Otherwise he would have used it, or tried to. Of that, Battles was certain.

Durham said, "I hate to, Giles, but I've got to put you under arrest. Ranger Battles has got a warrant."

The young woman came out sobbing. She threw her arms around Pritchard. Durham was apologetic. "I'm sorry, Alicia, but I've got to abide by the law. Maybe the witness was mistaken. It'll all come out in court."

The woman's gaze moved to Battles, crackling with unspoken accusation. Battles wished he had an explanation that would ease her mind, but the law was the law. He was here to serve it. The longer she glared at him, though, the less he regretted not having something comforting to say. He considered her loyalty sadly misplaced.

He saw then the way the sheriff looked at the woman, and he thought he understood some of the reason for Durham's reluctance. The boy has gone blind. He's in love with her himself. Hell of a note this is.

Durham asked, "Do you want to go to Comanche with us, Alicia?"

Pritchard spoke quickly, "No, Alicia, you stay and take care of the stock. Send your brother to town."

Brother. Battles chewed hard on that. Nobody had

identified Pritchard's helper, who had remained outside with their horses during the holdup. He was
probably someone unknown in Waco. Witnesses had
described him as a clean-faced boy, probably under
twenty. The whole thing had happened so fast that
nobody had taken a good look. Most had hunkered
down, hoping not to be struck by a bullet.

Battles had found over the years that excited eye-
witnesses to such affairs rarely saw everything the
same way. He had known of black horses being described as white.

He was relieved that the woman would not be going to town with them. Women's tears had always
been bad for his digestion. They were one reason he
had never seriously contemplated marriage.

As they rode, Battles quietly asked the sheriff, "Do
you know anything about her brother?"

Durham shook his head. "Never knew she had
one. Could be a black sheep they don't like to talk
about."

Black sheep. Possibly one who wouldn't mind
being a partner in a bank robbery, Battles thought.

Durham was evidently thinking along the same
lines. "I still can't believe it was Giles did that bank
job. But if he did—if, mind you—then it might be
that her brother was the one ridin' with him. Makes
sense, sort of. I can't see Giles doin' such a thing on
his own. If he did it, I'll bet her brother coaxed him
into it."

Durham was still resisting the notion that his long-
time friend was an outlaw. Battles thought it better for
a peace officer not to have many really close friends. It
put him in a painfully tight spot if he had to bring the
weight of the law down on one of them.

He said, "If you're harborin' any doubts about

Pritchard bein' guilty, you'd just as well put them out of your mind. He's got the rattlesnake smell all over him."

Durham continued to resist. "Somebody had to've led him astray."

"For your sake, I'd like to think you're right and I'm wrong." Battles didn't, though, not for a moment.

Durham said, "I feel awful sorry for Alicia. This'll be terrible for her."

"That teller may have had a wife. It's not easy for her, either."

Battles was tempted to say, *Look at the other side of the coin. With Pritchard out of the way, maybe you'll have a chance of winning her for yourself.*

He had the good judgment to keep his mouth shut. Dusk was giving up to darkness when they led the handcuffed Pritchard into the jail. Battles gave the cell door all his strength so it would clang hard. The windows rattled loose in their frames. The sound had a finality about it like the dropping of a trapdoor in a gallows. The sound had always brought him a warm satisfaction when he locked away an outlaw.

Sheriff Durham stared through the bars at his friend. "Giles, if you needed money I wish you'd come to me. You and Alicia could have anything I own, and I'd go on your note if that wasn't enough."

Pritchard slumped on the hard cot. "Damned old dry ranches, I don't see why anybody would want one in the first place. First they work you down to a nub, then they starve you the rest of the way to death."

To Battles that was as good as an outright confession, but he knew Durham, though swaying, was still looking for a different answer.

Durham's aging jailer turned the key in the lock.

He said, "John, I expect you and the Ranger are hungry. You-all go get you somethin' to eat. I'll be here."

Durham shook his head. "I couldn't eat. Low as I feel. I'd choke on the first bite. Fitz, you and him go."

The jailer was a gangly old man, thin as a willow switch, and looked as if he needed a meal. Several of them, in fact.

Battles cast a glance back toward the prisoner. "John, I know he's been your friend, but you can't look at him that way anymore. The longer he thinks about what's ahead of him, the more desperate he'll get. He'd kill you if it meant he could get away."

Durham nodded a sad acceptance. "I won't give him the chance."

"All right." Battles jerked his head at the jailer. "Come along. I'm hungry enough to eat a mule."

The restaurant—that term was too high-toned to fit the reality—was manned by a chuckwagon cook who had decided he liked life in town better than camping under the open skies every night. The food was tasty and filling, though far from fancy. The jailer lit into it as if he had not eaten in a week. Battles wondered what kind of wages Comanche County paid its employees.

The jailer said, "Odd name, Battles. Where'd you get it?"

"From my daddy and granddaddy. They said it came over from Ireland with some of my ancestors. Said they were fighters of the first water. Guess that's why they took the name Battles."

"Or maybe they favored strong drink and the name was supposed to be Bottles."

"That's possible. I doubt they were much hand at writin' and spellin'."

Battles was never one to eat heavily. He was used to long rides, and those were best taken on a lank belly. He leaned his chair back and watched the jailer finish everything on the table. It had been a stressful day. He was about ready to find a bed somewhere.

He heard the shots and knew instinctively where they came from. He jumped up, knocking his chair over, and took three long strides toward the door. He hit the dirt street on the run. Down toward the jail, people were shouting. Against the lamplight he saw two dark figures jump up on horses and spur away. One looked back just long enough for Battles to know he was Giles Pritchard.

He drew his pistol but realized a shot at this distance would be useless. More than likely he would simply hit some innocent bystander. There were not enough innocent people in the world as it was.

He saw that the second rider was slumped in the saddle. Pritchard brought his horse up even with him and held him in the saddle.

Battles ran for the jail, gratified that John Durham had hit one of them, anyway. It stood to reason that Pritchard's helper on the bank robbery had broken him out. Send your brother, Pritchard had told his wife. Several townsmen were inside ahead of Battles. Two knelt over Durham, stretched out on the floor. Battles felt a chill as he saw blood pumping from a hole in Durham's chest. He knew the sheriff had no chance.

One of the men saw Battles's badge. "You a Ranger?"

"I am."

"One of the boys went for the doctor. Don't you think you ought to be out chasin' whoever it was done this?"

"I'd just lose them in the dark." He dropped to one knee and leaned over Durham. "How'd it happen, John?"

Durham struggled to speak. The words came slowly and painfully, with long breaks between as he struggled for breath. The gist of it was that Pritchard's partner had burst in from the street, face covered by a neckerchief, pointed a pistol and demanded that Pritchard be set free.

"Anybody you ever saw before?"

Durham weakly shook his head. "Couldn't tell." He coughed. "I opened the cell . . . grabbed my gun . . . then he shot me."

"Pritchard?"

"His partner." Durham coughed again, spitting up blood. "But I hit . . . I know I did."

Battles raised up, voice raw with impatience. "Where's that doctor at?"

Even as he spoke, he knew a doctor could do little.

Battles clenched a fist. Outlaws. He wished he could string them all up, one at a time, slowly, letting them kick and choke to the last feeble heartbeat. He blinked away the burning in his eyes.

The doctor came, carrying a small black bag. Nothing in it was going to help much. A rattling sound came from Durham's chest. His hands flexed, he groaned, and life left him. The doctor closed the sightless eyes and looked up. "Can some of you boys carry him over to the livery? I'll rouse up the undertaker." He turned to Battles. "What're you going to do, Ranger?"

"I'll follow their tracks as far as it takes, even if that's plumb to Argentina."

"You'd better get yourself some sleep, then. It's a long way to South America."

Battles considered rolling out his blankets on hay at the wagonyard, but he knew he would never go to sleep. The images of Durham and Pritchard and the woman Alicia would keep running through his mind, along with the imagined face of Alicia's brother. If Durham's aim had been up to his capabilities, Alicia would have two men to mourn—her brother and her husband. He wondered if she was aware of Durham's feelings for her. If so, that made three.

Either by gun or by rope, Giles Pritchard would pay for this.

Several townsmen had chased after the fugitives. Battles reasoned that they had probably trampled out any nearby tracks that might have been helpful. Sleepy-eyed, his stomach in a turmoil, Battles played a hunch and rode in darkness, westward in the direction of Pritchard's place.

He figured it was a good bet that Pritchard and his partner would head there to pick up provisions and, more than likely, the Waco loot. Pritchard would know he could no longer remain here. It was anybody's guess where he would try to go. Mexico, perhaps, though it was far to the south. The Pecos River country, maybe, and beyond it the Davis Mountains. Or he might head north for the Red River and Indian Territory.

He would go to hell, if Battles had his way. Dawn's first light revealed the Pritchard house ahead. Battles drew the rifle. It was more dependable than the six-shooter except at close range. He considered firing it into the house to try to rattle Pritchard if he were still inside. He decided that would present too great a danger to Alicia. This was none of her doing. She had made a poor choice in picking a husband. She had had no choice in her brother.

Battles bent low in the saddle to present as small a target as possible and let his horse plod on toward the house. The rising sun was at his back, a point in his favor. A rifle flashed in a front window, and he jumped to the ground, running for the protection of a large oak tree. He fired at the window, regretting the danger to Alicia Pritchard but seeing no alternative.

The tree's trunk was not thick enough to hide him completely, though it made him less of a target. He waited for a second shot, then fired immediately upon seeing the flash. He heard a cry and hoped it was from Pritchard or his partner, not the woman.

Several long strides carried him to the small porch and into the house. Holding his arm, Pritchard sat on the kitchen floor amid shards of glass. Blood seeped between his fingers. "You busted my arm," he screamed. "Busted it all to hell."

Battles picked up the rifle Pritchard had used. The barrel was hot. "One arm'll do you where you're goin'. Where's your partner?"

"My partner?" Pritchard blinked at him, eyes watering.

"The man who was with you. Your wife's brother, if my guess is right."

Pritchard cried in pain but jerked his head toward a doorway that led to the bedroom. Battles checked the load in his rifle, then dashed through the door, holding the weapon ready.

On the bed lay Alicia Pritchard, her oversized shirt soaked with dried and drying blood. He could not bring himself to touch her. The claylike color in her face told him she was dead.

Trembling, he returned to Giles Pritchard. "The blood's too old. My shots couldn't have killed her."

Pritchard gritted his teeth, his voice bordering on a shriek. "John Durham, damn him. All he had to do was let me go. He didn't have to grab a gun. Wasn't nothin' she could do but shoot him."

Battles's jaw dropped. "She shot him?"

"And then he shot her. I had to hold her in the saddle all the way here."

"I don't understand. Where was her brother?"

"She never had no brother. It was her all the time. Kept her hair hid under her hat. Covered her face before she went into the jail."

The rest of it came clear to Battles without Pritchard having to tell him. Alicia had been his partner on the Waco trip, passing herself off as a boy. She had held the horses while he robbed the bank.

The irony of it made last night's supper rise up in his throat, burning like Mexican peppers. John Durham had been in love with her, but she had killed him.

At least Durham would not have to live with the fact that he had killed her as well.

"Why did you let her do it?" he demanded. "How could you turn your wife into an outlaw?"

Pritchard's face twisted in agony. He looked as if he might faint. "*Let* her? It was her fault all the time, wantin' things this little old ranch never could pay for, whisperin' about how easy it would be to rob a bank somewhere that we wasn't known. A demandin' woman, she was. But I loved her all the same."

Battles started to say he was sorry, but the words stuck in his throat. Like hell he was!

He declared, "Every damned hoodlum I ever knew blamed somebody else for his troubles. I wish just one of you grubby sons of bitches would stand up like a man and accept the responsibility for what you've done."

His hatred for the breed swept over him like a brush fire out of control. He did a rough job of wrapping the shattered arm while Pritchard whined and cried. He intended to save Pritchard's life so the authorities in Waco could hang him.

When he got time, Battles would take pleasure in writing *apprehended* alongside Pritchard's name in his fugitive book. When the hangman had done his job, Battles would add the word *executed*. Then, with the warmest satisfaction, he would scratch a heavy line through the name.

One more down. But there were still so many to go.

# JAILBREAK

**S**ome people claim they can tell a lawman as far as they can see him. Grant Caudell was not a lawman, but he had the look of one about him as he trotted his sorrel horse into the dusty, lamplit street of Twin Wells. It had been a long ride, a relentless search that had driven a deep weariness into his bones and put a heavy slump in his wide shoulders. But his stubbled jaw still kept a grim, determined set. And he sensed somehow that his search was done, that he had at last caught up with Slack Vincent.

An undefined tension hung in the air, taut and ominous. Grant Caudell caught its electric tingle as he eased his horse along among the scattered knots of men. He felt it in the way they stood together quietly, saying little to each other except in muttered undertones that did not carry beyond their tight circles.

Most stood with eyes fixed on the ground, or on their rough hands, or on the warped planks of the splintered, tobacco-stained sidewalks. Seldom did they look up into each other's faces, made unnaturally grave by deep shadows from the lamplight.

Far up the street Caudell made out the shape of a frame jail, its barred front starkly illuminated by lanterns hung over its short porch. Before it three men stood with guns in their hands and stolidly kept watch on the street.

It was as if the whole town waited for some signal, some spark. A shudder worked up between Caudell's shoulder blades, adding bleakness to a face already pinched and wrinkling from forty years in the hot sun and the dry wind of Texas.

He reined up at the livery barn and stiffly swung down. The old livery hand stood in the wide door, smelling of sour whiskey and dry hay and unwashed horse sweat.

"What's happened here?" Caudell asked the whiskered, dusty man.

"Fixin' to be a hangin'," came the reply in a quick, eager voice. "Soon's that bunch of folks from the L4 gits in here. Sheriff thinks he can stop it, but he's got another think comin'."

Dull dread settled in Caudell. "What's it all about?"

A slight stir down the street made the little man step forward in expectation. The stir died, and he slumped back, disappointed. "Feller held up the bank today. Girl in there got hysterical and run for the door. He shot her.

"They caught him before he got a mile out of town. They'd've strung him up right there if the sheriff hadn't been so quick. But they'll git him tonight, don't you doubt it."

Grant Caudell's heart quickened in dismay. "This robber—what did he look like?"

"Tall feller, stooped a little, got gray eyes that

drive through you like a tenpenny nail. Scar low on his cheek. Regular killer if ever I seen one. And," he added proudly, "I've seen a many of them." The description couldn't fit anyone but Slack Vincent.

Caudell felt sick at his stomach. For five months he had hunted Slack Vincent, trailing him up into Kansas, then all the way back into Texas, from cow outfit to cow outfit, from one gambling hall and fancy place to another. Now, at last, he had found him. And a lynch mob had first call!

Grant left his sorrel hitched to somebody's picket fence near the back of the jail. If a mob did come, he reasoned, there was no use letting it booger his horse clear out of the country.

Quickly, his spurs ringing to the hurried strike of his boots, he strode around to the jail's front. Instantly three shotguns were shoved into his face. Purposeful, worried-looking men stood behind them. Lantern light struck a reddish reflection from a badge.

"I've got to see the sheriff, quick," Caudell said.

The shotguns eased back a little, but one of the men shook his head. "Now? Look, friend, you'd better drift before this pot comes to a boil."

Caudell held his ground. "It's about your prisoner. I think I know him."

One of the deputies leaned forward to peer distrustfully into Caudell's face. "Go on in, then, but leave us your pistol. And you'd better make it quick. When the L4's hit town there's goin' to be hell. That was Old Man Longley's daughter he killed."

The sheriff was middle-aged, not many years older than Caudell. Troubled lines were etched deeply under his tired blue eyes, and his stubbled face sagged in weariness. He stared at Caudell with incredulity.

"You say you want to speak to the prisoner? There's a mob gatherin' out yonder. They want to speak to him too."

A clock was ticking in Caudell's mind, and he knew it was almost time for the alarm to go off. "I'll tell it to you quick, Sheriff. His name is H. W. Vincent. They call him Slack. I hired him to help me with a bunch of cattle we trailed up to the railhead. Everything I owned was ridin' on those steers. Even my wife's dad and mother had all their money in them.

"When I got the cattle sold, Vincent shot me in the back and rode off with the money. I was laid up in bed for sixty days before I could even climb on a horse. As soon as I could ride, I took up his trail. I've been on it for five months. Now I've got to talk to him before that mob gets here. If he's still got any of our money left, hidden someplace, I've got to get him to tell me."

The sheriff studied him thoughtfully, plainly not entirely believing. "All right," he said, his reluctance strong, "but you'd better be quick. I'm afraid there ain't much time."

Caudell frowned. "You goin' to let that bunch have him?"

The sheriff's voice was bitter. "Not without a fight. But I ain't goin' to kill any of my friends to save *him*."

He led Caudell back through a narrow, short corridor. He stopped at a cell door, hesitantly jingling the keys in his pocket. "Guess you better stay outside here and talk."

Slack Vincent's looks had not improved much. His eyes burned with a fearful desperation. "Thank God you got here, Grant. You know they're fixin' to hang me?" His hands trembled.

Caudell made no effort to cover his pent-up hatred. "I can't do anything about that. I just came for my money."

Vincent's bearded jaw fell. His bony hands gripped the steel bars. His eyes were wild as he stared into Caudell's face. "You'd just stand by and let them have me? My God, Grant, we was friends!"

"Friends? You shot me in the back and robbed me."

"I didn't *kill* you." The wildness gave way to a look of cunning, like a trapped wolf seeing a way out. "Sure I've got your money, Grant. And more besides. Luck's been runnin' with me, till today. But I ain't tellin' you where that money's at. Not as long as I'm in here. If you let them kill me, the secret dies too."

Anger ripped through Caudell, and he grabbed the bars. He realized his anger was futile. "What do you think I could do, Slack? I'm just one man. There must be a hundred out yonder waitin' to get their hands on you."

Slack Vincent wiped a dirty, ripped sleeve across his sweat-beaded forehead. "That's for you to figure out. It was you that figured how to get the cattle across the river when it was runnin' high. It was you that outsmarted them nesters and their quarantine line. So you get me out of here. Save me from that mob and I'll take you to your money. I stashed it away before I tried for this bank. It ain't far.

"Fail me, and it's good-bye to everything."

Grant Caudell stepped back, half sick to his stomach. He knew Slack Vincent meant business. The outlaw had all his chips in the game, and he was playing for his life.

In the outer office Caudell desperately faced the lawman. "Sheriff, can't you slip him out of here to

someplace safe? You know you and those three deputies can't keep him long."

Wearily the sheriff threw up his hands. "We
couldn't get him out of this jail without gettin' him
shot. There's men watchin' out there from every side.
If we was to make a run for it, chances are they'd
shoot one or two of us as well.

"If there was any question he was guilty, I'd try it.
But there ain't. If somebody has got to die tonight,
it's goin' to be him, and nobody else."

Despairing, Grant Caudell looked through a
barred window into the lamp-spotted darkness. He
pictured Molly as he had kissed her good-bye that
morning months ago, and as she had stood on the
porch, lantern in her hand, watching him start his
cattle herd north. Later she had traveled all the way
in a wagon to be with him while he recuperated
from the gunshot wound. She had tried to beg him
off of Slack Vincent's trail, even though it meant losing their ranch, their home.

"You're a cowman, not a peace officer," she had
argued.

But he had been desperate, for the ranch was likely
to be the only big chance of their lives. If they lost
it, he knew he would work for cow wages the rest
of his life, and she would cook and scrub for hands.
"I'll get our money back," he had declared, "or I'll
put a marker on Slack Vincent's grave."

Now it looked as if he could start building that
marker. He saw no answer.

Suddenly, he did. Upon the sheriff's desk lay
Caudell's pistol, where one of the deputies had placed
it. Caudell recoiled from his first impulse. But he
considered, and he knew it was the only chance he
had . . . the only chance Molly had.

He waited until a noise outside distracted the sheriff, then he picked up the pistol. The sheriff was looking through a rip in the window shade, trying to see what was happening down the street. Grant eased up behind him and poked him gently with the gun barrel.

"Don't make any noise. Just walk back into that corridor like nothin' was wrong."

The sheriff started to say something but choked it off. At the cell door Caudell took his gun. "Open that door, quick."

The lawman complied slowly, his face grave. "You're a fool. They'll cut you down when they see you come out with him."

Caudell did not answer. There was no answer to give.

Slack Vincent was out of the cell the instant the lock opened. A weak grin spread over his face. "I knowed that money would fetch you. Let me git a gun, and we'll ride out of here."

Grant shook his head. "One gun's enough. And *I'll* carry it."

He motioned the sheriff into the cell and closed the door behind him. "Sorry, Sheriff. I just can't see any other way."

The sheriff faced him grimly. "I don't know if you was tellin' me the truth or not, about him shootin' and robbin' you. If you wasn't, the hell with you. If you was, you better watch tight. He'll find a way to do it again."

Caudell tested the back door and found it locked. Glancing quickly over the sheriff's key ring, he found the key to fit it. Carefully he pulled the door open and looked outside. The back of the jail was unlighted, and he saw nothing. But he knew someone would be watching, out there in the pitch-black shadows.

He pointed. "My horse is over yonder. Let's run for it."

They jumped out the door abreast and struck a hard run toward the picket fence where he had tied his sorrel. Instantly someone shouted. A gun barked, and a bullet snarled overhead. Another shot followed, but the two men were quickly concealed in a black pool of darkness.

Caudell's horse shied as they ran up to him. Caudell grabbed the reins, rammed a foot into the stirrup and mounted. He reached for Slack and helped him swing up behind. Spurring out away from the excited shouting and the pounding of feet, Caudell kept a firm grip on the pistol in case Slack might try to grab it from his hand.

A horseman loomed up in front of them. Caudell saw the man raise a gun. He spurred the sorrel and rammed the man's horse. The rider's pistol exploded into the air as he tumbled back out of the saddle.

Slack jumped down, grabbed the loose horse, and mounted him. The two men bent low over their saddle horns and spurred.

Pursuit was immediate. But the darkness of the back street worked in the fugitives' favor. Caudell and Vincent hauled up quickly behind a building. A dozen riders whipped by, shouting angrily, one or two tossing wild shots ahead of them into the darkness.

Caudell realized suddenly that the building was a church. Catching his breath, he peered through the back window into a small room, then looked away. His conscience welled up inside him like an accusing judge.

He had seen a gray-haired woman sitting in dry-eyed grief beside a long pine box, a handkerchief crushed in her work-roughened hands.

For a moment Caudell considered calling the whole thing off and letting them have Slack Vincent. But years of hard work and desperate hope had gone into that ranch, that herd of cattle. At his age there would be no starting over.

More riders spurred by. Watching their dim outlines as they passed in the darkness, Caudell murmured, "Now, whichaway's that money?"

Vincent pointed his narrow, bearded chin in the general direction the riders had taken. Caudell motioned with the pistol. "Move out, then. We'll follow along with them a ways and drop out. They won't be lookin' for us to be amongst them."

A sudden thought struck him. He shook down his rope and dropped a loop over Vincent's shoulders.

"What the hell?" Vincent exploded.

"Just to make sure you don't take a notion to get away from me in the dark. Try it and you'll break your neck."

Within a couple of miles the riders gave up the chase. "Have to wait for mornin'," Caudell could hear one of them say as the men and horses milled around. "We'll get us a couple of good trackers."

When the group turned toward town again, Caudell and Slack Vincent held back. Unnoticed in the darkness, they soon were alone in the scattering of brush. The hoofbeats rapidly faded away into the distance.

The long period of tension left Caudell weak for a time, his heart struggling. It required strong effort for him to keep up his guard, but he knew he must.

To take his eyes from Vincent for even a moment might lead to losing him. "Let's be after what we came for," he said. "We can't afford to be here in the mornin' when they come back with somebody who can read tracks."

He made Vincent lead out. Caudell stayed close behind him, keeping the rope taut, for it would be easy for Vincent to slip the loop and spur away into the night.

For an hour they rode south and west, in as straight a line as the brushy terrain allowed. Whenever they ran into a thicket, Caudell made Vincent go around, though it meant extra distance. It would be too easy for Vincent to break loose and hide in the brush.

Once Caudell caught Vincent taking up slack in the rope and attempting to slip it over his narrow shoulders.

Furious, Caudell jammed the muzzle of the pistol into Vincent's ribs so hard that the gaunt man grunted in pain. "Drop that rope before I blow a hole in you!"

Vincent hesitated, shrugged, then once more let the rope settle about his flat stomach. "You wouldn't kill me, Grant. You need me too bad."

Caudell gritted his teeth. "I'd cripple you. I'd do it with pleasure."

Presently they dropped into a brushy draw where the silted turf was soft and yielding to the horses' hoofs. On the ground Grant detected a sign of an old wagon trail that crossed over, one that wasn't used much anymore.

"Old road back to town," Vincent said. "We're almost there."

The shack came up unexpectedly out of darkness. Its rough, whipsawed siding was warped, badly split in places. Most of the sections in the old glass windows had been broken, and the window frames had weathered out of shape. A night-feeding jackrabbit skittered away from the front door as the two horses plodded up.

"Don't look much like a bank, does it?" Vincent drawled.

Nervously Caudell motioned with the pistol. "Come on, come on. Let's find the money and get this over with."

Vincent stepped down. "All right if I take this rope off? Ain't like I was a horse that's got to be kept tied."

"All right, all right." Caudell nodded impatiently, looking for signs of first light in the eastern sky, though he knew it was still hours too early. "Hurry up."

After they had tied their horses, Vincent pushed open the sagging front door. Caudell was quick to follow him. He heard the crunch of rotten wood and felt the floor give way beneath his right foot. Falling to his knees, he forgot the pistol for a moment, then excitedly brought it back up to cover Vincent. In the scant light he saw Vincent take a quick step forward, then think better of it and stand back.

"Aimed to warn you about that hole," Vincent remarked. "Just slipped my mind."

Muttering, Caudell worked his foot loose and shakily stood up again, his hand tight on the pistol. "I'll bet it did. You got a lamp in here? If you have, light it."

Vincent grunted. "What if somebody was to spot it?"

"We'll take that chance. For all I know you could have a gun stashed in here. I want to be able to see."

Slack shrugged. "Trustin' soul, ain't you?"

Caudell heard the rattle of a lantern as Vincent slid it off a dusty shelf. Its smoky flame revealed a dirt-covered, disheveled shack with the beginnings of a pack-rat's nest in one corner. There was not even an old stove.

"The money," Caudell said sharply.

"Money!" Vincent replied. "I never saw anybody so hell-bent for money."

"It's not the money," Caudell said. "It's what it stands for. It's what I lose if I don't get it back." He did not expect Vincent to understand, and he wondered why he even tried to explain. He supposed he was trying to justify to himself what he had done, freeing a murderer who might murder again.

Slack Vincent hesitantly ran his tongue over his lips, plainly hating the thought of parting with the money. He carried the lamp over to the corner and shoved the rat's nest to one side with his boot. He knelt and pulled up loose boards. He lowered the lantern through the hole he had made in the floor.

"Might be a rattlesnake under there," he commented.

He brought up a lard bucket. Caudell's heart quickened.

"There's your money, Grant," Vincent said. "You been huntin' it for months. Now look at it."

Kneeling, Caudell nervously held the bucket with one hand and tried to push off the lid with the muzzle of the pistol. Glancing at Slack, wishing the man weren't so close, he laid the gun between his knees and put both hands to work on the tight lid. It sprang off and rolled across the floor with a sudden clatter.

Caudell looked inside the bucket, his whole body

a-tingle. It was all there, from what he could see. All there—in his hands—after that long search, after all those sleepless, worrying nights.

He sensed a sudden movement. He jerked his head up just as Vincent hurled the lantern at his face. Caudell ducked and felt the missile bounce off his shoulder. Shouting something unintelligible, Vincent sprang after the lantern. He slammed his body into Caudell and sent him sprawling backward onto the rough floor.

"That's *my* money!" Vincent shrilled.

Caudell grunted at the crushing weight of the man's body. He lunged to one side and felt the weight shift. Vincent went out of balance. Caudell grabbed the man's collar and gave him a quick heave. Vincent went down.

They struggled on the floor. Caudell was vaguely aware that the flickering yellow flames had begun to feed on the dry wood where the lantern had spilled its kerosene. Somehow Caudell managed to get to his feet, swapping blows with Vincent.

A cold, silent fury drove at Caudell, a fury that had begun far away and long ago, that had steadily grown during a heartbreaking search across a long stretch of trail. It had swelled to a climax beside a little church, where he had seen a gray-haired woman sitting in anguish.

In blistering heat from the blazing shack, Caudell pounded his fists without mercy at Vincent's body. At last Vincent reeled senselessly out the door to stagger and fall on his face in the sand.

Only then did Caudell fully realize that the shack was ablaze around him, that his clothes were smouldering. His heart leaped in panic at the thought of that money going up in flames after all he had been through to retrieve it. He grabbed up the pistol and the bucket, oblivious to the heat that blistered his hands. He jumped out through the door, caught the half-conscious Vincent under the arm, and dragged him away.

While the fire still afforded light enough, he dumped the contents of the can and began to count. When he had figured off twenty-one thousand dollars, he rolled it and put it into his saddlebags. The rest he shoved into Vincent's pockets.

Vincent stirred. Caudell cut a short piece off of his rope and roughly bound the man's wrists.

Vincent pleaded, "That's too tight. It's cuttin' me."

Caudell's face was clouded. "Shut up and be glad it isn't your throat. Now get back on your horse."

Vincent staggered to his feet and wavered uncertainly. Caudell prodded him with the pistol. "Get on." He tied the man's thin wrists securely to the saddle horn.

Vincent queried fearfully, "Grant, what you fixin' to do?"

Caudell stared at him without mercy. "You know, Slack, for a little while there I had a crazy notion about lettin' you go. But not now. I'm takin' you back to town."

Suddenly Slack Vincent was trembling. "No, Grant, you promised!"

"I promised nothin'. And if I had, the promise would've been off after you tried to jump me."

Leading Vincent's horse, he found the faded wagon trail and followed its meandering course northeastward.

The town was quiet as they returned. A dim promise of dawn was beginning to show in the east. Here and there a lamp sent its weak yellow light against the darkness. Caudell noted a dim glow in the jail windows as he rode up behind the building and dismounted. He tied the reins of Slack's mount to a fence.

"Listen to me, Grant," Vincent pleaded. "You can take my money too, all of it, if you'll cut this rope off of me."

Caudell shook his head. "I'm takin' just what's comin' to me, Slack. And you'll take what's comin' to *you.*

"Maybe the lynchin' fever's burned out by now. Things generally look different in the daylight. You can use your money to hire you a lawyer, if you think it'll do you any good. I doubt that it will. Adios, Slack."

Slack Vincent's jaw dropped. He was almost crying. "Grant, for God's sake—"

Caudell drew his pistol and fired three times into the air. He held back his fidgety horse until he heard a shout and the quick strike of boots upon the jailhouse floor.

Then he reined the horse around and spurred him out into the darkness.

```
┌─────────────────────────────┐
│                             │
│         BISCUITS            │
│          FOR A             │
│          BANDIT            │
│                             │
└─────────────────────────────┘
```

**I**t started out as just another day for the Slash
R's wagon cook. It might have been, too, if the gun-
slinging stranger hadn't shown up.

Old George Simmons frowned as he looked at
the early-morning sun beating down on the West
Texas sandhills. It'd probably get hot after a while.
His frown grew bigger as he looked at the tub full
of dirty dishes that sat beneath his chuck box, and
he cursed the fate that had ever made him a chuckwagon cook.

He hung a bucket of water on the crossbar over
his cook fire and hoped it would be a long time getting hot. He dreaded washing the dishes. He poured
some potatoes out of a sack and brought a bucket of
water from one of the barrels in the hoodlum wagon.
Carefully he washed the spuds, then sat down on an
old five-gallon bucket and began to peel them.

He listened for the horse wrangler's voice, but apparently the kid was out of earshot. The Slash R
cowboys had ridden out on drive about an hour

before. The kid had taken the extra horses toward the corrals a mile away to loose-herd them until the cowboys would come in off drive wanting fresh mounts.

Old George wished he hadn't had to camp so far from the corrals, but the country around the pens was sandy, making it a hard pull for the teams, getting the wagons in and out. It was better for the cowboys to leave the cattle in the corrals at dinnertime and ride to the wagon for chuck.

Still, it got pretty lonesome hanging around the wagon by himself all day except when the cowboys came in to eat. George always liked to have someone around to talk to.

The sun had gotten a pretty good start on its day's ride when George finished peeling the potatoes. He washed them again and put them in a pan of water to wait until he was ready to fry them for dinner.

He saw a jackrabbit in front of the wagon tongue, standing stone-still, his ears sticking straight up. A perfect shot. George glanced at an ivory-handled .45 lying in his chuck box, under the knife-and-fork drawer. But he knew it was empty. The cowboys had used up the last of the ammunition days ago, shooting at tin cans. Regretfully he whistled at the rabbit. The little animal jumped up and bounded away into the shinnery and bear grass.

The water was hot now. George took a bar of soap and cut half of it into thin shavings, scattering them around over the dishes in the tub. Then he poured the hot water in and cooled it with a bucket of cold water. The suds were quick to rise to the top. George stuck a finger in the water to test it. It was still a little too hot. But he didn't mind waiting a few minutes for it to cool.

As he looked up he saw a rider approaching. He wondered if something had happened to one of the men out on drive. He knew it couldn't be the wrangler, for the kid always alternated riding a bay and a dun horse. This fellow was astraddle a sorrel.

As the rider came closer the cook saw that he was not one of the boys from the ranch crew, but a stranger. George was glad he hadn't poured out the coffee yet. Here was somebody he could "auger" with for a while.

Then he began to wonder. That was a fine-looking sorrel the man was riding, but it was hanging its head and its legs quivered; the mount was completely tired out. Surely nobody would have ridden a horse down this early in the morning.

The stranger stopped a hundred yards away from the wagon and surveyed it for a minute. Then he rode in a little closer. Ten yards out from the fire he stopped again and looked around the campsite carefully, ignoring George.

"You here alone?" he asked at last.

"Yeah," George answered, puzzled. "Why?"

The stranger didn't bother to answer. He swung down from the saddle and tied his horse to a little mesquite tree close to the fire—closer than George liked for riders to bring their horses to his chuckwagon. But the cook said nothing. This man's actions worried him, and he decided it was best to keep quiet.

George stood motionless at the chuck box as the burly stranger slowly circled the wagon, his eyes taking in every bedroll, every extra piece of equipment, every tin can.

George glanced at the .45 in the chuck box. He would feel much better if it were loaded.

The stranger stalked back around to the chuck box and faced George. The man's face was dirty and was covered by a beard that hadn't been shaved in a couple of weeks. Bags under his bloodshot eyes showed that either he hadn't had much sleep lately or he had been hitting the bottle pretty hard. Maybe both.

The cook didn't like the looks of the gun the man wore slung low around his waist and tied down. It had been a long time since he had seen men wearing guns like that, but he remembered that when they did they usually meant business.

"What you got to eat?" the stranger asked gruffly.

"Haven't got anything left from breakfast but the coffee," George answered, pointing to the pot. "The boys ate up all the beef, and there weren't but a couple of biscuits left. I threw them out."

The stranger grunted. "Give me a cup."

George handed him a cup. The man went over to the pot and dipped out a steaming cupful of coffee.

"What you got in the wagon that a man could eat?" he demanded.

George could feel his hands begin to shake.

"Well, there's tomatoes, or peaches, or—"

"To hell with that! I want somethin' to eat! Fix me up some steak and some biscuits."

"Look, feller," George protested, trying to hold back the sweat he could feel popping out on his forehead, "I was just fixin' to wash these dishes. I've got plenty of work to do if I'm goin' to have dinner ready for the boys when they come in off drive."

The stranger whipped out his gun. "I said fix me some steak and biscuits, and I meant it. Now!"

"All right," George murmured. "Hold your horses!"

He took a shovel and poured some hot coals out

on the ground by the fire. He put an empty Dutch oven over them to be getting hot.

As he sifted the flour and baking powder into a pan he watched the stranger. The man was looking around the camp carefully. He picked up an extra bridle that was lying on a bedroll and examined it. Then he threw it down on the ground.

From another bedroll he picked up a fancy pair of spurs that George remembered had changed hands a dozen times in poker games since the roundup had started. The stranger shined one of the spurs on his sleeve and jingled the rowel. Something resembling a smile broke out through his matted beard and he took off his own spurs. He strapped on the fancy pair. They fit. He threw his old ones down on the bedroll and returned to the cook's end of the wagon.

"How you comin' with them biscuits?"

"I've got the dough about ready to put in the oven," George answered. Nervously he lifted the dough out onto the chuck box lid, rolled it flat, and cut it into round pieces with an empty can. He poured a little grease into the Dutch oven and put the pieces of dough in it. Then he covered the oven lid with coals.

After setting a pan of grease on the fire to be getting ready for the steak, he unwrapped the hindquarter that was hanging from the side of the wagon and cut off a few slices of meat. He pounded them with the blunt edge of a butcher knife, rolled them in flour, and placed them in the hot grease.

George was very conscious of the stranger sitting beside him, watching closely every move he made.

Suddenly the man jumped up from his seat cursing. He ran to the chuck box and shoved George aside. He grabbed the ivory-handled .45 from under the knife-and-fork drawer.

"You old devil," he snarled, his face livid with rage, "I don't see how I missed this. It's a wonder you didn't try to use it on me while my back was turned."

George's hands began to tremble a little more, and he could feel his mustache twitch.

"It ain't loaded," he said quietly. "The boys shot up all the shells."

The stranger searched through the chuck box anyway, apparently making sure there wasn't any ammunition there. Then he turned the pistol over in his hand again and again. He twirled the cylinder and squeezed off some dry-run shots.

"Pretty nice. I can use this." He shoved it in his waistband.

"Look, mister," George pleaded. "That pistol ain't mine. It belongs to one of the boys workin' here with the wagon crew. He blew in two months' wages buyin' that thing."

"Too bad," the stranger sneered.

He sat back down and began to watch George again. George looked at the sorrel horse.

"Kind of run-down, ain't he?"

"Yeah. Been ridin' him two days straight. Rode all night last night."

George nodded. He had thought so.

"How far is it to the New Mexico line?" the stranger asked.

"About ten miles," George answered.

"I can make that easy in two or three hours." The man smirked. "That fool sheriff hasn't got a chance."

Sheriff! George had known it would be something like that.

"How long has he been after you?" he asked.

The stranger sat up straight, a threatening glint in his eye. "You askin' me questions?"

George shook his head and started washing dishes. The water was cold, but he didn't much care.

"I guess it won't hurt you to know," the stranger said. "He's been after me since yesterday mornin'. If this horse had been fresh we'd have outrun him to start with. But Red was kind of tired, so about the best we could do was stay ahead. Last night, instead of stoppin' like the sheriff probably expected us to, we kept movin'. I'll bet he's back there now, hours behind, wonderin' where I spent the night."

The stranger laughed gruffly. "I'll be over the line in two or three hours. He hasn't got a chance."

George kept quiet. The steak was soon done. He lifted it off the fire and set it on some coals. In a few minutes the biscuits were brown. He lifted the lid off them and said, "It's ready."

The stranger grabbed a plate and loaded it down with steak and biscuits. As he bit into his first biscuit he scowled.

"You're a hell of a cook! These are the sorriest biscuits I ever ate!"

"Sorry," George said apologetically, "I can't help it if I can't cook. You can throw them away if you want to."

But the stranger didn't throw them away. He wolfed them down, one after another. He probably hadn't eaten in a day or two, George thought.

As he washed the dishes George watched the man disgustedly and a little fearfully. He wished there was some way he could signal the boys. But none of them were wearing guns, and there would be nothing they could do except go after a sheriff. George looked at the shiny spurs and the ivory-handled gun the stranger had stolen from the camp. He wished the man would leave before he found something else he wanted.

Then George saw a rider off in the distance. It wouldn't likely be the sheriff, for he would be far behind the stranger. It was too early for any of the cowboys to come in off drive. It must be the kid. He was probably after a horse that had strayed away from the remuda. But the stranger wouldn't know that.

"You say the sheriff is hours behind you?" George asked, a thin smile beginning to curl his lips.

"Yeah. Why?"

"Then who is that comin'?"

The stranger dropped his plate and sprang to his feet, gun in his hand.

"It can't be. He couldn't have trailed me all night."

Desperately he glanced back and forth from the chuck box to the horse.

"Put them other biscuits in a sack and hand them to me," he ordered. He ran to his horse, untied him, and swung into the saddle.

George scooped the remaining biscuits out of the Dutch oven and dropped them into an empty flour sack. The stranger rode over, grabbed the sack, and spurred his horse into a fast lope out of the camp and toward the New Mexico line.

George grinned faintly as he watched the man's dust. Good riddance. Then he looked for the kid. The boy was heading back the other way, driving a horse before him. The cook chuckled as he thought how the kid would brag when he found out that he had scared a bad man away.

It was about two hours later when George saw two riders swinging up to the wagon in an easy lope.

They were riding Slash R horses, but the cook saw something metal flash on one of the men's chests. They were lawmen, all right. They had probably commandeered a couple of fresh horses from the kid's remuda.

"I'm Sheriff Cole," the larger of the two men announced. "This is Bill Watson, my deputy. We're lookin' for a feller who robbed the bank over in Greasewood. He was ridin' a good-lookin' sorrel horse. Have you seen him?"

"Yeah," George answered. "He left here about two hours ago." He told about the stranger's visit and how he had been forced to cook a meal for the man.

The sheriff was plainly discouraged.

"We might as well go back," he said sadly. "We lost the trail after dark, but we kept ridin' all night, hopin' to head him off before he got to the line. It looks like he beat us. He'll be in New Mexico before we can get started good."

"I don't think he will, Sheriff," George disagreed.

The sheriff snapped his eyes to George's face. "What did you say?"

"I said I don't believe he'll get as far as the line. I think that if you'll go after him, you'll find him down the trail a little ways, lyin' flat on his back, sicker'n a dog."

The sheriff looked at George quizzically for a moment. Then he motioned with his chin.

"Come on, Bill. We can sure try."

They loped away following the stranger's tracks.

George began mixing dough for the cowboys' dinner. He could see clouds of dust in the direction of the corrals, and he knew the boys were bringing in a herd for the day's branding.

He had already put the biscuits on the coals and

was slicing up the potatoes when he saw the sheriff, the deputy, and the stranger coming back up the trail toward the wagon. The two peace officers were both smiling.

The stranger's face showed pale, even under the thick mat of whiskers, and he bent low over the saddle horn, rolling from side to side.

The sheriff waved to George. "Well, we got him all right. You'd better come get the stuff he took from your wagon."

George walked over and retrieved the spurs. The sheriff handed him the ivory-handled pistol.

"Where'd you find him?" George asked.

"About five miles up the trail," the sheriff answered. "He was lyin' on his belly, clutching at his stomach and carryin' on somethin' awful."

The lawman's eyes twinkled. "You said we'd find him like that. How did you know?"

As he looked at the pale outlaw, George grinned like a cat full of canary.

"Because I didn't put any milk in that biscuit dough," he answered. "There wasn't room with all the dishwater I dipped in there while he was lookin' off toward his back trail. Lye soap has been known to give a man a powerful bellyache."

# THERE'S ALWAYS ANOTHER CHANCE

**S**omething about the tall stranger's appearance attracted the old sheriff's attention immediately. The man came riding in through the thick, mesquite-choked draw on the south side of town and trotted slowly up the dusty main street of Greasewood.

The sheriff moved casually to the edge of the springy wooden sidewalk to have a good look at the stranger as he rode past. Both horse and man were covered with dust, and the stranger had a two- or three-week beard. But his pistol was shining, and his holster was freshly cleaned.

Probably harmless, the lawman told himself, but since the bank was robbed last year, I'm not takin' any chances with suspicious-lookin' strangers.

The tall man looked searchingly at the signs in front of all the buildings on the street, and he slowed his horse down to a walk as he passed one of the saloons. The lawman knew what the sign said: *Rainbow Saloon, Adam Norse, Proprietor.*

He had been on his way to that rowdy place when

he saw the stranger. He was going to tell Norse again that there had been many complaints about the gamblers he kept in the saloon. But he already knew what Norse would say, the same thing he had said a dozen times before: "Let the men who gamble with them watch out for themselves."

The sheriff wanted also to tell him to stop pestering Sally Neal, for he knew she resented Norse's attentions. But maybe that wasn't an old lawman's business.

The stranger spurred his horse back into a trot and headed for the livery stable at the end of the street. The sheriff watched him for a moment, then leisurely sauntered after him. At the end of the plank sidewalk he stooped over and picked up a short piece of soft wood, leaned against the wall, and began to whittle. He paused and pushed back his hat for coolness. A lock of gray fell over his wrinkled forehead, and he stuck out an angular chin as he tried to blow the hair back out of the way.

After a few minutes the stranger came out of the stable afoot. He paused a moment, looking up the street, then strode toward the sidewalk.

Now the sheriff had a good chance to look at him. Tall and somewhat lanky, the stranger walked with a slight limp. As he went by, the sheriff could see a thin streak on his chin where the whiskers did not grow. That meant a small scar of some kind. The combination seemed a little familiar, the lawman thought. He had probably seen it on some dodger that had come into his office from another town.

The stranger went into Jake's Barber Shop. The sheriff strolled by and heard Jake telling him where the bathtub was. Then the lawman crossed the street and walked down to his own office.

He took out all the WANTED notices from a drawer in his desk and slowly thumbed through them, looking for one that fitted the stranger's description. At last he paused, stared at one for a moment, then pulled it out of the stack and began to read it at length. Two years old, it was from the sheriff's office in Franklin, Texas.

> WANTED: *Pete McLane, in connection with the death of Cory Nestor, in Franklin, Texas, August 24, 1893. McLane is six feet, three inches tall, with dark-brown hair, blue eyes almost gray, walks with a limp, and has a scar on the left side of his chin. He is 29 years old. Served five years in the state penitentiary for cattle theft. No reward.*

The sheriff looked at the notice for quite a while.

"Might bear a little watchin'," he said to himself, "but Franklin's too far away for me to worry about. There isn't any reward, so it must not've been cold-blooded murder."

At last he slipped the dodger back into the desk drawer, put on his hat, and stepped out to the sidewalk. He looked down the street and saw the stranger, now clean-shaven, coming out of the barber shop. The man moved briskly enough, except for his slight limp. He paused for a moment outside Norse's saloon, gave his gunbelt a light tug, then moved through the batwing doors.

The lawman stepped down off the board sidewalk and angled across the dusty street toward the saloon. He paused at the doors. Usually there was at least a little noise in the saloon, even in the middle of the day, but now there was not even the jingle of a spur.

The sheriff pushed through the doors and stopped. Nothing was out of place, but there was a tension in the room, something ominous that he felt immediately.

A tall mirror beside the door threw a dull, shimmering reflection on the ceiling. Two card games had been in progress, but the players had stopped and were looking intently toward the bar, where the stranger stood fingering a full whiskey glass and glaring at Norse. Norse's pudgy face, usually red, was now pale, and his eyes were opened wide.

The stranger gave the sheriff a swift glance and looked back at Norse. Then he downed the drink and swung away from the bar, but the lawman knew he was watching Norse through the mirror as he stalked out.

Norse stared after him until the sound of his footsteps had faded away. Then he nervously poured himself a drink and took it all in one gulp.

"What's the trouble, Norse?" the sheriff asked.

"Nothin', Sheriff," the saloonman answered weakly. "Nothin'." He clunked the whiskey glass down on top of the bar and quickly pulled off his apron.

"Speedy!" he called urgently. "Speedy!"

A fat little man stepped out of the tiny kitchen.

"Take over the bar, Speedy," Norse ordered. "I'm goin' home for a while."

He walked swiftly out the back door.

Trying to hide his confusion, the sheriff looked about. The gamblers had started their games again, and the little bartender was wiping the bar. The lawman walked back out to the street. He nodded to a cowboy and asked, "Have you seen a tall stranger around here in the last few minutes?"

"Yep. He went into Sally's cafe."

"Thanks." The sheriff strode down the street to the little restaurant. A tiny bell jingled as he opened the door. He saw the stranger at a table with his back to the wall. Sally Neal stepped out of the kitchen.

"Come in, Uncle John. What'll it be?"

He grinned at the pretty blonde girl who stood smiling at him. "Just a cup of coffee, Sally."

She went back into the kitchen. The sheriff moved over to the stranger's table.

"Mind if I sit down?" he asked pleasantly.

The stranger eyed him suspiciously. "Have a seat."

"Thanks." The sheriff pulled up a chair and settled down comfortably. "I'm John Cole, county sheriff. Everybody just calls me Uncle John."

The stranger was silent. The sheriff's smile faded.

"I saw what happened in Norse's place while ago. I'd like to know what it's all about."

The stranger looked at him blankly, but said nothing. Sally brought them two steaming cups of coffee and set them down in front of the men.

"It took me fifteen years to make a peaceful town of Greasewood," Sheriff Cole continued, "and I'd like to keep it that way."

"So?" The stranger began to stir his coffee.

The lawman leaned forward and said forcefully, "So, I know who you are, Pete McLane!"

The stranger dropped his spoon. It struck against the side of the cup and rang a moment. Then he picked it up and nervously began once more to stir his coffee.

"I guess now you'll be wantin' to put me in your jail," he said resignedly.

"No," Cole replied, "not so long as you don't raise a ruckus. Just what was the trouble between you and Norse?"

McLane hesitated a moment. Then his reserve seemed suddenly to break. "It's a long story, Sheriff."

He took a big swallow of the black coffee and set the cup down. "You see, Norse's real name is Nestor. He and his brother, Cory, used to own a big ranch down close to Franklin. I had a little place too, and one side of it adjoined their outfit. We were always havin' trouble with one another, because they used to run off my stock at night. One day they caught me over on their range tryin' to find some of my lost cattle. That's where I got this limp and scar. They gunned me down and left me for dead.

"I was married then." McLane stared blankly at his cup and absentmindedly turned it around and around. "Jeanie was worried when I didn't come home that night, and when my horse came back the next mornin' without me, she backtrailed him and found me almost dead. Somehow she got me onto him and took me home.

"The Nestor boys found out I wasn't dead, so they decided to get rid of me another way. They ran a bunch of their cattle onto my place and penned them in a wire corral I had built for wild stock I drug out of the brush. Then they went to town and reported that some of their cattle were stolen. Naturally they didn't have any trouble findin' them on my place, and they charged me with rustling.

"I had lots of friends around Franklin, and most of them didn't believe I was guilty. But the Nestors had friends, too, and I had to be tried. The jury was doubtful, but the evidence was too strong. They gave me the lightest sentence they could get by with.

"I spent five years in the pen, Sheriff, five years on a framed-up charge. Jeanie almost went to pieces at first, but she tried to keep the ranch up by herself. It finally killed her."

McLane's hand trembled. He stopped talking and drank the rest of his coffee. The sheriff tugged at his mustache and looked uncomfortably down at the floor.

"The friendly neighbors helped her all they could," McLane continued, "but there was still too much for a girl like her to do. She was just wearing herself down. Then one day she got caught out in the rain and went down with pneumonia. She lived only a few days."

McLane clenched his fist. "It wouldn't have happened if I'd been there. It was the Nestor brothers' fault. They killed my wife just as surely as if they had shot her. I swore right then that when I got out I would kill them both, even if I had to hang for it.

"When I finished my sentence I went back to Franklin. I found Cory in a saloon that he and Adam had bought, and I made him shoot it out with me. It was a fair fight, but he had some good-for-nothin' friends who claimed it was murder, so I had to leave town quick. Adam disappeared as soon as he heard about it. Now, after two years, I've caught up with him."

McLane looked straight into the lawman's eyes. "I hate to disturb the peace and quiet of your town, Sheriff, but I'm gonna kill him!"

He stopped talking then, for he noticed Sally standing beside the table, staring wide-eyed at him.

"Here is the dinner you ordered," she said softly, placing a large plate of food in front of McLane. "I'll bring you both some more coffee."

McLane stared after her. "I hadn't noticed it before, Sheriff, but she looks a lot like Jeanie. Who is she?"

"Her name is Sally Neal. Her dad used to be a deputy of mine. He died a couple of years ago, and Sally bought this cafe with the money he left her. She's a fine girl, and a wonderful cook."

McLane said nothing more. He started eating. Sally brought more coffee, and the sheriff began to stir his slowly.

"Why didn't you kill Norse in the saloon while ago?" he asked. "You had a perfect chance."

"He didn't have a gun. Besides, I want to give him time to sweat. I want him to know I'm after him and that I'm gonna kill him. I want to make him suffer, like *she* must have."

Cole carefully sipped his hot coffee. "It's not that I mind you shootin' Norse, or Nestor," he said. "Lord knows he deserves it about as much as anybody I know. But he's got a lot of two-bit friends who would call it murder. And your record from Franklin would catch up with you. I'd have to send you back there. And somewhere down the line somebody would surely kill you, even if you didn't hang.

"You seem like a nice fellow, McLane. Why don't you just move on someplace far away, where nobody knows you, and forget all about this? There's always another chance for a young man like you. But if you kill Norse you'll never get that chance!"

"I've known that from the day I started out, two years ago," McLane replied bitterly. "And I'm not quittin' now."

Sheriff Cole silently drank his coffee, as McLane finished his meal. Then he arose, put on his hat, and said grimly, "All right, McLane, but when it happens, I'll be comin' after you!"

Fifty yards down the street he was stopped in his tracks by the deafening roar of a gunshot behind him.

He whirled around and saw McLane slump down in the doorway of the cafe. A thin column of gunsmoke curled up from behind a building a few doors down the street. Sally suddenly appeared in the doorway and started dragging McLane back inside.

"Take care of him, Sally!" Cole shouted, and he ran to the alley after the ambusher. He caught a glimpse of someone dashing in the back door of Norse's saloon.

He trotted down the alley and threw open the saloon door. Everything seemed normal. Norse and Speedy were both behind the bar. Two of Norse's gamblers were seated at separate tables conducting games with the usual crowd which could always be found in Norse's during the daytime.

"Which one of you just came in here?" the sheriff demanded.

Norse stepped out from behind the bar. "I'm afraid you've made a mistake, Sheriff," he said, almost insolently. "They've all been in here for hours."

Cole noted that Norse was not wearing a gun. If he had fired the shot at McLane he had quickly hidden the pistol so it could not be checked.

"I thought you were goin' home while ago," Cole said, eyeing Norse cooly.

"I came back. Ask any of the boys."

Cole nodded disgustedly and walked out. He knew they would all say the same thing. At the cafe he found the doctor examining McLane, who was lying on the floor. Sally knelt beside him, her face pale and tears glistening in her pretty eyes.

"You're lucky, fellow," the doctor was saying. "If you hadn't heard the gun click and started to duck, he'd have gotten you in the heart instead of the left shoulder."

McLane's face was pale from shock, and the skin was drawn tight with anger. "I ought to've known he'd pull something like that. I should've killed him while I had the chance."

"Don't talk like that," Sally was saying softly. "You'll be all right. Uncle John will take care of him."

The sheriff looked regretfully down at McLane. "We'll take you over to my house till you get well," he said. "There isn't a decent hotel in town."

McLane started to protest, but didn't.

"I'll bring you your meals," Sally said. "Uncle John can't even boil water without scorching it. That's why he always eats at my place." She winked mischievously at the sheriff.

The doctor wrapped his roll of gauze. "You'll be ready to ride in two or three weeks," he announced.

The sheriff borrowed a buckboard and carried McLane to his house on the edge of town. "Got to keep you off your feet so you'll be able to get up and ride out of here as soon as possible," he said meaningly. McLane made no reply.

Late that afternoon Sheriff Cole went into his office and took out the dodger about McLane. He looked it over for a few minutes and then began to write a letter. When it was finished he took it to the post office and handed it to the postmaster.

"I want that to get out as quickly as possible," he said. "It's important."

The sheriff kept a close watch on Norse, for he was afraid the man would try to finish the job he had already bungled once. But Norse stayed close to the saloon and the ill-kept shack he called home.

The days slowly went by. McLane began to walk around the house a little, although the doctor had told him to stay off his feet. Every night he would pull the shade down and move the bed to a new position so Norse could not shoot him as he slept.

Three times a day Sally carried food to McLane. She always refused to let the sheriff take it for her. "You'd steal the dessert and drink up half the coffee," she chided him jokingly.

One day Sheriff Cole met her carrying McLane his dinner. "What you got in that basket?" he grinned.

"Sowbelly and beans," she joked, trying to keep the basket out of his reach. But he caught it and lifted the cloth cover she had spread over the food.

He whistled mirthfully. "A whole pie! You never do that for any of your regular customers, not even your Uncle John. Reckon that's a good thing to be takin' a sick man?"

Sally blushed and tried vainly to make some sort of reply. The sheriff tucked the cloth back over the food and smiled.

"Just be careful that when he leaves here he doesn't take you with him."

Sally turned quickly and began walking again toward the house. But Cole noticed a new spring in her step, something he hadn't seen since her father had died. He chuckled to himself as he started back to his office.

A few days later as he sat leaned back from his desk reading some new dodgers, a shadow fell across the room. He looked up and saw Sally's slender figure silhouetted in the door.

"Come in, Sally. What's the trouble?"

"No trouble, Uncle John," she replied smiling. "I just want you to get Judge Winters to draw up some legal papers for me."

"Legal papers? What on earth for?"

"I'm selling the cafe to Widow Watkins. She's been wanting to buy it for a long time."

The sheriff started to protest, but Sally held up her hand.

"And I want to get a marriage license."

The sheriff dropped the dodger back onto his desk and let the front legs of his chair hit the floor with a bang.

"You mean you and McLane . . ."

Sally nodded. Then she threw her arms around his neck and said, half laughing, half crying, "Oh, Uncle John, I've talked him out of shooting Norse. As soon as he is ready to ride we are going away someplace where he has never been heard of, like Arizona, and start all over again.

"After—after his wife died he had a friend sell his ranch for him. He still has most of the money. We'll buy a new place, and someday I'll make him forget."

Proudly the sheriff took hold of her hand and squeezed it. "Sure you will. But what's Norse gonna say? He's sort of had his eye on you, you know."

"I don't care what he says, so long as he leaves us alone," she answered contemptuously. "I've never liked him."

"Everything will be all right," Sheriff Cole said optimistically. "I'll take care of the papers. You'd better get back over to the cafe and fix supper for your star customers."

She kissed him lightly on the cheek and went out. The sheriff stared after her, but his smile faded, and a deep frown took its place.

The next day, shortly after the stage had come and gone, Cole walked over to the post office to get his mail.

"Just one letter for you today, Uncle John," the postmaster said. "Postmark says Franklin."

The sheriff thanked him and started toward the house to see McLane. He tore the envelope open and read the letter as he walked. Then he folded it and put it in his vest pocket.

As he neared the house he could hear an argument inside. He recognized Sally's voice. Then McLane angrily strode out and slammed the door behind him. His left arm was in a sling. He was wearing his gun, and his face was flushed with rage.

"Hey, McLane," the sheriff protested, jumping in front of him, "you ought to stay inside. Where are you goin'?"

"I'm goin' to kill a skunk!" McLane thundered, shoving the lawman aside.

Cole heard Sally's voice behind him and turned as she desperately grasped his arm.

"Uncle John," she pleaded, "stop him! He's going to fight Norse!"

The sheriff put his arm around her shoulder comfortingly. "The only way I could stop him now would be to shoot him. What happened?"

"Norse stopped me as I was bringing dinner to Pete," she sobbed. "He twisted my arm and threatened me. He said if I didn't stay away from Pete he would kill him. When I got here Pete could see that something was wrong, and he made me tell him. Oh, Uncle John, Norse will know he's coming. He won't give Pete a chance. Please stop them."

"I can't stop the fight now," the sheriff told her, "but maybe I can make sure it's a fair one. You'd better stay here."

He turned and ran back to the main street. Then he went into an alley and trotted down it until he was almost at the back door of Norse's saloon. The door suddenly flew open and a flood of men began to spill out. Apparently Norse was getting ready for the fight, and these men wanted no part of it. As the last man came out the door the sheriff drew his gun and silently stepped inside.

Quickly he scanned the room. Only three men were left, Norse and his two ace gamblers. Their attention was on the front door, and they had failed to notice the sheriff's entrance. Norse was holding a sawed-off shotgun behind the bar, out of sight. The gamblers were seated on either side of the room, each holding a pistol under the table, trained on the door.

"All right, you two," the sheriff barked, "pitch those pistols out to the middle of the floor!"

The three men jumped, startled by the lawman's voice. The gamblers hesitated a moment. Then one of them pitched his gun out on the floor. It landed with a thud. The other glared at him, then threw away his own.

"That's better. Now both of you put your hands on the tables, where they can be seen." The two complied.

Norse was still standing behind the bar, holding the shotgun, but the sheriff's unexpected appearance had shocked him so that he did not move.

"You, Norse," the sheriff ordered, "put that shotgun up on top of the bar where everybody can see it."

Norse set the shotgun down, muzzle pointed toward the door. Footsteps thumped on the walk outside. Then the swinging doors parted and McLane stepped in, his right hand poised over his gun. His gaze quickly swept the room—over Norse and his shotgun, the two gamblers, the guns on the floor, and the sheriff, standing at the rear wall.

Then his eyes flashed back to Norse. "I see you've got your shotgun cocked and ready. You killed my wife, Norse, and now you're threatening Sally. But you'll never hurt anybody again. Reach for that gun!"

Norse didn't move.

"All right, then," McLane said angrily. "The sheriff is gonna start countin', and when he says 'three,' I'm reachin' for my gun. You'd better do the same. Start countin', Sheriff."

"Not me, McLane. I'm just a bystander."

McLane nodded impatiently at one of the gamblers and ordered, "You! Start countin'!"

"One."

The gambler paused and caught a deep breath.

"Two."

Norse's hands trembled and almost started to reach for the shotgun.

"Three!" Both gamblers dived under their tables, and the sheriff dropped to the floor. McLane's pistol seemed to leap from its holster as Norse grabbed the shotgun off the bar. McLane's gun barked once and the shotgun exploded harmlessly in the air, blowing a jagged hole in the ceiling. Norse dropped the gun and clutched at his chest, then slumped forward onto the bar and slowly slid to the floor.

"All right, McLane," the sheriff ordered gruffly, "get back to the house, quick. I'll be there in a minute."

McLane limped out the door. The sheriff strode across the room and picked up the gamblers' pistols. Swiftly he unloaded them and pitched them behind the bar.

"Don't you fellers get any smart ideas about shootin' people in the back," he warned. Then he backed out the door and ran to the house.

There he found McLane holding Sally tightly to him with his good arm. She was crying softly.

"We haven't got much time," Cole said anxiously. "Sally, have you had the papers signed by Widow Watkins and gotten your money yet?"

"Yes," she answered, wiping the tears from her eyes. "It's in the bank."

"Well, run up there and draw out all your money, quick. I'll get the justice of the peace to come over here and read the marriage ceremony, and I'll get a buckboard for you two to leave in."

"But what's the hurry?" McLane protested.

"Norse has a lot of good-for-nothin' friends who'll be after your scalp if you stay here long."

"I'm not afraid of them," McLane argued.

"That's just it. You'd stay around here and fight them till they finally killed you. Maybe you'd get a few of them, but they'd kill you sooner or later. You've got to get out of here, son, while you still can."

"I won't run away," said McLane stubbornly. "No cheap bunch of gamblers can make me."

Uncle John Cole was silent for a moment. "McLane," he said finally, "you've got to leave—for my sake. Somebody here is bound to know about that Franklin incident. They could charge me with neglecting my duty. And if the sheriff there is notified he'll force me to arrest you. Then where would Sally be?"

"I guess you're right," McLane agreed after a pause. "When do we start?"

While Sally withdrew her money from the bank and hurriedly packed her things, the sheriff went to the livery stable and bought a buckboard for the couple. He knew that the constant jar of riding a horse would be hard on McLane's unhealed wound.

The marriage ceremony was held in the sheriff's house. Then everybody helped load the buckboard, and Cole tied McLane's horse on behind as the couple climbed up.

McLane shook the old man's hand.

"Thanks for your help, Sheriff. We'll be across the line into New Mexico by this time tomorrow. Then you can send out the alarm for me."

There were tiny turkey-track wrinkles beside the sheriff's gray eyes as he grinned. "And thank *you* for ridding me of Norse's crooked place."

Sally leaned over and kissed him. "Good-bye, Uncle John. Thanks for everything."

McLane picked up the reins.

"That's a good team you've got there," the lawman said meaningly. "You can drive them easy with one hand. And they can take you a long ways before dark. See that they do it."

McLane flipped the reins and the team trotted away. Sally turned and waved back until the buckboard went around a curve and was lost to sight in the thick mesquite.

"Fine-looking couple," the justice of the peace said. "But we'll miss Sally. I'll bet the widow Watkins can't cook pie like she can." He shook his head sadly as he walked away.

The sheriff stood gazing at the road as he took from his pocket the letter he had received earlier in the day. He unfolded it and read it again.

Dear Sheriff Cole:

In reply to your letter of August 3, it has been proved to the law's satisfaction that the fight in which Pete McLane killed Cory Nestor was a fair one, and that his motives were justifiable. I inform you with pleasure, therefore, that all charges against McLane have been dropped.

Respectfully yours,
Andrew H. Todd,
Sheriff of Franklin County

Sheriff John Cole smiled as he ripped the letter to bits and let them flutter to the ground. There wasn't another chance for him here, he thought. Then he turned and walked slowly back toward town, whistling as he went.

# BORN TO BE HANGED

Old outlaws were never allowed to die. Just about every Western badman worth his salt supposedly survived his "official" death and was seen alive long after he was reportedly buried. These legends have grown up about such people as Jesse James, Billy the Kid, Butch Cassidy, and many others of less notoriety.

Judge Orland Sims, who wrote a couple of books about West Texas characters, told me once that he planned to write another to be entitled *Dead Outlaws I Have Known*. He never did, but he could have. One in particular who piqued his interest was Blackjack Ketchum. Blackjack first gained notice in the Knickerbocker community west of San Angelo, Texas. Even as a youngster, he developed a reputation for lawlessness.

The official story is that Blackjack was hanged in Clayton, New Mexico, in 1901, having been wounded and captured in an aborted effort at train robbery. During his long imprisonment, the many appeals and delays, he was fed well and gained considerable weight. The generally accepted version is that the hangman did not take this gain into proper account and dropped Blackjack too far. The grisly result was that the impact severed the outlaw's head from his body.

The late Glenn Tennis told me that as a teenager he helped his undertaker father move bodies from the old Clayton cemetery to a new site. They found Blackjack's body well preserved. He said the features still looked like photographs he had seen of Blackjack. Moreover, the head was indeed separate from the body. Nevertheless, a couple of San Angelo oldtimers who had known Blackjack were convinced that the hanging was rigged to allow him to survive. One told me he was sure he had seen Blackjack ride up to his brother's ranch house near the Pecos River some years later.

Though I am confident of Glenn's account, it is interesting to fantasize that Blackjack survived through some arrangement with the local law. For those who believe in the inexorability of fate, his story might have gone something like this:

Blackjack thought for a moment that he was indeed dead. The rigging hidden beneath his coat had absorbed the impact of the fall and allowed him to land on his feet atop a stack of sand bags, hidden from view behind canvas sheets that screened the bottom of the scaffold. But he had been unable to stand. As he lurched forward, the false noose drew tightly around his neck and choked him. A deputy posted out of sight beneath the scaffold quickly grabbed him. Holding the rope taut above the noose, he loosened its grip enough to allow Blackjack to breathe. He wheezed, struggling for air.

"Quiet," the deputy whispered urgently. "You want to give the whole thing away?"

Blackjack knew the crowd out there would not give him a second chance. They had come here hungry to see a hanging, and they thought they had. He managed slowly to fill his lungs. His neck burned, blistered by the rope's rough caress. There was an old saying that some people would complain even if they were hanged with a new rope. He wished this had been an old rope. It would have been more pliable, and easier on his neck's sensitive skin.

"Hold steady," the deputy whispered. "We've got to keep this rope tight till the crowd breaks up, or they'll know somethin' is haywire."

Presently the deputy was joined by another, and by a doctor who had been brought from out of town because the local physician was too honest to be involved in this kind of subterfuge. They removed the noose and let Blackjack ease his bulk to a sitting position on the sandbags. Blackjack heard the rattle of trace chains. The hearse was pulling up next to the scaffold.

The second deputy said, "You'd better play real dead, or somebody out there will see that things ain't on the up-and-up. Then there'll be hell to pay."

Blackjack held his breath as the doctor leaned over him, pretending to make an examination. "I detect no breath," the doctor said. "I pronounce him dead."

One of the deputies helped the undertaker carry a plain wooden casket beneath the scaffold. "He's too heavy for us to lift," he said. "Mr. Ketchum, you'll have to crawl into the coffin yourself." He looked back to be sure no one could see from outside the canvas.

The thought of lying in that casket brought a surge of nausea. Blackjack wished he had not eaten the hearty breakfast they had brought him as a last meal. He feared he would vomit but knew he must not.

"Take a deep breath," the undertaker told him. "Then hold it till we get you into the hearse. A lot of people will be watching."

He noticed that one of the deputies was scattering a red liquid beneath the scaffold. "Chicken blood," the man said. "There's a good reason for it."

Though Blackjack's eyes were closed and a thin cloth was laid across his face, he was aware of the bright sun as the coffin was lifted and he was carried out into the open. He heard excited murmuring from the crowd that pushed in for a look. His lungs burned like fire, but he could not afford to breathe. He was aware of darkness as the lid was placed over him. Even then he feared to take a deep breath. He opened his eyes but saw only black. Feeling suffocated, he fought against a sudden panic that threatened to engulf him. He had always hated tight places. This one gave him a stifling sense of being buried alive. He fought against a desperate desire to cry out, to beg for someone to open the box and set him free. Judgment prevailed, and he managed to hold silent, though his lungs threatened to burst.

He felt the coffin sliding into the rear of the hearse. In a minute the horses moved and the wheels were rolling beneath him. Sweating heavily, he pushed the coffin lid up just enough to let in a little light. Black curtains did not allow him to see outside, but on the other hand they kept bystanders from seeing inside.

The hearse pulled in to a shed that he surmised belonged to the undertaker. Someone closed the outside doors and said, "All right, you can climb out now."

Blackjack trembled, his legs threatening to collapse. The undertaker gave him a half pint of whiskey. Gratefully he downed half of it without pausing for breath. It helped relieve the cold knot that had built in his stomach. On a wooden slab he saw what appeared to be a body covered by a sheet. "Who's that?" he asked.

The undertaker said, "A hobo. He fell trying to catch a freight. As far as anybody needs to know, he's Blackjack Ketchum."

Blackjack had made a specialty of robbing trains. He shuddered to think how it would be to fall under the wheels of one. "Must've been an awful mess."

"It was. That's why we scattered the chicken blood. We gave out a story that the noose pinched your head off."

The deputy who had waited beneath the gallows said, "You'll have to stay here till after dark. Then I'll bring you a horse. We want you to ride as far and as fast as you can go, over Raton Pass and into Colorado. If anybody around here was to recognize you, you'd go right back on that scaffold, and the rest of us'd all be in one hell of a fix."

Blackjack was puzzled. "Why go to all this trouble for me? I've got no money to pay you with."

"A feller up at Trinidad has got a job for you. He's paid us good to keep you alive and kickin'. We had figured on buryin' some rocks in your coffin, but that hobo was a lucky break. If anybody ever takes a notion to dig you up, they won't know but what he's you."

Blackjack shuddered. "That's a damned grisly thought."

He had slept but little last night, dreading the morning and the strangling grip of the noose, knowing he was on the verge of a long sleep from which he would never awaken. They had not told him of this scheme until just before they took him out of the cell. Now he stretched out on a cot and made up for lost time, sleeping through much of a long day, awakening eager for night so he could put this oppressive town and everybody in it far behind him.

At dark the deputy brought him a little money and a plate of food. "Eat hearty," he said. "It's a long ride up to Trinidad."

"Several days. What do I do when I get there?"

"You won't go into town till dark. After midnight you'll find a saloon known as the Colorado Miner. After it closes, you'll knock on the back door. A gentleman will be expectin' you."

"What's his name?"

"You don't need to know. He'll know *you*. Just listen and do what he says. When the job is done, he'll give you travelin' money. Afterward, if I was you, I wouldn't stop ridin' till I got to Canada, or maybe whatever is north of that."

Blackjack was uncomfortable about going into a mission without even knowing what it was, but he swallowed his misgivings. He considered himself deeply in debt to the unknown benefactor who had saved him. Without that help, he would by now have been buried in the coffin the hearse had carried out to the graveyard.

Thank God for unlucky hoboes, he thought.

He finished his supper and took a long swig of whiskey. "Now where's that horse?"

Keeping off of the roads, it had taken him several days to ride from Clayton up through the high pass and down the long slope to Trinidad. There weren't many towns of consequence between here and Montana that he had not seen at one time or another, including this one. He thought he remembered the Colorado Miner, though it was but one of many dram joints in town. He waited as instructed until he judged midnight to have come and gone. He had no watch. His had disappeared along with most of his other personal possessions during the two years or so that he had languished in jail. It seemed that no matter how much everybody had hated him, they had been eager to collect whatever souvenirs they could get their hands on.

He tied the horse to a fence in deep shadows behind the saloon and rapped his big knuckles against the back door. He listened to the floor creak as someone walked across. The door's hinges squeaked, and it opened just enough for him to see one eye peering out suspiciously. The room was dark.

He asked, "Are you the man I'm supposed to meet?"

"Step inside, quickly. The blinds are down. I'll light a lamp."

In the dim glow Blackjack took a long look at the face, and in particular at squinted eyes that seemed to bore a hole through him. The man appeared well-to-do by the cut of his clothes. He said, "You probably do not remember me, but I was in the courtroom, watching your trial. And I was present when you dropped through the scaffold. I have to say right up front that I believe you deserved the sentence they gave you. You appeared to be a man born to hang."

Blackjack felt offended. The man was contemptuous of him, but not so much that he would not use him. "Then why go to the trouble of gettin' me out of it?"

"Because I saw that you are not a man who flinches easily. The task I have in mind is simple, but it requires a determined man who will not flinch or let soft feelings stay his hand."

By the tailored suit, Blackjack made a wild guess that his benefactor might be a banker. He had known of a few who arranged the robbery of their own banks to cover up shortages, or simply for self enrichment at the depositors' expense. "You got a robbery that needs doin'?"

"No. I have a man who needs killing."

Blackjack frowned. He had killed, but it was not a thing lightly undertaken. He said, "You could hire any thug who happened to drop off of the train. You wouldn't have to go to all the trouble and expense of savin' my neck."

"But if such a man were identified and caught, he would gladly betray me to save himself from the hangman. In your case, you have the strongest possible incentive not to let yourself be captured. You've already felt the choking of a noose about your neck. You will do anything to avoid another." The man poured Blackjack a drink. "Moreover, no witness could properly identify you. Everybody knows Blackjack Ketchum is dead."

That made sense. "What're you goin' to pay me?"

"You've already been paid. I have bought you your life. Nevertheless, I will pay you three thousand dollars when you are done. That should get you at least a thousand miles from here before you stop for breath."

Single robberies had netted Blackjack more money, but under the circumstances he decided it was not appropriate to quibble. At least he was not six feet under the ground. "I'll do the job for you. Who is the hombre I'm supposed to kill?"

"His name is Wilson Evans. He's a prosecuting attorney."

Blackjack warmed to the notion. He had been at the mercy of more than one prosecuting attorney. He had lain awake many nights, dreaming of artful ways to help them shuffle off the mortal coil. Unfortunately he had never had the opportunity to carry out any of these schemes. "I suppose this Evans is givin' you trouble?"

"Let us just say that this man has shown far too much opposition to certain areas of my business. You see, I own this establishment and several others of similar nature. It is his fervent desire to see my businesses ruined and myself housed in the penitentiary at Canon City. I do not find that prospect appealing."

Blackjack poured himself another drink without invitation. "Any special way you want the job done?"

"I am interested in the result, not the means. My only stipulation is that you do it thoroughly and elude capture. I would regret seeing you back on the scaffold."

"Not half as much as I would." The whiskey was not strong enough to shut off Blackjack's terrifying memory of the noose tightening around his neck. It was a death he would not wish upon a sheep-killing dog. He asked, "Where will I find Evans, and how will I know him?"

The man gave Evans's address to Blackjack and described his appearance. "He is tall, and he usually wears a black swallowtail coat and a black wool hat. I judge that he is about forty years old."

"That probably describes a lot of people."

"I would not advise your doing the deed in the heart of town. Too many law enforcement officers would be quick to respond. I would suggest catching him leaving home or returning there. You could be well on your way before anyone could organize an effective pursuit."

"Home it is, then."

The man handed Blackjack a few greenbacks. "This is on account. You will receive the rest afterward. And one more thing: you still have the beard you wore on the scaffold. You would look considerably different without it."

Regretfully Blackjack rubbed his chin. The beard had appealed to his vanity, but he could grow another when he was far enough away.

"I never did hear your name," he said.

"No, you never did, and you will not. You may call me Lazarus, if you wish."

"He's the one got raised from the dead, ain't he?"

"In this case, he is the one who raised *you* from the dead. Good night, Mr. Ketchum."

Clean-shaven, Blackjack took a room in a cheap hotel away from the center of town and tried vainly for a good night's sleep. He was haunted by a recurring dream which had him falling through the open trap door and choking to death at the end of the rope. He awoke wide-eyed and in a cold sweat.

Later he caught his horse and took a ride up the

street where Evans lived. He picked out a modest red brick house with the number he had been given: 326. It stood next to a church. He studied it intensely, mentally picturing Evans coming out the front door, down the short steps, and into the dirt street which would lead him a few short blocks to the town's center. Blackjack could waylay him anywhere along the route, though he had rather do it as near to his home as possible. A vacant lot on the other side of the church would afford him quick passage off of the street and out into an undeveloped area where he could lose himself in a stand of timber. By the time pursuit could be organized, he should be well ahead of it.

He would have to put in several days of hard travel when this job was over. He decided to give himself and his horse a day of rest before he got the town all stirred up. He remained in the hotel room all day except for meal times. He found that he slept well on his second night in Trinidad. He arose early, had a large breakfast, and saddled his horse at the livery stable.

He had lost track of the days and had not realized that this was Sunday. Evans would not be likely to go to the courthouse, though Ketchum decided it was unlikely he would remain at home all day. He rode up the street and dismounted where he could watch the front of the small brick home. Before long people began moving toward the church. After a time someone opened the front door of the house he was watching. As the man who called himself Lazarus had said, Evans was wearing a black coat and a woolen hat. Carrying a Bible under his arm and walking with a cane, he stopped at the church steps and began greeting visitors as they arrived.

Blackjack realized with a start that this man was a minister. The house in which he lived must be the parsonage. He swore under his breath. Why all that nonsense Lazarus had told about Evans being a prosecuting attorney?

He knew one thing for certain: he could not kill a minister. He was sure hell must have an especially hot corner reserved for men who committed a crime that serious. He mounted his horse and rode back to the Colorado Miner. Tying the animal behind the saloon, he tried the back door but found it locked. He threw a heavy shoulder against it and broke it open. No one was inside.

He had nothing but time. He could wait. After a while he heard voices and heavy footsteps in the front of the building. The saloon had opened for business. Though he knew his pistol was loaded, he checked it again to be doubly certain. He heard someone walking toward the office from inside the saloon. He drew his pistol and sat with gaze focused intently on the door.

Lazarus stopped in surprise, seeing Blackjack sitting in his desk chair. He closed the door behind him and said testily, "I've heard no shooting, no commotion in the street. I have to assume that you have not yet fulfilled your agreement."

"You told me Evans is a prosecuting attorney. Turns out you lied. He's a preacher. I never agreed to shoot no preacher."

"I told you that because I thought you might be hesitant about killing a man of the cloth, whereas you should have no qualms about a prosecutor. This man has influenced much of the town against me and cost me considerable business. His being a minister makes no difference. He is mortal like the rest of us.

All his prayers and preachments will not save him from one well-placed bullet."

"You'll have to be the one that places it. I won't."

"All I have to do is to raise a holler that Blackjack Ketchum is still alive. The whole country will be down on you like a pack of wolves."

"But they'd find out how the hangin' was rigged, and who paid to rig it. You'd have to get out of town so quick that your shadow couldn't keep up with you." Blackjack pointed the muzzle at Lazarus. "You promised me travelin' money. I want it."

"You haven't earned it."

"Only because you lied. I figure you still owe me. Now fork it over." He poked the pistol closer to Lazarus's face.

The man's eyes widened in a mix of fear and anger. "I don't have much on me."

Blackjack had noticed a small safe in the corner the first time he was in the office. It was the sort of thing that always caught his attention. "I'll bet you've got some in there. Open it."

Grumbling, Lazarus knelt reluctantly in front of the safe. He began turning the dial, first left, then right, then left again. "You won't get away with this."

"I'm bettin' I do. What're you goin' to say, that a dead man robbed your safe?"

Lazarus swung the safe's door open. "No, but I can say that he died trying." He whirled around, a derringer in his hand, and fired.

Blackjack felt as if a horse had kicked him. By reflex he fired the pistol. Through the smoke he saw Lazarus fall back against the safe, shock and disbelief in his eyes. Blackjack fired again, and Lazarus slumped to the floor.

Blackjack took a long step toward the safe, eager

to grab whatever money he could find and get out of here. But his legs betrayed him. He fell forward on his knees, then on his face. He rolled half over and placed his hand over his stomach. It came away bloody. He tried to rise up but could get no farther than his knees.

A derringer might be considered a woman's weapon, but its bullet could kill a man. He realized Lazarus had put one through his lower chest. It burned like the furnaces of hell.

He heard excited voices in the saloon. The door burst open, and half a dozen men rushed in. Some almost knocked others down in their haste. One wore a bartender's apron. He shouted, "He's shot Diamond Joe!"

Blackjack presumed that was the name by which people knew Lazarus, not that it mattered. His vision was blurred, but he pointed the pistol in a way that he covered everybody. "You-all stand back. I'll kill the first man that comes any closer."

It was a hollow threat. Someone grabbed the pistol and wrested it from his grip, then used its barrel to strike a hard blow against the side of his head. Blackjack sank to the floor.

He heard the bartender say, "The safe is open. This jaybird was tryin' to rob the place."

Someone examined Diamond Joe's body. "He's dead. Took two straight to the heart. Who do you reckon this man is?"

The bartender said, "Never seen him before. Probably dropped off of a freight and figured on grabbin' some easy money before the next train comes through."

"We'd better send for the sheriff."

"No sir," the bartender argued. "Diamond Joe was

a friend of ours. You know how bad the courts are about turnin' prisoners loose. We'll take care of this killer ourselves and tell the sheriff afterwards. Grab ahold of him. Somebody find somethin' to tie his hands with."

Blackjack struggled, but the wound had made him too weak to put up much defense. He felt himself manhandled by rough hands. His arms were twisted behind his back, and he felt the bite of a coarse rope around his wrists. He argued, "He shot me first. I just defended myself."

Somebody struck his face with a hard fist. He saw an explosion of light and felt the salty taste of his own blood from a split lip. He was jerked to his feet, then slammed back upon the floor again.

He cried, "It was him that fired first. I'm shot, can't you see?"

They might have seen, but it was obvious they didn't care. They began pulling him across the floor. His knees bumped painfully over the threshold as they dragged him out into the morning.

He had no strength to mount his horse, but rough hands lifted him into the saddle. They held him there as they led the horse down the alley to a telephone pole with crossbars which supported several lines. Through burning eyes he saw someone pitch the end of a rope up in an effort to lay it across a crossbar. It took three tries to get it done.

Strong hands pulled him far enough down the horse's left side that the bartender could reach him with the open loop and drop it over his head. It chafed his neck as it pulled tight.

Tears burned his eyes, and his heart pounded in panic. Blackjack cried, "For God's sake, you can't do this. You can't hang me again."

He felt the horse fidgeting beneath him, caught up in the wild excitement of the crowd. This was the nightmare of Clayton, all over again. His tongue seemed swollen and dry. He started to scream from deep in his throat when he heard a slap and felt the horse surge out from under him. His head seemed to explode. The scream was cut off abruptly at its highest pitch.

The crowd grew quiet, watching the body swing back and forth.

The bartender looked up in satisfaction at the morning's work. "Can't nobody blame us for doin' this. He had it comin'. Some people are born to hang."

Someone said, "It was a peculiar thing he said, that we couldn't hang him again. What do you reckon he meant?"

The bartender said, "There ain't no tellin'. One hangin' ought to be enough for anybody."

# O'MALLEY'S WIFE

Larkin O'Malley had a streak of recklessness in him a yard and a half wide. He must have, to have stood in front of a shotgun held by Mary Donovan's father and tell him flat out that he was going to marry her whether the scowling old Irishman liked it or not.

Old Michael Donovan had the hard head of a freighter's mule. But he had grudgingly lowered the shotgun, knowing that this young Texas sheepman was as stubborn as himself, and that he couldn't shoot him.

"She'll leave you," old Donovan had warned darkly. "Mary is a town-raised girl, and she'll not long stand for the sheepherder's life you're taking her to. I'll give your marriage six months. Three months if she's as smart as I know she is."

But Larkin O'Malley had seen the strength of Donovan in the face of his daughter, and he had been confident she could make the change to his kind of life. He had almost forgotten the old man's warning in the rosy glow of the honeymoon.

Now, with the blistering heat of the summer sun heavy upon him, he was plodding along on horseback in the low-hanging gray dust behind a band of black-top merino ewes with their leggy March lambs. And the words kept coming back to him.

"She'll leave you. She'll leave you."

He remembered them each time he saw Mary trying vainly to brush away the clinging dust, or blinking her burning blue eyes against the fiery bite of mesquite smoke from an open campfire, or scrubbing her town-bought clothing by hand on the banks of every half-muddied waterhole they came to, until the color was faded and the fabric was beginning to unravel.

Four days west of San Angelo came the first hint of new trouble. Helping Mary pull the wagon around for evening camp, O'Malley saw two bands of some-one else's sheep ahead, moving eastward toward him—east, when they should be drifting west. Gently he touched Mary's sun-blistered hand.

"I'll be back," he said, and swung into the saddle.

He spurred into a long trot, going past his own band of sheep and reining up near the next band he came to. He found these sheep gaunt and dragging. So was the bent, bewhiskered old man who owned them.

The old-timer licked his dry lips to soften them before he spoke, and his prune-wrinkled face squinched up at the bitter taste of the dust. "You'd better turn back," he said. "There hasn't been rain out yonder in six months. There isn't a drop of water in fifty miles, except for the river. And Hodge Guy-man has that."

Larkin O'Malley frowned, feeling a tug of sympathy for the old man and his suffering sheep, and thinking of his own. A few more days of this and they would look as bad.

"I can't turn back now. I'm taking them to the Howard's Draw country."

"So was I, but you can't get through this way. Guyman wouldn't leave enough of your sheep for a mutton stew. Me, I'm going back to San Angelo and drift south. Maybe I'll work into the Howard's Draw country from somewhere below."

O'Malley stiffened, looking westward into the slowly shifting dust. "That could take all summer."

The old man shrugged. "Time doesn't mean much to a sheep." He edged his horse on and started turning his flock so it would not mix with O'Malley's.

O'Malley worriedly rubbed the back of his sun-browned neck and looked up into the hot, dry sky. The sun bore down relentlessly, the heat waves rippling across the rolling scrub mesquite and grease-wood land. Three dancing whirlwinds boiled up dust at one time, two to the west, one east of him. There was still a fair turf of short grass. Though the long dry spell had left it brittle and brown, sheep could survive on it, provided they had water.

Mary had already shoveled out a pit and kindled a mesquite fire when O'Malley returned to camp and prepared to unsaddle. Watching this lithe girl he had married, as the lowering sun picked up a glint of red from her hair, he felt a warmth start inside him.

She had not seen him. She was too busy trying to chop down a half-dead mesquite tree for firewood. It had just enough greenness left to yield each time the ax struck it, then it would spring back. In a surge of Irish temper she swung extra hard. A branch whipped out and struck her. The thorns bit into her arm. She dropped to one knee, letting go the ax.

O'Malley rushed to kneel beside her, gripping her arms. "Did it hurt you, Mary?"

Her pretty lips were cracked from the sun and wind. They pulled tight as she shook her head. "It didn't hurt me. Just made me mad, that's all—mad and disgusted. I'm sick of this bouncy old wagon, sick of cooking over a campfire, sick of eating dust. Will we ever get there, Larkin?"

She tried to hold back tears, but one cut a trail down through the thick layer of dust on her comely face. He took her grimy hand and kissed it, and felt the calluses rough against his lips. It was not like the hand he had held when they had stood before the priest during the wedding ceremony.

"It won't be much longer now, will it, darling?" Mary asked, a note of desperation in her voice.

He looked westward toward the Guyman range and knew there was no choice for him. He shook his head and kissed her. "No, Mary, it won't be long now."

They came to the river late the next day, and he knew they were on Guyman's Two Bar range. He remembered Hodge Guyman well, for once—before he had saved his money and bought his sheep—O'Malley had worked on a ranch above San Angelo where Guyman had moved a herd of cattle through. He had not asked permission, nor had he given any thanks. He had picked the best grass and the best water and had shoved the owner's cattle aside. He had taken what he wanted and had gone on as if it were no more than his due, for he was the son of old Colonel

Tom, who had come here in the day of the Comanches and had built an empire of rawhide and steel.

No one had ever dared cross the father, and now no one crossed the son. How could O'Malley cross him now—just himself, a woman, and one old Mexican sheepherder as peaceful as a collie dog?

O'Malley eased his horse down the wide slant of the riverbank beneath the deep spreading shade of huge old native pecan trees. He saw that the river was barely running. Where in normal times the water was thirty or forty feet wide, there were now only sand and gravel bars, and green grass poking up through the hardening mud. Occasional potholes still held water, but the actual running stream was in most places only a step or two wide, and inches deep.

Suddenly O'Malley thought he saw a way. It was a chance, at least, if a man had luck and guts enough to bluff his way through. "Julio!" he called, waving his grease-spotted hat at his herder. "Take the sheep down into the riverbed."

The riverbed wandered crookedly across the range in a generally east-west direction. Following it westward, against the flow, O'Malley could keep his sheep on water for some thirty miles. Beyond that he would have twenty or so of dry, waterless range to cross before he reached the Howard country and home. But sheep were dry-weather animals; they could survive that last twenty miles.

The hard part would be this first thirty.

By the end of the second day he began to hope he was going to get by without being discovered. Up ahead, old Julio occasionally trotted forward afoot to throw rocks at Guyman's cattle so they would leave the river and not mix up with the sheep. There was no sign of any Two Bar men.

But early the afternoon of the third day, trouble came. A cowboy rode down over the edge of the riverbank and reined up sharply, staring in disbelief. With firm purpose he started his horse toward Julio, then saw O'Malley and turned back to meet him. The cowboy was a kid, perhaps eighteen or nineteen, the soft fuzz on his face just beginning to show a dark whisper here and there.

With all the ingrained haughtiness a cowboy could muster against his inferiors, he thrust his jaw forward. "How did you get here, sheepherder?"

O'Malley sat rigidly in the saddle, not yielding an inch. "Straight up the river."

"Hasn't anybody told you this is Two Bar range?"

"I've heard."

The young cowboy stared incredulously, as if O'Malley was by far the most stupid pilgrim he had ever met. "Then, mister, you're asking for it." He pulled his horse around and roughly spurred him up the steepest part of the riverbank.

O'Malley watched him a moment, then drew a slow breath and let his shoulders slump. It wouldn't be long now. He glanced down at his saddle gun, glad for its reassuring feel beneath his leg.

Three hours later the cowboy was back, with company. Six riders slid their horses down the riverbank, almost over-running some of the startled sheep. One of the men glared at the ewes and lambs as if he were about to tear them apart with his hands. Then his knife-sharp gaze pivoted to O'Malley.

"You're fixing to lose a flock of sheep!"

This was Hodge Guyman. O'Malley remembered him. Young, not over thirty, he was notoriously hotheaded, strong-willed, overbearing. He never forgot or let anyone else forget he was the colonel's son. He tried to carry himself with the stiff pride of an aristocrat, but somehow, to O'Malley, he looked more like a hill-country sheep thief.

O'Malley could see the outraged pride in Guyman's dark eyes and knew the urge that made the young man's hand drop to the butt of the .44 in a hand-tooled holster at his hip. O'Malley reached down and eased up his saddle gun, leisurely laying it across the saddle before him. The muzzle pointed at Guyman.

"You might have time to shoot *one* sheep," he said flatly.

Color flowed into Guyman's face at this unexpected defiance. He glanced quickly at a gray-haired, thin-shouldered rider beside him, his eyes asking. The son of Colonel Tom was begging for advice.

The man said quietly, "Go easy, Hodge. He's liable to kill you."

Guyman's hands cupped over the saddle horn, away from mischief. He slumped a little. But his eyes glowed like those of a caught wolf at the end of a trap chain.

Once, years ago, O'Malley had seen Colonel Tom Guyman angry, and it had been a sight to remember. It struck O'Malley that there was little of the colonel about the son except for what the younger man had consciously copied. Here was all of the arrogance, all of the fire—but none of the judgment. That could be a dangerous shortcoming.

Guyman said, "You don't really think you can get away with it, do you, sheepherder? If six men aren't enough to run these sheep out of here, I can get twelve. If twelve aren't enough, I can get twenty."

There wouldn't be any use talking to him about the dry water holes. It was foolish to try and reason with him about O'Malley's need to get to his home range as quickly as he could. Guyman just wouldn't care.

So O'Malley simply said, "I'm not on your land."

That shook Guyman. He turned his head a little, as if unsure he had heard right. "What do you mean, not on my land? It's *all* my land, a hard day's ride in any direction."

O'Malley shook his head. "All but the riverbed. That belongs to the state of Texas."

Guyman blinked, started to reply, then stopped. Glancing at the older man beside him, he jerked his head back toward O'Malley. His hand inched toward the .44.

The graying rider leaned across and caught his hand. "Hold on, Hodge. He still has that gun. And what's more, I have a notion he's right. This riverbed belongs to the state. They all do."

Guyman swore. His horse sensed the tension and began fidgeting. Hand flexing in rage, Guyman jerked savagely on the reins. "State or no state, no greasy sheepherder is making a monkey out of me. I'll kill him and his sheep both!"

An edge of impatience arose in the graying rider's face too, the slow anger of the tutor who must keep discipline but is not allowed to punish the master's brats. "Use your head, Hodge, like the colonel would have done. That new sheriff's been itching for you to make a mistake."

This cooled Guyman down some. But in stubborn resentment he said, "The Two Bar used to tell the sheriff what to do."

In the old puncher's face O'Malley could see the faintest trace of contempt. "Your father was still living then."

Hodge Guyman took the full implication, the

unstated comparison, and made no reply. But the anger deepened in his eyes. "All right, Newt, what can I do? If I let him get away with this, the whole country'll be thinking the Two Bar can be taken. They'll be down on us like a pack of wolves."

The old rider, Newt, shook his head. "I'm no lawyer, but I'd say there's not much you *can* do, as long as he stays in the riverbed."

It was then that Mary pulled the wagon up to the river's edge to look down and determine what was wrong. Guyman stared at her, the corners of his mouth lifting a little, like the grin of a coyote. Guyman liked women. From Del Rio to Fort Worth, they could tell you about this woman or the other, and Hodge Guyman. He got around. He looked at Mary, and his tone changed.

"Have it your way then, Newt. He can drive his sheep on state property, but we'll escort him. Any sheep that steps up over the bank, we'll shoot."

O'Malley did not like what he saw building in Guyman's eyes as he looked at Mary.

"And get that wagon down here too," Guyman said. "It's not going to travel on Two Bar land."

"The bank's too steep," O'Malley argued, glancing apprehensively up toward Mary. It was not the bank he was worried about.

"There's a place ahead where it can come down. See that it does."

Guyman split his men, half riding on one side of the river, half on the other, back from the unpleasant drift of sheep dust. When they reached the spot where the bank flattened out, O'Malley rode up and helped Mary bring the wagon down. She did not ask him any questions, except with her eyes. The whole thing had been obvious enough.

Once a ewe pulled away from the band and headed up the bank, her lamb following. O'Malley touched spurs to his horse, but the ewe reached the top before he could stop her.

Two shots roared, frightening the other sheep. O'Malley reined up in helpless anger, the sharp smell of gunpowder reaching him on the stifling hot breeze. Hodge Guyman made a dry, triumphant grin with no humor in it and calmly thumbed two new cartridges into the cylinder of his .44. Julio watched with tears in his brown eyes, for the sheep were like his children.

The riders stayed until almost dark. They stood by silently while Julio and O'Malley brought the strung-out sheep together to bed them down.

Guyman's eyes lingered on Mary. "We're going home now, but we'll be back bright and early in the morning. You keep that coffee hot."

Not until after supper did Mary ask O'Malley, "Why did we get into a fix like this?"

He told her how long it would have taken had they turned back and headed south from San Angelo.

"But this way you might lose all the sheep," she argued.

"It's better to lose the sheep than to lose you."

Her mouth dropped open. Her eyes were wounded. For a moment she stared at him in hurt silence. "Did you think I would be leaving you, Larkin?"

He stared morosely into the campfire, poking aimlessly at the coals with a burned-off mesquite stick. "I couldn't have blamed you. You're a town girl, like your father said. This life is hard enough on men sometimes, but for a girl, a girl from town . . ."

His voice trailed off. He looked up and saw her temper change from deep hurt to a proud anger.

"Why did you marry me then, Larkin, if you had so little faith in me?"

She arose stiffly and turned away from him. Pleading, he followed after her, but she would not listen to him. For a long time, then, he sat brooding at the dying campfire, watching the flashes of lightning that built in the west. He watched them, but he did not really see them at all.

Next morning the wind came out of the west, bringing patchy lead-gray clouds hurrying low overhead. The west wind was damp and cool, foretelling of rain somewhere. O'Malley's pulse quickened at the thought of rain. But there was an irony to it that did not escape him. Had it come a week earlier, he could have skirted around the Two Bar country. Now he was in the middle of it, and no amount of rain could change that.

Hodge Guyman arrived early. Arrogantly he rode into the middle of camp, heedless of the dust kicked up by his skittish, ear-twitching dun. It was a nervous young bronc with a hackamore over its head instead of a bridle and bit. That would be Guyman's way of making a show. And O'Malley knew who the show was for.

Guyman stepped down, took a tin cup without asking, and poured himself some black coffee. He did not have his crew with him, just Newt. Newt stopped outside of camp and led his horse in, as an old-time cowboy of good manners would do. He tipped his hat to Mary.

Guyman eased up to O'Malley's horse. Before O'Malley could move to stop him, he slipped the saddle gun out of its scabbard. He smashed the stock against an iron wagon rim and pitched the rifle into the wagon. Grinning, he stationed himself beside the wagon, where Mary had to pass close as she loaded the camp gear.

O'Malley clenched his fists, knowing he had to put up with it or see his flock wiped out. But he knew he could not put up with it long, sheep or no sheep. He gave Julio a signal, and they started the flock moving.

To the west the gray clouds darkened almost to black. The wind, so hot yesterday, now was cool with the stirring smell of rain that a drouth-hardened Texan can truly appreciate. Somewhere ahead, O'Malley thought, it must be raining torrents.

They had not been on the move long before a ewe up near the lead decided to take off on a cow trail that led up the bank. Seeing her, Julio Ramirez trotted heavily over to head her off.

Guyman was riding far back, near Mary and the wagon. Seeing Julio and the ewe, he jabbed spurs into the dun bronc. It made a couple of pitching jumps, but Guyman held its head up. Another time, maybe, he would let the bronc pitch its damnedest and put on a show. Right now he was more interested in beating the Mexican to that ewe.

But Julio had a head start. He was up on the bank first, waving his arms and shouting. The ewe wheeled and skittered back down to the flock. Guyman came charging up too late, his pistol out. In frustration he reined the bronc straight toward Julio.

The old Mexican tried to dodge, and the dun horse tried to miss him. But Guyman firmly jerked on the reins and slammed his mount into the herder. The impact flung Julio over the edge. He rolled down the steep incline.

Loping fearfully to him, seeing how crookedly the old Mexican lay there, O'Malley thought surely he would have some broken bones. For a moment his eyes stabbed at Guyman. He had to force down a wild urge to drag the man out of the saddle. But he had to take care of Julio. While he was doing that, Guyman rode away.

The old rider Newt came up and peered down the bank, shame in his eyes. "Your man hurt?"

The breath had been knocked out of Julio. When he tried to stand, he winced at the pain of it.

O'Malley said, "You'll do no more walking. You'll have to use the wagon."

Newt watched without comment as Mary brought the wagon. With Julio riding the wagon and O'Malley taking Julio's place afoot at the head of the band, it would be Mary's job to take O'Malley's horse and follow behind, keeping the drags moving. She accepted without saying anything. Her eyes were still angry. She did not look at O'Malley.

She retreated beneath the wagon's canvas cover and came out moments later wearing a pair of O'Malley's rolled-up trousers belted tightly around her slim waist. She swung onto the horse without accepting a foot lift. Her small boots, with Mexican spurs jingling on the heels, were far short of the stirrups when she sat in the saddle.

Looking back often from his place in front of the slow-moving flock, O'Malley could see her riding back there, and Julio bringing up the wagon. His face twisted in worry as he saw Hodge Guyman riding beside Mary, following her like a persistent dog when she tried to pull away.

The rain started, gentle at first but gradually beating heavier. The tiny pencil-thin stream slowly widened, its trickle of clear water turning chocolate with mud. As the water deepened, O'Malley could see that soon it would be impossible for his sheep to cross it. He began working back afoot, shoving all of them to the north side. Before long the stream was ten feet wide and moving rapidly.

O'Malley knew he could wait no longer. He led the sheep up the slanting riverbank, out and away from the water.

Guyman wasted no time in getting there. "What do you think you're doing?"

"This river's fixing to flood. I have to get these sheep up on the bank or they'll drown."

Hodge Guyman wore that grin again, cold as ice in January. "This up here is the Two Bar. That down yonder is the state property. You get back on it!"

He drew his pistol and sat there with it in his hand, looking like a coyote that had just caught a lamb. O'Malley took an angry step toward him, ready to force a showdown. The pistol lifted. O'Malley's mouth went thin with the fury that welled up in him.

"You can't afford to shoot me, Guyman."

"Maybe not, but I can shoot your sheep."

The gun barked twice, sending the sheep scurrying back down the bank, toward the water. All but two that would never go anywhere again.

O'Malley turned away, defeated. He could drag Guyman down and whip him up one side of the riverbank and down the other. He knew he was man enough to do it. But in the end Guyman would still be the winner. It would take two days at best before O'Malley could get his flock off of the Two Bar land. Guyman could bring his men and kill every sheep long before then.

All O'Malley could do now was to let the sheep string out as high up the bank as possible, hoping the water would not rise enough to sweep them away.

One thing he knew—if he lost his sheep, he would take their price out of Guyman's hide. He would make Guyman eat that six-shooter, piece by piece.

The sheep edged ever higher as the water lapped up near their thin cloven hoofs. Once O'Malley looked back to see a big lamb slip down the muddy bank and tumble into the brown water, floundering helplessly until its heavy wool dragged it under.

Julio had taken the wagon up above, and Guyman had not tried to restrain him. Guyman was too busy. He was riding beside Mary, telling her all she might do, all she might have, if she would go with him. He reached across and touched her arm, and this time she did not pull away.

O'Malley stopped suddenly, his mouth open, the hot, jealous anger rising to his face.

He heard the faint rumbling noise somewhere upriver, obscured in the heavy beat of rain on the muddy ground, the rolling of water close to him. He sensed that a wall of it was coming down from somewhere ahead. But at the moment he cared mostly about Mary.

A black fury in him, O'Malley started back in a stiff trot, his fists knotted. Then he saw why Mary was letting Guyman ride up beside her, stirrup to stirrup.

Mary turned her foot outward, ever so little, and raked her big Chihuahua spur rowel down the bronc's sensitive flank. The dun went straight up as if he had a fire in his tail. Caught by surprise, Guyman grabbed desperately at the saddle horn and managed somehow to catch hold of it. But his left stirrup was flopping free.

The bronc jumped again, sideways this time, as Mary sailed her wet hat under its nose. The right stirrup was flopping now. Guyman was up one side and down the other, helpless. The .44 sailed out of his holster and landed with a splash in the foaming water.

For one brief moment it looked as if Guyman would hang onto the saddle. Then he went down, his eyes and mouth wide open, into the dirty, churning water. The bronc pitched across the river and up the far bank, headed for home. Mary spurred along behind it, shouting, keeping it on the run.

Guyman pulled to his feet, swaying, coughing, the water swirling around his hips. He demanded that Newt catch his horse.

Newt eased through the rising water, in no hurry. Smiling, he looked back over his shoulder. "I'll try to catch him, Hodge. Don't you go away." He set off in a slow trot, taking his time.

Still boiling mad, O'Malley waded after Guyman, swinging his fists. Guyman was strong, and he was mean. But he had a bellyful of dirty water, and O'Malley had the wild strength that comes from an Irish rage. Guyman never had a chance.

The third time O'Malley dragged Guyman up out of the mud and water to pound him some more, Mary pushed her horse between them. "There's a big rise of water coming yonder. Even the sheep have got sense enough to get up out of the way."

O'Malley had to half carry Guyman up the north side because the man had so little strength left in him. Before long the river was bank full. Heavy clouds to the west promised to keep it that way. Guyman did not look like the colonel's son now. Afoot, his hat gone, his muddy clothes clinging to him, his lips blue with cold, he looked like a half-drowned banty rooster.

"It may be a couple of days before you can get back across," O'Malley told him. "Even if your friends come to help you, they can't do much from the other side. And maybe by then we'll be off of the Two Bar country for good."

There wasn't any fight left in Guyman now. "Two days is a long time to go without grub. You ain't going to pull out and leave me here to starve, are you?"

A malicious gleam came to O'Malley's eyes, and he began to smile for the first time in days. "We're not leaving anything here for you. But if you want to come along and help us drive the sheep, we'll see that you eat."

O'Malley thought Guyman was going to die right there in front of him. He shrugged. "Suit yourself," he said, and turned away.

But when he looked back later he saw Guyman trudging along in muddy boots, shoving wool-soaked sheep before him.

O'Malley walked slowly beside his wife, trying hard to think of the right thing to say. All that came was, "Forgive me, Mary."

She smiled the smile that had drawn him to her the first time he had seen her in San Antonio. "That I will, Larkin O'Malley. But remember this—I have the blood of Michael Donovan in my veins, and there's no quitting in the Donovans. Many a time I've seen my father mad and disgusted almost to busting, the way I was. And then he would go on and do a better job than he'd ever done before.

"You've seen me mad, and I've no doubt you'll see me mad again. But it doesn't mean I'm quitting you, Larkin. It just means you'll have to get a move on you if you want to keep up with me."

Smiling, Larkin O'Malley squeezed her hand and pulled her down from the horse to kiss her. Then he looked toward his sheep, strung out atop the river-bank, and he got a move on.

```
IN
THE LINE
OF
DUTY
```

**T**he two horsemen came west over the deep-rutted wagon road from Austin, their halterless Mexican packmule following like a dog, its busy ears pointing toward everything which aroused its active curiosity.

Frontier Texans always said they could recognize a real peace officer a hundred yards away and a Texas Ranger as far as they could see him. Sergeant Duncan McLendon was plainly a Ranger, though he customarily wore his badge pinned out of sight inside his vest. He rode square-shouldered and straight-backed, his feet braced firmly in the stirrups of his Waco saddle. He wore a flat-brimmed hat and high-topped black boots with big-roweled Petmecky spurs. His gray eyes were pinched and crow-tracked at the corners, and they pierced a man like a brace of bowie knives.

Those eyes moved restlessly, missing little. Quietly, without turning his head, he spoke to Private Billy Hutto. "Two men yonder in that live oak motte."

Hutto, in his early twenties and as yet simply a cowboy with a commission, let his hand ease cautiously toward the Colt .45 his Ranger wages were still paying for. "I see them. Reckon they're with us or agin us?"

Firmly McLendon said: "We're not here to be with anybody or agin anybody. We've come to arrest one man and stop a feud."

The two men did not follow, but the grim frown never stopped tugging at the corners of McLendon's gray-salted black mustache. It was still there when they skirted the crest of a chalky hill and came in sudden view of the ugly sprawl of picket shacks and rock cabins known as Cedarville.

Disappointment tinged Billy Hutto's voice. "I sure thought there'd be more to it than this."

It was common knowledge from here to the Pedernales River that Cedarville had stolen the county seat by voting all its dogs and most of its jackrabbits in the election. McLendon said: "For what it is, there's more than enough." Maybe next election the courthouse would go to somebody else.

For now, though, the courthouse was here, a frame structure long and narrow, facing a nondescript row of stone and cedar picket and liveoak-log buildings that dealt in all manner of merchandise but specialized in hard drink, by the shot or by the jug. Beside the courthouse squatted a flat-roofed stone jail which appeared more solidly built. The kind of prisoners they brought in here, it had better be. McLendon pointed his chin. "This is where we'll likely find Sheriff Prather."

He swung down and stretched his back and his legs, for it had been a long ride. He cast one wishful glance at a saloon, for it had been a dusty ride, too. But drink had to wait. He looped his reins over a cedar-log hitching rack and pointed at the packmule, which swiveled its neck as its curious eyes and ears took in the sights. "Tie the mule, Billy. She'll be all over town stirrin' up mischief."

A broad man with the beginnings of a middle-age paunch stepped to the open doorway, darkly eyeing McLendon and Hutto with a look just short of actual hostility. "Rangers?"

McLendon nodded. "I'm Sergeant McLendon. This is Billy Hutto."

"Where's the rest of you?"

"We're all there is."

"I asked for a whole company. We got bad trouble here."

"The two of us is all that was available. The legislature saw fit to cut the Ranger appropriations. I take it you're Sheriff Prather."

The man was not pleased. "I am. Come on in." He dropped into a heavy chair behind a wooden desk without inviting the Rangers to be seated. Noting the snub and filing it away for future reference, McLendon dragged up a hide-bottomed chair. He gave Billy a silent order with a nod of his head, and the young man stood in the doorway to keep watch on the street.

The sheriff bit the end off a black cigar and lighted it without offering one. "You come to kill Litt Springer?"

"We come to *arrest* him."

"There'll be no peace in this county till he's dead. But I didn't much figure you Rangers would have the stomach for it. Didn't really want to call in the Rangers in the first place, but folks in town pressured me." His eyes narrowed with suspicion. "You're sidin' with him because he was a Ranger himself."

"*Was!*" McLendon put emphasis on the word. "He's not anymore. We'll treat him like anybody else if he's committed a crime."

"*If?*" the sheriff exploded. "Damn right he's committed a crime. Why the hell do you think folks wanted to send for help? He murdered my deputy, Ed Newton."

"Any witnesses?"

"One. Freighter comin' up from Menardville seen the whole thing. You can doubt the citizens of Cedarville if you want to, but that freighter's got no friends here, and no ax to grind. Your friend Litt Springer is a cold-blooded killer."

Billy Hutto turned from the door, face red. "Way I heard it, Sheriff, he had a good reason."

McLendon said sharply: "Billy, you just keep watch. *I'll* talk to the sheriff." He rubbed his fist as if a pain had come in it. "The story we heard was that Litt's brother Ollie was arrested on some jumped-up horse-stealin' charge, and that your deputy turned him over to a hangin' mob."

"Aroused citizens!" the sheriff corrected. His eyes did not meet McLendon's. "Anyway, my deputy tried to protect his prisoner. There was just too many of them."

Billy Hutto snorted, and McLendon had to flash him another hard look. McLendon said: "Sheriff, our information was that Litt has gathered a bunch of friends around him and that there's danger of open warfare between them and the people here who back the mob. Our orders are to arrest him and take him to Austin."

"To Austin?" The sheriff stood up angrily. "If you arrest him you'll bring him here! His crime was committed here. It's the right of the community to see justice done. We'll give him a fair trial."

"And then hang him?"

"You damn betcha. Unless you was to shoot him first and be done with it. That'd be the best thing for all concerned."

McLendon's eyes narrowed. "I understand *you've* been tryin' to shoot him, and you've had no luck at it."

"That's a tough bunch he's got gathered. We can't get close."

"*We'll* get close."

"And fall right in with him, no doubt, seein' as he was a Ranger himself." The sheriff savagely chewed the cigar. "Was he a personal friend of yours, McLendon?"

McLendon stood up and pushed his chair back. "He was sergeant before I was. We rode together."

The sheriff sniffed. "About the way I had it pictured. Folks ought to've known we wouldn't get no help out of Austin."

Coldly McLendon opened his vest and showed the star pinned beneath it. "We're Rangers, Sheriff. That comes first—before friends, and before enemies. Come on, Billy, let's ride."

He knew the way out to Litt Springer's place on the north end of the county. He had visited there a couple of times after Litt had resigned from the force and had bought it. Litt had tried to talk him into doing the same, and many a long night under a thin blanket and a frosty moon he'd done some serious thinking on it.

He drew his rifle and laid it across his lap. Billy Hutto's eyebrows went up in surprise. "Litt ain't goin' to bushwhack us."

"He's got friends who don't know us. *They* might."

Billy Hutto swallowed and brought out his saddle gun too.

But they saw no one anywhere along the wagon trail that meandered lazily among the hills and across the mesquite-lined draws. Even so, McLendon was sure their passage had not gone unnoticed. At dusk they drew rein in front of Litt's liveoak-log house. A thin curl of smoke drifted out of the stone chimney. Though he knew within reason that Litt wouldn't be there, McLendon called anyway. "Litt! Litt! It's me, Duncan McLendon!" Nobody could accuse him of sneaking in.

A face showed briefly behind a narrow window. The door opened hesitantly, and a woman stood there, a woman of thirty who looked forty; her eyes vacant and without hope. "He's not here, Duncan."

McLendon swung slowly to the ground and took off his hat. "I don't suppose you'd tell me where he's at?"

She shook her head. "Are you here to visit, or is this official?"

"Official, Martha. I wish it wasn't."

She stared at the Rangers a long, uncertain moment. "Come in, Duncan. I'll fix you some supper."

Billy Hutto dismounted, smiling. He was always hungry. McLendon said: "Billy, you stay out here and watch. I'll tell you when supper's ready."

He followed Martha Springer into the small cabin, hat in hand. It was all one room, kitchen on one side, table in the middle, bed at the other end. McLendon doubted Litt had been in bed that much lately.

"It grieves me to come here this way, Martha."

"They want to kill him, Duncan."

"I know. And they'll do it if he stays out long enough. If I can arrest him, he'll have a chance. He's got friends in Austin."

She shrugged futilely. "What good would it do? This thing has been building a long time. Their stealin' the county seat was a part of it. Then what happened to Ollie. Now this." Her lips pinched. "Litt killed that deputy, just like they say. He doesn't deny it. He rode over there and found him and shot him. What's more, he's got a list of names in his pocket. He says he's going to kill the rest of them too."

"The people who hung Ollie?"

She nodded.

McLendon's stomach went cold. He hadn't heard about the list.

Martha Springer rolled a slice of steak in a panful of flour. "This county's been like a keg of powder ever since the county seat election. If Litt does what he says, he'll set off the fuse. There won't be a stop to it till they fill up the graveyard."

McLendon's face twisted. "He ought to know better. He was a Ranger long enough to understand how things go wild thataway."

Tears welled up before she blinked them away. "That's just it, Duncan, he *was* a Ranger a long time. Do you have any idea how many people he killed in the line of duty?"

He looked away. Yes, he knew, but he didn't know if *she* did, and he wasn't about to tell her. "Several. It was his job."

"It got too easy for him. The first time or two, it bothered him. After that . . ." She shook her head. "He should've gotten out a long time before he did."

Her gaze came back to him. "*You* get out, Duncan. Don't you stay in there till it's too late for you too."

Billy Hutto came through the door. McLendon turned. "Billy, I wanted you to stay . . ." He cut off in mid-sentence, for he saw that Billy's holster was empty. And he saw a tall, gaunt man step in behind Billy, pistol in his hand.

"Howdy, Dunk."

"Hello, Litt." McLendon made no move for his own pistol. He couldn't make it anyway if Litt Springer didn't intend him to. And he wasn't ready to test Litt's resolve. Other people had done that with disastrous consequences.

Springer held his empty left hand out, palm up. "I believe I'd best just take your six-shooter, Dunk. At least till we've had us a little talk." His voice was pleasant, but a hardness showed in his eyes—a hardness some border bandidos had learned they had good cause to fear.

"I'm not in the habit of givin' up my gun."

"You don't need to worry about me. I'm your friend. I wouldn't shoot you, Dunk."

"I'm *your* friend, too."

"But you're still a Ranger. Let's have it."

McLendon eased the .45 out of the slick holster and carefully handed it over butt first. Springer pointed his chin at the chair. "Set yourself back down, Dunk. I'm awful proud to get to see you again. I take it Martha's fixin' you some supper. I'm hungry too."

"You haven't been home much lately?"

Springer shook his head. "We got enough help to keep a posse out, but there's not enough to guard against a single man sneakin' in here in the dark and maybe shootin' from ambush. I'm not ready to die yet."

"You *will* die, Litt, if you stay here and keep this thing goin'. Sooner or later one of them is bound to get you. That's why we've come. We want you to go with us to Austin. We'll get this thing cleared up."

"Too late. I've killed a man now. I'd just as well go on and finish what I've started."

"I heard about your list. You think killin' those men is goin' to solve anything? All it'll do is open up a war."

"*They* opened a war the day they took Ollie and strung him up. Called him a thief, but it was a lie. They hated him because he tried to keep them from stealin' the courthouse. They knew he'd keep on fightin' them and maybe get the election recalled. That'd be the death of Cedarville."

"You didn't have to take it on yourself to start killin' them, Litt. You been a Ranger long enough to know you could go to the law."

"They *are* the law in this country. *You* been a Ranger long enough to know how it goes when a mob like that takes over the law. You know it usually takes force to root them out, and that force ain't always used accordin' to the statutes. These hills are a long ways from an Austin law library."

McLendon studied his old friend regretfully. Litt seemed thinner, older, grayer. There was more of a fierceness in his eyes now than McLendon remembered seeing there before. "We come to take you back with us. I'd hoped I could talk you into it. But if I can't, we'll use force, Litt. You know I mean what I say."

Litt Springer's gaze was level. "I know you'll *try*. But *you* know I got help out there. Even if I didn't have your gun—which I do—you couldn't take me out of here against my will. They'd stop you."

McLendon had no answer to that. Springer's gaze lifted to his wife, who was putting food on the table. She moved numbly as if she had already given up and was shutting the world out. Springer said: "Dunk, you and Billy set yourselves down and we'll eat."

They ate, and the tension lifted a little. Litt Springer's eyes lighted and smiled as he talked of the old days on the Ranger force. "Remember that time we went out to trail those Comanches, Dunk, and you took the midnight watch and saw that Indian standin' in the moonlight and shot him? And shot him, and shot him? And in the mornin' we found that tree stump with all those bullet holes in it?"

McLendon nodded, spirits lighter as he remembered. "And that time, Litt, when you were takin' a nap in winter camp on the San Saba, and a couple of us climbed up on the roof and dropped a handkerchief full of gunpowder down the chimney to wake you up? Like to've blown you through the wall."

Springer laughed. "Remember, they used to say that us Rangers could ride like a Mexican, trail like an Indian, shoot like a Tennessean and fight like the devil."

They sat there and spun old yarns as if nothing had come between them. Billy Hutto was too young on the force to add to the conversation. He just listened, grinning, holding his silence out of respect for the two older men whose experience was greater than his own.

After a while Litt began recounting the story of his long, dogged hunt for an outlaw named Thresher who had killed a Ranger. His smile died, and his eyes went grim as he recounted the days and weeks and months of tireless searching, the long miles and the hardship and the sacrifice. "They ordered me to quit. They threatened to discharge me from the service if I didn't drop the search and get on to other things. But I told them the man he'd killed was a friend of mine, and I'd go on and hunt him whether I was a Ranger or not. I swore I'd get him, and I did. I shot him like he'd been a wolf. That's what he was, really . . . just a wolf."

McLendon frowned. "This thing now, this thing with the mob from Cedarville . . . it's the Thresher case all over again, isn't it?"

Hatred came into Springer's eyes. "Just like that. I won't quit till the last one of them is dead."

"Nothin' I say is goin' to stop you, is it?"

"Not a thing, Dunk."

"Then stand warned, Litt. I'll be comin' after you. I'll stop you whatever way I have to."

Litt Springer stared at him in regret. "I'm sorry it's thisaway, Dunk. We been friends a long time. But all I can say is, you watch out for yourself. I don't intend to be stopped." He stood up and backed away from the table. "There's a wagon out yonder by the barn. I'll drop your shootin' irons in there where you can pick them up." His eyes lifted a moment to Martha's, then he backed out the door into the night. McLendon could hear his boots pounding across the yard. He moved to the door but couldn't see. He could hear the clatter of the guns falling into the bare wooden bed of the wagon. From out there came the sound of horse's hoofs, loping slowly off into the night. McLendon listened, his hands shoved all the way down into his pockets.

Billy Hutto said, "We can't follow him in the dark, can we, Dunk?"

McLendon shook his head. "No. We'll wait till

first light and pick up the tracks." He turned back to Litt's wife. "It was a good supper, Martha. I wish I could say I'd enjoyed it. I reckon we'll sleep in the barn. We won't disturb you, gettin' out of here in the mornin'."

Tears glistened in her eyes. "You won't disturb me. I haven't slept since I don't know when."

They were up as soon as the first color showed over the twisted old liveoak trees east of the barn. It was still too dark to see the tracks well, but soon as he satisfied himself of their direction, McLendon started out. Billy Hutto followed him silently, and the mule trailed after them. Not until long after sunup did McLendon call a halt by a small creek so they could boil coffee and fix a little breakfast. Billy Hutto had been holding his silence, but it had been an effort.

"Dunk, I always liked Litt. You knew him a lot longer than I did, and you liked him even more. So, what you goin' to do if you finally catch up with him?"

McLendon was slow in answering. "I'll know when I get there."

"You said you'd do whatever you had to. Does that mean you'd even shoot him?"

"I hope it won't go that far."

"But what if it does? Would you shoot him, Dunk? *Could* you?"

McLendon gave no answer. He didn't know the answer.

The tracks bore generally eastward. It didn't take much concentration to follow them, for in the night no effort had been made to cover them up. The morning wore away, the sun climbing into a cloudless blue sky. Riding, watching the tracks, McLendon oc-

casionally took out his pocketwatch, verifying what
the sun told him. About ten o'clock he reined up,
shaking his head.

"Looks like he's ridin' plumb out of the county,
Billy. That don't hardly figure."

Billy Hutto had no comment. He sat on his horse,
his face solemn. McLendon stared at him a moment,
as if waiting. When he saw Billy was going to have
nothing to say, he moved on. Presently he came to
a place where the rider had stepped down for a few
minutes. McLendon dismounted and examined the
tracks, running his finger along the edge of a boot-
print.

"Billy, did you notice Litt's boots last night?"

"Don't know as I did. Why?"

"Seems to me he had high, sharp heels—cowboy
heels. These are rounder, and flatter." He looked up
expectantly. "What does that suggest to you, Billy?"

Billy was slow in answering. A smile played about
his lips. "That Litt run in a ringer on us. He never
left his place. We been followin' somebody else."

McLendon pushed stiffly to his feet. "It couldn't
be that you've known it all along, could it?"

Billy Hutto shook his head. "I begun to suspect it
awhile back, but I didn't know."

McLendon's eyes narrowed. "Seems to me Litt
Springer slipped up on you awful easy last night.
Could it be that you *made* it easy for him?"

Billy tried to appear surprised, but to McLendon
he looked more like a kid caught swimming while
school was on. McLendon pressed: "Billy, did you
talk with Litt outside the house, before you-all came
in?"

"A little while, Dunk."

"And he didn't tell you he was fixin' to do this?"

"Not in so many words."

"Where do you reckon Litt would be right now?"

Billy's smile was gone. He took off his hat and wiped sweat from his forehead onto his sleeve. "Could be he's over somewhere around Cedarville, scratchin' names off of that list. With this, on top of the things he *did* tell me, it kind of adds up."

McLendon closed his eyes, a helpless anger swelling in him. "You better tell me all of it, Billy, and tell me quick."

Billy Hutto didn't look at McLendon. His gaze was on the ground. "He said we'd come a day too early for him. Said if we'd come a day later he'd of finished what he intended to do and it wouldn't make no difference anymore. Said he had a bunch comin' to help him. He was goin' to ride over to Cedarville and bait that sheriff to come after him. He was goin' to lead him into a box, him and everybody from town who went with him."

"The sheriff?"

"The sheriff's right at the top of Litt's list. Seems like he told that deputy the mob would be along, and to let them have Ollie Springer."

McLendon's voice was taut. "Billy, I thought you were a Ranger."

"I am. But I'm a friend of Litt Springer's, too."

"Right now you can't be both. Which way is it goin' to be?"

A stubborn anger flared in Billy. "That bunch of rattlesnakes . . . old Litt's got a right to do what he's doin'."

"Not by law."

"Law be damned. There's times when the law is wrong."

McLendon turned and looked regretfully over their

back trail. "I know. But it's still the law. You better go to Austin, Billy."

Billy was incredulous. "And leave you?"

"I don't want a man with me unless he's with me all the way. You took an oath, Billy. If you can't live up to it you better turn that badge in."

Billy stared at him, not believing at first. Finally he shrugged. "All right, Dunk. But he's your friend too."

"You don't have to remind me of that." McLendon unpacked the mule and took what little he thought he would have to have. He tied the meager supplies on his saddle, swung up and reined toward Cedarville in a long trot, alone.

The temptation was strong to push the horse into a hard lope, to rush for Cedarville. But it was a long way, and a horse ridden too hard might not make it. Years of Ranger experience had taught McLendon restraint. He had spent as much as two days carefully following an Indian trail, always within striking distance but always holding back, waiting for the right place and the right movement. Once he had spent three weeks patiently tracking a Mexican border jumper who, if not pressed or alarmed, would eventually lead him to the headquarters of an entire bandido operation.

All manner of images blazed in his mind, things that could be happening in Cedarville, or somewhere out among these limestone hills. But McLendon held himself back. He would swing into an easy lope for a way, then ease down to a trot, putting the miles behind him much too slowly.

Well past noon, he rode down Cedarville's dusty street and found it quiet. Hearing the ring of a hammer, he reined in at a blacksmith shop. The blacksmith was shaping a shoe against an anvil. Leaning out of the saddle, McLendon called, "You seen the sheriff?"

The grimy blacksmith pointed the tongs, the hot shoe still gripped in them. "That Litt Springer, he showed up at the edge of town this mornin'. Sheriff got a few men together and took out after him. Last I seen, they disappeared yonderway."

McLendon rode in a wide arc until he came across a trail he took to be the posse's. Spacing and depth of the tracks indicated the horses had been running. He put his horse into an easy lope. Trailing this was no effort. He could have followed this one in the middle of the night. An hour later he brought the horse to a stop. The warm wind had carried a sharp sound. He dismounted to get away from the saddle's creak so he could hear better. Presently it came again. A gunshot. And another.

*Litt's working on that list,* he thought darkly. He remounted. This time he didn't hold back. He spurred into a hard lope and held it. *Damn it, Litt, why couldn't you have listened?*

Ahead lay a range of broken hills, and amid those hills, a gap. McLendon could see horses, a single rider herding them a short way from the gap, away from the angle of fire. He halted awhile, studying the layout, determining where Litt and his men were scattered, and where the posse seemed to be bottled up in that gap. The firing was sporadic, just an occasional shot fired by one side or the other.

McLendon paused, looking at the gap but not really seeing it, listening to the shots but not really hearing them. He was seeing other battlegrounds, and other times. He was seeing a Litt Springer far different from the one down yonder.

He brought the rifle up from its scabbard, levered

a cartridge into the breech and lay the rifle across his lap. He unpinned the badge from inside his vest and transferred it to the outside where no one could miss seeing it. *Good target,* he thought. But it had been used for a target before. Gently he touched the spurs to the horse and moved into an easy trot again.

The horse herder rode forward, six-shooter in his hand. He wasn't a man, McLendon saw; he was only a boy, perhaps fifteen or sixteen. The boy stopped squarely in McLendon's path, the pistol aimed but the barrel wavering. The boy's voice was unsteady. "Ranger, ain't you? Litt won't be wantin' you in there."

"I'm goin' in there, son. I'm going to see Litt." McLendon kept riding, gazing unflinchingly into the boy's eyes. He could see uncertainty. "Son, you move out of my way."

"Ranger, I'm tellin' you . . ."

McLendon didn't slow. He kept staring the boy down. The boy's horse turned aside, the boy trying to rein him back around. McLendon rode past. He never turned his head, but he could feel the gun aimed at his back. He tensed, but he was almost certain—the boy wouldn't fire.

He rode into the opening of the gap. Now he could see Litt's men, perhaps a dozen of them, scattered among the rocks. He couldn't see the sheriff's crowd, for they were keeping their heads down, but he could tell where they would be. A man turned and saw McLendon, and he swung his rifle to cover him.

McLendon said evenly, "I come to see Litt."

"Ranger, you got no business here."

"I come to see Litt."

A call went down the line. Presently McLendon saw Litt Springer moving toward him, crouching to present less of a target to the men bottled up back yonder. Litt straightened when he thought he was past the point of danger. He walked out, flanked by a couple of his backers, carrying rifles. Litt looked surprised. "Wasn't expectin' you, Dunk. Thought you'd still be followin' that false trail. Where's Billy Hutto?"

"I sent him to Austin to turn his badge in."

Litt frowned. "I'm sorry about that. He's a good boy, Billy is. He'd of been an asset to the force."

"Not if he couldn't learn to put duty first. And he couldn't."

Litt's eyebrows knitted. "But you do, don't you, Dunk? Duty always comes first with you."

"The day it doesn't, I'll turn in my *own* badge."

"You shouldn't have come here, Dunk. Most of the men we got hemmed down was with that mob the day they hung Ollie. This is as far as they're goin' to go."

"I told you before, Litt, leave it to the law. Lynchin' is a form of murder. We'll take care of them the way it's supposed to be done."

"The law lets too many fish get out of the net. We've got these caught. There ain't none of them gettin' away."

"You're makin' yourself as bad as they are. Worse, even, because you've been a Ranger. I'm askin' you one more time. Let the law punish them."

"The law's too uncertain. *I'll* punish them."

"And start a war. I reckon Martha was right, Litt. You stayed with the Rangers too long."

"What do you mean?"

"You should've quit when it still gave you nightmares to kill a man. Killin' comes too easy for you now."

"When this is over I'll be satisfied."

"No you won't, Litt. There won't be any satisfyin' you because these killin's will lead to more. There'll be other deaths to avenge. There won't be any stop to it till half the men in this county are dead, and you among them. There won't be any rest for you this side of the cemetery gate."

"What do you figure on doin' about it, Dunk?"

"I got to stop you if I can."

Litt held out his hand. "I want your guns."

"Not anymore, Litt. I gave you my gun last night, but I won't do it again. You want it, you'll have to shoot me."

Litt Springer tried to stare him down, but McLendon held against him. Litt shrugged. "Then turn around and ride out of here, Dunk."

"I'm sorry, Litt. Your friendship has meant a lot to me. But from now on I'm not your friend. I'm a Ranger, and I got a job to do."

"Good-bye, Dunk."

"Good-bye, Litt."

McLendon reined the horse around and started away in a walk. The wind had stopped, and the still heat seemed to rise up and envelop him. Another shot came from the gap, but McLendon didn't hear it. He was hearing muffled echoes of old voices and old laughter from beyond a door he had shut behind him.

Gripping the rifle, he suddenly reined his horse around. He spurred him into a run. Ahead of him, he saw Litt Springer stare in surprise, eyes wide, his mouth open. Litt started bringing up the pistol he had held at arm's length. One of the men with him shouted a warning and dropped to one knee.

McLendon leveled the rifle. He saw fire belch from

Litt's pistol but knew Litt had missed by a mile. McLendon squeezed the trigger and felt the riflebutt drive back against his shoulder. Through the smoke he saw Litt Springer stagger backward, the pistol dropping from his hand. McLendon leaned over the horse's neck as the man on his knee brought his rifle into line.

Litt coughed an order, and the man lowered the rifle. McLendon levered a fresh cartridge into his own and stepped to the ground, letting the horse go. Litt Springer was on his knees, arms folded across his chest, his face going gray. He stared at McLendon in disbelief.

"Dunk . . . I didn't think you could."

Some of Litt's men came running, and McLendon could see danger in their eyes. One grabbed at the Ranger, and another shoved a pistol into his belly.

Weakly Litt said, "Let him alone, boys . . . He's a friend of mine."

"Friend?" one of them shouted angrily.

"A friend," rasped Litt. "He done what he figured he had to."

Litt crumpled. McLendon let his rifle fall and eased Litt onto his back on the ground. Throat tightening, he said: "I didn't want to, Litt. I kept tellin' you . . ."

"And I ought to've known. You're a better Ranger than I ever was, Dunk."

Litt's friends were gathering, leaving their places around the men they had trapped in the gap. Litt started to cough. McLendon could see blood on his lips. "Litt," he said, "call them off. Let this be the end of it."

Litt blinked, his vision fading. "You told me you'd see that the law took care of them."

"I meant it, Litt. I'll see that every one of that mob pays."

Litt nodded. "And you ain't never lied to me. Boys, go on home."

A few of them wanted to argue, but Litt waved them away with a weak motion of his hand. "We got his promise. Go home, boys."

Litt was gone then. Slowly the rest of the men came down from their positions. Openly hostile, they honored Litt's order. They caught up their horses and soon were gone, the dust settling slowly behind them.

Cautiously the sheriff crept out of the gap, rifle in his hands. Behind him the others followed, some still crouching, suspicious. Finally satisfied, the sheriff straightened and let his rifle arm hand loose. He strode over and looked down on the still form of Litt Springer.

"I seen what you done, Ranger. To be honest with you, didn't think you would. I reckon we owe you."

Curtly McLendon said, "You owe me nothin'."

The sheriff shrugged. "Have it the way you want it. Takes a special breed of a man who can shoot down his own friend thataway. I'll remember it. If ever I got another cold-blooded job that needs doin', I'll call on the Rangers."

McLendon didn't even think. In sudden rage he swung the riflebutt around and clubbed the sheriff full in the face. The lawman fell, surprised and cursing, the blood streaming from his broken nose.

The others stood frozen in shock. "Get him up," McLendon shouted. "Get him up and out of here before I kill him!" As they hauled the sheriff to his feet, McLendon said, "Wait!" They paused. McLendon gritted: "I'm takin' Litt home to bury him.

But I'm comin' back. I got his list, and every man on it is goin' to answer to a judge. Now git!"

They caught their horses and helped the sheriff into his saddle and rode off toward Cedarville. Looking down on Litt Springer, Duncan McLendon unpinned the Ranger badge from the front of his vest and put it back on the underside, where he usually wore it. They wouldn't need it to know who he was.

# RELICS

**T**he deputy sheriff sat hunched on the wagon tongue, tin plate in his hand, wolfing down cold beef, cold beans, and the morning's biscuits as if he hadn't eaten in a couple of days. Wagon cook George Davenport, standing by the chuck box, watched dourly as he kneaded sourdough for noon biscuits. He considered how disappointed that kid horse wrangler was going to be in an hour or so when he rode in for his midmorning snack of cold biscuits and leftover breakfast steak; there wasn't going to be any.

The deputy washed down a big mouthful with black coffee—that was one thing always hot around George's campfire, no matter what time of day it was—and said for the third time at least: "If he should happen along this way, don't you be tryin' to make a hero out of yourself, old-timer. You just give him anything he asks for and then send for us right away. He'd kill you in a minute if you was to give him cause."

George Davenport nodded passively and went

on with his work. He wasn't fixing to try to do anything about Enos Foxley if he happened by this chuckwagon, nor would he send for the law. George was going to be sixty years old next October, Lord willing, and one way he had gotten this far was by minding his own business. Over the years he had fed more than one outlaw at his wagon and had given several a bunk in whatever ranch shack, dugout, or tent he happened to be living in at the time. He had never felt an obligation to say anything about it. As long as Enos Foxley did neither him nor the T Bar Cattle Company any harm, George looked upon him as the law's worry, not his own. He couldn't remember any of the back-trail breed had ever done him any personal injury, something he couldn't say for those jerkwater "laws" that was always looking to lock a man up and fine him his whole month's pay for cutting loose a little.

The deputy went back to the cold Dutch ovens to refill his plate, and finished cleaning out what little he hadn't taken the first time. George looked over east toward the hills; he was expecting the kid to come in from the horse herd just about any time now.

Well, the boy would just have to listen to his stomach growl this morning and hold out till dinner with the rest of the men. It had been so long since George had had that young appetite, he found it hard to remember anymore. One disadvantage of growing old was loss of appetite. Or maybe it was an advantage; he hadn't quite decided which. He had lost his old appetite not only for food but for whiskey and women as well. That lent to tranquility in his downhill years. It also lent to his being able to save a modest nest egg to buy him a little house on the edge of town, where he could live out his time doing something light, like maybe running a ten-by-twelve chili joint. He had begun to fancy that idea lately, especially during the cold winter months just past. The greatest luxury of all would be sleeping until six or maybe even seven o'clock any morning he felt like it. A good wagon cook was never in the blankets past four in the morning. It was getting so his rheumy bones hated to leave that warm bedroll and get up to the black morning chill.

The deputy took the last piece of the last biscuit and wiped his plate clean with it, getting every remnant of the beans. George half expected him to wipe the pot too, but he didn't.

"You got a gun?" the deputy asked.

"You ever see a chuckwagon that didn't have a gun someplace? I keep a pistol in the chuck box."

"Well, you stay clear of it if Enos Foxley comes along. He won't give you no chance. You sure you know what he looks like?"

George assured him for the third or fourth time he had seen Foxley around the saloons last winter and would know his hide in a tanyard. "All right," the deputy said, walking toward the horse he had tied much too close to George's wagon, "you remember what I told you; he killed that storekeeper over by Midland for the sixty-seventy dollars in his cashbox. A man like that'll do anything. He comes by here, you let us know."

George was beginning to glower. The deputy was using that patronizing voice people save for kids and old folks; George didn't consider himself either one. He watched the man swing into the saddle and thought quietly he was beginning to run to gut. Seemed like a lot of these town laws had a tendency in that direction. George remembered cooking through spring roundup for the 07's five or six years ago when this same hombre was on the payroll as a cowpuncher. He hadn't been much of a cowboy; he wasn't much of a deputy sheriff either, George judged. He was relieved when the man finally rode through a spring patch of yellow and purple flowers and disappeared over the greening hill to the south, in the general direction of Midland.

George gave one more moment's thought to Enos Foxley, decided the man had probably lit out for Old Mexico, and put him out of his mind. He walked over to the coffeepot and found to his relief that it was still half full; the deputy hadn't been able to drink it all after stuffing himself on the leftover breakfast. George wouldn't have to put any fresh coffee on for a while.

He lost himself in his work, scrubbing up the morning's breakfast ovens and last night's bean pot the deputy had emptied. The dough sat on the hinged-down chuck-box lid, rising for the biscuits he would pinch off later and cook in a Dutch oven, hot coals shoveled over top and under bottom.

Presently he heard a rattle of trace chains. He turned, wondering for a minute what that fool kid Jug was up to. He saw a hunched figure riding a deep-bodied old farm wagon drawn by a pair of work-horses that had seen better days. Sam Weaver, face hidden by a month's growth of tobacco-stained gray whiskers, waved faintly and drew his team to a halt a respectable distance from George's wagon, where they wouldn't stir dust to drift into George's fixings. That was more thoughtfulness than the deputy had shown.

"Howdy, George," Sam hailed in a voice rough

as cedar bark. "Thought I'd stop by and see how you're doin'."

*Thought you'd stop by and get some of my cooking instead of fix for yourself,* George thought. He wouldn't have said it aloud for fifty dollars in silver. He had known Sam Weaver for too many years.

Sam had a heavy tarp drawn tightly over the wagon bed and tied down so no horse would work its nose under there and eat any of what he carried—grain soaked in a strychnine poison. He looked back to make sure the tarp had in no way worked loose, then stiffly, carefully began to crawl down from the old spring seat. He winced, and George knew Sam's knees hurt him with every step he took. Sam was even older than George, by maybe five or six years. At one time or another during the long years he had worked as a cowboy, he had broken just about every major bone in his body, except perhaps his neck. So, for that matter, had George. But at least George had finally developed some proficiency as a cook, so he could stand off and watch some other poor devil climb up there and do battle with those owl-headed broncs.

Sam had never known anything but punching cows. Now he was too old for that and they had given him the job of running that poison wagon, killing prairie dogs off of the T Bar. A new state law had been passed in Texas, with the concurrence of most landowners, requiring every owner to eradicate prairie dogs from his property or pay an assessment for the state or county government to do it. It had been decided the prairie dog did too much damage to the grasslands and caused too many crippled horses and men. The easiest way to get him was simply to shovel some poisoned grain down the hole in which the prairie dog lived. It was a job even a worn-out old puncher like Sam Weaver could handle.

Sam had a camp of his own, but he was always hungry when he came by George's wagon. Sam never could boil water without making it taste scorched. "What you got that's good to eat?" he asked as he limped up to George's smouldering fire and looked hopefully at the ovens.

George said testily, "You're too late if you've come to eat. I just fed it all to one of them laws from town."

Sam didn't take his word for it; he poked around all the ovens, lifting the lids off with a long black pothook. When he turned, he was trying to cover his disappointment. "Must've been a hungry one."

*No hungrier than Sam,* George thought. He felt his impatience ebb. *Hell, I'll be old myself one of these days.* "Get you some coffee and set down someplace. I'll fry you up a strip of beef and a little bread, squaw style."

"I don't want to be no bother," Sam said apologetically. "I was just ridin' by."

George knew he had probably ridden a right smart out of his way. He partially unwrapped a section of tarp from around a quarter of beef hanging off of the chuck box. He sliced a generous strip of steak. He hoped that kid wrangler didn't ride in here and catch him at it; he would be pestering George every day to do the same thing, and George wasn't about to start any new bad habits. He had enough already.

Sam sat on a big mesquite trunk that George had been using for a woodchopping block. He nursed a tin cup of coffee in his stiff hands. He had a weary look about him—a man who had long since earned the right to sit in the shade but never had been able to afford it. George heated grease in an open Dutch

oven, then dropped the steak and a big pinch of
bread dough into it. He straightened, pressing his
hands against the small of his back where the rheu-
matism had been getting at him. He looked first at
Sam's patient old horses, standing droop-headed in
the traces, then at the wagon itself.

"You ever carry anything to eat when you're out
workin'?"

"Sometimes, when I think of it. Mainly I just carry
me a jug, and a bucket to fix coffee in."

"You ever get scared foolin' with that poison? Ever
think what would happen to you if you was to get
a little of it mixed up in your food? Just a pinch off
of your hands might be enough to—" He broke off.
The thought was painful to contemplate.

"I just have to watch what I'm doin'." Sam
shrugged. "A man could hurt himself with a wheel-
barrow if he didn't watch."

George used a long fork to turn over the steak
and the wad of dough. "It ever bother you, Sam,
what you're doin' to them poor prairie dogs?" He
frowned. "They was here even before *we* was, and
*we* been here since they built the mountains and dug
the Pecos River."

Sam shrugged again, but George could see he
had touched him in a spot that hurt. "Somebody's
goin' to do it, George. It's the law. There ain't much
anybody'll hire me for anymore. I got to turn my
hand at *somethin'*."

"It's goin' to be a different-lookin' country when
all them prairie dogs are gone. It won't seem right
without them."

"It's the law," Sam said defensively.

George nodded, recognizing the inevitability but
saddened by it. The prairie dog was a relic of the

past, a relic nobody wanted anymore. They were using another relic, Sam, to get rid of it.

*What'll they do to get rid of Sam?* he wondered, knowing the answer even as the question crossed his mind. They would simply ignore him, and one day he would be gone.

It probably wouldn't be much longer before they would be trying to ignore George too. But they would play hell doing it. He had money—damn near seven hundred dollars stashed in the Midland bank—and people didn't ignore a man who had money.

George made Sam wash his hands before he would let him start on the steak and fried bread; he was afraid Sam might have some of that strychnine on his fingers. Sam made a good start on the food. George knew that he probably hadn't had anything except coffee since yesterday. He wondered why it was that some old people hated so badly to cook. It beat hell out of riding broncs, or trying to.

The horse wrangler came in when Sam had about half finished eating what George had cooked for him. The boy rode a good stout young sorrel horse the boss had let him break during the slow time last winter and had kindly left in the kid's string. When an outfit let a kid keep a really good horse, that was a sign he was working his way up in the world. The boy called the horse Red, appropriate enough in view of the color. Jug would have stuck both bare feet into a bucket of hot coals rather than let anything happen to that horse.

He was tying the reins to the rear wheel of Sam's wagon when George hollered, "Git that horse away from there! Don't you know that's full of poisoned grain?"

Jug yanked the reins free and walked the horse out to a mesquite tree well away from the wagon.

George grumbled, "Young boys and young horses . . . not a lick of brains in either one of them."

"You got no patience," Sam said, "and no memory either."

Jug Adams walked to the cookfire, whistling expectantly. *Happy as if he had good sense,* George thought. He figured Jug to be about sixteen; Jug claimed twenty. George was dubious about the "Adams" part too. In all likelihood Jug was an East Texas farm boy who had run away from home and didn't want to be found until he had made good on his own, a full-fledged cowboy drawing a grown man's wages and drinking a man's whiskey. George had seen fifty like him over the years. Hell, he had *been* one like him a long time ago. He remembered, despite what Sam had said.

Jug found the pans empty and turned to George in dismay. "How come you threw everything out?"

"I didn't. I had company."

Sam Weaver's dull gray eyes brightened as he watched the boy hunt around the chuck box in vain. He looked down at the plate in his lap, then back to the boy. "Jug, I got more here than I can eat. Come share it with me."

George protested, "He ain't goin' to starve between now and noon." Sam needed the food more than Jug did.

Sam replied, "You're too old and cranky to remember how hungry a boy can get. But I remember. Come on, Jug, finish it so I don't get the bellyache."

When Jug had finished Sam's steak and bread, he gave vent to his curiosity. He had to know who had visited the camp and why. George told him about the deputy and that the laws were all hunting Enos Foxley.

The boy perked up. "I've heard about Foxley. They say he can be a mean one. They got any reward out for him?"

George frowned. It was not healthy for boys to get overly interested in such things; pretty soon they would get to thinking the world was made of easy money and they wouldn't want to sweat anymore. "He didn't mention no reward."

"I'll bet there is one. I sure wish he'd come by here. I could use a little extra cash."

Sam smiled. "What would you do with it, son?"

"I'd buy me a new saddle to put on Red. That's one thing. Then I'd—" He stopped. He had already covered the important part.

George said crustily, "Man like Enos Foxley comes by, you'd better just look off and whistle a tune so you don't see nothin' or hear nothin'. If the laws want him, let the laws find him."

After a bit the young wrangler drifted off toward the scattering remuda, which was his responsibility. It would be his job to take the horses to the morning gather when the cowboys bunched the herd. They would change to fresh mounts. A little after the boy left, Sam decided he had better leave too; he had a prairie dog "town" to work.

"You come back by when you get done," George told him. "I'll see that you have somethin' to eat."

"I'll do that," Sam said, and put his team into an easy trot, jingling the chains as he made his way around the hill.

The cowboys came in at noon, eating by relays so some of the crew could always be with the cattle herd. It was out of sight to the east, but now and again when the breeze came just right, George could hear the bawling. They were branding the calves, whittling ears, turning prospective bulls into a better prospect for beef.

When the cowboys were all gone and the dishes were washed, George stretched out under the shade of the wagon for the siesta he normally took when he wasn't on the move between camps. The breeze was cool, and it didn't take him long to drop off. He didn't know how long he slept, but when he awoke it was suddenly and with a start. He sat upright, nearly bumping his head on the belly of the wagon.

A man stood by the chuck box. George couldn't see much of him above the belt buckle, but he saw the six-shooter shoved into the waistband of the striped California-style pants. He first thought it was another of those hungry laws. He crawled stiffly out from under the wagon, taking his time about straightening up because of a nagging pain in his back.

He saw the face then and knew this was no lawman. This was Enos Foxley.

"Didn't go to wake you up," Foxley said. The words were apologetic, but the voice wasn't. The words were merely form, an obligation. George knew if he hadn't awakened by himself, Foxley would have awakened him. Foxley asked, "Could I trouble you for somethin' to eat?"

George told him there was coffee in the pot, but Foxley had already found it. His rummaging for a cup was probably what had brought George out of his nap. "The coffee's fine," Foxley said, "but it ain't enough to carry me far. I'd be obliged if you could let me have somethin' more substantial." The words were polite, but the eyes were commanding and cold.

George told him to help himself to what was in the pots, left over from dinner. He remembered there had been several high-rise biscuits in one Dutch oven, and a pot of beans usually lasted at least two meals. A couple or three strips of steak had been left; he had put them in the oven on top of the bread, knowing Jug would surely come by during the afternoon, and maybe Sam too.

Foxley was nervous in the way he watched George, so George made it a point to stand out in the open, several steps away from him, hoping to demonstrate his own peaceful intentions and set the man's mind at ease. Several of this twisty breed had crossed his trail over the years; he had found it prudent not to cause them anxiety. Most were like a badger—pure hell when they thought they were in a corner.

Thank God, he thought, there weren't many of this kind left. They belonged to another time, and that time was gone. George might grieve a little over the prairie dog or the passing of the open range, but he would feel relief when the last Enos Foxley was gone.

Foxley ate with a hunger that bordered on ferocity. He was even hungrier than that soft-bellied deputy. His gaze stayed on George most of the time but periodically made a long sweep around him, making sure nothing came near that he didn't see. When his worst hunger had been appeased, he slowed a little, taking more time with the second plate. He studied George intently and without trust. "Ain't I seen you before?"

George admitted, "I spent some time in Midland around Christmas."

Foxley's eyes narrowed. "Then I reckon you know who I am?"

George figured a lie would be worse than the truth; it would be too obvious. "I know you."

Foxley held his silence a minute, eating. "I didn't go to kill that storekeeper. Damn fool tried to pull a gun out of a drawer. That made it self-defense, the way I see it."

That the storekeeper had been a damn fool, George had no doubt; the fact that Foxley was robbing him at the time made it difficult for George to accept the notion of self-defense. He chose not to make an issue of it, however.

Foxley finished the plate and went back to the pans. He couldn't really be hungry anymore, but he was probably going by the old Indian adage that when a man had the chance to eat, he ought to take all his system could absorb; he never knew when the next meal might come to him. The breeze brought the sound of the bawling cow herd, a long way off. Foxley turned his ear to it, listening.

He said, "That horse of mine is about caved in. Whichaway's your remuda?"

For the first time George lied to him. "I don't rightly know. The wrangler ain't been in since dinner."

What Foxley had done to a reckless storekeeper a long way from here was none of George's business. But when he contemplated taking a T Bar horse, that was getting too close to home. What's more, that fool kid would probably put up a fuss and get a gun barrel applied over his ear.

Foxley's eyes bored into George; he didn't know whether to believe the cook or not. "Old-timer, I do need me a fresh horse."

George stared silently at him with the best poker face he had.

Foxley turned suddenly, startled, and drew the six-shooter. George heard the trace chains again. Sam Weaver was coming back with his wagon. Foxley glanced urgently at George, his eyes asking.

George said, "It's nobody that'll bother you. It's just old Sam Weaver. The company's got him poisonin' prairie dogs."

Foxley kept his hand on the pistol just the same, until Sam had drawn the team to a halt and was climbing down on the right front wheel, taking his time. He stopped and squinted, trying to get a clear image of Foxley. Sam's eyes were none too good. Either he was too proud to wear glasses or he didn't have the money. George eased out toward him, trying to head him off.

"Sam," he said roughly, "I got nothin' for you to eat. You'd just as well be gettin' back to your own camp."

But Sam Weaver was close enough now for a good look at Foxley. George knew from Sam's eyes that the old man recognized him. The presence of two men in camp would make Foxley more nervous than he already was, even if the two were old.

"Sam," George said, "I ain't got time to mess with you now."

Sam said stubbornly, "You already got company. A little more ain't goin' to hurt you."

George understood then. Sam had the notion George was in danger and that by staying here he might somehow protect him. "Sam . . ." he protested, then ran out of words. There was no use in arguing. Old men like that had a way of being unreasonable.

Enos Foxley took a few steps toward the wagon, his eyes on Sam's horses. George could see him weighing the proposition, then deciding against it.

His own horse, even tired, was better than either of Sam's. Foxley shoved the pistol back into his waistband.

George knew he could do nothing now except stand here with Sam and hope Foxley would soon decide it was time to be riding. He thought about the pistol in the chuck box, but he wouldn't have gone near it for a thousand dollars in gold coin carried to him in silken bags by twelve naked maidens on horseback.

For a minute he thought Foxley was fixing to go. The outlaw walked out to where his horse was tied, then stopped there, looking to the west. George cursed under his breath. "That damn fool kid. I swear, that appetite of his will be the death of him before he has a chance to outgrow it."

Jug Adams came riding in, whistling. He was on Red again; George wondered sometimes if that poor horse ever had a rest. Jug waved at Sam as he rode to the same mesquite where he had tied Red earlier in the day. "Howdy, Sam, you back already? Hope you got ol' George to fix us somethin' fresh to eat."

George wanted to holler at the kid to get the hell out of there, but it wouldn't have been any use. He would have asked "What?" twice and "Why?" afterward.

Jug didn't know Enos Foxley from Abraham Lincoln. He waved in his thoughtless, friendly way and said, "Hello, friend, you another one of them lawmen?"

George closed his eyes and said some cusswords he hadn't been using much of late.

Foxley said, "No, son, not a law. Just a passin' stranger. Good-lookin' horse you got there."

"Best horse in the whole outfit," Jug said proudly.

"I'd stand him up against anything in this country or any of them that adjoins it."

*Goddammit, Jug,* George thought, *I wisht you'd shut up!*

Foxley said, "I've got a pretty good one here myself, if he wasn't tired out. He'd make a nice swap for that sorrel of yours."

Jug hadn't begun to catch on. "Red's not for tradin'."

Foxley had been walking slowly toward Jug while he talked. He reached out and took Red's reins. "I'm makin' the trade, boy. You'd better stand back over yonder with them friends of yours and be good so I don't have to do anything unpleasant."

Only now did it soak in on Jug that this man intended to take his horse away from him. He grabbed at the reins, gripping them above Foxley's hands, near the bits. "Mister, I don't know who you think you are—"

"You know, if you'll think about it."

Jug thought about it, and George could tell that he finally realized who he was dealing with. But it made no difference. Jug grabbed the reins with both hands and held tight.

"You ain't takin' my horse!"

Foxley glanced toward George as if asking him for help. "Damn it, man, I ain't got time to mess with a fool kid."

George said, "Jug, you'd better come here to me!"

Jug had no such intention. He held bitterly to the reins. Foxley's face darkened. "Oh, hell," he said, and pulled the six-shooter from his waistband.

George's heart went to his throat. He thought Foxley was about to shoot the kid. Foxley swung the barrel and struck Jug a glancing blow to the side of his head. Jug went to his knees, his floppy old felt hat sailing off, but he didn't let loose of the reins for long. He groped and caught them.

"Damned hardheaded kid!" Foxley said angrily, and swung the gun barrel again.

Sam cried, "George, he's killin' that boy!" Sam turned and ran for the chuckwagon.

George called, "Sam . . ."

Nothing he could have done would have stopped what happened. Sam reached into the chuck box and came up with the pistol George kept there. But he didn't know that George always kept a chamber empty to avoid an accident. Sam brought the pistol around and trained it on Foxley.

George heard the click of the hammer falling on a spent cartridge, then heard the roar of Foxley's six-shooter. Sam Weaver slammed back against the wagon wheel, then went down like he had been struck by a sledgehammer. He never moved.

Jug lay on his stomach, his head bleeding. He was trying to crawl but getting nowhere.

"What about you, old man?" Foxley demanded of George. "Am I goin' to have trouble with you too?"

George pulled his eyes away from Sam, shuddering from a hard and sudden chill. "No trouble."

"Worst bunch of damn fools I ever come up against," Foxley complained. "I didn't come here to kill anybody. I just come for somethin' to eat and a horse. I'm takin' the sorrel."

Frozen, George stood watching him. He fought an urge to turn and look again at Sam. He knew it was useless to try to help. Sam was dead.

Foxley swung into Jug's saddle, tried the stirrups, and stepped down again. "Too short for me. I'm goin' to change my saddle onto him. You put some food into a sack, old man, so I'll have somethin' to eat along the way."

George couldn't seem to move his feet. Foxley waved the six-shooter at him. "I'll tell you just one more time. Get me some food to take along."

George found his feet and turned toward the wagon.

The sheriff was older than his deputy and assumed none of the younger man's superior airs. He was strictly business as he lifted the blanket back over the bearded face of old Sam.

George sat hunched on a bedroll, chilled and numb, as if he had been kicked in the stomach. He studied the kid lying on a blanket beneath the wagon, stirring a little but not rising up. Jug hadn't been clear in his head yet; he didn't remember what had happened to him. He would have time later to remember, a whole lifetime.

The deputy said defensively, "I told them, Joe; I told them not to mess around with Foxley. I told them to leave him to us."

The sheriff cut him a sharp, quick look that told him to shut the hell up. He turned back to George with sympathy in his eyes. "I'm sorry about old Sam. And I'm sorry about the long head start Foxley got on us. Three hours . . . we'll never make that up."

George hadn't said much; he hadn't felt like it. He had given short answers to direct questions, and that was all. He shook his head. "You can catch up to him all right. All you got to do is to follow that sorrel's tracks."

"We been pushin' our horses hard. His is probably fresher."

"Won't matter," George said flatly. "Sooner or later he'll stop to eat what I packed for him. That's where you'll find him."

The sheriff's eyes narrowed, asking a question. George said, "I put the food in a sack out of Sam's wagon."

The impact hit the sheriff like a fist. "My God! You poisoned him!"

George shrugged, looking back at Jug Adams and Sam.

The sheriff hurriedly swung into his saddle and motioned for the deputy to follow him. They rode out of camp in a long trot, following Foxley's tracks. The sheriff was saying maybe if they hurried they would get to Foxley before he stopped to eat. But they wouldn't, George knew.

The T Bar wagon boss stood slack-jawed, staring at George in disbelief. George explained, "He killed Sam. Sam's poison has killed *him,* or will. Seems right enough to me."

"But he's a man, George."

George shook his head again. "He's a relic." He stared at the blanket that covered Sam Weaver. His voice was cold. "Who's got time or use for relics anymore?"

```
┌─────────────────────────────┐
│                             │
│        NORTH                │
│        OF THE               │
│        BIG RIVER            │
│                             │
└─────────────────────────────┘
```

**I**'d always looked down my nose at ranchmen hiring wetbacks. That's the people who swim over into Texas from the south of the Rio Grande. They generally come in the dark of the moon, looking back over their shoulders for the border patrol.

Folks call me Ike Ballantine. For forty years I've been ranching ten miles north of the river. The way I figured it, cheap wetback labor was unfair to workers on our own side of the river. Besides, hiring wetbacks was breaking the law, just like their swimming over had been. But then Pedro Gonzales came along.

It all commenced one evening when I was sitting in a rawhide chair on my front porch, glancing over the stock news in the San Angelo paper. I happened to look up over my reading glasses and spot this feller slipping up through the brush afoot. I stepped into the house and grabbed my .30-.30. As I levered a cartridge into the breech I watched the man bend low and sprint up to the house. He disappeared under a window.

Little Juanita Chavez was fixing supper in the kitchen. Her eyes got as big as the biscuits she was cutting when I slipped through there with the rifle. I stepped out the door and waited on the back porch.

When the fellow came around the corner, I shoved the gun barrel under his nose. He dropped a little bundle he was carrying. His brownish skin turned a shade lighter, and he licked his lips.

"Please, sir," he said nervously, in good English. "I mean no harm."

I saw then that he was young, not much older than Juanita.

All of a sudden he slumped over onto the porch. I was so surprised I dropped the rifle and grabbed him. That was when I saw the bloodstains on his shirt, and the knife-slit in his sleeve.

I yelled for Juanita to go get her dad, but old Trinidad was already running up from the barn. His soft belly bounced up and down over a low-slung belt. Neither one of us was as young as we used to be, but we managed to carry the boy into the house and lay him down on a couch.

Juanita hustled some hot water. Her pretty face got a little pale as she cleaned up the knife wound. It wasn't too deep, and it hadn't struck an artery. She held a warm, damp cloth on the boy's forehead while I poured rubbing alcohol into the wound. Busy as I was, I couldn't help seeing the way Juanita's dark eyes melted when that boy began to flinch.

I'd known Juanita ever since she was born, and I'd never seen her look that way before. Her dad had been working for me for thirty years. He was nearing middle age when he brought a young wife to share the little house he lived in, out back of mine. The woman had died when Juanita was born. My own wife was gone, too. So between old Trinidad and me, we'd managed to raise Juanita ourselves. Now, watching the way she handled the man, I guess we both felt proud of ourselves.

The young man looked startled as he opened his eyes and saw Juanita bending over him. Waking up and seeing a girl like her would be apt to make any man think of heaven.

We heard the rattling of a pickup truck on the road leading up to the house. The young Mexican's eyes got wide as if it was the hangman coming.

"It's Señor Barfield," he exclaimed. "I must get away!" He jumped up and almost fell to the floor. I helped Juanita put him back on the couch.

"Keep him still," I told her. "I don't know what this is all about, but Barfield won't get him."

I walked out front as Clint Barfield braked his pickup to a stop. Although he was my neighbor on the south, it was the first time he had been on my place since I'd caught him trying to cheat me in a cattle trade a couple of years back.

He crawled out of his pickup like a mad bull coming through a barbed-wire fence. Another man was with him, his dark-skinned *segundo* named Salazar.

"I'm looking for a damned wetback that left my place this mornin'," Barfield boomed. "If he's come over here, I want him right now!"

Barfield's face had always made me think of a grizzly bear, especially when he was mad.

"What do you want him for?" I asked.

"He stole one of my horses. If you got him here, bring him out."

I could feel a fire kindling up in me. I wished I'd brought my gun along.

"There's nobody here but me and the Chavez

family," I told him flatly. "And I'd just as soon you'd git off my place."

Barfield stood glaring as if he wanted to take an ax handle to me. He was big enough to whip me without any help.

Just then Salazar came around the corner of the house. I hadn't noticed him sneak away. He was carrying the bundle of clothes the young Mexican had dropped by the back porch.

"I won't fool with you, Ballantine," Barfield thundered. "Drag that boy out here or I'll tell the border patrol you're harborin' wetbacks!"

I couldn't help snickering. "But you'd have to tell them how you come to know. You probably had him grubbin' prickly pear, then refused to pay him, like you do so many wetbacks. If he took a horse, he'd probably earned it."

Barfield and Salazar began to move toward me. Then they stopped and looked up on the porch. I glanced back. Old Trinidad stood there like a bulldog, the .30-.30 rifle in his hands.

Barfield swallowed hard, and his face got the color of a ripe apple. He raised his fist. "All right, Ballantine, but we'll be back."

They crawled into the pickup and drove off so fast the dust didn't settle for ten minutes.

The boy felt a lot better then. His name was Pedro Gonzales, he told us. He had worked as a vaquero on ranches down in Chihuahua. But the outbreak of foot-and-mouth disease and the quarantine laid against Mexican cattle by the United States government had been hard on Mexican ranchmen, and Pedro couldn't find work anymore. He had decided to swim over and try the Texas side.

He had hit Barfield's ranch, which lay on the river.

Barfield and Salazar had offered him a nice chunk of money to help them with a job and keep his mouth shut.

Under the light of the moon Salazar had led Pedro and a couple more vaqueros across the river. They had picked up about forty steer yearlings from a Mexican ranchman and pushed them back across the river. A few hundred yards to the north, on rocky land where tracks wouldn't show, Barfield had a movable sheep-panel corral and a couple of bobtail cattle trucks waiting for the contraband steers. Bought cheap, the cattle would at least triple his money on Texas markets.

By the time Pedro realized what serious trouble he was letting himself in for, it was too late. Next day he bundled up the few clothes he had. He found Salazar in the barn and asked to be paid off.

Salazar knew the boy was pulling up stakes. He slipped out his knife and sprang at Pedro. Pedro grabbed the man's arm and held the knifepoint inches away from his throat. The two pitched and rolled on the barn floor.

Sweat was popping out on Salazar's swarthy face as Pedro held him on the floor and struggled for the knife. Pedro saw a big, rusty gate hinge under a saddle rack. He grabbed it with one hand and slung it at Salazar's head. The knife blade cut into Pedro's arm, but Salazar was stunned.

Holding his wounded arm, Pedro grabbed his bundle and ran out the barn door. A saddled horse stood tied to a fence. It was Salazar's. Pedro swung up and lit out the only open gate.

He should have headed south of the river, he realized later. But the pasture lay to the north, and Pedro's only thought was to get away.

Men came after him, but he stayed clear of them. Finally the tired horse stumbled, and Pedro sprawled on the ground. He was weak, and couldn't get up in time to catch the mount, so he started out afoot.

As he got his strength back, Pedro turned out to be a lot of help to us. At first he worked around the houses and corrals, helping old Trinidad finish up a lot of jobs that there hadn't been time for before. He fixed up the kitchen for Juanita, rearranging shelves and building new ones to save her a lot of steps. He fixed the leaky faucets and cleaned out the stove-pipes. I could see Juanita's eyes go soft every time he came around her. It worried me a little.

By the time Pedro had been on the place three weeks, I was ready to let him stay, border patrol or no border patrol. I'd just about forgotten the trouble I'd had with Clint Barfield, and Pedro was a top-notch cowboy.

But then it all came back to me in a hail of hot lead.

Pedro and I were out horseback, looking for wormies in the south pasture which neighbored Barfield's place. I didn't think much about riding across the flat close to the fence. I'd done it ten thousand times before. All of a sudden a bullet zipped between us and whined off into the brush. My horse reared up and like to've spilled me. Another shot came from over past the fence, and a third bullet hit the horse. I sailed out over his shoulder and lit rolling in the sand. The rifleman was really after me now. A bullet thudded into the ground in front of my face as I got up. I started running, and another hit behind me.

Pedro yelled. I turned and saw him spurring after me. He reined up, grabbed me, and helped me swing up behind him. Then we rode for better cover, the rifleman still shooting. Pedro's horse, Snorter, didn't like the double load, but I managed to hold onto Pedro.

We rode straight to the house. I stomped in, grabbed my .30-.30, and got another gun for Pedro.

"From now on this gun is yours," I said, my blood hot enough to melt the watch in my pocket. "If you ever catch any of Barfield's bunch on my place, use it!"

We caught fresh horses and headed back, me ridin' Trinidad's old saddle. Nothing happened when we got to where we'd been shot at. The man was gone. We tied our horses to the fence and crossed over afoot. I was still mad enough to've bit the wires in two.

All we could find was spent cartridge cases, an empty Bull Durham sack, and a penny-size Mexican matchbox.

"Salazar!" Pedro gritted, half spitting the word out.

"The sheriff'll be interested in this," I said angrily. Then I thought better. He would be *too* interested. I'd have to tell him about Pedro. By this time I knew I sure didn't want to lose that boy.

Juanita didn't want to lose him either. She was waiting by the gate when we rode in. Tears of happiness rolled down her cheeks as she saw that we were both in good shape. She threw her arms around Pedro and clung to him, and I noticed he held onto her pretty tight.

Old Trinidad was standing in the barn door. He shook his gray head. The wrinkles in his face looked deeper than ever. "What do we do when he must go back to Mexico?" he asked me sadly. "Juanita, she has Mexican blood, but she is American. She not happy south of the river."

I felt like there was a heavy rock on top of my heart. "She won't be happy here, either, Trinidad—not without him."

That night I began to get some hope. I read in the Angelo paper that Mexico was taking Texas off its labor blacklist and the ranchmen and farmers could make applications to keep any wetbacks that were already on their places.

I didn't tell Pedro or the Chavezes. No use getting their hopes up for something that might not work out.

The next morning I got into the pickup and drove to town. I hunted up a border patrol officer and asked him about the piece in the paper. It was right, he said. I'd have to go to an employment commission office and file an application to keep Pedro.

It was midafternoon when I finally hit the long road back to the ranch, and not long before sundown when I drove up to the house. Juanita came running out the door when she heard me. Tears were streaming down her face.

"He's gone!" she cried. "He's gone!"

She was so broke up I couldn't get any sense out of her. While she cried on my shoulder, old Trinidad told me about it. Pedro had saddled up Snorter and left a couple of hours before. He had felt he was to blame for me getting shot at. He had told Juanita he loved her, but he knew she couldn't be happy in Mexico. And he didn't want to be torn away from her later, the way he would be if the border patrol got him. So he was going back to Mexico now, before it was too late.

He had taken the rifle I had given him, and a pocketful of shells, on the chance that he might strike some of Barfield's bunch on his way to the river. If we couldn't head him off before he got to the river, there wasn't much chance of ever getting him back. The Mexican government had a habit of throwing Americans in the calaboose for going down there soliciting labor.

I told Trinidad we'd get the pickup and try to overtake him. I took the .30-.30 down off the rack and got my deer-hunting rifle out of the closet for Trinidad.

We took out across country, hoping to beat him to the river. We might have, too, if we hadn't hit that rough stretch and got the pickup stuck on high center. We fumed and fussed for an hour before we got the blamed thing loose. It was dark then, but the moon was coming out.

Way ahead of us, and off to the right, we could see car lights moving. We cut our own lights off and felt along in the dark. A mile from the river we heard shots, and I recognized the peculiar sound of that old rifle Pedro had taken.

"Pedro's run onto Barfield's bunch," I said, my heart climbing up in my throat. I gunned the old pickup, and we bounced across that rough country like a matchbox behind a bicycle. I didn't dare turn the lights on now.

A little way from where the shooting was, I pulled to a stop.

"I'm goin' down to haul Pedro out of there, Trinidad," I said. "You better stay here. If somethin' goes wrong, it'll be good to have you out here where you can help us. If we make it, we'll pick you up."

Trinidad protested, but he got out. As I drove off he was still arguing with me, using his hands as much as his mouth.

I stepped on the gas again, heading for that rifle. Soon I saw Pedro.

Jamming on the brakes, I tooted the horn and hollered: "Over here, Pedro! It's me, Ike!"

Pedro fired one more shot and came running. Guns flashed back in the darkness. A bullet slammed through the top of the pickup. Pedro jumped in, and we spun back around.

"Thanks to God you have come," he breathed. "My shells were about gone."

Barfield was bringing cattle across the river again, he told me breathlessly. Pedro had accidentally run into one of Barfield's sentries, stationed down the river a ways to keep a lookout for the border patrol.

When the shooting had started, Pedro had got down behind cover, and his horse had run off.

They were after us on horseback now. Pedro smashed the back window and fired through it with his rifle. Bullets clanged into the pickup. Every time Pedro levered a hot shellcase out of the rifle, I flinched, expecting it to flip down my collar.

That's why I didn't see the ditch ahead till it was too late. A front wheel cut into it. We came to a sudden jolting stop.

By the time our heads had cleared, Barfield, Salazar, and another rider had us covered.

"Crawl out of there with your hands up," Barfield growled. "This is where we even up the score."

There wasn't much else we could do. Salazar and the other rider tied our hands behind our backs.

"What do we do with the pickup, Señor Barfield?" asked Salazar. "Nobody cares about this wetback, but they look for Ike Ballantine."

Barfield grunted. "Nobody'll ever know what happened if they can't find no sign. I know a gully close to here where we can cave a bank in on top of the pickup and cover it up, with them two in it."

Barfield got in the pickup, started racing the motor and rocked back and forth till the pickup came out of the ditch. He left the motor running and jumped out.

"Put them in the back and keep an eye on them, Salazar," he ordered. "We may need them to push if we get in a ditch again." To the rider he said, "Follow along behind us with the horses. We got to have them get away from the gully."

They forced us to get in the bed of the pickup, then Barfield commenced driving slowly across country in the moonlight. Salazar sat there by the endgate, watching us like a cat does a mouse he's playing with.

Behind us, down by the river, we saw three sets of car lights. A few shots rang out, then there was silence.

"The border patrol, Salazar," I said. Any other time I'd have laughed. "The shootin' must've brought them. They'll be roundin' up your friends with the trucks and cattle."

Even at the distance I could see fury cross over Salazar's swarthy face. "They will be too late to help you, señor."

I glanced sideways at Pedro. He was sitting in one corner, his back to the side of the pickup. I noticed he was working his wrists up and down a little. Barfield's bullets had left jagged holes in the pickup. Pedro was sawing his ropes in two on the rim of one of them.

Behind us I could see a rider following along. In the darkness I couldn't tell much about him, but I figured it was Barfield's man.

All of a sudden Pedro shook his ropes loose and

sprang up at Salazar like a panther after a horse. The outlaw was too startled to do anything for a second. His gun went flying as Pedro hit him. Then the two plunged over the endgate and sprawled out on the ground.

Barfield braked the pickup to a sudden stop and piled out, a gun in his hand. Pedro wouldn't have a chance, I thought. Although my hands were behind my back, I stood up and jumped out at Barfield, hoping a bootheel in his belly might stop him. He dodged. As I went down on my knees he fetched me a blow with his gun barrel that flattened me out.

My heart seemed to stop beating as I raised up a little and saw Barfield trying to draw down on Pedro. But Pedro and Salazar were rolling on the ground like a couple of mountain lions. For a moment Pedro was on top. Barfield leveled the gun, and I closed my eyes.

But it wasn't a pistol that spoke. It was my deer rifle. I opened my eyes to see Barfield slump to the ground. Old Trinidad was there, the rifle in his hand. He was fighting to keep hold of a boogered horse.

I managed to get to my feet and walk over to him. Pedro and Salazar were still locked together on the ground. I caught the glint of a knife in Salazar's hand, and saw that Pedro was holding the man's wrist like a vise. Inch by inch Pedro forced the knife back around. All of a sudden he shoved it downward.

Salazar stiffened, shuddered, then kind of relaxed. He was dead.

Pedro arose slowly, looking at the knife. He dropped it in the sand and turned to look at us. His face gleamed with sweat.

"I should have killed him on that day at Barfield's," he said bitterly. "The chance was mine."

Car lights moved toward us, and a spotlight played back and forth across the brush. It was the border patrol. Pedro limped over to the pickup and turned on the lights to guide the patrolmen.

Old Trinidad picked up the knife and cut the ropes that my wrists were bound with.

"That was you that was follerin' us horseback," I said. I still couldn't savvy. "I thought it was Barfield's man."

Trinidad grinned a little. "When you drive into the ditch I run to help. But I see the riders get there before me. I think it is better I wait. As soon as the pickup go, I slip up and take the man's horse away from him."

I began to savvy. "Where's the man now?"

Trinidad broke into a broad grin that reached from one ear to the other. "He's still there, I think. He have one awful headache."

Well sir, to make a long story short, the government was grateful to Pedro. It had suspected that cattle was being pushed across the river. Government riders had secretly searched over Barfield's place, but hadn't found any Mexican stock. That was because Barfield trucked them off.

Old Trinidad moved into the main house with me, putting his gear in the back bedroom. Then we all pitched in and started fixing up the house he and Juanita had been living in.

By the time we got through with it, it was a right pretty little place. Just right for a young couple to start out in.

# THE GHOST OF TWO FORKS

A railroad was often a blessing to early Texas towns, but it could as easily be a curse. Many new towns sprang up and thrived along the rights-of-way as track layers moved into new territory eager for improved transportation. But other towns, once prosperous, withered and died because the Eastern money counters and the surveyors favored a route that bypassed them.

Such a town was Two Forks, for years a county seat. Its voters had approved a bond issue that built a fine new stone courthouse with a tall cupola that sported a clockface on each of its four sides. From the day its doors first opened for business, it had been Sandy Fuller's job to sweep its floors and keep its brass doorknobs bright and shiny. In winter he kept wood boxes full for the several potbellied heaters. All these were tasks he enjoyed, for he had hand-carried many of the stones that went into its building, and he felt he owned a share of it.

Most people would say Sandy was not among the

brightest members of the community, that his limited skills restricted him to the most menial of tasks. At fifty his back was beginning to bend. Toting all those heavy stones had not been good for his arthritis, either. But whatever his own shortcomings might have been, his two Jersey cows gave more milk than any in town, and his three dozen laying hens kept much of the community well fixed for eggs. He also kept a dandy little garden, selling much of its produce to his neighbors, giving it to those who could not pay.

Those assets, along with his housekeeping job at the courthouse, yielded everything Sandy needed for the good though simple life. He told his cowboy friend Cap Anderson that he hoped it would last all of his days and that Heaven would be just like Two Forks. He and Cap had ridden broncs together in their younger years, until too many falls forced Sandy to find less strenuous work. Cap still held a steady ranch job, though now he rode gentler horses.

Everybody in town knew Sandy, but a thousand miles away, in a cloud of cigar smoke at the railroad directors' conference table, decisions were made by men who had never heard of him. All they knew of Two Forks was that it was in the wrong place. The surveyors had marked a route that would miss the town by at least six miles. They were about to strike a death blow to the prosperous little community, but that was Two Forks' misfortune and none of their own.

Sandy had every reason to remain where he was, among friends, working in a courthouse he had helped to build. Among other things, he visited the cemetery almost every day, carrying a bucket of water to sprinkle on wildflowers that grew over two graves. One tombstone marked the resting place of Ardella

Fuller, loving wife and mother. Beneath the shadow of the other, topped by the carved figure of a lamb, lay the infant daughter of Sandy and Ardella. The date of death was the same on both stones.

For months Sandy had heard rumors that the railroad was coming. He shared his neighbors' early enthusiasm, because the shining rails could bring fresh enterprise to the town he loved. Sandy's thin wage might not increase, but it pleased him to think it would be a boon to his friends and neighbors. Meanwhile, he kept the courthouse spotless and clean. It was the town's crowning glory, and his own.

He paid little attention to whispered rumors that surveyors were placing stakes across the Bar M ranch far south of town. It seemed unreasonable that the railroad's builders would not want to make the fullest use of a promising community like Two Forks. It was already a landmark of sorts, its courthouse clock tower standing proudly three stories high, visible for miles across the open prairie. The striking of the clock was music to Sandy's ears.

Not until he heard the county judge talking to two of the commissioners did he begin feeling uneasy. He stopped pushing his broom to eavesdrop.

The judge said, "I met with the railroad people. They tell me we've got no chance to change their minds. The Bar M offered them the right-of-way cheap because Old Man Mathers figures to sell town lots. The graders are already at work."

A commissioner asked, "What kind of a county seat will this be then, six miles from the railroad?"

"Old Man Mathers figures sooner or later we'll have no choice but to move it to his town."

"We can't move a stone courthouse, and this one ain't half paid for."

"No, but you can be sure Mathers will try to convince the voters to build a new one over on the railroad."

The commissioner declared, "He'll play hell doin' it. Most of the county's voters live right here in Two Forks."

That sounded reasonable to Sandy. He went back to his sweeping and put the worry behind him.

That night as he watered the wildflowers on Ardella's grave, he talked to her just as he had talked to her when she was alive. "Don't you be frettin' none, honey. The folks ain't goin' to go off and leave a good town like this, especially one with such a pretty courthouse, and it not paid for yet."

But it played out like the judge had said. The graders followed the surveyors, and the rails followed the graders. Old Man Mathers had a crew staking out town lots along the right-of-way. He donated a large town square for the building of a new courthouse. He put up a big new general store and guaranteed that his prices would be lower than those in Two Forks because he could obtain his goods directly from the railroad without the extra cost of freighting them in by wagon.

Sandy refused to acknowledge the writing on the wall, even when he stood with Cap Anderson and watched skids being placed beneath the Jones family's frame house. He watched a six-mule team slide the structure across the prairie toward the new town of Mathers.

"They'll wish they hadn't moved," he told Cap. "They'll get awful lonesome over there without their old neighbors."

But one by one, the old neighbors moved too. House after house made the six-mile drag to a new site on the railroad or rode over there on wagon beds extended in tandem. In time, Two Forks began to look as if a tornado had skipped through, taking out structures at random, leaving behind only cedar-post foundations and falling-down sections of yard fence. Weeds grew where flower beds and gardens had been.

"Town's not the same anymore," he told Ardella. "But the courthouse ain't changed." He swept every day, for dust from the abandoned lots made it more difficult to keep its floors clean. He polished the doorknobs and, as he could get to them, washed the windows.

Cap Anderson sympathized. "You can't blame folks for leavin'. They've got families, most of them. They've got to go where they can make a livin'." Cap lived north of Two Forks. The new town was a hardship for him because it meant he had to travel six miles farther than when he could do all his business here.

Time came when almost the only people still living in Two Forks were those who worked in the courthouse: the judge and his wife, the county clerk, the sheriff, a deputy, the jail keeper, and Sandy. The operator of the last general store loaded his goods on wagons and hauled them to a new building in Mathers. His old place stood vacant. It made Sandy think of a dogie calf. One night some young vandals from the new town sneaked in under the cover of darkness to break out the store's windows, and those of what had been the blacksmith shop.

The judge was the first of the courthouse crowd to surrender. He had his big house sawed in two and hauled over to Mathers. Sandy heard that one section was sprung a little during the trip so that the two never fit back together just right. After some loud cussing, the judge grudgingly accepted the patching job, though his wife was never again satisfied with the house. The county clerk was not long in following the judge to Mathers.

The sheriff and his crew had to stay because the jail was still in Two Forks, though the lawman spent most of his time enforcing the ordinances in the new town. The few residents remaining in Two Forks were not given to crimes and misdemeanors.

The judge became increasingly vocal about the nuisance of living in one town and working in another. Sandy heard his voice ringing down the hall. "There is no longer any question about it. We've got to move the county seat to Mathers."

Sandy almost dropped his broom.

The sheriff agreed with the judge's opinion but pointed out that such a move would require a vote of the county's citizens.

The judge said, "Most of them are in Mathers now. Who is left to vote for staying in Two Forks?"

As it turned out, the only dissenting votes were Sandy's and those of some farmers and ranch people like Cap, afraid of higher taxes. Sandy listened disconsolately as the ballots were counted in the clerk's office. He quickly saw that his vote was being crushed beneath the weight of all those others.

He heard the judge say, "Now we've got to have a bond vote so we can build a new courthouse."

The sheriff was skeptical. "The county still owes ten years' payments on this one. Do you think the landowners are goin' to vote another tax burden on themselves?"

"The people in town outnumber the country voters," the judge argued. "They're tired of having to come all the way over here to do business with the county government."

And so it was. The new citizens of Mathers were overwhelmingly in favor of a new courthouse, especially after the judge pointed out that most of the added tax burden would be levied upon landowners and not themselves. Old Man Mathers was especially pleased. His son-in-law was a builder and a cinch to get the construction contract from the commissioners' court. The stone would be quarried from the south end of the Mathers ranch. It was a foregone conclusion that the price of building stone was going to run high.

Watering the flowers, Sandy told Ardella, "It's goin' to take them a while to get that new courthouse built. I'll bet it won't be nothin' like as pretty as this one here."

He was right. He sneaked over to Mathers one Sunday afternoon to steal a peek at the construction work. The side walls were up, and the roof was half built. He took a measure of satisfaction in the fact that this courthouse was going to be butt-ugly. It offered no imagination in its architecture, no adornments, just four plain square walls and a row of deep-set windows that reminded him of the eye sockets in a skull.

What was more, he had been told that this courthouse was costing twice as much as the older one. There would be hell to pay for the judge and some others when the next election rolled around. But that was still more than a year off.

From people who came to the old Two Forks courthouse to do business with the county, Sandy heard rumblings of discontent. Cap led a petition drive, demanding that the county refuse to accept the new structure on the basis that it was badly designed, shoddily built, and uglier than a mud fence. But the judge ruled that the petition did not represent a large enough percentage of the voters and thus was invalid.

Construction was completed, and the new courthouse was approved by the commissioners' court. The next step was to move the records from the older building. Sandy's hopes soared when a dozen ranchers and their cowboys, including Cap, surrounded the Two Forks courthouse and vowed to stop, at gunpoint if necessary, any transfer of documents.

The judge and the sheriff foiled that attempt by bringing in two Texas Rangers to enforce the court order. The ranchers and their cowboys might have gone up against the United States Army, but they knew better than to oppose the Texas Rangers. Sandy and Cap watched crestfallen as the county records were placed in a line of wagons and hauled away.

That night he told Ardella, "I don't know what I'm goin' to do now, except for one thing. I ain't leavin' you and the baby, and I ain't leavin' my courthouse."

The judge came to him the next day with a proposition. "You'd just as well give it up, Sandy, and come on over to Mathers. We need a janitor to take care of the new courthouse like you've taken care of this one."

Sandy knew one reason they wanted him was that they could not find anyone else willing to do the job for the same low pay.

"No sir," he said. "I'm satisfied where I'm at."

"But there's nothing for you to do here."

"This courthouse is still here, and it needs somebody to care for it."

The judge began to show impatience. "Don't you

understand? This courthouse is vacant. Retired. We don't need anybody to take care of it."

"But it still belongs to the county, don't it? We're all still payin' for it, ain't we?"

"That is beside the point. We can't pay you to sweep out an abandoned building. We will pay you to take care of the new one."

"One way and another, I reckon I'll get by. If anything ever happens to that new courthouse, you'll be glad you've got this one sittin' here waitin' for you."

The judge shook his head in disgust. "A man who would argue with a fool is a fool himself." He turned away but stopped to say, "Your paycheck ends today."

Money had never been an important issue with Sandy. He could get by on very little. Between his garden, his chickens, and his milk cows, he would not go hungry.

He told the judge, "If you ever need me, you'll know where to look."

"Damn it, man, don't you realize that Two Forks is a dead town?"

"It ain't dead as long as somebody lives in it. That'll be me."

Sandy cooked his meals and slept in a plain frame shack. It would be a stretch of the language to say he actually lived there. He lived in the courthouse. He was accustomed to going there before daylight and making sure it was ready for business. In winter he built fires in all the stoves to take the chill off before the first of the staff arrived. Now, though, it was summer. He opened windows so a cooling breeze could freshen the air. Everything continued the same as before with one important difference: no one was in the courthouse except him.

With all the desks and chairs removed, the sweeping chore was easier because he did not have to work around the obstacles. The empty rooms looked larger than before. In the county clerk's office the shelves were bare where once they had been full of records of land transactions, court decisions, marriages and births and deaths. Sandy did not need the records to help him remember, however. He had been a witness to almost everything that had happened here.

Having more time on his hands, he spent longer at the cemetery, talking to Ardella. He wiped dust from the carved lamb atop the baby's tombstone. "It's awful quiet here now," he said, "but in a way I kind of like it. Sometimes I got tired of all that noise. And I don't have a lot of people throwin' their trash around. You ought to see how clean the courthouse is."

He almost never went to Mathers. The sight of that squatty new courthouse made his eyes hurt. He still bartered enough butter and eggs to trade for the few groceries he needed, mainly coffee and bacon and such. Every two or three days, Cap or some other rancher or cowboy took his produce to town for him and brought back whatever he ordered from the general store.

He had noticed that the new courthouse did not even have lightning rods like the old one. Maybe one day lightning would strike, the building would burn down, and they would have to move the county seat back to Two Forks. The county could not afford to be paying for three courthouses at the same time. Well, when it happened, they would find the old one as good as when they had left it. Better even, for Sandy made improvements on it here and there.

But lightning did not strike. Time went dragging on. A windstorm took most of the roof from Sandy's shack. He decided to move into the jail, which stood in the shadow of the courthouse. He reasoned that a building always fared better when someone lived in it than when it stood vacant. They would need the jail again someday when they returned to Two Forks. He kept it as clean as the courthouse.

One by one, his rancher and cowboy friends died or moved away. Cap remained, but he did not often go to town anymore. No longer could Sandy depend on someone else to carry his butter and eggs to town. He had no choice but to walk the six miles to Mathers, carrying his goods in a cloth sack, then walking back with food he could not produce for himself. Most of the townspeople had forgotten about him. Now they talked about him again. He was "poor, feeble-minded old Sandy," who didn't have the sense to give up and quit beating a dead horse.

He became the ghost of Two Forks, a ragged apparition who showed up briefly on the dirt streets of Mathers every three or four days, said little or nothing to anybody, and disappeared like a wisp of smoke. A few of the more superstitious even suggested that he had died of lonesome and that what they saw was a wraith, a will-of-the-wisp. Town boys dared each other to visit the Two Forks cemetery after dark and see if the ghost would appear.

He did, on a few occasions. Sandy was as protective of the cemetery as of the courthouse. He was afraid vandals might topple some of the tombstones, especially Ardella's or the baby's. After several town boys hurried home shaking with fright, talking about the ghost that appeared out of nowhere, the nocturnal visits stopped. Hardly anyone except Sandy came to the cemetery anymore.

The few abandoned frame houses gradually succumbed to time and the weather, sinking back to the ground or giving up to the wind which scattered them in pieces across the old townsite. Only the grand old courthouse remained, and the jail. The ghost of Two Forks continued to care for them, to keep up repairs.

Then one day a cowboy happened by on his way to town. It was a hot summer day, but the courthouse windows remained closed. Sandy had routinely opened them each morning from spring into late fall.

Maybe the old man was ill, the cowboy thought. He rode up to the courthouse and tested the front door. It was locked. He led his horse to the jail and went inside. Sandy was not there. The stove was cold. Sandy's coffeepot sat empty except for yesterday's grounds. Alarmed, the cowboy went outside and called. The only response was the echo of his own voice. A circle through the townsite yielded no sign.

He rode to town and went directly to the office of the new sheriff. A small delegation of townspeople—mostly older ones who remembered the heyday of Two Forks—accompanied him back to the ghost town. They searched every room, every closet in the old courthouse, half expecting to find Sandy dead in one of them. They even climbed up into the clock tower. They did not find him.

"It's like the wind just lifted him up and carried him away," the cowboy said.

"Or maybe he wasn't nothin' but a ghost to start with," a townsman suggested. "Maybe he died when the town died."

So now Two Forks was officially dead. The last

person to have lived there was gone. The tall old courthouse stood as silent testimony to the town that once had been, and to the man who had stubbornly refused to accept that it was gone.

But as Sandy had long predicted, the courthouse did not die. It refused to submit to the wind and the rain and the ravages of time. After many years, some former citizens of Two Forks decided it was time to honor the town's memory with a big reunion, a barbecue and dance. Where better to have it than in the courthouse? No one knew where to find the keys, if they even existed anymore, so someone had to pick the lock so the committee could go inside and clean up the place for the benefit of the expected crowd.

To their amazement, the courthouse was as clean as if it had just been swept. Tight windows, they reasoned, had not let the dust in. There should have been cobwebs, yet they saw none. Even the windows sparkled as if freshly washed.

The ghost of Sandy Fuller, some said. He had never given up his job.

The state placed a historical marker beside the front door of the old Two Forks courthouse. The reunion and barbecue became an annual affair, and dances were a frequent event. From time to time the old building pulsed with life as it had long ago. Visitors came often in hope of glimpsing the ghost of Two Forks, but none ever saw him. They knew only that occasionally he still swept the courthouse by night and kept it clean. No one ever knew how Sandy Fuller had disappeared.

Well, almost no one. Cap Anderson knew, for he had found Sandy lying dead beside Ardella's grave. Knowing Sandy's love for the courthouse, and knowing the law would not allow it if anyone knew, he secretly buried him in the basement.

He kept Sandy's keys. He also kept Sandy's broom until he wore it out and had to replace it with a new one.

# LONESOME
# RIDE
# TO PECOS

Cautiously watching the dust settle, Deputy Sheriff Andy Hayes holstered his smoking six-shooter and walked to the fallen and dying man. The young robber stared up at him with wide and frightened eyes. One hand over the growing red splotch on his chest, the gasping outlaw turned his head toward the little plume of hoof-churned dust that hid his escaping partner. His lips moved, but only a groan came. In a moment Hayes forced himself to kneel and close the sightless eyes.

He shuddered in revulsion for what he had had to do. He would not sleep tonight. Wishing he were somewhere else, doing anything else in the world for a living, he reluctantly searched the robber's pockets for identification. It was a bitter thing to kill a man, leaving a scar that he knew would always be with him. It was even more bitter because the man had been so young, by the look of him probably an impatient cowboy wanting to make his stake in one day.

Hayes found a letter inside the worn vest. Finished but never sealed, it was addressed to Pecos and signed *Tommy Clyde*.

The deputy's big hands trembled as he read what the cowboy had written to a girl named Julie, pouring out his love, telling her he was on a cattle trade which would stock their little ranch and give them the start for which they had waited.

Hayes found himself visualizing the girl named Julie. He saw her—painfully—in the image of another whose name had been Mary, disapproving of guns and men who wore them, marrying a young minister who, like her, would never have use for them.

He heard running horses, and he slipped the letter into his shirt pocket. Placing the cowboy's dusty hat over the still face, he pushed to his feet. He blinked stinging eyes as the possemen reined up in a swirl of dust.

A grim-faced Elton McReady gave the dead man a glance that was without compassion. He said to Hayes, "Killed one, I see. Did you get the money back?"

Hayes raked a quick glance over the riders. Reluctantly he brought his gaze back to McReady, trying not to react to the man's eternal baiting. "His partner must've been carryin' it. He's took to the tall brush."

McReady bit hard on the dead cigar clamped between his teeth. "Then you ought to've killed *him* too."

Hayes's face warmed. "One dead man ought to be enough."

"Not when the other has got the bank's money." He pointed in the direction in which the survivor had fled. "How come you stopped here? Why didn't you keep on after him?"

Someday, Hayes promised himself, he was going to mash that cigar across McReady's face. "My horse is wounded."

"You could've caught this man's and kept on goin'."

Hayes said, "Yes, I could've. But I didn't. You go on after him if you've a mind to. His horse is faster, so you won't catch him, any more than I would've. But you can make a chase out of it, and maybe you'll feel like you've done your do."

McReady said gruffly, "I reckon I'll just do that." He glanced around him. "Come on, boys, let's get after him."

Hayes found a friendly face and beckoned with his chin. "March, would you mind goin' back to town and fetchin' a wagon?" The rest of the posse spurred out. Hayes watched them, knowing they would drag back after a while, exhausted and empty-handed. Not a horse in the bunch could catch the fast bay the second outlaw had been riding.

Hayes turned his back on them and saw after his own horse, standing braced in mute agony, head down. Hayes gathered his strength, unsaddled, drew his pistol and fired.

A couple of hours later old Sheriff Tol Murphy limped to the wagon in the street and lifted the tarp to look. He muttered bitterly about waste and gently let the tarp settle back into place. "The pity is that he died for so damned little," he said. "The teller kept his wits about him and didn't give them nothin' but blank checks and bills of low denomination. They didn't get more than three hundred dollars. Not near enough to die for."

Hayes asked himself silently, *How much is enough to die for?* He said, "It could be enough to leave *us* in bad shape, though, me and you. McReady'll see to that."

The sheriff did not seem to have considered McReady. He shrugged, indicating he could do nothing anyway.

Hayes told him McReady had led the posse on what was sure to be a futile chase. "He'll make the effort look good, at least, to help him run against you in the summer election."

Murphy nodded, his eyes sad. "I hope you know another trade, son. You may not have this one after the vote's counted." He stared at the wagon, his mind returning dutifully to the more immediate problem. "Any idea who he is?"

Hayes took the letter from his pocket. Murphy held it to arm's length but had to carry it back into the office and get his glasses. Sitting at his desk, he mulled over the letter in silence a long time. "Nothin' said here about his partner. Think you'd know him if you saw him?"

Hayes shook his head. "Not to hold water in court."

The sheriff read the letter one more time. "Then I think it'd be a good idea if you went out to Pecos. Don't tell anybody a damned thing. Just find an excuse to hang around there and watch. Maybe you'll get lucky." The frown returned. "If you don't, ain't much use you comin' back. I'll probably be swampin' out old Emery's stable for a livin'."

The county furnished Hayes a new horse, a long-legged sorrel that reached out and gathered in the miles with an easy trot that carried him halfway across West Texas in less time than Hayes expected . . . less time than he wanted. He was in no hurry, for he dreaded Pecos. He toyed with a temptation to send back a written resignation and payment for the sorrel. He might have done it had he not felt an obligation to Murphy.

He crossed the Concho, then rode westward across the dry desert country, following a wagon road that set him a crooked path through stunted mesquite and greasewood country. In Pecos City a saloon-keeper gave him directions to the Slash C. "If I was lookin' for a job, that sure wouldn't be my choice of the place to go. One of these days they're goin' to have a contest to find the sorriest ranch in Reeves County. That one and about three more will tie for first place."

"A job's a job."

"Well, come the end of the month, be sure they pay you in cash money. Don't take no promises."

Hayes sat on the edge of a hill west of the narrow river. He stared down toward two wooden windmill towers, a little cluster of corrals, and a few small frame buildings at the edge of a scrub-brush draw. Between him and the ranch headquarters stretched a broad and nearly barren alkali flat. If this place tied for first prize, he thought, he would not care to see the others. He had hardly seen even a jackrabbit the last two or three miles. He could understand why.

Then he saw the girl sitting on the edge of a narrow porch at the front of a small box-and-strip house. She was tiny, hair light brown, done up in a bun on the back of her head. Not until he was near enough to speak to her could he see that she held a kitten in her lap, gently washing its eyes with milk. She looked up. Her face was not that of the girl named Mary after all, but it did not matter. Mary's image faded from his mind. It was as if this face was the one he had been seeing all the time. A pretty face, to be sure, but it brought him a chill. This had to be the Julie of the letter.

He forced a thin smile. "Kind of fudgin' on Nature, ain't you? That kitten may not be *ready* to see yet." Three more were in a squirming mass beside her.

She said, "The world won't be any prettier for puttin' it off." He sensed a bitter edge in her voice.

He said, "I was told in town that I might find a job here. They said you-all had . . . lost a man."

She looked at the ground, so he could not see her eyes. "The owner's son . . . outlaws killed him."

Outlaws. Well, he thought, that was as good a story as any, if the family wanted to spare a wayward boy's memory.

The girl stroked the kitten a moment before she trusted herself to look up again at Hayes. She said, "Maybe if you'd talk to Mr. Clyde . . ." She looked toward the brush corrals.

Hayes saw the outline of a man beyond a fence built of mesquite branches stacked between double rows of heavy posts. The man did not seem to be moving. Throat tight in sympathy, Hayes touched the sagging brim of his hat and led the sorrel toward the corrals.

A rifle shot stopped him. He reached instinctively for his pistol as the horse jumped back in fright. He saw a movement at the edge of the alkali flat. A coyote ran a few steps, fell, threshed a moment and went still. Shaky, Hayes slipped the pistol back into its holster and walked to the fence. A short, stocky man hobbled toward him on the opposite side. "Hope I didn't give you a fright," the ranchman said. "Damned coyote comes after the chickens every time we turn our backs." He tried to meet Hayes's gaze but could not hold it. His eyes seemed haunted.

Hayes gave him time to collect himself. "I heard in town you might be lookin' to hire a hand."

The rancher was probably not so old as he looked at this moment. "Bad news travels fast, don't it?"

Hayes was not sure how to answer. "Always seems like."

The rancher looked again toward the coyote, hiding his eyes as the girl had done. "They tell you about my boy?"

Hayes thought about his answer. "Said he had been killed, was all."

Hatred crept into the man's voice. "Someday maybe I'll face the man that done it. I'll shoot him with no more compunctions than I shot that coyote." His eyes showed a moment of fire. When that burned away, a bleakness remained. He looked Hayes up and down, making a quick judgment. "Amos Worth is the foreman. Go tell him I've hired you."

He turned away, then back. "That shack yonder is the closest thing we've got to a bunkhouse. You'll be the only hand in it till Duff Daggett gets back."

Hayes swung into the saddle and rode to the bunkhouse to throw his bag and roll of blankets onto an empty steel cot. Someone stepped into the doorway, blocking much of the light. Cautiously, thinking of the second robber, Hayes turned. He saw a tall, gaunt man almost as old as Clyde, wearing the weathered, dried-out look of a man who seldom let daylight catch him under a roof.

"I'm Amos Worth," the man said, withholding welcome until sure of Hayes's business there.

Hayes said, "Mr. Clyde told me to hunt you up. I just hired on."

Worth extended his hand. "We can use the help. But you've come at a sad time."

"So I gather." Hayes did not want to ask too many questions, but he already harbored a suspicion. "Mr. Clyde told me there's supposed to be another hand here."

"Duff Daggett. Him and Tommy Clyde left a while back to buy some cattle on the Llano. We got a message from him that robbers killed Tommy. Duff taken a bullet himself, but he sent word he'll be back soon's he's able to ride."

Guardedly, Hayes asked, "Where did this happen?"

"Duff's letter didn't say. Old John's sent messages to every sheriff in two hundred miles, tryin' to find out."

The foreman's eyes showed no sign he was covering up the facts. Hayes concluded that Worth was telling the truth as he knew it. Sheriff Tol Murphy had evidently sent no word to John Clyde. He was leaving Hayes a chance to work things out in his own time.

Hayes fingered the badge, hidden in his pocket, and wondered if he—or somebody—had actually hit Duff Daggett as he was getting away from the bank. One dead, one wounded, for less than three hundred dollars.

He asked, "That girl . . . is she Mr. Clyde's daughter?"

"Not his, *mine*. Tommy Clyde had it in his mind to marry her soon's he got the land John was fixin' to give him."

Hayes's eyes narrowed. "Then *you* lost a son too, in a manner of speakin'."

Worth nodded grimly. "I ain't sure Julie was as set on it as Tommy was. The boy had his rough spots, but I felt like he'd've made my girl happy."

From the only window in the little shack, Hayes could see the girl in a chicken yard back of her house, feeding grain to a wing-flapping cluster of brownish hens. Wind tugged at the full skirt of an old gray cotton dress, but it barely lifted the hem as high as her ankles. It was not possible, he thought, that he could be in love with a girl he had met only once. But he had been seeing her in his mind since he had first read that letter.

*Careful, Hayes,* he told himself. *She'll hate you when she finds out. And she'll have to find out.*

Duff Daggett had been the second man in the bank. Of that Hayes was already convinced. The teller would make the identification easily. All Hayes had to do was stay here and wait for Daggett to come back.

He had cowboyed for years before he had gone to work for the county, but he did not remember that the work had ever been as hard as following old John Clyde. The rancher was a furious engine of a man, pushing himself and Hayes and Amos Worth at a backbreaking pace from daylight until dark.

Once when the old man loped his horse out of hearing to push some shaded-up cattle from a brushy draw, Hayes observed, "He must be drivin' himself to help him through his grief."

Worth shook his head. "No, fact is he's slacked off some. You ought to've seen how he used to work . . . before."

Hayes frowned. "Maybe he drove the boy too

hard." He had been about to say *drove the boy to what he did.* That might have spilled the whole story.

"A man has to be hard and tough to make it on the Pecos River," Worth said. "Somebody called the Pecos the grave of a cowman's hopes. John just does what the country demands of him."

Despite the grueling pace, Hayes came to respect John Clyde and Amos Worth. The harsh days were tempered by his anticipation of seeing Julie in the evening. Around sunset each day he would ride a weary horse into the big corral with Amos and the brooding John Clyde, his nerves tight with dread that this would be the day Duff Daggett had come back, that this would be the time all facts must be revealed and the acceptance he had earned from these people would turn to hatred.

Julie had begun to smile, sometimes. Hayes avoided telling her anything that would make her realize he was or ever had been a lawman, but he told her stories of his upbringing on the San Saba, of hunting wildcats and wolves, of falling into the river while trying to retrieve a big catfish, of horses that he had broken and that had come near breaking him. The stories often brought light to her eyes and crowded out the grief he so hated to see there.

Evenings, sometimes, he milked the cow for her, something he had not done since he had left the family homeplace. Because she was the only woman in the foreman's house, it was expected of her that she cook for whatever single men were on the ranch, which at this time meant her widowed father, Clyde, and Hayes. Hayes took it for granted that Clyde's wife was dead, but Amos told him she was not. She had decided years ago that life on a Pecos River ranch was too hard for her, and she had gone to El Paso, leaving her husband and son behind.

Often Hayes followed Julie into the kitchen after supper and dried the dishes as she washed them. Watching her, he knew he did not want to live the rest of his life a bachelor. He told himself it was reckless to let this girl arouse these feelings in him, for it was inevitable that the warmth he saw more and more in her eyes would turn one day soon to contempt.

But one night, as he gazed at her, he let a wet cup slip out of his hand and fall to the floor with a clatter. Both reached for it, and their hands met. For a moment he clutched her fingers, not wanting to turn loose, and she made no effort to pull away. He tried for words that would not come. Color flushed her cheeks, and then she was in his arms. He told her without words what he had wanted to say from the beginning.

He went to the bunkhouse in a black mood, wishing he had never come here. He lay awake a long time, torn. At one point he went to the barn, intending to saddle the sorrel horse and ride away, to avoid the black day that must come.

Any other night the horse would have been there, staying close for the morning's welcome bait of oats. This night he had strayed off into the pasture, far out in the darkness. Hayes went back to the bunkhouse, his resolve weakening. By morning, when he saw Julie again, he knew he could not leave her that way, at least not yet a while.

By night it was too late. Duff Daggett came back.

He was standing beside the little saddle shed when Hayes and Amos Worth rode in that evening. At

some other time, in some other place, Hayes would
not have recognized him. But here, he could be no
one else. Walking out to meet Amos, Daggett carried
himself stiffly. He had not lied about being wounded,
only about the circumstances under which it had
happened. Somehow, Hayes was disappointed. He
had pictured Daggett as some callous outlaw, riding
away with the spoils, coldly leaving his partner to
die. But Hayes saw here a guileless face, a cowboy
as young as the one who had died.

Daggett stared at Hayes with suspicion, even after
Amos explained how Hayes came to be there. Amos
placed his hand on Daggett's shoulder, and Hayes
sensed the old foreman's fondness for the youth.
"You been over to tell John how it happened?"

Daggett nodded grimly. "Hardest thing ever I
done, Amos. Made me wish it had been me instead of
Tommy."

Amos said sympathetically, "I imagine you done
all a man could, under the circumstances. Old John's
been tryin' for a month to find out where his boy is
buried. You tell him?"

Daggett replied, "I told him. Now he wants me to
take him and fetch Tommy's body home." He glanced
at Amos in apprehension. "I wisht you'd talk him
out of the notion."

"The boy belongs here, buried at home."

Daggett argued weakly, "It'll be an ordeal for the
old man."

"He's already been through his worst ordeal.
Maybe this would give him peace."

Daggett seemed unconvinced. He looked to Hayes
as if for help, as if forgetting he was a stranger. A little
suspicion came back into his eyes. "Ain't I met you
somewhere?"

Hayes's heart made a little jump. It stood to reason that Daggett and Tommy Clyde had spent time in town before the robbery, looking over the layout. Daggett might have noticed him then because of his badge. Hayes tried to bar the worry from his eyes. "You ever been in the San Saba country?" he asked.

"No," Daggett said. "You must just look like somebody."

"Poor feller," Hayes replied, "whoever he is."

Daggett turned his attention back to Amos Worth. "I wisht you'd talk to John. I don't want to go back there. I just *can't* look at the place again where it happened."

Amos again placed his hand on the cowboy's shoulder. "I wouldn't ask you to go through a thing like this for *me*. But this is for *him*. You don't know what he's been through."

"I *do* know, Amos. I been through it too." Tears brimmed in Daggett's eyes.

Hayes turned away. Because of John Clyde and Julie, he had known this would be a hard thing to do. He had not considered that it would be hard because of Daggett too.

Supper was somber and quiet, nobody wanting to talk. Hayes watched Julie, wishing he could tell her, knowing he couldn't.

Sleep was out of the question. He lay staring into the darkness, again considering the possibility of simply riding away from there, of writing Tol Murphy a letter saying the trail had gone cold. Even as he pondered that option, he knew it was something he could not do.

Upwards of midnight he heard the gentle creaking of a steel cot as Duff Daggett swung his legs over the side. Hayes turned his head slowly and watched

Daggett quietly putting on his clothes, stuffing his few belongings into a canvas bag, rolling up his blankets. Barefoot, Daggett carried the things outside and paused on the moonlit step to pull on his boots.

Hayes quickly dressed, then brought his six-shooter from its hiding place beneath his pillow. He eased the door shut and made his way from one dark patch of shadow to another until he reached the corral. Duff Daggett awkwardly swung his saddle up onto a horse's back, his stiff arm limiting his movement.

Hayes said, "You'd just as well slip that saddle off. You ain't goin' anywhere till daylight."

Daggett whirled, eyes widening as he saw the pistol in Hayes's hand. He tried to speak, but the words seemed to catch in his mouth. He reached up with his good hand and gripped the arm that had taken the wound. Finally he managed to ask, "You some kind of law?"

Hayes nodded. "You owe a debt back there where you-all robbed that bank. Looks to me like you owe a debt to that old man too. You was fixin' to run out on both of them."

Daggett seemed about to buckle at the knees. He leaned against his horse for support. "You the one that put a bullet in my arm?"

Hayes nodded. "Probably. I didn't know I'd done it."

"Then you'd be the one that shot Tommy too."

Hayes felt his throat tighten. "I wish I could say otherwise. I've wished a thousand times . . ."

"So have I. I ain't had a minute's rest since it happened."

"Where's the money, Daggett?"

"Never was much of it to start with. What I didn't

spend for the doctorin' I've still got in my bag. I swear
to God, I'll send them the rest of it soon's I can find
me another job. Just let me get away from here so I
don't have to tell John."

Hayes said with regret, "I can't do that. If I could,
I'd do it for myself."

"Then if you've got to take me back, do it now,
tonight, while he's asleep."

"No, Daggett. We've *both* got to face him. We'll
wait till daylight."

Daggett looked up at the position of the Big Dipper. "Goin' to be a long night."

"There's already *been* a lot of long nights."

Hayes walked him back to the little bunkhouse.
"You'd just as well lay down," he said. "*One* of us
ought to get some rest." Daggett would be easier to
watch, lying on his back. Hayes lighted the lamp and
sat in a rawhide-bottomed chair to wait the night
through. He heard every nightbird that called in the
darkness, every howl of a coyote far down toward
the Pecos. His eyes burned, and his eyelids were
heavy.

Daggett lay still most of the time, but Hayes knew
he did not sleep. Once he asked, "What do you think
they'll do to me?"

"There wasn't any citizen killed, or even hurt.
We'll be takin' part of the money back. If you behave
yourself, maybe they won't give you too long a sentence."

Miserably Daggett said, "I've got a *life* sentence
ahead of me, just rememberin' what happened."

Hayes had no comfort to offer him.

Daylight seemed three nights in coming. At last
Hayes saw the rose glow of dawn breaking through
the window. Lamplight was yellow in the kitchen of

the Worth house. He pushed to his feet and found his legs stiff, reluctant to move. "We'd better be gettin' it done," he said.

He kept the pistol in his hand, but he did not point it directly at Daggett. He had a feeling he would not need to fire it. He let Daggett walk ahead of him.

Julie had a smile for them as they came through the door. "Mornin', both of you." The smile died as she saw the pistol.

"Julie," Hayes said, "I wish you'd fetch Mr. Clyde over here. Duff Daggett and me have got somethin' to tell him."

Amos Worth came through the door of his tiny bedroom, stuffing his shirttail into his trousers. He stared at the pistol but asked no questions. Hayes had an idea from the dismay in his face that he was already sensing the truth. He watched his daughter hurry out the door, then said, "If you boys got anything to tell me before John gets here . . ."

Hayes said, "Be ready to help him. He'll need a friend."

Tears were in Daggett's eyes again.

John Clyde stopped in the doorway and stared wide-eyed at the two young men, at Hayes's pistol pointed vaguely toward the ceiling. Julie came in behind him and stood at his side. Hayes said, "Mr. Clyde, you'd better sit down. This boy has got somethin' to tell you."

Clyde stepped toward Daggett, but Hayes motioned him back. "I'd rather you stood clear of him." He fished the badge from his pocket and showed it, then put it back. John Clyde seated himself heavily in a straight chair, his shoulders drooped. Like Amos, he seemed to sense some of what was coming.

In a broken voice Daggett explained. "It didn't

happen like I told you, Mr. Clyde. Me and Tommy went to buy them cattle, but we didn't know the market had taken a big jump. We didn't have near enough money for what Tommy wanted to buy. We seen a high-stakes poker game in a dramshop over there, and the players acted like a bunch of amateurs. Tommy taken a notion he could run up that bankroll and get his cattle after all.

"They wasn't the amateurs; *we* was. That roll didn't last no time, hardly, and Tommy was broke. He was scared to come back to you and Julie and own up to what he'd done. Well, there was this little crackerbox bank. We taken a notion it'd be easy pickin's, but it wasn't. One of them lawmen killed Tommy and put a bullet in my arm. I thought I'd got away, till last night." He glanced at Hayes, then looked at the floor.

Hayes reached in his shirt pocket. "Julie, this is for you." He gave her the letter from Tommy Clyde.

Her hands trembled as she realized what it was. Tears came, and she could not read it. "How did you come to have this?"

"I found it in Tommy Clyde's pocket, after . . ." He swallowed. "I'm sorry, Julie. I wish it'd been different."

John Clyde sat with head bowed, shoulders shaking. "Scared to come and tell me. I thought I'd raised my boy not to be scared of anything. I reckon I made him scared of *me*." After a time he lifted his burning eyes to Hayes. "He said a lawman killed my boy. Are you that man?"

Hayes forced himself to hold his gaze to those terrible eyes. "Yes, sir. I am."

John Clyde pushed to his feet and staggered across the little room, apparently without aim or purpose except to give his emotions an outlet in movement instead of in a cry. But he had purpose. Too late to stop him, Hayes saw the rifle standing in a corner. Clyde grabbed it and spun around, swinging the muzzle toward Hayes. He cocked back the hammer.

Julie cried out in fear. Amos shouted, "John, don't . . ."

Hayes's stomach went cold. His hand seemed paralyzed on the pistol. He had killed *one* Clyde.

Duff Daggett jumped from his chair and threw himself between the old man and Hayes. "No, Mr. Clyde! Me and Tommy made a bad-enough mistake. Don't you make another."

"Out of my way, Duff," Clyde shouted, trying to shove past him.

Daggett grabbed the barrel and pushed it upward. The blast shook the thin walls. For a moment everyone seemed frozen. Then Daggett sighed and sank slowly to his knees.

John Clyde dropped the rifle and grabbed the sagging cowboy. "My God!" he rasped, "I didn't go to shoot you." Holding to Duff, he looked up pleadingly. "Somebody help!"

Hayes took two long strides, picked up the rifle and threw it out the door. Then he knelt beside Duff Daggett, whose face was graying like clay as shock set in. John Clyde was tearing desperately at Daggett's shirt. "Duff! Boy! I didn't go to do it!"

Hayes said, "Bullet went up through his shoulder. Same arm that was hit before."

The wound bled badly, but the slug had gone through. Julie rushed out of the room and appeared again with some cloths. Hayes said, "If we can just stop the blood . . ."

"Damn fool kid," Amos Worth gritted. "But his heart is in the right place."

John Clyde made his way back to his chair and sat down, silent, shattered, while Hayes and Amos and Julie worked on Daggett. They stopped the blood, soaked the wound with kerosene, then wrapped it. Amos said, "I'll bring the wagon around. John, me and you better haul him to town." Clyde nodded. His eyes were closed, tears on his face.

Julie's eyes pleaded with Hayes. "What'll you do to him?"

"Nothin', for now," Hayes said. "I couldn't take him back, the shape he's in. Maybe they'll take into account the price he's already paid. It's a chance anyway."

John Clyde stared at Hayes, and Hayes knew Clyde could never entirely forgive. It was too much to expect of him. Clyde said, "Whatever the bank is short, I'll make it up. This good boy won't be left beholden. My boy either." He paused, trying not to cry. "But don't come back for it. I'll send it. Better for both of us if we don't set eyes on one another again."

Amos brought the wagon up to the door. Julie spread blankets in the wagon bed, and the men carefully placed Daggett on them. Amos climbed back onto the seat. John Clyde knelt beside the cowboy. He was saying quietly, "You rest easy, son. Ain't nobody goin' to hurt you again as long as I'm here to do somethin' about it." The wagon started out upon the town road, Amos clucking the team into a brisk trot.

Hayes walked to the bunkhouse and gathered his few belongings, then went to the barn and saddled the sorrel horse.

Julie stayed at the house, watching him. He rode back to her and dismounted, struggling for the words to keep him from losing her. "I reckon this changes everything between us."

She said, "You'll have to give me time."

He swallowed. "How'll I know when it's been time enough?"

She tried to smile but could not quite make it work. "You'll know. I'll come lookin' for you."

"I won't be hard to find." He swung into the saddle. When he looked back, she was still watching. She waved, and some of the weight of the past weeks lifted from his shoulders. He knew someday he would look around, and she would be there.

# APACHE
# PATROL

**S**unrise promised a typical peaceful desert day, with the early morning cool and pleasant before a blazing sun would beat the desert into fevered submission and cloud the distant mountains with devilish, dancing heat waves.

But the sun was hardly an hour high before Apache hoofbeats drummed destruction, Apache knives dripped red, and curling brown smoke told of sudden death.

The first signal the military had of disaster was when an Apache scout the white men called Charlie Longknife spurred through the front gate and cut arrow-straight across the bare parade ground toward the headquarters building. His heaving bay horse was flecked with sweat foam and caked alkali.

Out in the G Troop corral, twenty blue-clad troopers saddled and packed horses in preparation for patrol. Only Corporal Hadley watched the scout's arrival, and his interest soon turned back to the troop's officer. The lieutenant sat alone on a stool in the shade of G Troop stable.

"Looks like the Apache fever's working on the lieutenant again," he remarked quietly.

Big Sergeant John Bell leaned against the corral fence, absently riffling with his thumb the well-worn deck of cards he always carried.

"Yeah, he's been eating his heart out for the last six months," he said in a long Southern drawl. "Ever since the day old One-Ear's band cut us up over on Massacre Creek."

He looked intently at the corporal, and in his eyes was a warning to keep quiet about it. "But by Jasper he's still the best officer you'll ever see, boy."

To a casual passerby Lieutenant Monte Fowler might have been asleep. But a careful look would reveal the pinched, quivering lines at the corners of the closed eyes, the hard set of the mouth that almost hid its youth, and the fists clenched so tightly that the knuckles showed white.

It had been like this for Monte every time he'd started a new patrol the last six months. His eyes closed tightly, he could see again the screaming Apache band sweeping down on his undermanned troop along the dry creek bed, covered by a murderous hail of snarling bullets from above. Again Monte could feel the painful, nose-pinching smell of gunsmoke. He was hearing the triumphant shouts of the savages as they broke through and overran part of the troop.

There were belching guns, flashing knives, the desperate cries of wounded and doomed men. Most of all there was the blinding red haze, the choking in his throat, the crazy desperation that had made him jump into the fray, swinging his jammed carbine by the barrel and crushing the brown ribs of Apache horsemen until something had crashed down upon his skull and dropped him into merciful oblivion.

Then he was remembering the terrible quiet that followed. He almost thought he could feel again big, graying Sergeant Bell wiping his face with a wet, dirty handkerchief, trying to bring him to. He remembered the sickening sight of half his troop sprawled in horrible death along the creek bed.

His fault! His men slaughtered because he had forgotten caution. A pretty girl with brown eyes and dark hair had spoken harsh words of contempt, and Lieutenant Monte Fowler had angrily led his men into ambush.

"Lieutenant Fowler, sir!"

Monte opened his eyes and blinked against the bright desert sun that reflected off the powdered alkali of the corral. He became conscious of a young trooper standing at attention before him.

"Lieutenant Fowler, sir, Colonel Stiles wants to see you immediately."

Monte stood up, returned the salute and mumbled his thanks. He followed the trooper at twenty paces, trying to shake the last ragged edges of the memory from his mind. Almost at the headquarters building he remembered to button his blue field uniform all the way to the top and to straighten his yellow neckerchief.

In the colonel's office Scout Longknife was tracing on a wall map with the wicked-looking knife that had given him his nickname. Scout or not, he was Apache, and Apaches loved their knives.

Colonel Stiles worriedly returned Monte's salute. Major Davenport, the adjutant, sat in a corner, watching Longknife and frowning darkly.

"Trouble, Mister Fowler," the colonel said. "One-Ear's jumped the reservation again. He has a hundred renegades with him this time."

One-Ear! Monte silently let the dreaded name roll off his tongue. A bronco Apache from way back. It had been the custom among some Indian fighters to cut off the ears of a renegade, to make him an object of ridicule among his own people. But the man who had touched the knife to this Indian had never lived to finish the job.

Colonel Stiles's hands shook. "He's headed for Mexico. The worst of it is, he's going to pick up guns on the way. The way Longknife tells it, the renegades joined One-Ear last night. A lot of them brought along their women. They drank tulapai until their blood thirst got the best of them.

"On the way out they raided a camp of peaceful Apaches, killed some of the men and stole some women and horses. That started the alarm. The word is that they're headed straight for Santos Mountain. A gunrunner is supposed to meet them there with a wagonload of guns."

Monte frowned. "Any idea who the gunrunner is?"

The colonel took the pipe out of his mouth and stared at it, scowling. "Beecher Garrett, most likely."

Monte felt a bitter taste in his mouth. Garrett had been an Indian agent here. He had been so crooked that even the Indian Bureau had not been able to stand the stench. After his discharge he had stayed around the fort and gambled troopers out of their pay. He had been chased off the post two or three times.

The colonel straightened. "With the new settlers that keep filling in between here and the Border, Mister Fowler, I don't have to tell you what bloodshed such a group of armed, raiding Apaches could cause if they use Old Mexico as a sanctuary.

"Your troop is ready for patrol anyway," the colonel went on, "so you're to take the field immediately. You're to make a forced march to Santos Mountain and try to get to Garrett first. If you're too late, you will race One-Ear to the Border. Whatever the cost, engage him before he can get over. Hold him until we get there."

Monte's breath came short as alarm arose in him. "But, sir, G Troop was short even before Massacre Creek. Now I have only twenty men. You said One-Ear has a hundred."

"I'm alerting three troops to be ready to ride with full field equipment and rations within three hours. So whatever happens, we will be only a few hours behind you.

"Now proceed as ordered, Mister. And take Charlie Longknife with you."

Monte saluted, a sickening dread making his sun-browned face perhaps a shade lighter. "Yes, sir."

As Monte's bootheels clicked off the veranda, Major Davenport arose from his chair in the corner.

"Do you think it was wise, Colonel, leaving Fowler in command on a mission as important as this? You know how he's been since that ambush."

The colonel bit down on his pipestem. "I've told him a dozen times he was blameless for that affair. Any officer might have ridden into it."

"But just the same, sir, it has preyed on his mind, and he still blames himself for the deaths of those men. If he faces another battle like that one, he may fold up. He may not fight."

The colonel stood up angrily. "Blast it, Davenport, Fowler's a good soldier. He'll do all right."

"But if he doesn't—what then?"

The colonel sank into his chair, looked down at his desk and clenched a big fist. "If he doesn't, I'll make him wish he'd never heard of the Army!"

With Sergeant Bell and Corporal Hadley beside him, Monte led the blue-clad troop out of G corral without ceremony. As they passed the row of small, stingily built houses used by enlisted men's families, a young woman stepped down from a small porch and walked rapidly out to meet them.

She waved her hand briefly to catch Corporal Hadley's attention. But Monte could see that she had had that from the instant she stepped out the door. He raised his hand for the troop to stop a moment.

"Scott," she said quietly, urgently, her small hand on the shoulder of the corporal's horse, "please keep a watch out for Chester. He may be out there somewhere, needing help."

Scott Hadley swallowed. "Sure, Polly. I'll watch for him."

Monte noted the forlorn look in the young corporal's face, despite his attempt to cover it up. There was pleading in the slender woman's blue eyes, enough to jolt any man's heart. Monte knew it hurt Hadley worse than anyone.

He saw the pain spreading in Hadley's face. "We'd better be moving, Corporal," he said quickly, wanting to end it.

Clear of enlisted quarters, Monte glanced at Hadley again. "You still haven't told her that her husband is a deserter?"

"No, sir," Hadley answered tightly, not looking at the lieutenant. "Everybody knows he's an expert with Indians, so I've told her he's out on a special mission. And if any man tells her different, I'll whip him to within an inch of his life."

Hadley set his jaw solidly and rode on without another word.

The fort was seven dusty, sweaty, sun-tortured hours behind them now. Just ahead, Santos Mountain rose lonely and jagged from the desert. A small mountain compared to others farther south and west, but it loomed large because it stood alone.

It loomed even larger than usual to Monte now as the troop moved closer to it, first in a gallop, then in a hard trot. In its shadow a white man had come to trade the blood of other white men for gold.

Were the troopers in time, or had the guns already passed into savage hands? Monte wondered and trembled a little, for the taste of Massacre Creek was still with him.

Suddenly he raised his hand for the small troop to stop. Ahead a rider spurred toward them. Monte quickly took out his binoculars. Charlie Longknife all right. He had ridden on to scout.

"Many tracks, many horses," Longknife said breathlessly. Sweat stained the bottom of his greasy headband and trickled down the brittle, leathery skin of his brown face.

"They pass maybe half hour ago. Go straight to mountain. We maybe too late."

Monte clenched his fists and let himself curse a little. Twenty troopers against a hundred renegade Apaches, all armed now. Ambush would not be difficult, for an Apache could spring an ambush in broad open desert. And here there was cover enough.

He hesitated, remembering the other ambush and feeling the clammy hand of fear catch his throat.

Sergeant John Bell seemed to sense Monte's indecision, and he knew there was no time to waste.

"Did the lieutenant say to proceed?" Without waiting for an answer, Bell waved the troop on at a gallop. Monte spurred his mount and knew a tinge of shame for letting his sergeant make the decision for him.

They saw the tiny spiral of smoke first. Then there was the wagon, still burning to prevent identification. Hoofs of more than a hundred horses had beaten a solid mat of tracks around the spot where the trade had been made. Splintered remnants of packing cases lay scattered. Here and there the sun was reflected off a brass cartridge case dropped by an Indian in haste to ride on.

Charlie Longknife signaled urgently. He showed Monte a set of tracks leading off to one side. "Two white men," he declared. "They maybe ride off on horses that pull the wagon."

Monte gritted his teeth as he thought of the gunrunners. They couldn't be many minutes ahead.

Bell seemed to be outguessing him again. "Colonel's orders were to catch the *Indians,* sir," he drawled.

Shame warmed Monte's face. He had to admit to himself that one reason he wanted to go after the gunrunners was that it might delay contact with the Indians a little.

A grin broke across Bell's broad, wrinkling face. "But as you say, sir, the runners' trail don't seem to be much out of our way."

Monte hadn't said. But before he could say anything, Bell had waved the troop on. Hoofs drummed across the desert, rustled the sage, veered around clutching cactus. One mile behind them, then an-

other. Searing wind, parched throats, burning eyes
were forgotten in the fast ride, the sudden thrill of
the chase.

Then the troop topped a low rise, and the quarry
was seen not three hundred yards ahead. One of the
two men looked back and discovered the pursuit. He
spurred his horse.

But raw anger fanned high among the troopers
as they saw the men who had run guns to warring
Apaches. They spurred harder. The gap quickly narrowed. Then they were close enough so that Monte
could yell: "Pull up there or we'll fire!"

The fugitives reined up, and one of them, a broad
man, turned his horse around. Monte instantly recognized him. It was Beecher Garrett, all right, his
fleshy, sun-reddened face scowling belligerently.

The other man had stopped his horse but still faced
the other way. The rider bent over the saddle horn,
his lean shoulders sagging.

"All right, you," Bell shouted, "turn around here!"

The man turned. Monte heard a sharp gasp from
Corporal Hadley. It was Private Chester Millard, the
deserter, in civilian clothes. Millard kept his head
down.

Sergeant Bell was the first of the shocked troopers
to speak. "Chester," he said, his strong voice so quiet
that its contempt rubbed like a curry comb, "I wish to
God we'd found you with an Apache arrow sticking
in you. At least there'd've been some honor in that."

Garrett blustered, "Now see here, Fowler. You've
got nothing to hold me for."

A hot tide of hatred surged through Monte.
"You've just sold a wagonload of guns and ammunition to a bunch of blood-thirsty renegades, and you

say we have nothing to hold you for. If I were anything but a soldier, Garrett, I'd kill you right where
you're sitting."

Garrett's face flushed. "I'll remind you, Fowler,
that I have friends in the Indian Bureau, powerful
friends. They can make their weight felt in the Army,
too."

Monte spurred up beside Garrett's horse and
quickly untied the flap of one of the gunrunners'
bulging saddlebags. He pulled out a small Indian-
made rawhide bag and knew by the feel that there
were more. He loosened the tie-string, reached in and
let the yellow dust spill between his fingers.

"Gold," he said quietly. "Your saddlebags and Millard's too are full of it. Ten to one it's gold the Indians took from a stagecoach weeks ago."

Garrett shook his fist. "You'll never make any
charges stick, Fowler," he shouted. "I'll have your
bars for this. I'll see you stripped of that uniform."

Rage choked Monte, rage he couldn't swallow
down. He leaned forward in the saddle and drove
a hard fist into Garrett's flushed face. The gunrunner almost fell off his horse. Grabbing the horn, he
weakly pulled himself back up. A trickle of blood
stained his chin.

Sergeant Bell ended it. "Corporal Hadley, tie the
prisoners' hands," he ordered. "We can't lose any
more time."

For almost an hour the troop kept up a hard pace,
following the tracks of the large band as it headed
almost due south. Charlie Longknife stayed well in
front, following the trail carefully and watching for
ambush.

Presently Monte saw Longknife draw rein and
study the ground, slowly walking his horse in a small

circle. The Indian straightened in the saddle and waved the troop in.

"Here Apache break up, go two ways. Some go southwest. Other bunch, it go southeast."

Even before the Indian spoke again, Monte knew what was coming, and his heart was sick.

Longknife pointed off into the distance. "Two ranches here. One to southeast, they call him George Porter."

Porter! The name brought a picture flashing into Monte's mind. A picture of a pretty girl with brown eyes and dark hair. Virginia Porter, her name was. Virginia Porter, whose angry words had sent him charging into ambush on Massacre Creek.

"You think they split up to raid both ranches?"

Longknife nodded. "Later maybe they come back together. More new ranches between here and Border. Maybe steal lots horses, kill lots white people, then go Old Mexico and have big laugh."

The picture of Virginia Porter was burning in Monte's mind. Maybe he should have hated her for driving him into the massacre. But she couldn't have known about that. And the thought of her dying under Apache guns or dragged into Apache captivity turned his blood to ice.

"Begging your pardon, sir," Sergeant Bell spoke. "Not wanting to tell you what to do or anything like that, but a good gambler like myself always takes the chance that looks best. It's only three or four miles to the Porter ranch. If our luck is good we could go on to the other ranch."

It occurred to Monte that as an officer he should resent any advice from an enlisted man, even a noncom. But he didn't. Sergeant Bell was a man an officer could lean on.

If our luck is good! If it isn't, Monte told himself bitterly, there will be weeping in enlisted quarters tonight. But he found himself nodding and heard Sergeant Bell shout, "Forwar-r-d! Ho-o-o!"

More hard riding. Hot wind seared the lungs. Red eyes peered vainly through the tortuous heat waves that distorted the horizon. Hearts leaped at every twisting dust devil that danced across the desert with its false signal of the bloodthirsty Indians.

Then, from over the last rise came the rattle of gunfire, a film of dust and a thin column of light brown smoke rising up into a sky turned copper by a blazing sun.

As they topped the rise, Monte motioned for the men to spread out in a skirmish line. For a moment he held his binoculars to his eyes and looked down at the flaming scene a half mile away. Apaches crawled there like so many ants. They weren't using the circling technique of the plains Indians. The Apaches liked to fight afoot, close in.

Only a few horseback Indians could be seen, those mostly trying to hold mounts belonging to the others. Indians lay in protection of corrals, brush clumps and the few outbuildings that weren't already in flames. Gunflashes still jabbed at them from the ranch house, the last stand of whatever whites might be left. Any minute now there would be a final rush.

Monte lowered the binoculars and swallowed hard. He felt more than saw Sergeant Bell ride up and stop beside him.

"Ready, sir?"

Monte looked at his troop. Twenty men—twenty good men. He remembered Massacre Creek and dreaded this. But he also remembered a pretty girl with dark hair.

"I'll never be ready, Sergeant."

To a trooper who waited near him, Monte said painfully, "Bugler, sound the charge. Make it loud enough for every Indian to hear."

A crooked line of blue-clad men surged forward in a pounding of hoofs, a chorus of defiant yells. Hot wind tugged at Monte's hat, burned his face, dried his throat.

Ahead, the Indians had heard the bugle. For a moment they held their ground and watched the tide of mounted men sweeping toward them. Then they broke and began running toward their horses. Even a superior force of Indians caught afoot in the open had little hope against cavalry.

Within range now, the troopers began pouring fire into the Apaches. Gunflashes from the ranch house increased, too. Renegades still afoot stumbled and lay where they fell. Many tumbled from their horses. But in a moment all those who had not been hit were on their horses and riding west.

Monte slid his mount to a dusty stop and raised his binoculars again. Off to the west another group waited, one he hadn't seen from the rise. It included a number of loose horses and very few men. Mostly it was squaws, many of them captives. He wished he could free them, but he knew the soldiers could not get there in time.

Part of the troopers, led by Corporal Hadley, kept after the Indians long enough to drop a good many more from their horses. Finally the troopers regrouped and came riding back toward the ranch house.

With Sergeant Bell behind him, Monte reined in at the ranchyard. Warily he watched the fallen Indians. There might still be a live one or two. It was ancient tribal law for a dying Apache warrior to take as many enemies with him as possible into the land of the shadows.

The front door opened and a big ranchman wearily stepped out onto the bullet-scarred gallery. There was a smear of blood on his hard, wrinkled face and even in the end of his thick, graying mustache. He stood there, staring thankfully at the troopers.

"Never thought I'd ever live to see the day I'd be glad to have a Yankee yellow-leg come to my house. But God himself must have sent you."

Monte kept watching the door, hoping to catch a glimpse of her. Anxiety throbbed in him. "Virginia— Miss Porter, is she—"

The man nodded. "She's all right."

Suddenly Monte heard Bell's desperate shout. Instinctively he grabbed for his pistol. He felt himself being shoved. Even as his shoulder hit the gallery floor he heard the shot explode. He saw Bell spin around and grab his huge arm. Then Monte spotted the Indian, cocking his new rifle for another shot.

Hardly taking time to aim, Monte squeezed the trigger. The Indian jerked, dropped the rifle and slowly relaxed, sinking facedown to the ground.

Hands shaking from the sudden excitement, Monte pushed himself back up onto his feet. Bell stood there gripping his left arm. Blood slowly trickled out between his fingers.

"Better get in the house, trooper," George Porter said. "The womenfolks'll take care of that wound."

Monte followed the sergeant into the house. Two cowboys stood with rifles in their hands, sweat, blood and dirt mixed on their faces. A couple more sat on the floor, arms or legs bandaged. In a corner a tautly pulled sheet revealed the outline of a body under it.

Then she stepped out of the kitchen. Virginia Porter. The same girl he had met at the officers' and noncommissioned officers' ball in the fort, when she had been a guest of an officer's family. That had been a night he could never forget. Her warm smile, the feel of her warm body close to his as they danced—it had been with him, a part of him, ever since.

But he had seen her another time, too, weeks later. His troop had ridden to investigate a column of smoke and had found two wrecked, burning wagons, their contents scattered, their occupants dead. While the troopers were still there, another group of riders had come up. Cowboys, George Porter—and Virginia.

"We got here too late," Monte had explained simply.

The girl had looked at the bodies, then fire flashed in her brown eyes. "Too late! The Army's always too late! Never in time to save the living, but always on hand to bury the dead and parade their blue uniforms.

"I used to laugh at Dad when he said the only thing lower than a buffalo hunter was a Yankee yellow-leg. But I won't laugh any more, Monte Fowler. Because I know now that he's right!"

Her words had burned in him like a shovelful of coals from a campfire. He had swung into the saddle and led his troops in pursuit of the savages. Blinding anger had pulled him into the ambush at Massacre Creek.

Now Monte stood facing her again. The old anger was not in her eyes anymore. There was blood on her dress from bandaging the wounded. A lock of disheveled brown hair hung down over her forehead. A dark smear showed across one side of her face. Her lips were pale. But somehow she was as lovely as she had been that night at the fort.

"Monte," she breathed. Then she fell into his arms.

An hour ago it would have given him much satisfaction to say, "We got here in time." Now it didn't seem appropriate. Nothing seemed appropriate except to hold her like this. Without either one saying a word, something passed between them that said that any grievance one had held against the other was forgiven, forgotten.

He broke the silence. "I've got a wounded man here. He saved my life."

Virginia seemed to come out of a trance, and she pulled out of his arms. "I'll see after him," she said, her voice as warm as it had been that night at the fort.

Monte stepped out onto the gallery as the rest of the troopers rode up. They scattered to look over the fallen Indians, to make sure none were playing dead.

Corporal Hadley swung down and saluted. "They've routed, sir. We seem to've killed fifteen or twenty. We've lost one man killed, two wounded."

"Who's dead?" the lieutenant asked painfully.

"O'Malley, sir."

Monte looked at the ground and clenched his fists tightly. He could already see himself knocking on Mrs. O'Malley's door, to offer his weak condolences, just as he had knocked on so many doors after Massacre Creek.

The manual was explicit on such forms of etiquette as an officer's introducing himself to the new commanding officer's family. But it didn't tell you what to say to a woman newly widowed. It didn't tell you how to say you had led her husband to his death and that you were very sorry and that arrangements would be made for her trip home. It didn't tell you how to shut your eyes to the anguish in her face or how to shut your ears to the weeping of the children.

Monte tried to shake the sickness out of him as the corporal spoke. "The Indians that got away are heading straight for the other ranch, sir. It may be that One-Ear doesn't know we're so close behind him. But he'll know it when they get there."

Monte nodded bleakly. "Right, Corporal. We can't waste any time."

He glanced toward a trooper bringing up the prisoners, Garrett and the deserter.

"We'll have to take the prisoners with us, Corporal. These people here already have all the trouble they can handle."

Hadley saluted. "Yes, sir. I'll get the men together."

Monte noted the aching look in the corporal's eyes as he glanced at Millard. Then Hadley swung his horse away and started calling his men.

Back in the house, Sergeant Bell had taken the deck of cards out of his pocket and was playing solitaire to keep his mind off the pain as the girl cleaned his wound.

"We're going on to the Baker ranch, Sergeant. You'd better stay," Monte said regretfully.

"But it's just a flesh wound," Bell protested. "And begging your pardon, sir—" he paused a moment— "I believe you need me."

Monte swallowed. Bell had hit the truth there. Monte knew that there were some commanding officers who would cashier a lieutenant for letting a sergeant shield him as Bell had done.

"I'm sorry, Sergeant."

Bell started to raise his left arm in argument, then

grimaced miserably and lowered it. He managed a weak grin. "But, sir, the cards show my luck to be with me. I've been reading my fortune."

"And what is your fortune?"

"Good luck, sir. Good luck and a long life."

Monte managed to smile, but he was sick inside. "I'm still sorry, Sergeant." He turned quickly to go. He wanted desperately to have the sergeant with him. But it just wouldn't do.

Virginia Porter stepped in front of Monte as he started for the door. "Monte, the sergeant says the other Indians were headed for the Baker ranch." He nodded and she added, "My sister lives there. You've got to take me with you."

Monte looked at her, his smile gone. "There'll be another fight. It's impossible."

"But it's my sister, I tell you. And they'll need me to help take care of the wounded."

The anguish in her brown eyes held him, formed a knot deep inside him. But he managed another no, and stepped outside quickly.

The soldiers faced into a setting sun, eyes weary, faces grimy. Their blue uniforms were turned gray by dust, caked in spots by sweat. The horses were beginning to be jaded, too, but there was no time for rest. Somewhere ahead Apache guns were speaking of death.

Back in the column Corporal Hadley had gotten up nerve enough to speak to the deserter Millard. Up front, Monte could hear their quiet voices.

"How could you ever do this, Chester—to Polly, to yourself?"

Millard was silent a moment. "It was Garrett. I got to gambling with him. First thing I knew I owed him more than I could hope to pay in ten years. He had his eyes on Polly all the time. He hoped my debt would give him some freedom with her. I was always afraid of what he might do when I was away from the fort. I ought've killed him, I know, but I'd've gotten hung for it.

"Then he offered to forget the debt if I'd help him line up this gun deal with One-Ear. He'd found out how well I knew Indians. There didn't seem to be much else I could do. I figgered on leaving the country afterwards and sending for Polly."

Monte felt anger burning his face. Another score to settle with Garrett. But with the Indian Bureau the way it was, there was a good chance the gunrunner would get off free.

It was almost dark when the troopers heard the gunfire behind them. For a split second Monte remembered Massacre Creek and wished desperately for Sergeant Bell.

"It seems to be about half a mile behind us, sir," Corporal Hadley said. Monte waved the troop back in a gallop.

They found Sergeant Bell and Virginia Porter taking refuge behind a boulder. With his good right hand the sergeant was firing his pistol into a clump of brush. Virginia was triggering the sergeant's carbine.

Quickly the troopers fanned through the brush, flushed out two straggling Apaches, and dispatched them.

"Sergeant Bell," Monte declared angrily, "you were ordered to stay behind. What do you mean by disobeying that order, and bringing Vir—Miss Porter with you?"

"It wasn't really such a bad wound, sir," the sergeant said defensively. Monte noted that somehow it had broken open again, and that a spot of blood showed on the bandage.

"As for Miss Porter, sir, she's a shrewd trader. I couldn't get her to get me my horse without promising to let her come with me."

Monte chewed on the inside of his lip. "Well, it's too late to do anything about it now. I guess she'll have protection with us. As for your disobedience, Sergeant, we'll take that up when this mission is over. Now let's move out."

A thought kept running through him, chilling him. Those stragglers had been there when the troop went by. They hadn't been seen. What if somewhere ahead a larger group waited to pounce on the small troop as the stragglers had fired on the sergeant and Virginia?

Monte's heart jumped as he heard a whoop from Charlie Longknife half an hour later. Monte yelled for a halt and jerked out his gun. Then he heard Longknife call the men on.

They saw the scout kneeling beside a figure who lay on the hard alkali ground. Dismounting, Monte found that it was a young squaw. There was still a breath of life in her, but the sticky blood which stained her dress showed she didn't have much time left.

Virginia Porter stepped down from her horse, her mouth tight. Without a word, she took Monte's canteen, soaked a handkerchief and pressed it to the woman's burning lips. She brushed the black hair back from the dark, pain-filled face.

With terrible effort the Indian woman began to speak. Longknife bent low to catch her words. In a moment he raised up.

"This *estune,* a married one, was stolen from the reservation. She see Apache kill her husband with knife. A while ago she try run away. They shoot her to show other women what happen if they try to run away."

The woman spoke again in a faint whisper. The whisper died away, and the glazing dark eyes slowly closed. The squaw was dead.

After an uncomfortable silence, Longknife interpreted her last words. "She say all One-Ear's group meet at ranch, the one they call it Baker. Then they ride to San Miguel Pass."

San Miguel Pass! Monte's heart leaped. There were many places a man afoot could go, but the pass was the only place for ten miles or more either way which would allow horsemen to get through the rugged mountain range. Once through it, the Indians would have a clear path to the Border.

If Monte's troop would get to the pass first, and hold it until Colonel Stiles could get there with a bigger force—

"Lieutenant," a trooper shouted excitedly, "look over yonder, to the southwest!"

Monte looked up. He saw a dull glow which must have been on this side of the mountains. The glow suddenly burst into a brilliant red. The awful silence that followed was a living, choking thing. Then Virginia Porter gasped and began to weep. Everyone knew what it was. The Baker ranch!

Monte was numb a moment. He put his arms around the girl's trembling shoulders and held her tightly to him.

"I guess there's nothing left to do now but race One-Ear to San Miguel Pass," he said finally. "I'll detail a couple of men to take you home, Virginia."

Wiping her eyes, she shook her head. "With only seventeen men left to face One-Ear and his seventy-five or eighty? You can't do it, Monte. I'll get home alone."

Monte looked at her warmly and wondered at her bravery. "I shouldn't have let you stay with us at all. I can't allow you to go back alone. Thomas! McCrorey!"

"You need every man, Monte," she declared as the two troopers rode up. "I won't let you waste them by sending them with me!"

Without a word, Monte lifted the protesting girl back into her saddle. Suddenly she spurred her horse and plunged out into the night. Stunned, Monte saw the darkness swallow her up. Then he yelled, "Catch her!"

But the search was futile. Somewhere out there she had apparently stopped and dismounted to keep from making any sound that the troopers could hear. They could have ridden within a hundred feet of her now and not seen her.

A big lump of fear choked Monte as he thought of her going back to the ranch alone. He remembered the stragglers and wondered how many more there might be.

He swallowed at the ache that cut through him. "Well, Sergeant, we've got to beat One-Ear and his band to San Miguel Pass!"

Monte could feel Bell's eyes appraising him in the darkness, and he wondered at the sergeant's verdict. Bell asked, "Do you think we can hold it until Colonel Stiles gets there?"

Monte licked his dry lips and felt the presence of the ghosts of Massacre Creek. "Only your cards could tell the answer to that one, Sergeant."

The word quickly slipped back through the ranks. The frightened voice of gunrunner Beecher Garrett yelped, "I'm a prisoner. You can't force me to go along and be butchered. There won't a man of us get out alive!"

The cries sent a chill down Monte's back and he felt Sergeant Bell's eyes on him again. The sergeant wheeled his horse around and spurred back down the line.

"Shut him up," Monte heard Bell order Garrett's guard. "I don't care what you do to him, but keep him shut up."

With ice all the way down to the pit of his stomach, Monte ordered, "Forwar-r-d! Ho-o-o!" and the column moved on into the darkness toward San Miguel Pass. Or was it another Massacre Creek?

The night was long, miserably long. Weariness and despair settled over the men like the dead weight of infantry packs. It was a race between a handful of troopers and a large band of Indians.

But it wasn't a rapid race, and that made it even more awful. For men can be driven on and on until they fall, and then they can be shot for not going farther. But you can't court-martial a horse that drops in exhaustion after being ridden a three-day distance in one day. A dead horse is of no use to a cavalryman, and these were almost dead.

So it was walk and lead, then mount and ride, then get off and walk some more, mile on weary mile. There were occasional stops for rest, with soldiers flopping down on the ground and half wishing they could die where they lay.

But always there was the maddening thought that perhaps the Indians were riding while the troopers rested. Perhaps they galloped while the troopers walked. We're ahead and they're behind, each man told himself. But always the doubt was there. And always the men forced themselves up off the ground and pushed doggedly on even before their short rest periods were up.

At last color began brightening the eastern sky. Footsteps quickened. Bent frames straightened. Even the horses, it seemed, began to pick up new strength as gray light fanned out over the desert.

Ahead of the troop the long mountain range stretched, reaching partly around them like a half moon. In its center, dead ahead, was San Miguel Pass—the only place for miles in either direction where One-Ear could take his horses through.

Hands trembling, Monte pulled his binoculars out of their case and focused them on the pass. No sign of movement. Slowly he half turned, looking for the renegade band. Then, northwest of the troop, he could see a thin, long column of dust rising in the crisp dawn air. Even without seeing the horses, he knew it was One-Ear's band, coming along Indian fashion, in single and double file.

"We're ahead of them, Sergeant. Not more than a couple of miles, but we're ahead of them."

At the pass Monte reined around and watched the dust of the Apache column. Sergeant Bell spurred on into the opening. It was hardly more than thirty feet wide at the mouth. He found a sheltered place and ordered the men to dismount and picket their tired horses there. While the dust column moved steadily closer and individual riders became visible, Bell spotted the troopers around at vantage points among the rocks.

Monte picked a high place for himself and the prisoners. From here he would look down and watch all his men. At last satisfied with the distribution of the troopers, Bell came up to Monte's post and settled down to eat some cold rations.

Garrett wouldn't eat. The gunrunner's face was as pale as its naturally reddish cast would allow it to be. Millard ate a little, however. He sat calmly, as if he held no fear of what was coming. He still had some soldier in him, Monte thought proudly.

Monte wished for some of that calmness. "It looks as if One-Ear still doesn't know we're here," Monte observed to Bell. "But he'll cut our tracks pretty soon now. He could pass us up and go ten miles down to another place."

Bell shook his head and watched the Indians coming closer. "I'll bet all my chips on One-Ear's cussedness, sir. He's come this far to San Miguel Pass, and when he reads our tracks he won't let a few troopers scare him off to another one. After we once engage him and kill a few Indians, he won't quit till we're all dead, or till Colonel Stiles comes. He's got too much Apache pride in him, sir."

Monte mulled it over. *He won't quit till we're all dead.* A hollow feeling spread in the pit of his stomach, and the shadow of Massacre Creek fell over him again. Twenty men had died there. Now here were seventeen more, not counting himself.

Bell fidgeted. "I hope you're feeling all right, sir."

Hands still trembling, Monte raised the binoculars. Four hundred yards from the pass opening, the Indians had found the tracks. A great flurry of movement started in the Apache column. Renegade warriors gathered into a bunch. Loose horses, the women and a small handful of bucks moved off well to one side. It wouldn't be long.

"I killed twenty soldiers at Massacre Creek, Sergeant," Monte said in a strained voice. "Now I'm killing seventeen more. I wish it could be just me."

Bell gave him a strange look. "You'd give your own life, sir, if you could save your men?"

Monte nodded bleakly. "After what I did at Massacre Creek, that would be a cheap payment."

He studied the ground a moment, then turned back to Bell. "You've sensed for a long time that I've been going to pieces, Sergeant. I've acted like a coward, yet you've shielded me at every turn. Why?"

Bell frowned. "You're no coward, sir. If it's cowardice to be afraid for your men, then the Army needs more cowards."

Embarrassed, Bell cleared his throat. "Begging your pardon, sir, and no flattery meant, but you're the best officer I've served under since I was wearing the gray for General Lee. That is, you were till Massacre Creek got the best of you. And I know you will be again, once you stop tearing yourself to pieces.

"I can help a friend lick any two-legged enemies he's got," the sergeant added, "but there's not much I can do to help you lick what's in your mind. Just remember this, sir. Some of us will die here, maybe all of us. That's a soldier's job, when you come right down to it. But it'll cost One-Ear a lot more than it costs us. Every one of us that dies may be saving the lives of a dozen settlers, or maybe even other soldiers. That's a mighty good trade in my book, sir. Now I better go see after the men."

Throat dry, Monte watched Bell go, his left arm hanging stiffly at his side. *One life given for a dozen saved. A mighty good trade.* The words echoed through his brain.

Suddenly a large knot of warriors split off and gathered into a skirmish line. Monte realized that they were going to charge and try to get a foothold in the rocks at the foot of the pass. Once there they could begin creeping in for hand-to-hand fighting— the kind of warfare in which Apaches excelled.

Monte felt the muscles tightening in his chest. He wiped his shaking, sweaty hands on his yellow-striped trousers a dozen times. The scene before him hazed over, and again he was seeing the savage, bloody battle at Massacre Creek, watching his men go down under Apache gunfire and flashing Apache knives.

He buried his face in his trembling hands and hoped to God no one was watching him.

Then he heard Apache war cries and the popping of guns. No dream this time. For a moment he sat there paralyzed, unable to breathe, his body aching.

Sergeant Bell's voice jolted him. "Don't shoot till I do, men!" the Southerner shouted.

It was a strong voice, a brave voice. Something in it sent a thrill through Monte. His tight muscles began to relax. His breath came easier.

An Army carbine barked. There was a sudden volley of gunfire that was painful to Monte's ears. Then came the fearless, defiant shouts of the troopers as they kept up rapid firing.

A dozen Indians sprawled in the dust and among the rocks a hundred yards out from the pass. Panicky, riderless horses galloped every which way. The ragged line of surviving Apaches was pulling back under heavy fire.

Triumphantly the troopers cheered and waved their hats. Monte counted them. Seventeen. Not a soldier killed.

He felt his fear slip away. Massacre Creek had been different, he realized. There, death had struck without warning, without giving a chance for defense.

Here his men were prepared. They had won the first skirmish and gained confidence. They weren't afraid. Why should he be? Whatever happened now, they would be ready.

And, Monte vowed to himself, he would be ready too!

For the first time in six months, confidence flowed through him. He walked down from his place and helped bandage two troopers who had been nicked. Sergeant Bell followed him.

"Like to play a little game, sir?" the sergeant asked, taking the deck of cards from his pocket. "It's great for settling the nerves."

"My nerves are settled, Sergeant," Monte said. "For the first time since Massacre Creek, they're settled. I thank you for that."

Bell stood looking at him, and a huge grin broke out on his kindly face. "I'm glad, sir. Looks like our luck's with us again. That old rebel luck."

Suddenly there was a loud thump, followed by a rifle shot from a fallen Indian two hundred yards away. Sergeant Bell buckled and fell forward, trying to catch himself with his good arm. The cards flipped from his hand and scattered out around him.

Choking, Monte grabbed him. He saw the red color spreading around the little round hole in the back of Bell's blue shirt. Carefully Monte turned him over. He could hear the heavy barking of Army carbines as troopers killed the Indian.

"John!" Monte called plaintively. "John!"

Bell's lips parted. "It's still—a good trade, sir." Then he was gone.

Kneeling beside the sergeant, Monte felt grief stab him. He picked up one of the fallen cards. Bitterly he remembered Bell's words at the Porter ranch. *Good luck. Good luck and a long life.* He shredded the card in his hands.

Monte glanced out at the Indians. They were ready for another charge. Some of that old dread came back to him, and he wavered. Bell was dead. The sergeant had helped hold him up, and now that prop was gone.

He heard the battle cries of the Apaches as they came again. He heard the staccato fire of their rifles. For a moment he thought he was going to fold up, to give in to blind despair.

Then he looked again at Bell, lying in eternal peace. Somehow the sergeant gave him strength again now in death, as he had in life.

Monte turned to face the charging Apaches. He raised his carbine and shouted for all the troopers to hear: "Pay them for Massacre Creek. Pay them for Sergeant Bell! Pour it to them!"

Carbines blazed with the fury of hell. Monte saw a trooper rise to aim, then slump forward, dropping his gun. Another grabbed an arm and fell back weakly against a rock.

But the Apaches were taking a licking. A few made it in to the very foot of the mountain, only to be killed or driven back by a deadly stream of bullets.

During the charge Monte's carbine jammed. It was the same one that had betrayed him at Massacre Creek. He hurled it away and grabbed up Bell's. Then the attack was over.

Some signal of alarm made him look up. Just above

him the gunrunner Garrett stood with an Army pistol in his untied hands. His eyes were wild.

"You brought me here to be butchered, didn't you, Fowler?" he babbled. "Well it won't happen that way. I'm going out to join One-Ear. He's my friend. The Indians will slaughter your troops, but I won't be here."

He laughed crazily. "You won't be here either, Fowler. Because I'm going to kill you right where you stand!"

His throat dry again, Monte looked higher. He saw the prisoners' guard lying on his face a little way above. An Indian bullet must have gotten him. Then Monte saw Millard, stealthily climbing down, his hands still tied. The deserter was awkwardly picking up the jammed carbine, not knowing that Monte had discarded it.

"Hold it right there, Garrett," Millard shouted. "I've got a gun on you."

Desperately Garrett swung his gun up toward the deserter. With a look of extreme satisfaction, Millard squeezed the trigger. The inevitable happened. The jammed gun clicked. Garrett's pistol thundered. Surprise whipped across Millard's face. Then he fell.

Monte took advantage of the moment to jump behind some sheltering rocks. Garrett cursed, then Monte heard his heavy footsteps jarring loose small rocks as the gunrunner scurried down the mountainside. At the bottom was an Indian pony which had entered the mouth of the pass after his rider was shot. Garrett jumped on him and spurred out.

Troopers farther down swung their guns around. Monte quickly jumped up. "Hold your fire!" he shouted. "Hold your fire!"

Surprised soldiers lowered their guns. Corporal

Hadley came up. He swallowed as he looked for a long moment at the dead Millard.

"Why didn't you let us shoot him, sir? It would've been easy."

"It would've been too easy, Corporal," Monte replied grimly. "His guns have caused too many good people to die in the last few hours. I think One-Ear gives traitors more appropriate treatment than we do."

Hadley was puzzled. "How's he a traitor to One-Ear?"

"He's with us. One-Ear is bound to reason that it was Garrett who betrayed him to us. Garrett was too hysterical to figure that out. Whatever the Indians do to him will be no more than he deserves. And whatever they do will take time. We need all of that we can get."

Half a dozen Apaches rode out to meet Garrett. They hustled him into the group. Through the binoculars Monte watched the gunrunner frantically gesturing to the ugly One-Ear. The Indian listened a moment, then jabbed out with his rifle butt and knocked Garrett off the horse.

Even at this distance, the troopers could hear the shouts and whoops as Garrett was passed from hand to hand for perhaps half an hour. He was tortured ingeniously, so that he never quite fainted. Finally it seemed that the renegades were wearying of their sport. Monte saw them catch two ponies. They tied Garrett's right foot to the tail of one and his left to the other.

Monte lowered the binoculars and looked away as the savages stampeded the two horses across the rocks. His stomach turned over, and he half wished he had let his troopers fire.

He expected another charge after the Apaches had finished with Garrett. But it didn't come. Instead the remaining Indians split up into two bunches. One group rode to the mountains half a mile up from the pass on one side. The others went to the mountains about the same distance in the other direction.

Realization of their plan struck Monte right between the eyes. The Apaches weren't cavalrymen and knew it. They were foot soldiers. Now they were getting into the mountains afoot, to creep in among the rocks and root the troopers out, one by one, on the Indians' own terms. The soldiers wouldn't have a chance.

The troopers figured it out about as quickly as Monte did. He could feel the fear begin creeping into them, settling over the little group like he remembered chill fog settling in on cold nights at the Point. Fighting at close range, slashing with knives, swinging rifle butts wasn't their kind of fighting. Why did they have to do it?

Yes, why did they? The question suddenly brought the solution. The troopers still had their horses hidden back in the pass. The warriors had left their horses with two tiny groups of guards, one of which also had to keep watch over the captive women.

"All right, men," Monte said just loudly enough for them all to hear. "We're going to slip back and mount up. Go easy, so they don't see too much movement at one time."

He sat and watched until the last trooper was out. Then, excitement tingling through him, he followed them and mounted his own horse. He divided his men into two equal groups. They picked up the few Indian horses which had drifted into the pass.

"Corporal," he said crisply, with a new confidence, "your men will move at a gallop and capture all the horses they've left on the east side of the pass. We'll get all those on the west. We'll meet with them a mile north of the pass. Pick up all strays as you go. Don't leave a single hoof for those renegades." He paused a brief second. "Now move out!"

With a new fire in them and rested horses beneath their saddles, the troopers spurred out of the pass.

It didn't take the Indians on the mountainsides many seconds to understand what was happening. They fired rapid, futile shots at the galloping troopers. But the soldiers were moving targets at too long a range.

Monte's troopers spurred up to the westernmost band, firing as they rode. The frightened horses bolted. Three Indian guards fired quick shots into the air, desperately trying to halt the runaways. Troopers' bullets knocked down one Apache, then another. The third fired a couple of wild shots toward the troopers. Then, in hateful spite, he aimed his rifle into a group of captive women.

Charlie Longknife slid his horse to a halt, raised his carbine and fired. The Indian toppled. Troopers circled the horses and headed them back toward the rendezvous point. The squaws went along, the captured ones jubilant, the rest sullen.

Now Monte rode in close to the mountainside and reined up for a long look. Dust far to the east showed that Hadley's group had had the same good luck. Now that these Apaches were afoot, still miles from the border, most of them would give up without much more trouble. Especially when Colonel

Stiles and his men arrived and began combing the mountains.

Monte heard something whistle by his ear, followed by the heavy roar of a rifle. Before he could move, the rifle roared again, and his horse fell. Monte's leg was pinned beneath him. So was his carbine.

He struggled to pull the leg out but could not move it. Desperately he grabbed for his sidearm. But the holster was empty. The pistol had been lost in the fighting.

An Indian arose from behind a rock. Stealthily he crept out and hesitated. Then he realized Monte's helplessness and stepped confidently forward. Only one Indian could own that hate-filled face—One-Ear!

Holding his breath, Monte looked at that sharp, fox face, the cruel, thin-lipped mouth, the mutilated ear half hidden by the stringy black hair.

Monte had heard it said that Apaches never grinned. He had long known it wasn't true, and he knew it again now. For One-Ear was grinning, a vengeful, merciless grin that revealed a row of crooked, stained teeth. A few feet from Monte the breech-clouted Indian stopped.

"White-eyed lieutenant," he hissed. "You die!"

Fear had been in Monte so long that it seemed to have burned itself out. He wondered vaguely why he felt so little dread now. A thought came to him, incongruous as it might have been. Wonder if anybody'll ever get that other ear?

A gun barked, but it wasn't the renegade's. One-Ear bent at the middle and pitched forward. Monte turned his head toward the sound of hoofbeats. It was Charlie Longknife.

Charlie helped Monte get loose from the dead horse. Monte swung up onto the scout's mount.

"You wait," Longknife said. He walked over to One-Ear's body, took out that long knife, and answered Monte's question.

Colonel Stiles reached the pass some time after noon. Renegade Indians began filing down out of the mountains to surrender. A few remained to fight, and the colonel's troopers went up into the rocks to oblige them.

Monte and his men, relieved of the duty of further fighting, waited with the captured horses and the freed Indian women. Monte found himself thinking of Massacre Creek again. Strangely the memory of it brought little pain to him now. It had been a defeat, surely. But the death of One-Ear and the quelling of his insurrection had avenged it in full.

Corporal Hadley took Monte aside.

"I was thinking, sir," he said, "that since Private Millard is dead, we might find some way of keeping Polly, I mean Mrs. Millard, from knowing how things really were."

Monte nodded. "I've given it some thought, Corporal. Private Millard made up for a lot when he tried to save me from Garrett. I'll speak to Colonel Stiles. Under the circumstances, I think he'll have Millard's desertion stricken from the record and mark him down for having been on a special assignment. I believe that's what you told Mrs. Millard."

Hadley looked down. "That'd be mighty kind of you, sir."

Monte hesitated. "I suppose Mrs. Millard will be going back to her people."

"She hasn't any, sir."

Monte rubbed his chin. "Well, then, come to think of it, ever since the sutler's daughter went off to finishing school, the sutler and his wife have been wanting to hire someone to help them around the store. I could suggest Mrs. Millard. That would give her a chance to stay on the post. Then, after a proper period of time—"

Hadley looked up and saluted. He was blinking rapidly. "Thank you, sir."

A good man, Monte thought as he watched the corporal walk away. And G Troop would need a good sergeant now.

While he watched for the colonel to return, Monte began to worry about Virginia Porter. He thought of the many things that could have happened to her.

Finally the colonel rode up.

"Sir," Monte pressed urgently, "I'd like your permission to ride back to the Porter ranch. There's someone there I have to see about. I mean, there's—"

The colonel laughed. "You're worried about that girl? Well, don't. She's all right. Instead of going home last night she came on to meet us. She found us just after daylight and told us to come straight to San Miguel Pass. I detailed a couple of troopers to escort her home."

Relief washed through Monte. Relief and pride.

The colonel went on, "Part of my men are going to march the renegades back to the reservation. The Apaches will walk every step of it. Your men will drive the horses." A brief smile flickered on the colonel's face when he added, "If you choose to take them by way of the Porter ranch, that will be satisfactory to me."

The colonel started to leave, then stopped again. "By the way, Mister, that's quite a girl. She'd make a fine Army wife. I think she'd marry you if you asked her.

"And if you don't ask her, I'll transfer you to the infantry!"

Grinning, Monte saluted. No, he told himself, the colonel wouldn't have to worry about that transfer.

In later times, Burkett Wayland liked to say he was in the last great Indian battle of Kerr County, Texas. It happened before he was born.

It started one day while his father, Matthew Wayland, then not much past twenty, was breaking a new field for fall wheat planting, just east of a small log cabin on one of the creeks tributary to the Guadalupe River. The quiet of an autumn morning was broken by a fluttering of wings as a covey of quail flushed beyond a heavy stand of oak timber past the field. Startled, Matthew jerked on the reins and quickly laid his plow over on its side in the newly broken sod. His bay horse raised its head and pointed its ears toward the sound.

Matthew caught a deep breath and held it. He thought he heard a crackling of brush. He reached back for the rifle slung over his shoulder and quickly unhitched the horse. Standing behind it for protection, he watched and listened another moment or two, then jumped up bareback and beat his heels against the horse's ribs, moving in a long trot for the cabin in the clearing below.

He wanted to believe ragged old Burk Kennemer was coming for a visit from his little place three miles down the creek, but the trapper usually rode in the open where Matthew could see him coming, not through the brush.

Matthew had not been marking the calendar in his almanac, but he had not needed to. The cooling nights, the curing of the grass to a rich brown, had told him all too well that this was September, the month of the Comanche moon. This was the time of year—their ponies strong from the summer grass— that the warrior Comanches could be expected to ride down from the high plains. Before winter they liked to make a final grand raid through the rough limestone hills of old hunting grounds west of San Antonio, then retire with stolen horses and mules— and sometimes captives and scalps—back to sanctuary far to the north. They had done it every year since the first settlers had pushed into the broken hill country. Though the military was beginning to press in upon their hideaways, all the old settlers had been warning Matthew to expect them again as the September moon went full, aiding the Comanches in their nighttime prowling.

Rachal opened the rough-hewn cabin door and looked at her young husband in surprise, for normally he would plow until she called him in for dinner at noon. He was trying to finish breaking the ground and dry-sow the wheat before fall rains began.

She looked as if she should still be in school some-where instead of trying to make a home in the wilder-ness; she was barely eighteen. "What is it, Matthew?"

"I don't know," he said tightly. "Get back inside."

He slid from the horse and turned it sideways to shield him. He held the rifle ready. It was always loaded.

A horseman broke out of the timber and moved toward the cabin. Matthew let go a long-held breath as he recognized Burk Kennemer. The relief turned to anger for the scare. He walked out to meet the trapper, trying to keep the edginess from his voice, but he could not control the flush of color that warmed his face.

He noted that the old man brought no meat with him. It was Kennemer's habit, when he came visiting, to fetch along a freshly killed deer, or sometimes a wild turkey, or occasionally a ham out of his smokehouse, and to stay to eat some of it cooked by Rachal's skillful hands. He ran a lot of hogs in the timber, fattening them on the oak mast. He was much more of a bagman and trapper than a farmer. Plow handles did not fit his hands, Kennemer claimed. He was of the restless breed that moved westward ahead of the farmers, and left when they crowded him.

Kennemer had a tentative half smile. "Glad I wasn't a Comanche. You'd've shot me dead."

"I'd've tried," Matthew said, his heart still thumping. He lifted a shaky hand to show what Kennemer had done to him. "What did you come sneaking in like an Indian for?"

Kennemer's smile was gone. "For good reason. That little girl inside the cabin?"

Matthew nodded. Kennemer said, "You'd better keep her there."

As if she had heard the conversation, Rachal Wayland opened the door and stepped outside, shading her eyes with one hand. Kennemer's gray-bearded face lighted at sight of her. Matthew did not know if Burk had ever had a wife of his own; he had never mentioned one. Rachal shouted, "Come on up, Mr. Kennemer. I'll be fixing us some dinner."

He took off his excuse of a hat and shouted back, for he was still at some distance from the cabin. "Can't right now, girl. Got to be traveling. Next time maybe." He cut his gaze to Matthew's little log shed and corrals. "Where's your other horse?"

"Grazing out yonder someplace. Him and the milk cow both."

"Better fetch him in," Kennemer said grimly. "Better put him and this one in the pen closest to the cabin if you don't want to lose them. And stay close to the cabin yourself, or you may lose more than the horses."

Matthew felt the dread chill him again. "Comanches?"

"Don't know. Could be. Fritz Dieterle come by my place while ago and told me he found tracks where a bunch of horses crossed the Guadalupe during the night. Could've been cowboys, or a bunch of hunters looking to lay in some winter meat. But it could've been Comanches. The horses wasn't shod."

Matthew could read the trapper's thoughts. Kennemer was reasonably sure it had not been cowboys or hunters. Kennemer said, "I come to warn you, and now I'm going west to warn that bunch of German farmers out on the forks. They may want to fort up at the best house."

Matthew's thoughts were racing ahead. He had been over to the German settlement twice since he and Rachal had arrived here late last winter, in time to break out their first field for spring planting. Burk Kennemer had told him the Germans—come west from the older settlements around New Braunfels and Fredericksburg—had been here long enough to give him sound advice about farming this shallow-soil land. And perhaps they might, if he could have understood them. They had seemed friendly enough, but they spoke no English, and he knew nothing of German. Efforts at communication had led him nowhere but back here, his shoulders slumped in frustration. He had counted Burk Kennemer as his only neighbor—the only one he could talk with.

"Maybe I ought to send Rachal with you," Matthew said. "It would be safer for her there, all those folks around her."

Kennemer considered that for only a moment. "Too risky traveling by daylight, one man and one girl. Even if you was to come along, two men and a girl wouldn't be no match if they jumped us."

"You're even less of a match, traveling by yourself."

Kennemer patted the shoulder of his long-legged brown horse. "No offense, boy, but old Deercatcher here can run circles around them two of yours, and anything them Indians is liable to have. He'll take care of me, long as I'm by myself. You've got a good strong cabin there. You and that girl'll be better off inside it than out in the open with me." He frowned. "If it'll make you feel safer, I'll be back before dark. I'll stay here with you, and we can fort up together."

That helped, but it was not enough. Matthew looked at the cabin, which he and Kennemer and the broken-English-speaking German named Dieterle had put up after he finished planting his spring crops. Until then, he and Rachal had lived in their wagon, or around and beneath it.

"I wish she wasn't here, Burk. All of a sudden I wish I'd never brought her here."

The trapper frowned. "Neither one of you belongs here. You're both just shirttail young'uns, not old enough to take care of yourselves."

Matthew remembered that the old man had told him as much, several times. A pretty little girl like Rachal should not be out here in a place like this, working like a mule, exposed to the dangers of the thinly settled frontier. But Matthew had never heard a word of complaint from her, not since they had started west from the piney-woods country in the biting cold of a wet winter, barely a month married. She always spoke of this as our place, our home.

He said, "It seemed all right, till now. All of a sudden I realize what I've brought her to. I want to get her out of here, Burk."

The trapper slowly filled an evil black pipe while he pondered and twisted his furrowed face. "Then we'll go tonight. It'll be safer traveling in the dark because I've been here long enough to know this country better than them Indians do. We'll make Fredericksburg by daylight. But one thing you've got to make up your mind to, Matthew. You've got to leave her there, or go back to the old home with her yourself. You've got no business bringing her here again to this kind of danger."

"She's got no home back yonder to go to. This is the only home she's got, or me either."

Kennemer's face went almost angry. "I buried a woman once in a place about like this. I wouldn't want to help bury that girl of yours. Adios, Matthew. See you before dark." He circled Deercatcher around the cabin and disappeared into a motte of liveoak timber.

Rachal stood in the doorway, puzzled. She had not intruded on the conversation. Now she came out onto the foot-packed open ground. "What was the matter with Mr. Kennemer? Why couldn't he stay?"

He wished he could keep it from her. "Horse tracks on the Guadalupe. He thinks it was Indians."

Matthew watched her closely, seeing the sudden clutch of fear in her eyes before she firmly put it away. "What does he think we ought to do?" she asked, seeming calmer than he thought she should.

"Slip away from here tonight, go to Fredericksburg."

"For how long, Matthew?"

He did not answer her. She said, "We can't go far. There's the milk cow, for one thing. She's got to be milked."

The cow had not entered his mind. "Forget her. The main thing is to have you safe."

"We're going to need that milk cow."

Impatiently he exploded, "Will you grow up, and forget that damned cow? I'm taking you out of here."

She shrank back in surprise at his sharpness, a little of hurt in her eyes. They had not once quarreled, not until now. "I'm sorry, Rachal. I didn't go to blow up at you that way."

She hid her eyes from him. "You're thinking we might just give up this place and never come back . . ." She wasn't asking him; she was telling him what was in his mind.

"That's what Burk thinks we ought to do."

"He's an old man, and we're young. And this isn't his home. He hasn't even got a home, just that old rough cabin, and those dogs and hogs . . . He's probably moved twenty times in his life. But we're not like that, Matthew. We're the kind of people who put down roots and grow where we are."

Matthew looked away. "I'll go fetch the dun horse. You bolt the door."

Riding away, he kept looking back at the cabin in regret. He knew he loved this place where they had started their lives together. Rachal loved it too, though he found it difficult to understand why. Life had its shortcomings back in East Texas, but her upbringing there had been easy compared to the privations she endured here. When she needed water she carried it in a heavy oaken bucket from the creek, fully seventy-five yards. He would have built the cabin nearer the water, but Burk had advised that once in a while heavy rains made that creek rise up on its hind legs and roar like an angry bear.

She worked her garden with a heavy-handled hoe, and when Matthew was busy in the field from dawn to dark she chopped her own wood from the pile of dead oak behind the cabin. She cooked over an ill-designed open fireplace that did not draw as it should. And, as much as anything, she put up with a deadening loneliness. Offhand, he could not remember that she had seen another woman since late in the spring, except for a German girl who stopped by once on her way to the forks. They had been unable to talk to each other. Even so, Rachal had glowed for a couple of days, refreshed by seeing someone besides her husband and the unwashed Burk Kennemer.

The cabin was as yet small, just a single room which was kitchen, sleeping quarters and sitting room combined. It had been in Matthew's mind, when he had nothing else to do this coming winter, to start work on a second section that would become a bedroom. He would build a roof and an open dog run between that part and the original, in keeping with Texas pioneer tradition, with a sleeping area over the dog run for the children who were sure to come with God's own time and blessings. He and Rachal had talked much of their plans, of the additional land he would break out to augment the potential income from their dozen or so beef critters scattered along the creek. He had forcefully put the dangers out of his mind, knowing they were there but choosing not to dwell upon them.

He remembered now the warnings from Rachal's uncle and aunt, who had brought her up after her own father was killed by a falling tree and her mother was taken by one of the periodic fever epidemics. They had warned of the many perils a couple would face on the edge of the settled lands, perils which youth and love and enthusiasm had made to appear small, far away in distance and time, until today. Now, his eyes nervously searching the edge of the oak timber for anything amiss, fear rose up in him. It was a primeval, choking fear of a kind he had never known, and a sense of shame for having so thoughtlessly brought Rachal to this sort of jeopardy.

He found the dun horse grazing by the creek, near a few of the speckled beef cows which a farmer at the old home had given him in lieu of wages for two years of backbreaking work. He had bartered for the old wagon and the plow and a few other necessary tools. Whatever else he had, he and Rachal had built with their hands. For Texans, cash money was in short supply.

He thought about rounding up the cows and corralling them by the cabin, but they were scattered. He saw too much risk in the time it might take him to find them all, as well as the exposure to any Comanches hidden in the timber. From what he had heard, the Indians were much less interested in cattle than in horses. Cows were slow. Once the raiders were ready to start north, they would want speed to carry them to sanctuary. Matthew pitched a rawhide reata loop around the dun's neck and led the animal back in a long trot. He had been beyond sight of the cabin for a while, and he prickled with anxiety. He breathed a sigh of relief when he broke into the open. The smoke from the chimney was a welcome sight.

He turned the horses into the pole corral and closed the gate, then poured shelled corn into a crude wooden trough. They eagerly set to crunching the grain with their strong teeth, a sound he had always enjoyed when he could restrain himself from thinking how much that corn would be worth in the settlements. The horses were blissfully unaware of the problems that beset their owners. Matthew wondered how content they would be if they fell into Indian hands and were driven or ridden the many long, hard days north into that mysterious hidden country. It would serve them right!

Still, he realized how helpless he and Rachal would be without them. He could not afford to lose the horses.

Rachal slid the heavy oak bar from the door and let him into the cabin. He immediately replaced the bolt while she went back to stirring a pot of stew hanging on an iron rod inside the fireplace. He avoided her eyes, for the tension stretched tightly between them.

"See anything?" she asked, knowing he would have come running.

He shook his head. "Not apt to, until night. If they're here, that's when they'll come for the horses."

"And find us gone?" Her voice almost accused him.

He nodded. "Burk said he'll be back before dark. He'll help us find our way to Fredericksburg."

Firelight touched her face. He saw a reflection of tears. She said, "They'll destroy this place."

"Better this place than you. I've known it from the start, I guess, and just wouldn't admit it. I shouldn't have brought you here."

"I came willingly. I've been happy here. So have you."

"We just kept dancing and forgot that the piper had to be paid."

A silence fell between them, heavy and unbridgeable. When the stew was done they sat at the rough-hewn table and ate without talking. Matthew got up restlessly from time to time to look out the front and back windows. These had no glass. They were like small doors in the walls. They could be closed and bolted shut. Each had a loophole which he could see out of, or fire through. Those, he remembered, had been cut at Burk Kennemer's insistence. From the first, Matthew realized now, Burk had been trying to sober him, even to scare him away. Matthew had always put him off with a shrug or a laugh. Now he remembered what Burk had said today about having buried a woman in a place like this. He thought he understood the trapper, and the man's fears, in a way he had not before.

The heavy silence went unrelieved. After eating what he could of the stew, his stomach knotted, he went outside and took a long look around, cradling the rifle. He fetched a shovel and began to throw dirt onto the roof to make it more difficult for the Indians to set it afire. It occurred to him how futile this labor was if they were going to abandon the place anyway, but he kept swinging the shovel, trying to work off the tension.

The afternoon dragged. He spent most of it outside, pacing, watching. In particular he kept looking to the west, anticipating Burk Kennemer's return. Now that he had made up his mind to it, he could hardly wait for darkness, to give them a chance to escape this place. The only thing which came from that direction—or any other—was the brindle milk cow, drifting toward the shed at her own slow place and in her own good time for the evening milking and the grain she knew awaited her. Matthew owned no watch, but he doubted that a watch kept better time than that cow, her udder swinging in rhythm with her slow and measured steps. Like the horses, she had no awareness of anything except her daily routine, of feeding and milking and grazing. Observing her patient pace, Matthew could almost assure himself that this day was like all others, that he had no reason for fear.

He milked the cow, though he intended to leave the milk unused in the cabin, for it was habit with him as well as with the cow. The sun was dropping rapidly when he carried the bucket of milk to Rachal. Her eyes asked him, though she did not speak.

He shook his head. "No sign of anything out there. Not of Burk, either."

Before sundown he saddled the dun horse for Rachal, making ready. He would ride the plow horse bareback. He climbed up onto his pole fence, trying to shade his eyes from the sinking sun while he studied the hills and the open valley to the west. All his earlier fears were with him, and a new one as well.

*Where is he? He wouldn't just have left us here. Not Old Burk.*

Once he thought he heard a sound in the edge of the timber. He turned quickly and saw a flash of movement, nothing more. It was a feeling as much as something actually seen. It could have been anything, a deer, perhaps, or even one of his cows. It could have been.

He remained outside until the sun was gone, and until the last golden remnant faded into twilight over the timbered hills that stretched into the distance like a succession of blue monuments. The autumn chill set him to shivering, but he held out against going for his coat. When the night was full dark, he knew it was time.

He called softly at the cabin door. Rachal lifted the bar. He said, "The moon'll rise directly. We'd better get started."

"Without Burk? Are you really sure, Matthew?"

"If they're around, they'll be here. Out yonder, in the dark, we've got a chance."

She came out, wrapped for the night chill, carrying his second rifle, handing him his coat. Quietly they walked to the corral, where he opened the gate, untied the horses and gave her a lift up into the saddle. The stirrups were too long for her, and her skirts were in the way, but he knew she could ride. He threw himself up onto the plow horse, and they moved away from the cabin in a walk, keeping to the grass as much as possible to muffle the sound of the hoofs. As quickly as he could, he pulled into the timber, where the darkness was even more complete. For the first miles, at least, he felt that he knew the way better than any Indian who might not come here once in several years.

It was his thought to swing first by Burk's cabin.

There was always a chance the old man had changed his mind about things . . .

He had held onto this thought since late afternoon. Maybe Burk had found the tracks were not made by Indians after all, and he had chosen to let the young folks have the benefit of a good, healthy scare.

Deep inside, Matthew knew that was a vain hope. It was not Burk's way. He might have let Matthew sweat blood, but he would not do this to Rachal.

They both saw the fire at the same time, and heard the distant barking of the dogs. Rachal made a tiny gasp and clutched his arm.

Burk's cabin was burning.

They reined up and huddled together for a minute, both coming dangerously close to giving in to their fears and riding away in a blind run. Matthew gripped the rawhide reins so tightly that they seemed to cut into his hands. "Easy, Rachal," he whispered.

Then he could hear horses moving through the timber, and the crisp night air carried voices to him.

"They're coming at us, Matthew," Rachal said tightly. "They'll catch us out here."

He had no way of knowing if they had been seen, or heard. A night bird called to the left of him. Another answered, somewhere to the right. At least, they sounded like night birds.

"We've got to run for it, Rachal!"

"We can't run all the way to Fredericksburg. Even if we could find it. They'll catch us."

He saw only one answer. "Back to the cabin! If we can get inside, they'll have to come in there to get us."

He had no spurs; a farmer did not need them. He beat his heels against the horse's sides and led the way through the timber in a run. He did not have to look behind him to know Rachal was keeping up with him. Somehow the horses had caught the fever of their fear.

"Keep low, Rachal," he said. "Don't let the low limbs knock you down." He found a trail that he knew and shortly burst out into the open. He saw no reason for remaining in the timber now, for the Indians surely knew where they were. The timber would only slow their running. He leaned out over the horse's neck and kept thumping his heels against its ribs. He glanced back to be sure he was not outpacing Rachal.

Off to the right he thought he saw figures moving, vague shapes against the blackness. The moon was just beginning to rise, and he could not be sure. Ahead, sensed more than seen, was the clearing. Evidently the Indians had not been there yet, or the place would be in flames as Burk's cabin had been.

He could see the shape of the cabin now. "Right up to the door, Rachal!"

He jumped to the ground, letting his eyes sweep the yard and what he could see of the corrals. "Don't get down," he shouted. "Let me look inside first."

The door was closed, as they had left it. He pushed it open and stepped quickly inside, the rifle ready. The dying embers in the fireplace showed him he was alone. "It's all right. Get down quick, and into the cabin!"

She slid down and fell, and he helped her to her feet. She pointed and made a cry. Several figures were moving rapidly toward the shed. Matthew fired the rifle in their general direction and gave Rachal a push toward the door. She resisted stubbornly. "The horses," she said. "Let's get the horses into the cabin."

She led her dun through the door, though it did not much want to go into that dark and unaccustomed place.

Matthew would have to admit later—though he had no time for such thoughts now—that she was keeping her head better than he was. He would have let the horses go, and the Indians would surely have taken them. The plow horse was gentler and entered the cabin with less resistance, though it made a nervous sound in its nose at sight of the glowing coals.

Matthew heard something plunk into the logs as he pushed the door shut behind him and dropped the bar solidly into place. He heard a horse race up to the cabin and felt the jarring weight of a man's body hurled against the door, trying to break through. Matthew pushed his own strength upon the bar, bracing it. A chill ran through him, and he shuddered at the realization that only the meager thickness of that door lay between him and an intruder who intended to kill him. He heard the grunting of a man in strain, and he imagined he could feel the hot breath. His hair bristled.

Rachal opened the front-window loophole and fired her rifle.

Thunder seemed to rock the cabin. It threw the horses into a panic that made them more dangerous, for the moment, than those Indians outside. One of them slammed against Matthew and pressed him to the wall so hard that he thought all his ribs were crushed. But that was the last time an Indian tried the door. Matthew could hear the man running, getting clear of Rachal's rifle.

A gunshot sounded from out in the night. A bullet struck the wall but did not break through between the logs. Periodically Matthew would hear a shot, first from one direction, then from another. After the first three or four, he was sure.

"They've just got one gun. We've got two."

The horses calmed, after a time. So did Matthew. He threw ashes over the coals to dim their glow, which had made it difficult for him to see out into the night. The moon was up, throwing a silvery light across the yard.

"I'll watch out front," he said. "You watch the back."

All his life he had heard that Indians did not like to fight at night because of a fear that their souls would wander lost if they died in the darkness. He had no idea if the stories held any truth. He knew that Indians were skillful horse thieves, in darkness or light, and that he and Rachal had frustrated these by bringing their mounts into the cabin.

Burk had said the Indians on these September raids were more intent on acquiring horses than on taking scalps, though they had no prejudice against the latter. He had said Indians did not like to take heavy risks in going against a well-fortified position, that they were likely to probe the defenses and, if they found them strong, withdraw in search of an easier target.

But they had a strong incentive for breaking into this cabin.

He suggested, "They might leave if we turn the horses out."

"And what do we do afoot?" Rachal's voice was not a schoolgirl's. It was strong, defiant. "If they want these horses, let them come through that door and pay for them. These horses are ours!"

Her determination surprised him, and shamed

him a little. He held silent a while, listening, watching for movement. "I suppose those Indians feel like they've got a right here. They figure this land belongs to them."

"Not if they just come once a year. We've come here to stay."

"I wish we hadn't. I wish I hadn't brought you."

"Don't say that. I've always been glad that you did. I've loved this place from the time we first got here and lived in the wagon, because it was ours. It is ours. When this trouble is over it will stay ours. We've earned the right to it."

He fired seldom, and only when he thought he had a good target, for shots inside the cabin set the horses to plunging and threshing.

He heard a cow bawl in fear and agony. Later, far beyond the shed, he could see a fire building. Eventually he caught the aroma of meat, roasting.

"They've killed the milk cow," he declared.

Rachal said, "We'll need another one, then. For the baby."

That was the first she had spoken of it, though he had had reason lately to suspect. "I shouldn't have put you through that ride tonight."

"That didn't hurt me. I'm not so far along yet. That's one reason we've got to keep the horses. We may need to trade the dun for a milk cow."

They watched through the long hours, he at the front window, she at the rear. The Indians had satisfied their hunger, and they were quiet, sleeping perhaps, waiting for dawn to storm the cabin without danger to their immortal souls. Matthew was tired, and his legs were cramped from the long vigil, but he felt no sleepiness. He thought once that Rachal had fallen asleep, and he made no move to awaken her. If trouble came from that side, he thought he would probably hear it.

She was not asleep. She said, "I hear a rooster way off somewhere. Burk's, I suppose. Be daylight soon."

"They'll hit us then. They'll want to overrun us in a hurry."

"It's up to us to fool them. You and me together, Matthew, we've always been able to do whatever we set our minds to."

They came as he expected, charging horseback out of the rising sun, relying on the blazing light to blind the eyes of the defenders. But with Rachal's determined shouts ringing in his ears, he triggered the rifle at darting figures dimly seen through the golden haze. Rachal fired rapidly at those horsemen who ran past the cabin and came into her field of view on the back side. The two horses just trembled and leaned against one another.

One bold, quick charge and the attack was over. The Comanches swept on around, having tested the defense and found it unyielding. They pulled away, regrouping to the east as if considering another try.

"We done it, Rachal!" Matthew shouted. "We held them off."

He could see her now in the growing daylight, her hair stringing down, her face smudged with black, her eyes watering from the sting of the gunpowder. He had never seen her look so good.

She said triumphantly, "I tried to tell you we could do it. You and me, we can do anything."

He thought the Indians might try again, but they began pulling away. He could see now that they had a considerable number of horses and mules, taken from other settlers. They drove those before them, splashing across the creek and moving north in a run.

"They're leaving," he said, not quite believing.

"Some more on this side," Rachal warned. "You'd better come over here and look." Through the loophole in her window, out of the west, he saw a dozen or more horsemen loping toward the cabin. For a minute he thought he and Rachal would have to fight again. Strangely, the thought brought him no particular fear.

*We can handle it. Together, we can do anything.* Rachal said, "Those are white men." They threw their arms around each other and cried. They were outside the cabin, the two of them, when the horsemen circled warily around it, rifles ready for a fight. The men were strangers, except the leader. Matthew remembered him from up at the forks. Excitedly the man spoke in a language Matthew knew was German. Then half the men were talking at once. They looked Rachal and Matthew over carefully, making sure neither was hurt.

The words were strange, but the expressions were universal. They were of relief and joy at finding the young couple alive and on their feet.

The door was open. The bay plow horse stuck its head out experimentally, nervously surveying the crowd, then breaking into a run to get clear of the oppressive cabin. The dun horse followed, pitching in relief to be outdoors. The German rescuers stared in amazement for a moment, then laughed as they realized how the Waylands had saved their horses.

One made a sweeping motion as if holding a broom, and Rachal laughed with him. It was going to take a lot of work to clean up that cabin.

The spokesman said something to Matthew, and Matthew caught the name of Burk Kennemer. The man made a motion of drawing a bow, and of an arrow striking him in the shoulder.

"Dead?" Matthew asked worriedly. The man shook his head. "*Nein, nicht tod.* Not dead." By the motions, Matthew perceived that the wounded Burk had made it to the German settlement to give warning, and that the men had ridden through the night to get here.

Rachal came up and put her arm around Matthew, leaning against him. She said, "Matthew, do you think we killed any of those Indians?"

"I don't know that we did."

"I hope we didn't. I'd hate to know all my life that there is blood on this ground."

Some of the men seemed to be thinking about leaving. Matthew said, "You-all pen your horses, and we'll have breakfast directly." He realized they did not understand his words, so he pantomimed and put the idea across. He made a circle, shaking hands with each man individually, telling him thanks, knowing each followed his meaning whether the words were understood or not.

"Rachal," he said, "these people are our neighbors. Somehow we've got to learn to understand each other."

She nodded. "At least enough that you can trade one of them out of another milk cow. For the baby."

When the baby came, late the following spring, they named it Burkett Kennemer, after the man who had brought them warning, and had sent them help.

That was the last time the Comanches ever penetrated so deeply into the hill country, for the military pressure was growing strongly.

And all of his life Burkett Kennemer Wayland was able to say, without taking sinful advantage of the truth, that he had been present at the last great Indian fight in Kerr County.

# UNCLE JEFF AND THE GUNFIGHTER

**O**ut in West Texas the old-timers still speak occasionally of the time my uncle Jeff Barclay scared off the gunfighter Tobe Farrington. It's a good story, as far as it goes, but the way they tell it doesn't quite go far enough. And the reason is that my father was the only man who ever knew the whole truth. Papa would have carried the secret to the grave with him if he hadn't taken a notion to tell me about it a little while before he died. Now that he's buried beside Mother in the family plot over at Marfa, I reckon it won't hurt to clear up the whole story, once and for all.

Papa was the elder of the two brothers. He and Uncle Jeff were what they used to call four-sectioners a long time ago.

Lots of people don't understand about Texas homesteads. When Texas joined the union it was a free republic, with a whopper of a debt. Texas kept title to its land because the United States didn't want to take on all that indebtedness. So in later years

Texas had a different homestead law than the other states. By the time Papa and Uncle Jeff were grown, the state of Texas was betting four sections of land against a man's filing fee, his hope, and his sweat that he would starve to death before he proved up his claim. It's no secret that the state won a lot of those bets.

But it didn't win against Papa and Uncle Jeff. They proved up their land and got the title.

Trouble was, their claims were on pasture that old Port Hubbard had ranched for a long time, leasing from the state. It didn't set well with him at all, because he was used to having people ask him things, not tell him. And there was a reckless streak in Uncle Jeff that caused him to glory in telling people how the two of them had thumbed their noses at Port Hubbard and gotten away with it.

It would be better if I told you a little about Uncle Jeff, so you'll know how it was with him. I've still got an old picture—yellowed now—that he and Papa had taken the day they got title to their four sections apiece, a little more than seventeen hundred acres the way people figure it in most other places. It shows Papa dressed in a plain suit that looks like he had slept in it, and he wears an ordinary sort of wide-brimmed hat set square on his head. But Uncle Jeff has on a pair of those striped California pants they used to wear, and sleeve garters, and a candy-striped shirt. He's wearing one of those huge cowboy hats that went out of style years ago, the ones you could really call ten-gallon without exaggerating much. The hat is cocked over to one side of his head. A six-shooter sits high on his right hip. The clothes make him look like he's on his way to a dance, but the challenge in his eyes makes him look like he's waiting for a fight. With Uncle Jeff, it could have been either one or both.

A lot of ranchers like Port Hubbard made good use of the Texas homestead law. They got their cowboys to file on land that lay inside their ranches. These cowboys would prove up the land, then sell it to the man they worked for. Plenty of cowboys in those days weren't interested in being landowners anyhow, and in a lot of West Texas four sections wasn't enough land for a man to make a living on. It wouldn't carry enough cattle. And farming that dry country was a chancy business, sure enough.

It bothered Hubbard when Papa and Uncle Jeff took eight sections out of his Rocking H ranch. But he held off, figuring they would starve out and turn it back. And meanwhile, they would be improving it for him. When that didn't work the way he expected, he tried to buy it from them. They wouldn't sell.

Hubbard might still have swallowed the loss and gone about his business if Uncle Jeff hadn't been inclined to brag so much.

"He's buffaloed people in this part of the country for twenty years," Uncle Jeff would say, and he didn't care who heard or repeated it. "But we stopped him. He's scared to lay a finger on us."

Papa always felt Port Hubbard wouldn't have done anything if Uncle Jeff hadn't kept jabbing the knifepoint at him, so to speak. But Hubbard was a proud man, and proud men don't sit around and listen to that kind of talk forever, especially old-time cowmen like Port Hubbard. So by and by Tobe Farrington showed up.

Nobody ever did prove that Port Hubbard sent for him, but nobody ever doubted it. Farrington put in for four sections of land that lay right next to Papa's and Uncle Jeff's. It was on Rocking H country that had been taken up once by a Hubbard cowboy who later got too much whiskey over in Pecos and took a fatal dose of indigestion on three .45 slugs.

Everybody in West Texas knew of Tobe Farrington in those days. He wasn't famous in the way of John Wesley Hardin or Bill Longley, but in the country from San Saba to the Pecos River he had a hard name. Folks tried to give him plenty of air. It was known that several men had gone to glory with his bullets in them.

A lot of folks expected to see Farrington just ride over and shoot Papa and Uncle Jeff down, but he didn't work that way. He must have figured on letting his reputation do the job without him having to waste any powder. Papa said it seemed like just about every time he and Uncle Jeff looked up, they would see Tobe Farrington sitting there on his horse, just watching them. He seldom ever spoke, he just looked at them. Papa admitted that those hard gray eyes always put a chunk of ice in the pit of his stomach. But Uncle Jeff wasn't bothered. He seemed to thrive on that kind of pressure.

I didn't tell you that Uncle Jeff had been a deputy once. The Pecos County sheriff had hired him late one spring, mostly to run errands for him. In those days the sheriff was usually a tax assessor too. The job didn't last long. That summer the sheriff got beaten in the primary election. The next one had needy kinfolks and didn't keep Uncle Jeff on.

But by that time Uncle Jeff had gotten the feel of the six-shooter on his hip, and he liked it. What's more, he got to be a good shot. He liked to ride along and pot jackrabbits with his pistol. Two or three times this trick got him thrown off of a boogered horse, but Uncle Jeff would still do it when he took the notion. That was his way. Nothing ever scared him much, and nothing ever kept him from doing as he damn well pleased. Nothing but Papa.

If Tobe Farrington figured his being there was going to scare the Barclay brothers out of the country, he was disappointed. So he began to change his tactics. Farrington had a little bunch of Rocking H cattle with a "vented" brand, which he claimed he had bought from Hubbard but which everybody said Hubbard had just loaned him to make the homestead look legal. He started pushing his cattle over onto the Barclay land. He didn't do it sneaky. He would open the wire gates, bold as brass, push the cattle through, then ride on in and watch them eat Barclay grass. It wasn't the rainiest country in the world. There was just enough grass for the Barclay cattle, and sometimes not even that much.

Uncle Jeff was all for a fight. He wanted to shoot Farrington's cattle. Papa, on the other hand, believed in being firm but not suicidal. He left his gun at home, took his horse, and pushed the cattle back through the gate while Farrington sat and watched.

"He couldn't shoot me," Papa said, "because I didn't have a gun. He couldn't afford a plain case of murder. When Farrington killed somebody, he made it a point to be within the law."

Farrington gave up that stunt after two or three times because Papa always handled it in the same way.

After that it was little things. Steer roping was a popular sport in those days. Farrington always rode across Papa's land to go to Fort Stockton, and while passing through he would practice roping Barclay cattle. It was a rough sport. Throwing down those grown cattle was an easy way to break horns, and often it broke legs as well. Farrington made it a point to break legs.

Uncle Jeff wanted to take a gun and call for a showdown. Papa wouldn't let him. Instead, Papa wrote up a bill for the broken-legged cattle they had had to kill and got the sheriff to go with him to collect. The sheriff was as nervous as a sheepherder at a cowboy convention, but Papa collected.

"Guns are his business," Papa tried to tell Uncle Jeff. "The average man can't stand up against a feller like Tobe Farrington any more than a big-city bookkeeper could ride one of Port Hubbard's broncs. You leave your guns at home or one of these days Farrington'll sucker you into using them. Second prize in his kind of shootin' match is a wooden box."

I reckon before I go any further I ought to tell you about Delia Larrabee. Papa might have been a little prejudiced, but he always said she was the prettiest girl in the country in those days. Uncle Jeff must have agreed with him. Papa met her first and was using all the old-fashioned cowboy salesmanship he had. But Uncle Jeff was a better salesman. It hurt, but when Papa saw how things were, he backed off and gave up the field to Uncle Jeff. Looking at that old picture again, it's not hard to see why Delia Larrabee or any other girl might have been drawn to my uncle. He was quite the young blade, as they used to say.

Tobe Farrington had drawn a joker from the deck every time he tried to provoke a fight with Papa or Uncle Jeff. Stealing grass or injuring cattle hadn't done it. But when he found out about Delia Larrabee and Uncle Jeff, he must have realized he had found the way. The big dance in Fort Stockton gave him his chance.

Papa didn't go that night, or he might have found a way to stop the thing before it went as far as it did. But it still hurt him too much to be around Delia Larrabee, knowing he had lost her. And he hadn't seen any other girl he felt comfortable with. Besides, he was tired because for two days he had been out with a saddle gun, trying to track down a calf-killing wolf. So he let Uncle Jeff go to town alone, though he made sure my uncle left his gun at home.

Tobe Farrington waited around till the dance had been on a good while. That way, when he did show up he would get more attention. And get it he did. Folks said the hall fell almost dead silent when Farrington walked in. Dancers all stopped. Everything stopped but the old fiddler, and his eyes were so bad he couldn't tell a horse from a cow at forty feet. Farrington just stood there till he spotted Uncle Jeff over by the punch bowl. Then he saw Delia Larrabee sitting at the south wall, waiting for Uncle Jeff to fetch her some punch. Farrington walked over, bowed, and said, "You're the prettiest girl in the crowd. I believe I'll have this dance."

Uncle Jeff came hurrying back. He had his fists clenched, but Delia Larrabee shook her head at him to make him stop. She stood up right quick and held out her hands as a sign to Farrington that she wanted to dance with him. She knew what Farrington really wanted. To refuse him would have meant a fight.

But Farrington didn't mean to be stopped. When that tune ended, he kept hold of her hand and forced her into another dance. Uncle Jeff took a step or two forward, like he was going to interfere, but she waved him off. That dance finally ended, but Farrington didn't let her go. When the fiddle started, he began dancing with her again.

Uncle Jeff had had enough. He hollered at the fiddler to stop the music.

By that time nobody was dancing but Farrington and Delia Larrabee anyway. Everybody else had pulled back, waiting.

Uncle Jeff walked up to Farrington with his face red. "Turn her loose."

Farrington gripped her fingers a little tighter. "This is too pretty a gal to waste her time with a little greasy-sack rancher like you. I'm takin' over."

Uncle Jeff's picture shows that he had a powerful set of shoulders. When he swung his fist on somebody, it left a mark. Tobe Farrington landed flat on his back. By instinct he dropped his hand to his hip. But he had had to check his pistol at the door, same as everybody else. With a crooked grin that spelled murder, he pushed to his feet.

Delia Larrabee had her arms around Uncle Jeff and was trying to hold him back. "Jeff, he means to kill you!"

Uncle Jeff put her aside and looked Tobe Farrington in the eye. "I left my gun at home."

Farrington said flatly, "You could go and get it."

"All right. I will."

Farrington frowned. "On second thought, Barclay, it'd still be nighttime when you got back. Night's a poor time for good shootin'. So I tell you what: I'm goin' home. Tomorrow afternoon I'll come back to town. Say at five o'clock. If you still feel like you got guts enough, you can meet me on the street. We'll finish this right." His eyes narrowed. "But if you decide *not* to meet me, you better clear out of this country. I'll be lookin' around for you."

They were near the door, where the guns were checked. Farrington took his, strapped the belt around his waist, then drew the pistol. "So there's no misunderstandin', Barclay, I want you to see what I can do."

Thirty feet across the dance hall was a cardboard notice with the words FORT STOCKTON. Farrington brought up the pistol, fired once, and put a bullet hole through the first O. Women screamed as the shot thundered and echoed.

Uncle Jeff waited a few seconds, till the thick smoke cleared. "Let me see that thing a minute." Farrington hesitated, then handed it to him. Uncle Jeff fired twice and put holes through the other two O's.

Folks always said afterward that Farrington looked as if he had swallowed a cud of chewing tobacco. He hadn't realized Uncle Jeff was that good.

Uncle Jeff said, "*I'll* be here. Just be sure *you* show up." Right then he would have taken on Wild Bill Hickok.

He didn't go home that night. He knew Papa would argue and plead with him, and he didn't want to listen. He stayed in town with friends. Next morning he was out on the open prairie beyond Comanche Springs, practicing with a borrowed pistol.

Delia Larrabee had tried awhile to reason with him. She told him she would go anywhere with him—California, Mexico—if he would just go, and do it right now. But Uncle Jeff had his mind made up. He would have done this a long time ago if it hadn't been for Papa. So Delia got her father to take her out in a buckboard in the dark hours of early morning to tell Papa what had happened.

"You've got to do something," she cried. "You're the only one who can talk to Jeff."

Papa studied about it a long time. But he knew Uncle Jeff. The only way Papa would be able to stop him now would be to hog-tie him. And he couldn't keep him tied forever.

"I'll try to think of something," Papa promised, "but I doubt that anything will stop it now. You'd best go on home." There was a sadness about him, almost a giving up.

He sat at his table a long time, sipping black coffee and watching the morning sun start to climb. It came to him that Farrington was only doing a job for Port Hubbard, and all that Port Hubbard really wanted was to see the Barclay brothers leave the country. If it came to that, Papa had rather have had Uncle Jeff alive than to own the best eight sections in Pecos County.

He knew Jeff wouldn't listen to him. But maybe Farrington would.

Papa saddled up and started for the frame shack on Farrington's four sections. He still had the saddle gun he had used for hunting the wolf. He didn't really intend to use it. But there was always a chance Farrington might decide to make a clean sweep of the Barclay brothers while he was at it.

Not all the wolves had four legs.

Farrington's shack had originally been a line camp for Hubbard on land inside Papa's claim. When Papa took up the land, Hubbard had jacked up the little house and hauled it out on two wagons. The only thing left at the old campsite was a ruined cistern, surrounded by a little fence to keep stock from falling in. Papa had always intended to come over and fill it up, when he had time.

*Now,* he thought, *there won't be any need to fill it up. It'll be Hubbard's again.*

He saw smoke curling upward from the tin chimney, and he knew Farrington was at home. "Farrington," Papa called, "it's me, Henry Barclay. I've come to talk to you."

Farrington was slow about showing himself, and he came out wearing his gun. Distrust showed all over him. His hand was close to his gun butt, and it went even closer when Papa's horse turned so that Farrington saw the saddle gun.

"It's past talkin' now, Barclay. There was a time we could've worked this out, but not anymore."

"We still could," Papa said. "What if we give you what Hubbard wants? What if we sell our land to him and clear out?"

Farrington frowned. "Why should I care what Hubbard wants?"

"We don't have to play games, Farrington. I know what you came for, and you know I know it. So now you've won. Leave my brother alone."

"You're speakin' for yourself. But your brother may not see it your way."

"He will, even if I have to tie him up and haul him clear to California in a wagon."

Farrington considered awhile. "You make sense, up to a point. Pity you couldn't have done this a long while back, before I had spent so much time here. Now you might say I got an investment made. What suits Port Hubbard might not be enough to suit *me* anymore."

"You want money? All right, I'll split with you. Half of what Hubbard gives for the land. Only, I don't want Jeff hurt."

"Half of what Hubbard'll give now ain't very much."

"All of it, then. We didn't have anything when we came here. I reckon we could start with nothin' again."

A dry and awful smile broke across Farrington's face. "No deal. I just wanted to see how far you'd crawl. Now I know."

"You're really goin' to kill him?"

"Like I'd kill a beef! And then I'll come and put you off of the land, Barclay. It won't cost Hubbard a cent. You'll sign those papers and drag out of here with nothin' but the clothes on your back!"

That was it, then. Papa turned his horse and made like he was going to ride off. But he knew he couldn't leave it this way. Uncle Jeff was as good as dead. For that matter, so was Papa, for he had no intention of leaving his land if Uncle Jeff died.

Seventy feet from the house, Papa leaned forward as if he was going to put spurs to the horse. Instead, he took hold of the saddle gun and yanked it up out of the scabbard.

Farrington saw what was coming. He drew his pistol and fired just as the saddle gun came clear. But Papa was pulling his horse around. The bullet went shy.

Papa dropped to the ground, flat on his belly. He had lessened the odds by getting distance between him and Farrington. This was a long shot for a pistol. It was just right for Papa's short rifle. Farrington knew it too. He came running, firing as he moved, trying to keep Papa's head down till he could get close enough for a really good shot.

Papa didn't let him get that close. He sighted quick and squeezed the trigger.

Papa had shot a lot of lobo wolves in his day, and some of them on the run. Farrington rolled like one of those wolves. His body twitched a few times, then he was dead.

Papa had never killed a man before, and he never killed one again. He knew it was something he had had to do to save Uncle Jeff. But still he was sick at his stomach. All that coffee he had drunk came up. Later, when he had settled a little, he began wondering how he was going to tell this. Uncle Jeff probably never would forgive him, for he had wanted Farrington for himself. Papa would never be able to convince him Farrington would have killed him. Hubbard would scream *murder,* and it might be hard to convince a jury that it hadn't been just that. Men had been known to murder for much less than a brother's life.

Then it came to him: why tell anybody at all?

Nobody had seen it. For all anyone needed to know, Farrington had just saddled up and ridden away. Gunfighters did that sometimes. Many a noted outlaw had simply disappeared, never to be heard of again. A new country, a new name, a new start . . .

Farrington's horse was in the corral. Actually, it was a Rocking H sorrel of Port Hubbard's. Papa put Farrington's bridle and saddle on him, then hoisted Farrington's body up over the saddle. The horse danced around, smelling blood, and it was a hard job, but Papa got the body lashed down. He went into the house. He took a skillet, a coffeepot, some food—the things Farrington would logically have carried away with him if he were leaving the country. He rolled these up in Farrington's blankets and took them with him.

He worried some over the tracks, and he paused to kick dirt over the patch of blood where Farrington had fallen. But in the north, clouds were building. Maybe it would rain and wash out the tracks. If it didn't rain, at least the wind would blow. In this country, wind could reduce tracks about as well as a rain.

Papa led the sorrel horse with its load out across the Farrington claim and prayed he wouldn't run into any Rocking H cowboys. He stayed clear of the road. When he reached his own land, he cut across to the one-time Hubbard line camp. There he dragged Farrington's body to the edge of the old cistern and dropped him in. He dropped saddle, blankets, and everything else in after him. Then he led the sorrel horse back and turned him loose in Hubbard's big pasture.

Papa was not normally a drinking man, but that afternoon he took a bottle out of the kitchen cabinet and sat on the porch and got drunk.

Late that night, Uncle Jeff came home. He had been drinking too, but for a different reason. He had a couple of friends with him, helping him celebrate.

"Howdy do, big brother," he shouted all the way from the front gate. "It's me, little old Jeff, the livest little old Jeff you ever did see!" He swayed up onto the porch and saw Papa sitting there. "Bet you thought they'd be bringin' me home in a box. You just been sittin' here a-drinkin' by yourself and dreadin' seein' them come. But I'm here, and I'm still a-kickin'. I won. Farrington never showed up."

Papa couldn't make much of a display. "You don't say!"

"I *do* say! The whole town was waitin'. He never

came. He was scared of me. Tobe Farrington was scared of *me*!"

Papa said, "I'm glad, Jeff. I'm real glad." He pushed himself to his feet and staggered off to bed.

Next day there must have been thirty people by at one time or another, all wanting to congratulate Jeff Barclay. They didn't see Papa though. He had gone off to fill up that old cistern before a cow fell in it.

It was told all over West Texas how Jeff Barclay, a greasy-sack rancher, had scared Tobe Farrington into backing down. Folks decided Farrington was reputation and nothing else. They always wondered where he went, because nobody ever heard of him after that. Talk was that he had gone into Mexico and had changed his name, ashamed to face up to people after backing down to Jeff Barclay.

Papa was more than glad to let them believe that. Like I said, he kept the secret till just before he died. But it must always have troubled him, and when finally he knew his time was coming, he told me. He kept telling me it was something he hadn't wanted to do but he had to because of Uncle Jeff.

The irony was that it didn't really save Uncle Jeff. If anything, it killed him. Being the way he was, Uncle Jeff let the notoriety go to his head. Got so he was always looking for another Tobe Farrington. He turned cocky and quarrelsome. Gradually he alienated his friends. He even lost Delia Larrabee. The only person he didn't lose was Papa.

Papa wasn't there to help him the day Uncle Jeff finally met a man who was like Tobe Farrington. Uncle Jeff was still clawing for his pistol when he fell with two bullets in his heart.

Uncle Jeff's four sections went to Papa, but he sold them along with his own—but not to Port Hubbard.

He bought a ranch farther west, in the Davis Mountains.

And Delia Larrabee? She married Papa. I was the oldest of their six sons.

# SELLOUT

The rattle of gunfire a mile away was in Jeff Brewster's ears as he reined his fidgety sorrel to a stop on a sandy little hill. The young Texan's narrowed gray eyes searched the brush ahead for movement.

He blinked, eyes stinging from a fast ride into the cold wind. Instinctively he felt for the silver star pinned to the pocket of his jumper, to make sure the brush hadn't ripped it off.

He stood up in his stirrups as he glimpsed the color of a red roan horse in the tangled mesquite ahead. Hand stiff from cold, he drew his .45, and then touched the spurs to the sorrel's side.

The sheriff hit the brush at full speed. Mesquite limbs popped. Thorns ripped through the jumper, burned into his skin. He fired two shots over the fugitive's head. The rider reined up, turned around, and lifted his shaking hands. Brewster slid his horse to a stop in the sand.

Then he recognized the rider of the red roan, and he felt as if he had been kicked in the ribs.

"Clay!" he breathed unbelievingly. "Clay Simmons! What're you doin' with Red Weaver's cattle-thievin' bunch, anyhow?"

Desperation was stark in Simmons's wide-open eyes. "I had to do it, Jeff!" he pleaded. His face, usually handsome, seemed ready to fall to pieces. "You can't take me in. They'll hang me!"

This would be a day folks in Dry Wells wouldn't forget in a long time, the lawman thought numbly—Sheriff Jeff Brewster bringing in his best friend for cattle rustling!

Brewster gravely holstered the gun. He wanted to turn around and ride away, but he brought out the handcuffs.

Simmons's voice shook. "Jeff, I won't ever do it again. I swear it!"

"This is a hard enough job, Clay. Don't make it worse."

Simmons choked. "I didn't want to tell you like this, Jeff, but now I've got to. Donna's promised to marry me."

Surprise again jolted Jeff Brewster. Feeling weak and uncertain, he rested his big hands on the saddle horn.

He thought back to the day more than a year ago when he and Clay had been riding together across the Frank Larkin ranch, and Clay had bet Jeff he could rope a calf before Jeff could. Jeff had won the bet, but pretty Donna Larkin had ridden up suddenly and judged the pair to be cow thieves. It took twenty minutes of shouted explanations and coaxing before the two men, flat on their bellies in the sand, could induce her to quit blazing away at them with her .30-.30.

Now Simmons was explaining how he had really

gotten mixed up with a band of rustlers. "I lost to Red Weaver in a poker game. It was more than I could pay," he explained. "I couldn't let him take my store. He gave me a chance to make it up. It was only this once. I swear it, Jeff. You can't let Donna find out now!"

Brewster's eyes stung. He swallowed hard, looking down at his saddle horn. "But she had almost promised *me*, Clay."

"I know, Jeff. That's why you've got to listen. You know how she'd feel if you dragged me in to be hung, or to be locked up at Huntsville till I'm hobblin' around on a cane."

Temptation was pounding inside Brewster. He could turn his back on Simmons. He could say the rustler had outrun him.

"You've got to promise me never to hook up with Weaver again," he said finally, his lips tight.

Simmons beamed, "I swear it, Jeff."

Brewster slipped the handcuffs back into his pocket. "This isn't for you, Clay. It's for Donna. You better hope that cattlemen's detective doesn't pick up your trail. Now get out of here!"

Guilt burned in Jeff Brewster as he watched his friend ride off into the brush. A sellout! He fingered the star and thought of the oath he had taken the day it was pinned on him. Not once in six years had he even thought of deviating. Now he had sold out!

He reined the sorrel around and started to spur back toward the point where the posse had jumped the rustlers. Then he glimpsed a rider who sat solemnly watching him, fifty yards away. Something akin to fear bolted through Jeff. The association man, Charlie Strickland!

The graying outlaw hunter was nearing fifty. But

if age had drooped his shoulders a little, it hadn't made the manhunter any less fearsome riding the trail of cattle thieves, in protection of his association's members.

Now his craggy face looked darker than ever, and his brown mustache was as forbidding as a thunderhead.

"Looks like your man got away, Brewster," he said flatly.

Jeff didn't answer.

Strickland glanced in the direction which Simmons had taken. "Maybe some of the other boys had better luck," he muttered darkly. "We better go see."

As they rode along, Jeff waited for Strickland to speak the thoughts that lay behind the brooding black eyes. The tension steadily mounted in him as he glanced at the man again and again, expecting him to lash out at any moment. But the association man rode silently, looking grimly toward the bleak storm warnings in the northern sky.

The rest of the posse hadn't done much better. Of more than half a dozen rustlers, all but one had escaped. That one was dead.

"My trap didn't spring fast enough," Strickland commented darkly. "I knew Weaver was our man. I knew he'd take the bait if I let him get the word that there was goin' to be a good-sized herd close to the New Mexico border—especially one poorly guarded."

He doubled his gnarled fist and drummed his knuckles against the rawhide-covered saddle horn. "That damned windmill! If that outlaw hadn't climbed the tower and seen us comin' while they was waterin' the herd, we'd've had them all!"

Jeff Brewster worriedly studied the brooding

Strickland's face as the detective learned of the posse's only casualty—one man wounded. He knew part of the older man's thoughts. Next time Weaver would be more wily, and likely more vicious. He wished he knew what else Strickland was thinking.

The handful of lawmen stopped at the windmill to water their thirsty horses. The wooden fan creaked as it turned slowly in the cold wind, pouring out a small stream of life that only recently had made this West Texas land usable for livestock. Let this little stream of water quit, and within a week the land would pass back to the jackrabbits, the hawks, and the lizards.

Yellow lamplight was pushing back the darkness from dozens of windows when the posse rode in to Dry Wells. Most of the tired deputies headed for a saloon.

Strickland went with Jeff to the chilly jailhouse. He settled his rangy body in a cane-bottom chair and studied the sheriff's face while Jeff lighted a kerosene lamp and adjusted the flame.

"Your friend Simmons," he said finally. "Tell me about him."

Jeff's pulse quickened. "Not much to tell. We grew up together around Menardville. We came out here together. I took up sheriffin', and Clay won a second-rate general store in a card game."

Strickland thoughtfully twisted his mustache. "Simmons runs a few cattle on the side, and usually lets somebody else run his store. Has he ever done anything out of line before? Never slipped his brand on anybody else's stock that you know of?"

Jeff slowly rolled a cigarette, spilling more tobacco than usual. He shook his head.

The detective frowned. "I happen to know you

once had to put up fifty dollars of your own money to get Simmons out of trouble, after somebody'd found five aces in a deck he'd been playin' with."

Jeff's hand shook as he lighted the cigarette. "Clay paid that back, soon as he was able."

Gravely, Strickland stood up. His black eyes were grim under thick, dark eyebrows. "I was a deputy, when I was young. A man I thought was my friend was brought in for murder. I slipped him a gun. Later he used it on *me*." The association man cleared his throat. "You better hope your friend keeps straight from now on, Brewster. If he jumps out of the pasture again, I'll have you jailed for sellin' out on your duty!"

Strickland tromped out into the chill darkness. Jeff sank back into his chair and threw away the half-smoked cigarette. He was as numb as if he had fallen into icy water.

He wished he could talk to Donna Larkin. For more than a year he and Simmons had been riding out to her father's ranch to pay her company. For much of that time they had both been proposing to her. It had looked as if their chances were about equal. It had, that is, until today.

Jeff and Strickland had expected trouble from Red Weaver, but they hadn't expected it to come as soon as it did. In the middle of the next afternoon, an excited, brown-skinned youngster slid his horse to a stop in front of the jail, swung down, and ran up the steps. The howling cold wind and choking brown sand pushed through the door with him.

He was a Mexican lad who worked for Donna's father. The violent story tumbled out in English mixed with Spanish. The ranchman and one of his cowboys had ridden up on Weaver's men rounding up cattle at a Larkin windmill, many miles from the ranch house. In the battle that followed, Larkin was killed and the cowboy wounded. Their horses ran away. The weakened puncher had trudged the long miles back to the house, facing a blast of wind and sand that had ground his face raw.

Within minutes Jeff had rounded up Strickland and half a dozen possemen. As he rode to tell the doctor to hurry out to Larkin's, he saw Clay Simmons riding up the street on his red roan, head bowed against the wind.

A gnawing fear ached in Jeff. Where had Simmons been? Could he have ridden with Weaver again today?

The lawmen headed straight for the mill where the shooting had occurred. The chill wind at their backs improved their time, although the sand burned their eyes and made their chests ache.

But it had done worse than that. The howling wind and moving film of sand just above ground level had smoothed out all tracks. There was no way to tell for sure which direction the herd had taken. And darkness was closing in.

Heading into the biting wind, the group turned back toward the Larkin ranch. Jeff felt as helpless as a man with his hands tied. Anger burned deep within him. Fine wedding present to take Donna Larkin—her father's body!

He thought of Simmons, and knew the old man-hunter Strickland was thinking along the same lines. Jeff half expected Strickland to slip a pair of cuffs over his wrists. But the association man rode silently, bowed against the cold.

With the coming of night, the sandstorm subsided.

The weary group reined up at the Larkin barns and left their horses in a corral. Jeff went ahead of the others to the house to make sure Donna didn't see her father brought in.

Anxiety and grief had cut deep lines in her pretty face, but they were lines that would fade away. Her cheeks showed sign of shed tears, but her eyes were dry now.

"You didn't find Weaver?" she asked.

Jeff shook his head.

Her small hands trembled as she clasped them to her slender body and looked down at the floor. Jeff ached to take her into his arms and comfort her.

Then she led Jeff, Strickland, and the deputies into a bedroom where the wounded cowboy, Slim Horner, lay.

Weaver and his men had had at least a couple of hundred cattle at the mill when Larkin and the cowboy had ridden up on them, the puncher said. Slim had been wounded in the first exchange of gunfire. His gun had been lost in the sand.

"Mr. Larkin seemed to go crazy when he seen me go down," the cowboy related. "He spurred into them outlaws like he had a troop of cavalry behind him. Even after they had shot him off his horse, he kept firin' till his gun was empty.

"Red Weaver started to shoot him then as he laid on the ground. One of the outlaws rode up and tried to stop Red. But Red hit the feller across the face with his gun barrel—like to've knocked him off his horse. Then Red went ahead and killed Mr. Larkin."

Strickland bent over eagerly, gripping the cast-iron bedstead. "Who was that man, Slim?"

"I couldn't tell," Slim answered. "The way the sand

was blowin', most of the rustlers had handkerchiefs tied over their faces. All I could tell was, he was ridin' a red roan horse."

Fear clutched at Jeff as Strickland turned on him, his craggy face dark as a storm cloud. "I reckon you know who rides a roan, Brewster."

Donna seemed to sense the tension that sprang between the two. "What's wrong, Jeff?"

Strickland answered her question. "He put too much faith in friendship, miss. He let an outlaw go yesterday when he found out the feller was his best friend."

Jeff clenched his fists. "Shut up, Charlie!"

Donna's face paled as the words sank in. "Best friend . . . a roan horse . . . you're talking about Clay!"

Strickland nodded.

Donna's voice broke. She sank down onto the edge of the bed. "Now they'll send you to jail too, Jeff. Why did you do it?"

Jeff tried to speak calmly. "He told me you were goin' to marry him. He promised to keep straight. I didn't want you to find out."

Tenderly he put his hand on her slender shoulder. "He tried to keep Weaver from killin' your dad, Donna. You've got to remember that."

The girl sat silently a moment. Then she stood and faced Strickland. "If Jeff could find out where Weaver went, and could help you catch him, would you clear him?"

Strickland shook his gray head. "I reckon I might, but I can't afford to give him that chance. He forgot his duty, but I ain't forgittin' mine. I'm takin' Jeff in tonight."

Donna moved so quickly that Jeff hardly saw her

snatch the gun from a deputy's holster. "Maybe not," she breathed. "You took a chance for me, Jeff. Now I'll take one for you."

Strickland made a motion to grab the gun the girl held, but he backed off as she cried, "I'm not afraid to use this gun. Put up your hands, all of you." She let two fast shots off toward Strickland's feet as she spoke.

Even Jeff was caught off guard. He stood uncertainly for a moment, as the surprised lawmen stared at the girl, then slowly raised their hands.

"I hate to do it, Donna," Jeff said reluctantly, "but it's the only chance we've got. I'll go to Clay. He's got to help me catch Weaver. See if you can keep these men here for at least an hour."

He moved quickly out the door. A minute later he was on his horse and spurring through the cold darkness, headed back to town.

Lamplight shone from one window in Clay Simmons's small frame house. Jeff hitched his horse, jumped up on the little porch, and pushed through the front door.

Clay sat slumped in a cowhide chair. His half-opened eyes stared dully at Jeff. He listlessly extended a nearly empty bottle toward the sheriff.

"Have a drink, pardner," he said drunkenly. "Help me celebrate. Yesterday I was just a cow thief. Today I'm a murderer!" Bitterness put a raw edge in his voice.

Jeff recoiled in anger as he saw the cruel blue mark across Simmons's face.

"Where'd Weaver go, Clay?" he asked, leaning eagerly forward.

"New Mexico!" Clay answered, louder than he knew. "An' I hope he never comes back."

"We've got to bring him back, Clay," Jeff pressed. "Strickland saw me turn you loose. We'll both be in jail if we don't stop Weaver!"

Simmons's eyes were bleak. "Don't make no difference. I helped Red Weaver steal cattle from Donna's dad. He said if I didn't go he'd frame me. I was there when Red killed Larkin. I'd rather be dead myself."

Desperation took hold of Jeff. He grabbed Simmons's shoulders, shook them hard. "Snap out of it, Clay. You've got to help me. Where was Weaver takin' those cattle?"

Simmons hunched forward in the creaky chair. "He took a long chance. Headed them northwest, up toward Grogan's mill. Figgered he'd water them there, then push them on across the New Mexico line."

Jeff stared incredulously. "But it's twenty miles without water up to Grogan's mill!"

"That's why he did it. Figgered nobody'd look for that. They'd be lookin' for him to follow the best waterin' places. He'll drive all night."

Jeff jerked Simmons up out of the chair. "If we ride hard we can beat him there," he declared. He scrawled a short note to Strickland and left it pinned under a kerosene lamp on the table. Then he half dragged the protesting Simmons out the door.

Quickly he saddled Simmons's red roan and caught up a fresh horse for himself from the corral. Alternating between a fast trot and an easy lope, he had to half hold Simmons to keep him in the saddle the first three or four miles. Finally the cold night air and the constant pounding of the saddle sobered the man.

The long, hard day in the saddle and the endless

miles of chilly night-riding tolled on both riders. By sunrise it seemed to Jeff that they had ridden over ten thousand sand dunes and across hundreds of mesquite flats.

All sleepiness vanished from him, though, when he saw the moving herd of cattle a mile to the south.

"Not a mile to the mill, Clay," he exclaimed. "We'll just beat them there!"

Minutes later the two riders reined up at the mill. After watering their horses, they hid them behind a dune.

"We've got to keep Weaver and the cattle here till Strickland comes," Jeff declared. "It's just a mile on to the New Mexico border."

Quickly he looked over the watering place. The one windmill pumped water out into a small tank, which was enclosed by barbed wire. The water flowed through a buried pipe from the tank out into a wooden trough.

"Those cattle are bone-dry by now, Clay," he reasoned. "If Weaver gets them watered out, he'll push them across the line in half an hour. If he doesn't, they'll be so thirsty he'll pay hell ever gettin' them away from this mill. They can smell water here."

The sheriff knelt beside the trough and examined the mechanism which regulated the flow of water. It was designed to cut itself off when the water reached within an inch of the trough's rim. Jeff took out his handkerchief and used it to tie the float lever to a bar across the top of the trough, so no water could enter it.

His skin tingled as he heard the thirsty cattle bawling, not far away.

"Get your hat off, Clay. We're goin' to dip the water out of this trough."

They worked feverishly, pouring the icy water out. The thirsty sand drank it up as quickly as it hit. Before long there was nothing but a little muddy water in the bottom of the trough. The two men slipped through the barbed-wire fence and knelt down behind the tank dam, out of sight.

They didn't wait long. A forward guard of gaunt cattle trotted out of the mesquite brush, their noses low to the ground as they smelled water ahead. Two outlaws followed them. They had been riding point, probably fighting the cattle back the last miles.

The first cattle crowded around the empty trough and nosed futilely in the mud. As more cattle came, they fought for positions at the trough. Thirsty, bawling cattle began to walk around the barbed-wire enclosure that barred them from the tank of water.

The dry outlaws didn't seem to notice. They dismounted, tied their horses to the wire, and climbed through the fence for a drink of the clean tank water.

Jeff raised up a little from behind the tank dam and leveled his gun on the men.

"All right, you two," he ordered gruffly. "Throw your guns in the tank!"

Startled, the outlaws hesitated, then complied. The guns splashed into the water and sank in the mud.

"Now move around here out of sight and git down on your bellies," the sheriff barked. By the time a couple more rustlers came in to water, Jeff and Simmons had the first two hidden from sight, gagged and lying in the cold sand with their hands tied behind their backs.

In a few minutes the second pair of cursing outlaws was in the same position.

Then Red Weaver rode in, two men with him. He

was pointing angrily at the milling, fighting cattle. One of the men with him galloped ahead and fought his way through the thirsty cattle to the trough. His excited signals brought Weaver and the other man in a lope. The first outlaw dismounted and knelt to look at the float.

Jeff knew that if the man untied the lever the trough would quickly refill. He leveled his gun and fired at a point just in front of the outlaw. Splinters flew. The surprised man started to reach for his gun, then froze. He slowly raised his bleeding hands, slashed by splinters.

Jeff fired quickly as Weaver and the last outlaw dismounted. Then the two rustlers were on the ground behind the milling cattle.

The sheriff, nodding with satisfaction at Clay Simmons, holstered his gun.

Simmons took charge of the outlaw at the trough. Jeff watched anxiously for Weaver to show his head.

A bullet whined off the tank dam, showering dirt into the sheriff's face. Before he could fire back, Weaver was hidden again. The frightened cattle were running in circles now, raising clouds of dust that hid the two free outlaws from sight.

Jeff glimpsed a man's figure through the dust. He fired quickly and saw the man double over. Flame lanced at him from another point. Dirt bit into his eyes, blinding him.

He blinked at the burning pain, struggled to clear his vision. Moments later, when he could see again, he squinted vainly through the dust for a sign of Weaver. But he saw only the running cattle, their tossing horns, and their trampling hoofs.

He shivered, his heart in his mouth. Weaver could be anywhere now.

Suddenly there was a knot in the pit of Jeff's stomach as he became aware that Clay Simmons had raised his hands. Throat dry and nerves tingling, the sheriff whirled. He saw Weaver rising to his feet just outside the fence, gun pointed steadily at Simmons's back.

"Drop your gun, Brewster," the outlaw gritted, "or I'll kill your friend!"

"Don't do it, Jeff," Simmons shouted. "Shoot him!"

An awful weight seemed to be crushing Jeff as he lowered the gun. He was licked, completely beaten. There was no choice.

Then, in a second, Simmons whirled and leaped at Weaver. The barbed wire sang as he hit it. A long moment the two men struggled, the ripping, gouging wire between them. Jeff tried vainly to get a bead on Weaver. His heart sank as he heard the muffled shot. Simmons slumped, trying vainly to hold himself up on the treacherous fence.

Jeff glimpsed the hatred that burned in Weaver's red face as he raised the smoking gun. Jeff raised his own gun and jumped to one side as the man's weapon winked. Then he squeezed the trigger. Weaver dropped his gun, swayed, and pitched headlong onto the fence.

The other five outlaws had bellied the ground during the shooting. They stayed that way after Weaver fell.

Jeff moved quickly to Simmons's side. "What did you do it for, Clay?" he asked quietly.

Simmons licked his dry lips and whispered, "You saved me once, Jeff. You shouldn't have. I couldn't let you do it again . . . and have you risk so much."

The thirsty cattle had watered out by the time Strickland and his posse got to the mill an hour later.

Jeff made one of the outlaws untie the handkerchief, so the trough would refill. While the posse took
charge of the outlaws, Jeff explained to the association man just what had happened.

"Clay did a few things he shouldn't have," he said,
looking at the still figure which lay in the sand, face
covered by a hat. "But he paid back a lot more than
he owed."

Strickland nodded. "Reckon you're a better judge
of men than I figgered, Brewster. If you'll forget what
I said about you sellin' out, I'll forget about swearin'
out charges against you."

Jeff held out his hand, and Strickland clasped it in
his strong one.

"We'll take Simmons's body back to town. You better go tell that girl what happened," Strickland said. A
thin smile creased the association man's leathery face.
"When she finally let us leave the ranch, we almost
had to use a gun on her to keep her from comin' with
us. She was worried sick—about *you*, Jeff."

So Jeff Brewster started out again, back across the
sand and mesquite country. His shoulders sagged
from weariness, and he hunched in against the cold.
But the warm thought of Donna waiting for him kept
him spurring the tired horse on.

# DIE
# BY THE GUN

**T**he sudden lift of his horse's head was Dolph Noble's first indication that the trail had run out. The dun's black-tipped ears pricked forward, and Noble's hand dropped to his gun. He jerked the dun to a halt and raised his left hand as a quick signal to the five riders behind him.

He squinted his windburned eyes against the hot glare of the Texas sun and searched out the thick brush on the hills ahead of him for sign of what the wind had carried to the sensitive nostrils of his horse. A tingle played up and down under the sweat-soaked back of his shirt. That thorny tangle of mesquite and catclaw could hide one man, or it could hide the whole band of Clayton Chasteen.

A bent-shouldered rider of fifty years eased up beside him. His narrowed eyes were chips of flint as his gaze probed over the rocky hills.

"They up there, you reckon, Dolph?"

Dolph Noble's mouth was a hard, straight line beneath three days' stubble, dirt and sweat. To most of the riders who sided him, he was still a young man. But already his gray eyes were old. The silver badge pinned to his shirt had done that for him.

"Can't say, Andy," he replied in a tight voice. "But we better fan out."

The horsemen pulled away from him on either side. There was no gallantry here, no romantic flourish. Just five broken-down old cowpunchers and a cautious sheriff, doing an unpleasant job.

The skin of his back still crawling, he pushed the dun into a slow walk. His right hand eased the gun out of its holster, and he thumbed the cylinder away from the empty safety chamber.

The bullet whined by him and ricocheted off the rocky hillside. The slap of the pistol shot echoed and reechoed from the hills. Before the second shot, Dolph was off his horse and onto the ground, sprinting stiff-legged into the scattering of brush.

He didn't look for the possemen. He didn't have to look to know they would be afoot, seeking cover as he was.

Fear was cold and clammy at the pit of his stomach, as it always was in a situation like this. But he never stopped moving up, working from bush to bush, putting himself closer to the gunman. His tense lips were dry as leather, and his eyes were desperately searching the brush ahead of him.

He got a glimpse as the man raised up from behind a mesquite and fired at him. The bullet tugged at Dolph's sleeve, raising a puff of dust. Dolph dropped behind a tiny cleft in the hillside.

Keeping his head down, he called, "This is Dolph Noble, the sheriff. You're surrounded. Better call it quits and come on down."

There was a long silence, and Dolph hoped the

gunman was taking his advice. But when he raised his head, the gun exploded again. This time he waited. He knew he wouldn't have to wait long.

Sure enough, in a few minutes he heard Andy Biederman's heavy voice boom from above, "All right, mister, how about it?"

There was one more pistol shot, followed by the heavy roar of a saddle gun before there was time for an echo. The sound of a choked groan brought Dolph up in a stiff run.

The gunman lay on his face, his body drawn up in agony. Dolph kicked the pistol far away from the cramped fingers and carefully turned the outlaw over onto his back. He blanched, his heart sickening. Suddenly he hated the badge he wore.

Andy Biederman came picking his way down the rocky hillside, carrying a smoking saddle gun. The old puncher took one look at the dying ambusher, whose glazing eyes bulged in terror as they beheld the smothering blanket of death. Biederman's face fell, and his shoulders suddenly sagged.

His gruff old voice was broken and miserable. "A kid, Dolph. Just a slick-faced kid."

Old Lew Matlock leaned a thin shoulder against the weathered siding of his big frame livery barn. He watched with narrow interest the six horsemen moving slowly across the brush-spotted draw and up the wagon road that led into the western end of Twin Wells' dusty main street. Squinting his pale eyes, he could see the heavy sag of the men's shoulders as the trailing sun sent their shadows searching far out ahead of them.

Sheriff Dolph Noble rode half a length in the lead

Dust set a gray cast to his shirt that had been blue, and sweat-salt showed dull white under the arms and down the back.

Noble reined up before the livery barn and turned stolidly in his saddle.

"We'd just as well break it up here," he said quietly, as if it was an effort even to speak. "My thanks to all of you."

His wrinkle-carved face still grim and sick, Andy Biederman lifted his gnarled hand in tired, wordless salute and pulled his long-legged sorrel aside. One by one the other riders peeled off and plodded their various ways, sagging in fatigue.

The last man moved up hesitantly, bringing a led horse behind him. "The button's horse, Dolph. What you want done with it?"

Noble's sun-cracked lips tightened. His big fist knotted, then he reached out and took the reins. "I'll take care of him, George. You go on home and get you some rest."

Lew Matlock stepped out of the broad open door as Dolph Noble stiffly eased down from the saddle. The liveryman eyed him levelly, knocking ashes out of his pipe on the heel of his hand. There was no word of greeting, just an understanding nod between them. That was all that was needed. They had been friends since Dolph was a short-pants kid, thirty years and more ago.

"See what you can get for the saddle, Lew," Dolph Noble said.

Matlock shoved his cold pipe into his shirt pocket. "You got one of them, did you?"

Dolph's tired gaze settled on the hard-tromped floor and the scattering of dry hay there. "Just a kid, Lew. Twenty, maybe, or twenty-one. About like my brother Tommy. He'd been wounded, and they'd gone off and left him. He wouldn't surrender. He had to fight it out."

Lew Matlock sensed the bleakness that ached in Dolph. "Lawing's a dirty business sometimes, Dolph," he said in sympathy. "But somebody's got to do it."

A bitter anger welled up in Dolph's throat and died there. He pointed at the brand on the hip of the young outlaw's horse.

Lew Matlock frowned. "Long L. Can't say as I'm surprised."

Dolph's lips were tight. "They'll lie out of it. They'll say it was stole."

Impatiently he unfastened his saddle girth and jerked at the cinch. Lew Matlock gently pushed him aside.

"I'll take care of the horses. You go on and get cleaned up, and catch some rest."

Dragging his worn boots down the sandy street toward the sheriff's office, Dolph tried to stretch the saddle stiffness out of him. It wasn't as easy as it used to be; he knew that only a long night's sleep would do it. He knew, too, that there would be little sleep for him tonight. They had killed a man today. With darkness the grim picture would rush at him a thousand times, as other such pictures had done in the past.

From his room in the back end of the office he picked up clean clothes and angled across to the barber shop. By the freshly painted peppermint sign he paused to grind out a tasteless cigarette with his bootheel.

The barber didn't ask any foolish questions. He was another old friend, like Lew Matlock, and he knew when not to ask too much. Anyway, the news had beaten Dolph in.

Daubing the lather on, the barber said regretfully, "Something I hate to tell you, Dolph, but you ought to know. Hoggy Truscott's been itching for you to get back. Seems like your brother Tommy got in a little jackpot over at Hoggy's saloon a couple of nights ago. Him and that wild compañero of his, that Herndon kid."

Dolph groaned inwardly, impatient anger growing in him. There was always a jackpot of some kind or other. "What was it this time?"

The barber frowned. "Now, Dolph, don't be hard on the boy. He's a good kid, just got a few wild oats to sow yet. You never had a chance to sow any. Maybe that's why you don't understand him." The razor was sharp and quick. "I got an idea Tommy was still peeved because you wouldn't let him go with you on that posse, Dolph. Anyhow, him and Pete Herndon sat in on a game with that long-legged gambler that's been hanging around Hoggy's lately.

"They got a notion the gambler was cheating, which most likely he was. They throwed it in to him, and he started to pull a gun. The two boys swarmed all over him then, mopped up the saloon with him good and proper. But they kind of busted up the place doing it. Now the gambler's left town. Hoggy's probably madder about that than he is about the damage. I think he was getting a percentage."

Dolph sat in angry silence, his hands gripped tightly on the arms of the chair. The barber was right. He didn't understand Tommy. But he had tried to. He had tried hard.

◈

A long soak in the shop's cast-iron tub had drained some of the fatigue out of Dolph Noble. Now, walking up the dusty street in the reddish glow of sunset, he felt fresher, and some of the weight was gone from his shoulders.

His whiskers gone, he was a smooth-faced man with features not young but not yet those of middle age. Wrinkles bit deep into the brown skin at the corners of his eyes, the result of years of squinting across a sun-drenched land. His squarish jaw bore a somber set, for he had been jolted up against hard reality at an age when most boys were still full of play. He had been there ever since.

His gaze swept far ahead of him and picked out the small frame house just at the edge of town, where the street began to dwindle into a powder-ground pair of wagon tracks. In front of it he paused for a moment, half in eagerness to go in, yet feeling a strong tug of regret.

His eye caught the quick movement of lace curtains in the side window of a house nearby, and an ironic grin broke across his cracked lips. He walked up onto the little porch and knocked.

Lila Chasteen opened the door and stepped back. She was a woman of thirty, with a slender grace and stoical dignity. There was much of youth left in her oval face, but trouble had brought maturity to her dark blue eyes. Silent welcome showed in the eyes now, as she stepped aside for Dolph. But with it was a desperate worry.

He took off his hat and tried a smile that somehow didn't materialize. An uneasy silence stood between them. Then she asked, "Did you see Clayton?"

He shook his head. "No, Lila. We didn't *see* him."

Her chin dipped a little, and she bit her lip. "But you're sure it was him?"

Again he nodded. "I wish I could say different, Lila. But there's no use lying to you about it. It was him, all right."

He sensed that she had known, even before he had come in, that there was no longer any hope. There had remained only the cruel formality of telling her.

He lowered his head. "It makes me hate myself, Lila, and hate being what I am. I wish it wasn't me that had to tell you. I wish—"

Bitterness welled into his voice. "I wish sometimes I was a cowboy again, or a merchant, or even a section hand. Anything but a gun-carrying lawman."

Her hand quickly lifted to his arm. "Don't, Dolph. It's not your fault. It was bound to happen. And I'm glad it's you who heads the law here, not someone else."

Then she said, "You're tired, Dolph. Sit down, won't you?"

He looked levelly into her eyes. "I guess I'd better not, Lila. I saw old lady Kittredge's curtains move aside as I walked up. Likely as not, she's timing us. I'd better go."

Color deepened in her face. "Then you've heard the gossip, too. There's been plenty of it—about the sheriff and the outlaw's wife," she said in quick sharpness.

"I ignore idle gossip," he told her.

Her eyes lifted. They were honest eyes, eyes that could tell of love, had they not already told of so much heartbreak. "A *man* can afford to," she said. "I guess you're right, Dolph. You'd better go."

At the door she reached out and caught his hand. She held it in her own for a long moment. "Thanks, Dolph, for coming by."

Dolph longed to pull her to him, to hold her tightly and never let anything hurt her again. But he was old enough to know the futility of it, and to keep tight rein on himself. He said simply, "Good night, Lila," and moved quickly into the street.

Back in his office he sank wearily into the straight, hard chair at his rolltop desk. He dug out the letter that had been found in the dead young outlaw's pocket. For the fifth or sixth time he read through it, his mouth straight and hard. It was a letter from the boy's mother. Smudged and badly creased, it evidently had been carried a long time.

Dolph took a blank sheet of paper out of a desk drawer and whittled a new point on a pencil stub. He stared at the paper a long time, his teeth biting deep into the pencil. Then he bent over the desk and began to write laboriously, a frown cutting dark lines across his leather-brown face.

Dear Mrs. Merchant:

As sheriff of this county, it becomes my most painful duty to inform you of your son's death. It was an accident, his horse falling on him while he was chasing a runaway cow. It was quick; he felt no pain.

Your boy had not been here long, but he was well liked and a hard worker.

Dolph paused a while, his fists knotted. He reached into his pocket and pulled out an old leather billfold.

He took most of the money out of it, counted it, and tucked it into the envelope.

Your son had a month's wages coming to him. His boss asked me to mail the money to you. Also, we are selling his saddle. Will remit payment as soon as the sale is made.

Your most sympathetic servant,
Dolph Noble, Sheriff

Dolph slipped the letter into the envelope, licked the flap, and stuck it down with pressure from his big brown hand.

He was so absorbed in the letter that he didn't know the girl had come into the office until she spoke. He looked up in quick surprise, his face warming. For a second he was afraid she might know what was in the letter. Then he realized she couldn't, and he was relieved.

"Howdy, Dolph," said Susan Lane. "You had supper yet?"

She was a slight girl of eighteen, with flaxen hair and honest brown eyes that could dance with laughter. Dolph shoved back from his desk, surreptitiously pushing the letter under a stack of papers. He really smiled, for the first time in a good many days. "I swear, Susan, you get younger and prettier every day, while I just get older and uglier."

Color crept into her pleased face, and she bowed in an exaggerated curtsy.

Dolph reached into his shirt pocket for his tobacco. Deftly she took it out of his hands, rolled him a cigarette and placed it in his mouth. She pulled a match from the band of his dusty old hat, which hung from the top of a cane-bottomed chair.

Dolph leaned back with a pleased smile and dragged long at the cigarette. "You oughtn't do things like that. You make an old bachelor see the error of his ways."

Laughter danced in her bright brown eyes. "Just practicing. A bride-to-be has to learn little touches like that."

Dolph grunted, a frown slowly forming on his face. "I'm afraid it may take more than that, Susan. The girl who marries Tommy needs to be tough as a bronc stomper, and still have the patience of Job."

Her brown eyes went serious. They looked at Dolph, and fearfulness showed in them. "Dolph," she said, "he's your brother. But in so many ways he's different. He's—"

Her gaze dropped to the floor. "I love him, Dolph. I want him more than I could ever tell you. But sometimes I wish—I wish he was you."

Dolph leaned forward and placed his hand on her shoulder. "I guess we're both going to have to give him time, Susan. We've got to remember that he wasn't raised with a mother to guide him, or a dad to teach him what he ought to know. I had to be brother and dad both to him, and most of the time I was working too hard to be much of either one.

"Besides, I guess I was too much older than him to teach him like a brother, and still not old enough to understand him like a father would. He grew up with a wildness in him that's going to work its way out in spite of both of us. We've just got to wait, and watch, and hope he finds the right road by and by."

She forced a quick smile. "I guess so, Dolph. I guess so."

She rubbed a hand across her eyes and said, "I didn't come here to tell you my troubles. I came to invite you over to the house for supper. We've got some fresh pie. And besides, Dad wants to talk to you."

Stiffly, the fatigue settling back into him, he arose from the chair. He grinned at the girl. "Well now, if it's pie you've got, just lead the way."

The Lanes lived in a big frame house in the south part of town. John Lane had built the place when Susan had gotten old enough to go to school and the family had to be moved in from the ranch. The Lanes were a big family. It looked as if they had a good many more years to spend here before the last of the youngsters had finished school.

Big John Lane sat on his wide front porch, contentedly drawing on his pipe and watching two of his youngest boys chasing each other up and down over the painted porch railing. As Dolph climbed the steps with Susan, the gray-thatched Lane took the pipe from his mouth and grinned genially.

"Sit down, Dolph. The womenfolks haven't quite got supper ready yet."

Dolph eased into a cane chair beside the big man. He watched the two rowdy boys and listened to their shrill yelping, and he knew a vague regret, a feeling of something missed.

Frowning, John Lane knocked the ashes out of his pipe and refilled it with fresh tobacco.

"Been some things happening around here lately, Dolph, things I don't like. Maybe you've got wind of them, and maybe you haven't. There's a big move shaping up to get you out of office."

Dolph showed no sign of surprise or regret. "I don't think I'd much care, John. I think I might be glad to turn it over to somebody else."

Lane said something under his breath as he failed to light his pipe with the first match. "But not to the one who'd get it, Dolph. If you lost out, the office would go to Rance Ostrander."

Dolph glanced quickly at Lane. "Rance? Now, who'd elect Rance? Everybody knows why I fired him as deputy. They ought to know how the law would degenerate around here if he was the sheriff."

Lane nodded grimly. "Ought to. But sometimes people get to wanting a change so bad they'll take anything, just so it's different."

Scowling fiercely, he flipped away a match that had burned his fingers.

"There are more people against you than you think, Dolph. Rance and his bunch are doing all they can to fire them up. Why they're even saying you don't really want to catch Clayton Chasteen. That his wife has you—" Sudden anger flared in Dolph's eyes. Lane broke it off and said apologetically, "I guess I shouldn't have told you that. But I figured you ought to know how far they're going with it."

His face clouded, Dolph leaned forward and doubled his fists. "I don't care what they say about me. But they'd better leave Lila out of it."

Mrs. Lane stuck her head out of the door and called:

"It's ready, men. And John, you leave that pipe outside."

John stood up with Dolph. His hand was on the sheriff's shoulder. "But they won't leave her out of it, Dolph. There's only one answer. You've got to bring in Chasteen. And you've got to do it soon."

They walked inside.

The sheriff sat in the straight chair outside the door of his office, watching the stars brighten against the deepening black of the sky. The night air had turned cool and pleasant after the baking heat of the day. From down the street came the faint tinkling of a piano at Hoggy Truscott's place, broken now and then by a howl of laughter. Dolph reminded himself that he would have to go down there in the morning and talk to Hoggy about Tommy's fight.

From far up the street came the leisurely thump of horse's hoofs in the soft sand. A horse hitched across the street from the office lifted its head and pointed its ears toward the sound.

Tommy Noble trotted up in front of the office and swung down from the saddle with the easy grace of a born cowpuncher. He wrapped the reins around a post and stepped up onto the wooden sidewalk, dusting the legs of his trousers as he walked. He was a slender youth, quick of wit and movement, and handsome enough that half the young girls of the town watched him covertly wherever he went. There was many a girl who didn't like Susan Lane anymore.

Tommy stopped abruptly as he saw Dolph sitting there in the near darkness. He nodded. "Heard you were back in."

Dolph grunted an answer. He felt an old tightening within him. He was going to try to hold himself down this time. He was going to try to keep from losing his patience.

The youngster said, "They say you didn't catch up with Clayton Chasteen."

Dolph's eyes were steady on his kid brother's face. "That's right."

The kid's reserve suddenly left him and he was bending over close, his voice intense.

"Well, what else could you expect, taking along a

bunch of old worn-out hands like that for a posse? Andy Biederman. Why, he can't even get on a horse by himself anymore. And George Castleberry. George couldn't hear a gun go off if you held it right by his ear. The rest are just about as bad."

Dolph's voice was tightening. "Andy's stiff, you're right about that. But he's still the best shot in this country. And George Castleberry can track a cat over bare rock.

"What's more, Tommy, they know what they're doing. They'll get there if anybody can, and they'll get back in one piece. They won't be out chasing after glory like half-baked kids and get their heads shot off. They'll be there when you need them, and they'll do whatever's got to be done."

Tommy pondered that. "But, Dolph, I'm a good shot, too; you got to admit that. I can even beat you."

Dolph nodded.

"And I'm twenty-one, Dolph. I'm already older than you were the first time they pinned a deputy badge on you."

The heat beginning to color his voice, Dolph said, "Some kids are grown by the time they're fifteen. And there are others who never do grow up."

Tommy stiffened. Dolph went on impatiently: "Tommy, I've told you a hundred times. A lawman's life is no good, not for me and not for you. I've wished to God I'd never started at it. Now I've been at it so long I can't quit.

"But I'm not letting you get trapped that way. You start living with a gun, and by and by you have to kill somebody. Then you get to where you can't live without a gun. Everywhere you go, it's got to go with you. You live by it, and one day you die by it.

I'd give all I've got if I could back up and start over. I can't. But I can see that you get a different start. That's why you'll never get a badge, Tommy. Not from me."

The boy's anger was almost crackling in the darkness. Tommy turned on his bootheel and stomped back toward his horse.

"Wait a minute, Tommy," Dolph called, his voice milder. The boy stopped.

"I was talking to John Lane about you. He still wants you to take over the running of his home ranch. Living in town and being a director of the bank keeps him too busy to take care of it himself the way he wants to. It'd be a fine start for you, Tommy. He'd pay well and you could go ahead and marry Susan. You ought to go talk to John, and tell him you want the job."

Even in the darkness, he could feel the boy's piercing glare. "I wish you'd let me alone, and quit telling me what to do. Maybe I'd like the kind of life you live. I'm of age. You've got no right anymore to try to stop me. If you won't give me a chance, I'll have to find it someplace else."

He jerked the reins loose from the post, swung into the saddle, and moved away at a stiff trot. Dolph stared after him until the boy had disappeared into the thick darkness of the street. He rolled a cigarette, took only a couple of puffs on it, then bitterly ground it under his heel.

Suddenly the night was no longer cool. The air was hot and close and uncomfortable, and he found himself soaking in sweat. He got up and started walking, hoping to find relief.

Hoggy Truscott's saloon was in a big false-fronted building that stood off apart from the others on the street. The front of it had been given a fresh coat of bright red paint the year before, but the sides and back were still dark and peeling, needing paint badly. Stopping in front of it, Dolph noted a front window broken out. He wondered if that was Tommy's work, or if some other fight had done it.

Hoggy was sitting at a table with Rance Ostrander. Their low-pitched talk stopped as Dolph walked in. Hoggy stood up quickly, shoving back his chair. Unconsciously he wiped his hands on the greasy apron hung around his middle. Although the morning was not yet really hot, Hoggy was without a shirt. Sweat stained his dingy underwear.

"Morning, Dolph," he said, his voice neither friendly nor hostile. "I been hoping you'd come by, so I wouldn't have to go see you."

Dolph halted in the middle of the floor, looking around him, trying to locate the source of the stale smell that seemed to ooze from every corner of the place. Hoggy was a poor customer of soap, and he kept only a small water barrel.

"I understand Tommy and Pete Herndon busted up some furniture," Dolph said. "What do you figure I owe you?"

Hoggy frowned. His little eyes set in their usual attitude of irritation. "Well, in the first place, they busted one table and two chairs. I figure that's worth, say, five dollars. I can get it fixed. Then they busted the corner out of the mirror behind the bar. It cost me twenty dollars new."

Dolph frowned. He remembered seeing that corner broken out a long time ago.

Hoggy pointed a thumb at the broken front window. "They busted that, too. That's the one they throwed Mr. Duckworth through."

Dolph said, "Tell you what, Hoggy. I'll give you twenty dollars to cover the whole thing, and we both forget about it."

Hoggy's mouth turned down at the corners. "Seems to me I'm entitled to more. I figured the damage twice that much."

Dolph's tone was firm. "Twenty's enough. I ought not to give you anything, you trying to get by me with that mirror."

He held out the twenty dollars. Hoggy grabbed it, counted it, and shoved it deep into his pocket. "If you wasn't the sheriff," he said grudgingly, "I wouldn't let you get away with this. But it wouldn't do me much good to sue you."

Rance Ostrander, the ex-deputy, spoke up for the first time. "Don't fret over it, Hoggy. Come election, he won't be sheriff no more."

Rance Ostrander was a lean, hungry-looking man in a dirty shirt. There was too much white around his eyes, making them look bigger than they really were. They were eyes that always smouldered with a brooding resentment.

"Yeah, Hoggy," he repeated with a wry grin, "after election, old Dolph's liable to come to you looking for a job swamping out the saloon." Rance's words were formed like a joke, but Dolph knew they were meant. "Dolph, they tell me you could've caught Clayton Chasteen if you'd really wanted to, if you'd taken some real deputies along. You had a good deputy once, if you'd had sense enough to keep him."

Dolph's anger began to build. "You know why I fired you, Rance. You wouldn't stay sober, and you couldn't stay away from these women down here. You know I couldn't keep a man like that."

Rance Ostrander stood up, a malevolent grin on his sallow face. "Listen to who's talking, Hoggy. I seen him last night, walking out toward the edge of town. Wasn't the first time, and ain't apt to be the last."

Dolph's face flamed. His fists balled, but he held himself in check.

Rance added, "There's only one way we'll ever catch Clayton Chasteen. That's to run that Chasteen woman out of town and then either make Dolph tend to his business or run him out too."

Dolph took a long step toward Rance, then stopped. He realized that that was what Rance was asking for. He sensed that other men had come into the saloon and stood behind him, watching. He dropped his fists.

"Don't you ever mention her name again, Rance," he said in a low voice. "If you do, I'll take off this badge and give you the whipping of your life."

He turned quickly and elbowed his way out, the whole outdoors a flaming red in front of him.

It was a hot ten-mile ride out to Brant Lawton's Long L. The ranch was isolated by a rough range of hills which divided the watersheds and sent the infrequent runoff waters from the Long L coursing down toward the Pecos.

But the Long L was well favored with lengthy draws which grew grass knee-high. It made a good place for raising horses, which was Lawton's principal business. He also raised some cattle, although some people said they weren't all his own. And there were some who said he wasn't always careful who he sold his horses to, either.

The house was a long, rambling affair, leisurely built and leisurely kept. A scattering of junk littered the whole place. A huge pile of rusted tin cans behind the back door of the kitchen marked it as a batching camp.

Brant Lawton stood on the front porch, leaning against a wooden post. "Git down and come in, Sheriff," he said affably. "Cook's fixing dinner. We got time for a quick snort if you're a mind to."

Dolph shook his head. "No, thanks, Brant. Just wanted to talk a little."

He dropped his reins over a sagging fence picket and sat down on the rough edge of the porch beside Lawton. Lawton was a friendly man of about fifty. That was one trouble with being a lawman. It wasn't easy, taking action against somebody you liked.

Dolph picked up a long stick someone had been whittling on and idly began to sketch in the sand.

"You heard the latest about Clayton Chasteen, I reckon," he said.

Lawton nodded. "You mean about him trying to hold up the train west of here. Yeah, I heard."

"Baggage messenger drove them off with a shotgun," Dolph went on. "But they killed one man before they gave up. We trailed them for a couple of days. We only caught up with one of them." He paused. "That one was riding a Long L horse, Brant. And the messenger said he saw the Long L on two of the other horses as they came by."

He looked directly at Lawton. "You real sure you haven't seen Chasteen? Haven't sold him some horses?"

Lawton's face flushed. "You meaning to accuse me, Dolph?"

"I'm not accusing anybody. I'm just asking."

Lawton sat stewing in angry silence. Then he said stubbornly, "A week ago we turned up missing a bunch of horses from down on Towson's Draw. They was good horses, all broke to ride and handle."

"You never did report it to me," Dolph said pointedly.

"I was busy. Anyhow, they left us as many horses as they took. They was good horses, too, only tired and ganted a little. I just counted it off as a trade and decided to keep my mouth shut. I always found it a healthy policy, keeping my mouth shut."

Dolph said dryly, "So I've noticed."

He remounted his horse and swung around to face Lawton once more. "Just one more thing I want to say to you, Brant. You know that Chasteen's bunch has blood on its hands. And you know that anybody who helps them gets his hands bloody too. He'll share in the punishment. Just remember that, the next time you get to swapping horses."

He pulled his horse around and started to spur him back toward town. Boisterous shouting made him pull up and look toward a grassy flat east of the headquarters. There he saw three men in a race, spurring their horses toward him as far as they could stretch, yelping at every stride. Behind them a couple of other riders followed at a more respectable pace.

The finish line appeared to be a big lone mesquite tree that stood a hundred yards from the corrals. Passing it, the three racers gradually pulled their horses to a halt and brought them around toward the house. The horses breathed hard and pranced nervously. The laughing men were red-faced and winded.

Dolph's mouth set rigidly as he watched them. The three riders were within a stone's throw before they noticed him. One of them reined up sharply, and his laughter hushed.

"Come on, Tommy," Dolph said. "We're going back to town."

Tommy Noble didn't speak. Young Pete Herndon brought his heaving horse up alongside that of his young partner. "Aw, now, Dolph," Herndon said. "Tommy's not hurting anything. We're just having us a little innocent fun. Just trying to show old Brant there that we've got horses as good as any of his."

"I'm not going to argue," Dolph spoke severely. "Tommy, you're coming along with me."

Tommy stubbornly held his ground a long moment, trying to stare his brother down. Then he shrugged his slim shoulders and moved up beside Dolph. The sheriff looked at young Pete Herndon.

"If I were you, Pete, I'd come along too. I don't think this is the right place for you either."

Herndon laughed, the devil dancing in his eyes. "Reckon I'll stay, Dolph. I'm having a right smart of fun. And I haven't got a bossy big brother."

The sheriff answered, "A pity you haven't, Pete. Come on, Tommy."

There wasn't a word between them for the first mile they jogged along the wagon trail under the heat of the noonday sun. Then Tommy said complainingly, "The least we could've done was wait for dinner. I'm starved out."

"Keep running with fast company like that Long L bunch, and you'll miss a lot of meals," Dolph retorted.

Tommy's face flashed in anger. "When're you ever going to stop treating me like I was a kid?"

"When you stop acting like one. Now shut up and let's ride."

According to the engraved gold watch the express company had given Dolph years ago, it was a little after two o'clock when they rode into town, the strained silence heavy between them. They moved down the street toward the hotel, their horses working along at a walk, their heads hanging a little.

"Hungry?" Dolph asked.

Tommy glared at him. "Drag me ten miles across country right at noontime and ask me if I'm hungry. Sure, I'm hungry."

They left their horses at Lew Matlock's big livery barn and walked back to the hotel, the Ranchers House. Tommy hung half a pace behind his brother. They went through the little lobby to the back porch, washed their faces in the washpan there, and dried on the same damp towel. The dining room was empty, for the other customers had long since eaten and gone on.

Dolph looked around for Lila Chasteen but didn't see her. An older woman came out of the kitchen to wait on them.

"Sorry we're so late, Mrs. O'Toole," Dolph said. "Got too far from home."

"That's all right," she said pleasantly. "We still have some good roast. I declare, in this hot weather it seems like we always cook too much."

Dolph shifted around uneasily in his chair before

he finally asked the question that was nagging him. "Where's Lila?"

Mrs. O'Toole looked down uncertainly. "She's not here, Dolph. Fact of the matter is, she quit. This noon. Pretty upset. If you ask me, it was something Rance Ostrander said to her. But she wouldn't tell me. Just said she had to leave."

Dolph stared at the clean tablecloth, his hands unsteady. He had been hungry a moment ago. Now he wasn't. He stood up and put aside the big napkin he had spread out across his lap.

"I believe I'll just let that roast go for now," he said. "Maybe I'll be in later."

Tommy's eyes were on his. He was anticipating a fight. "Want me to go with you?"

Shaking his head, Dolph paused at the door. "You just stay and eat your dinner."

The sun bearing down on him, he walked briskly down the street, dust rising with his quick stride. In front of Lila Chasteen's little frame house he turned in and stepped up onto the small porch. The front door was open. He knocked hurriedly, then walked in.

Lila looked up in surprise. She was packing clothes into a heavy trunk. Dolph glanced about the room. He saw that it was nearly bare of the things that had made the place her own.

"Lila," he said. His voice, forced to quietness, carried with it surprise and deep disappointment.

Her blue eyes were upon his face, filled with hurt. "Dolph," she said huskily, "I know what I'm doing. Don't try to talk me out of it, please."

He stood where he had halted, just inside the door. His face was pinched and drawn.

"You can't leave, Lila. Forget whatever it was they said to you. Please stay here, for me."

Her eyes lowered, and he saw a tear break along her cheek. "I can't. That's why I'm going, Dolph— for you."

He stepped forward then, just one step, and stopped again. "Lila, you said once you wouldn't let them crowd you out of town. You stood up stubborn and proud and said you'd stay till you got good and ready to go."

Her voice was tight. "But then it was only *me*, Dolph. Now they're using me as a means to hurt you. Can't you see? I can't stay and let them do this to you."

Dolph stepped forward again, this time right up to her. He gripped her shoulders and pulled her tightly against him. "Don't do it, Lila. There's nothing they can do to me or say about me that would hurt me half as much as losing you."

A quick sob broke from her. Her hands closed about his arms, and she held him tightly.

"Dolph, Dolph," she cried helplessly, "what's to become of us?"

A long moment he held her there, his throat tight and painful. He could think of no answer. He knew that with Lila he felt a sense of fulfillment, a feeling that there was something in life for him besides hard work and heartache and the solid, deadly weight of the gun that rode always upon his hip.

It was Lila who broke the silence. Her soft voice was strained to the point of breaking. "You know it's hopeless for us, don't you, Dolph? I'm a married woman. That I'm married to an outlaw, a man I no longer love, doesn't alter the fact. I'm still a married woman."

He said, "We could go away together. Any judge in the country would set you free."

She shook her head. "No, Dolph. You know how people would feel about divorce. They wouldn't accept it. Neither would I. Besides, they need you here, Dolph. As much as you may hate that gun you carry, they need it. So we have to be strong, Dolph. We have to make ourselves forget. You've got to pretend you never met me, that all this never happened."

Dolph's face was suddenly old. "It would be a lie, Lila. I did meet you, and everything changed. Nothing will ever be the same as it was, even if you leave now and I never see you again."

He turned half around, his head down, his misty gaze on the floor. "Please stay a while longer, Lila. I've got some hard times ahead of me now. Without you, I'd just as well give up at the start."

Their eyes met. "Please stay a while longer, Lila," he pleaded again. "I need you."

She melted into his arms and he had his answer.

Outside Lila's house, Dolph paused in thought, but only for a moment. His fists drew up, and he moved on grimly with long determined strides. He didn't slow up until he had walked through the open door of Hoggy Truscott's saloon.

His eyes raked the smelly room, then pounced on Truscott. "I'm looking for Rance Ostrander. Where's he at?"

Hoggy Truscott's little eyes widened in alarm. "Ain't seen him since dinner. He might be in any one of a dozen places."

Dolph's voice coiled back like a whiplash. "Don't tell me where he might be. Tell me where he's at."

A genuine alarm gripped Truscott's round face. "Don't go jumping on *me,* Dolph. If I was looking for him, I'd go to his room. He most generally takes a nap during the heat of the day—like now."

Rance Ostrander kept a room in an unkempt rooming house a little way down the street. He had a door opening to the outside so he could come and go quietly, without waking up the crotchety old man who ran the place.

Dolph found Rance's door ajar just enough to let in the air without letting in any stray dogs. He shoved it open. It dragged across the sandy, warped floor with a grating noise that made Rance Ostrander sit bolt upright on his cot. He blinked the sleepiness from his wide-open eyes. One long stride brought Dolph up against the cot. He grabbed Rance's collar and jerked the man upward.

"If you say a word to me, I'll knock you through that wall," Dolph breathed, his voice even and sharp as a skinning knife. "You just sit there and listen.

"I don't know what it was you said to Lila Chasteen. You better hope to God I don't ever find out. But let me tell you this, Rance Ostrander. If you ever bother her again—if you ever say another word to her—I'll find you wherever you are and beat you to death!"

With a rushing surge of anger he shoved Ostrander back so hard that the man's head bumped sharply against the wall. Ostrander's mouth hung open, and his lips were quivering. But sleepiness and sudden surprise had tied his tongue.

He huddled back against the wall and watched

with frightened, blurry eyes as Dolph stomped out and moved on up the street.

No one found any trace of Clayton Chasteen and his bunch. Small searching parties trailed west and southwest, cutting for sign in the rough brush country where a man could hide unseen in a clump of brush and shoot a rider at six paces. It was a fruitless search.

Dolph even enlisted the brief aid of a Texas Ranger who had been on another mission and was returning to headquarters. The Ranger, with a couple of cowboys from John Lane's ranch, never turned up a trace.

As always, Tommy Noble needled Dolph to let him go out with a posse. And as always, Dolph ruled him down. So Tommy rode out anyway and joined the Ranger and his two cowboy helpers.

Dolph was waiting when Tommy got back. Tommy stood at stiff attention while Dolph hotly unloaded the anger that had built up in him through these anxious days. An angry tremble in him, the boy said nothing. When Dolph was through, Tommy turned away, leading his horse toward Lew Matlock's stable.

By dark, Dolph knew there was no longer any doubt about it. Tommy had left. His clothes were gone, and he had taken both his good horses.

His conscience heavy, Dolph went to the Lane home and called for Susan. Her brown eyes still showed the sign of her crying.

"He wouldn't tell me anything," the girl said in a breaking voice. "He just said he was leaving. He asked me to wait. That's all, Dolph. He didn't say another word."

Dolph lowered his head. He felt only a foot tall.

"Don't blame him, Susan. Blame me. It was my fault. I've had so much to worry me, I rode him a little too hard. Maybe I ought to've stopped trying to force him into something he didn't want. Maybe if I'd let him alone, he'd have found himself by this time. As it is, he's still got it all ahead of him."

A few mornings later, Lila Chasteen didn't show up for work at the hotel dining room.

"Maybe you better go over and see what's the matter, Dolph," Mrs. O'Toole said, her brow knitted in worry. "She hasn't been feeling too good lately. She's fretted too much."

There was no answer to Dolph's insistent knocking on Lila's front door, nor to his calling her name. He walked in, and his heart sank.

There had been a struggle, that much was clear. A chair was turned over, and the framed picture of Lila's mother and father hung at a crazy angle on the wall. A bureau drawer was open, and clothing hung out over its edge as if someone had grabbed quickly for a few items and had left the rest where it fell.

Two long strides carried Dolph into the kitchen. The rear door hung ajar over the small back porch. The soft ground was marred by the tracks of milling horses.

Dolph stood numb, his gaze fastened on the horizon, which stood razor sharp in the morning air. A tormenting fear drained him of strength. Whoever had taken her, she hadn't gone of her own will.

Someone called his name. He turned jerkily, like a man caught up in a terrible dream. It was the kid who swamped out the livery stable for Lew Matlock.

"Dolph," the boy shouted breathlessly, "Lew say

you better come running. It's about Clayton Chasteen."

Trotting heavily, Dolph followed the youngster back to the barn. His heart was hammering against his ribs when he stopped in front of the big door. Lew Matlock's face was red with excitement.

"Dolph," Matlock said quickly, "Brant Lawton just rode in. He seen Clayton Chasteen and his bunch."

Lawton stepped out into the early morning sun. "That's right, Dolph. They came by my place about daylight. Five of them. And they had Chasteen's wife with them."

Dolph froze.

Lawton continued, "It was easy to tell she wasn't with them because she wanted to be. I seen Chasteen draw back and slap her once. They took fresh horses and rode on. They was headed west."

Desperation had hold of Dolph. But there was still room for a cagey distrust. "Why did you come in and report this, Brant? You've always been one to keep your mouth shut."

Lawton shrugged. "I changed my mind. Maybe it was what he was doing to the woman. Anyhow, I've told you. The rest is up to you."

Dolph whirled into action. "Max," he said to the boy, "you go round up my posse for me. Hurry. You know them. Andy Biederman, George Castleberry, and the rest. Tell them to get here as quick as they can."

He turned on his bootheel. "Lew, you get some horses caught up. I'll try to find a few more boys around here to go along."

He peered intently at Brant Lawton. "You coming, Brant?"

Lawton shook his head. "I've done my part already,

Dolph. Clayton's been my friend in the past. I won't help you run him down."

Dolph made a quick *vuelta* through the business end of Twin Wells and picked up a couple of stray cowboys to go along. In about twenty minutes his posse was saddled up and ready to ride, seven men strong.

Chasteen's tracks were as plain as if they had been left on purpose. But there was no need to follow them the first ten miles to Lawton's Long L. In a stiff trot the posse broke out over the rough divide and slanted down the head of a long draw, the curing brown grass yielding its settled dust.

Dolph swung down at a surface tank which Lawton had gouged in the edge of a draw to catch runoff from the rains and hold it for livestock water. He loosened his cinch and let his horse have its fill of water. Sweat speckled the dun's hide, but the day hadn't reached its peak of heat, and the horse didn't drink much.

Other possemen were afoot, watering their mounts the same way. Andy Biederman handed his reins to a younger puncher and hobbled stiffly around to another side of the tank, where mud had not been stirred up by restless hoofs. He pitched his hat to one side, flopped on his belly, and drank long and deeply of the brownish water.

"A little thick," he said at last, wiping his gray sprinkled mustache with his sleeve, "but it's wet."

A couple of the younger cowboys grinned sheepishly and followed his example. But it didn't take them long to get their fill.

Another time Dolph would have gotten a kick out

of it. But there was no humor in him now. His mind dwelt on Lila.

"Hurry up," he said impatiently. "Let's get a move on."

They circled the ranch house. Dolph briefly considered stopping and getting some fresh horses. But he saw none near, and it probably would take an hour to catch some. Their own horses hadn't been far enough to tire them much, he decided. They would go on.

George Castleberry was Dolph's tracker. But the youngest puncher in the bunch could have followed the trail Chasteen and his men left as they rode west from the Long L corrals. With the tracks so plain, it was all Dolph could do to keep from swinging into a lope to make time while the trailing was so easy. But when one of the young men suggested they do just that, Andy Biederman voiced the thought that had held Dolph back.

"A man on a wore-out horse had just as well be afoot."

Dolph swung into a stiff trot and held it for long stretches at a time. The pace had slowed considerably, however, by the time the men pulled up again at a creek which wound a crooked course in a generally southern direction. It was a spring-fed creek that was usually dry. But heavy rains a month before had pepped up the spring, and the flow had not yet quit.

The jolting of the heavy trot had beaten a stiff weariness into the men. They were glad to ease down to the ground for a few moments while their horses watered. Every man walked a few paces upstream and took a long fill of the clean water—every man but Dolph Noble. The impatience still dogged him.

He was hardly aware of the dryness of his mouth. He scooped up some water in the crown of his hat, gulped it down a little, and pulled the hat back on.

"Let's go," he said.

It had been many hours since the Chasteen horses had climbed out of the creek on the opposite bank and moved on west toward the rough country. The heat of the sun had dried the tracks cut deep into the creekbank.

Dolph noted that the Chasteen bunch seemed to be riding closer together since leaving the creek. He wondered at it, and decided they might have begun to fear pursuit, and were staying near one another. He pushed on harder, hoping the posse was making more time than had Chasteen.

Once George Castleberry pulled in close beside him. Like many men hard of hearing, he talked loudly. "Something funny about these tracks, Dolph. You see the night-crawler tracks in them? Lawton said Chasteen went by his place about daylight. But these tracks was made a heap sight earlier than that."

A nagging worry began to trouble Dolph. "Chances are Lawton was lying, George. The tracks have to be Chasteen's. We've been following them off and on ever since we left town. Chasteen probably went by the Long L in the middle of the night. Lawton lied so we wouldn't know how much head start Chasteen really had."

There wasn't much doubt in his mind that Lawton was still in sympathy with the outlaws. But maybe Dolph had scared him. He'd waited until he was sure Chasteen could get away. Then he had given the alarm to clear himself.

❖

The sun reached its fiery peak and began to slant down toward the west. The long ride had sapped the vitality from the posse's horses, and the men were beginning to sag a little. But in the lead Dolph Noble still sat his saddle straight as a gun barrel, his gaze always reaching to the skyline ahead. If his horse faltered or slowed, Dolph gently touched him with his spurs and picked him up again. The other riders gradually slowed down until at last they were a long file strung out behind the sheriff.

A hot breeze lifted from the west. As Dolph topped out over a rise and began on the downward slope, his horse lifted its head. The short ears poked forward. The horse slowed to a walk, and, before Dolph could stop him, it nickered.

An answering nicker came on the wind that touched Dolph's face with summer warmth. Dolph's nerves tingled, and he stood up in the stirrups, his eyes eagerly searching the brushy terrain ahead. He held up his hand, and the other possemen reined in beside him.

"Horses ahead yonder," he said. "It's probably Chasteen. Too late for us to slip in there without being seen. Spread out and go into that brush with your guns in your hands. Keep your eyes peeled. We don't want any of us getting shot."

Fanned out in a thin skirmish line, the posse moved into the brush in a slow walk. Tenseness was stretched through the men like a taut spring. Dolph's lips parted, and he became conscious of his own broken, fearful breathing.

He saw them as he broke out into a grassy clearing. At the same time he heard George Castleberry explode:

"Dolph, it's only loose horses."

For a moment he thought these were just strays, that Chasteen had merely passed them and gone on. But then the dread realization began to soak in. It was *these* horses they had been trailing. There was no other answer. There was only one trail leading out of here, a single horse headed on to the west.

Andy Biederman brought up the clincher. His face twisted in rage, he came riding up with a tangled mess of ropes on his saddle horn.

"Look what I found in that brush yonder. We been tricked, Dolph. These horses was haltered and led here on a rope by one man. He turned them loose here and skedaddled on by himself."

Desperation was a drum beating at Dolph's temples. "But we've been trailing the same bunch ever since we left town," he protested futilely. "There's no place they could have switched on us. No place but—the creek!"

It hit him then like a sackful of rocks. It *was* the creek. Chasteen had had a man waiting there with the horses haltered and tied on a rope. Chasteen and his men had ridden into the creek, and the other horses had been led out on the opposite side to continue the trail. Then Chasteen and those with him had ridden down the middle of the creek where they would leave no sign, until they had gotten far enough that Chasteen thought they could safely climb out.

Futile anger fired up in Dolph. It was too late now to do anything about it. There was nothing to do but go back. Maybe, with fresh horses, they could pick up the trail again. But chances were they wouldn't. Chasteen would cover up his trail and lose them somewhere, like he always did.

"Catch up those loose horses," Dolph ordered grimly. "Whoever's got the tiredest horses had better change. We can halter them and bring them on behind us."

While the change was being made, Andy Biederman reined up beside Dolph. "Don't take it so hard, Dolph. It ain't your fault. Chasteen was just too slick. Why, he even took in old George Castleberry."

He frowned then and changed the subject. "Guess you noticed what brand them loose horses was carrying."

Dolph nodded. "A Long L."

Biederman's mustache bristled. "Just something to remember, the first time we get a chance to do anything about it."

Still four miles from town, they saw riders coming toward them. The sun, almost at the horizon line, splashed a reddish cast across the rolling land and the men who approached them.

The oncoming riders spurred into a lope and didn't rein up until they were almost upon the posse. A length in the lead was a little dried-up man who operated a greasy eating place a little down from Hoggy Truscott's saloon. Many of Hoggy's customers were also his customers.

"From the looks of you, you didn't see anything of Clayton Chasteen," the man said, chips of malice in his voice.

Wariness in him, Dolph shook his head.

The cafe man grinned without humor. "We didn't think you would. You ain't heard the news yet, have you, Sheriff?"

Dolph's eyes narrowed. "I don't know what news you mean."

A smug triumph rose in the rider's hatchet face.

"While you was off chasing shadows, Clayton Chasteen rode in this morning and robbed the bank."

Dolph gripped the saddle horn and looked at the possemen behind him. His face drained white. A wordless oath escaped from him. He looked down at the ground a long moment.

"Baited," he spoke bleakly. "And we grabbed the hook like a catfish . . ."

Excitement still boiled in the town. Quick to seize an opportunity which might make him look good, Rance Ostrander had taken over the organization and operation of hasty, ill-prepared posses. Now, with darkness drawing down, small parties of searching men were drifting in, discouraged and angry, ready to fasten the blame on anybody who was handy to take it.

Angriest man was Phineas Towbridge, president of the bank.

"It's a lawman's solemn duty to be around to protect the people who pay the taxes and keep him in office," Towbridge stormed at Dolph Noble. "But did you do that? No, you were off on a wild-goose chase heaven knows where, while here at home we were all at the mercy of a vicious band of outlaws!"

Dolph listened in studied patience, his face warm. He couldn't really blame Towbridge.

"We thought we were after Chasteen," Dolph explained evenly. "We were fooled, and I'll take full responsibility for it."

Towbridge's face flared a violent red. "You'll never get a chance to make any more mistakes around here, Noble, if you don't catch Chasteen in a hurry. You'll be out hunting for a job."

John Lane stood by silently, his round face sympathetic but grave as he listened to Towbridge taking out his anger on Dolph. When the banker stalked away, Lane stepped up and put his hand on Dolph's arm.

"Let's go where we can talk a little, Dolph."

In a back office of the bank, John Lane told how Chasteen and four men had suddenly appeared on horseback in front of the building about ten o'clock in the morning and had swept through the door before anyone had a chance to move.

"They were all masked, but you could tell Chasteen anywhere by his voice and the way he carries himself. Funny thing, Dolph, they didn't take any gold or other coin. They just took paper money. Didn't want to carry the extra weight, I reckon."

Dolph frowned. "Paper money? You got the serial numbers?"

Lane nodded. "Yes, we had them listed on all except a few small bills. First thing we did was to send them out by wire. Every bank in the country will have a list of them before Chasteen has a chance to use the money. Most of what he got was big bills, too. He'd have to take them to a bank to break them." A grim confidence gleamed in Lane's eyes. "He's stuck with them, Dolph. He's got a bagful of money he'll never be able to use."

Dolph still frowned. "But Chasteen's no fool. He's bound to've known that's what would happen."

John Lane cut a sidewise glance at Dolph. "You mean he might've figured a way to get around it?"

Dolph beat his open palm with his right fist. "I don't see how he could. But I'd be willing to bet that he at least thought he did." Then eagerly, he leaned toward Lane. "John, was there—was there any sign of Lila?"

Lane nodded. "Lila's all right. On his way back

to town after he threw you off the trail, Chasteen dropped her off afoot on the Rafter T ranch. It was three miles, but she ran all the way to the house to give the alarm. She was almost dead with exhaustion when she got there. But she was too late. By the time anybody could get in from the ranch, Chasteen had already pulled the robbery and was gone."

Dolph was standing, his heart tripping. "John, where is she?"

"She's over at our house, Dolph. Wife thought we ought to keep her there. People are still pretty mad, and . . . you know how it is."

Dolph turned quickly and started for the door. Lane called him back.

"Dolph, before you go, there's a couple of other things you ought to know."

He pointed his chin toward Towbridge's desk. "There'll be some Rangers here on the morning train. Phineas sent for them. He's lost confidence in you. And one other thing. I'd rather cut my tongue out than to have to tell you. I haven't said a word about it to anybody else.

"I was in here when Chasteen came. I backed up against the wall like everybody else. I saw one of the robbers bend over to pick up a handful of bills, and I caught a glimpse of his face as his handkerchief dropped away from it. Dolph, it was that Herndon boy, the one Tommy has been palling around with ever since they were both in knee pants."

Dolph leaned back against a desk, his knees weak beneath him. He could guess what was coming.

"There was another robber I noticed, Dolph. I didn't see his face, and I didn't hear him speak. But he was just about Tommy's size."

John Lane balled his fists. His voice was drawn tight. "I could be wrong. I hope I am. But you know it's been about a week since we've seen Pete Herndon around here. And it's been just about as long since Tommy left."

Dolph closed his eyes, and he let his head ease weakly into his hands. For a long time he sat there, helpless, a knot in his throat. A thousand things ran through his mind at once—old memories of Tommy as a parentless kid running wild and loose because his big brother didn't have the time to take care of him. A hundred things he should have done and should have said—but hadn't. A wonderful girl named Susan Lane, who wanted Tommy more than anything else in the world and had lost him now because Dolph had driven the boy away.

"If it's true, John," Dolph said tightly, "it's my fault. It's not him that needs to take the punishment. It's me."

Dolph walked down the street like a drunken man, his eyes fastened hazily on the Lane house far ahead, his feet dragging lightly through the sand. He was barely conscious of the people who watched him. He vaguely heard someone call him a name, and it meant nothing to him.

He found himself on the front porch. Susan Lane was standing in the doorway, waiting for him.

"Lila's in here, Dolph," she said quietly.

Dolph stopped and stared at the young girl. "Susan . . ." he began, then broke it off short. He wanted to beg her forgiveness. But she didn't know yet. And he couldn't tell her.

The sight of Lila seated in a rocking chair broke him out of the daze. Her face was drawn, and she was trembling with the emotion she had held pent up within her. He knew that a weaker woman would have broken long before.

"Dolph," she spoke almost in a whisper. She arose shakily and stood there. He took a quick step toward her and bound her tightly in his arms. For a long time they stood that way, drawing strength from one another.

Dolph ached to ask her about Tommy, to find out if he really had been with Chasteen. But he was afraid to. He couldn't ask her, and he knew she wouldn't tell him.

He stepped back for a look at her. His fists tightened as he saw the faint blue color high on her cheek.

"What else did he do to you?" Dolph demanded.

Her stricken eyes were upon his just for a second, then fell. She was trembling. Color rose in her face.

"The law says he's still my husband, Dolph, and I'm still his wife."

Dolph's blood was ice. The fury mounted in him, a blind fury that quickly burned all else. There were two scores now.

His voice was like honed steel. "I don't think I could have killed him before, even if I had to. But I'm going to kill him now. I'm going to hunt him out and kill him like a wolf."

Weariness settled an almost unbearable weight upon him, but he could not sleep. He lay facedown on his cot, fully clothed, staring into the darkness while his mind roiled in torment. Sometime past midnight he managed to drop into fitful sleep. But he was up again, staring across a steaming coffeepot, before the first light of dawn broke in the east.

He walked down to the livery barn and saddled his horse. By daylight he was out alone, trying to pick up sign that would help lead him to Clayton Chasteen. But it was hopeless. Ostrander's irresponsible searching parties had tracked up the area so badly the day before that he couldn't have trailed a whole wagon train. Dolph muttered to himself about Ostrander and reined around toward town again.

The train arrived at nine-thirty. Dolph was back in time to meet it. The first man who stepped off was a pudgy, middle-aged man with an indoor pallor. The man's eyes fell upon Dolph and dropped to the badge on Dolph's shirt. Dolph thought he caught quick fright in the pale face, but decided he had been wrong. He lost interest in the stranger and turned away from him as the man took a fresh hold on the big leather grip he carried and hurried off.

Another man stepped off the train then and took all Dolph's attention. He was medium tall, with a trimmed black mustache, a broad-brimmed hat, and trousers tucked into high-topped boots. For a second a badge on his vest caught the flash of the sun. He glanced around him briefly. He saw Dolph and walked toward him.

"Sheriff Noble, I believe," he said pleasantly, extending his hand. He had a viselike grip. "I'm Captain Jim Barnhart, Texas Rangers."

"Dolph Noble. You come by yourself, Captain?"

Barnhart jerked a thumb back over his shoulder. "No, there's another man with me, a Ranger recruit. He's back yonder getting our horses from the baggage car."

Worriedly Dolph said, "I hope this won't turn out to be a wild-goose chase for you, Captain Barnhart.

I've had plenty of them lately. There's not much to go on."

A shadow of a smile crossed the Ranger's lips. His gaze moved down the street, where the man with the grip was entering Lew Matlock's livery barn.

"Maybe I've brought an ace or two with me, Sheriff. Did you see the man who got off the train just before I did?"

Dolph glanced quickly toward Matlock's. "Why yes, I saw him."

"His name is Danforth. He's a lawyer. And you know what he's got in that grip?"

Dolph shook his head. The Ranger said, "Well, I don't know for sure, but I'd bet a hundred dollars to a Mexican peso that it's full of greenbacks." The Ranger leaned against the station wall and rolled a cigarette. "You see, he's a dealer in stolen goods. We've known it a long time, but knowing and proving are two different things. He represents a rich old crook in San Antonio. He buys stolen goods at half what they're worth, keeps them till people have stopped looking for them, then sells them at a big profit."

Dolph's heartbeat quickened. "Now I see what you're driving at. He'll go to Clayton Chasteen and buy that stolen bank money from him, giving Chasteen money he can spend without having to worry."

The Ranger nodded. "That's right. He'll give him about fifty cents on the dollar. He'll lay the money away two or three years till the serial number lists have all been thrown away or forgotten. Then he can bring it out."

Dolph whistled softly. "How'd you get onto him this time?"

"Just luck. We happened to get on the same train

with him. I spotted him and asked the conductor where he was bound for. He told me this place, and I put two and two together." The Ranger looked past Dolph. "Here comes the recruit with our horses."

Dolph turned. His jaw sagged and he clutched a station post. "Tommy!"

Tommy Noble came up in his cocky, bowlegged walk, a grin plastered across his face. There was a high polish on the Ranger badge pinned proudly to his shirt.

"Howdy, Dolph. Hope you're not mad at me anymore."

"Mad at you?" Dolph swallowed, his heart thumping happily. A blessed relief flooded over him. "I thought . . . I thought . . . Well, never mind what I thought. When did you join up?"

"Right after I left here. I went straight to Austin. I was assigned to Captain Barnhart's company. Yesterday we got word of the robbery. The captain figured I was the best one to come with him, because I knew the country."

Dolph sat down weakly on the bench in front of the station. He began to laugh. It was a loud, half-crazy laugh, the draining of the dreadful anxiety that had swelled and grown within him until he had thought it would break him apart. The Ranger captain and Tommy watched him wonderingly, until at last the laughter was gone from him, and Dolph was silent again.

Still watching Dolph quizzically, the captain said, "Just to cinch the thing, we ought to go check with the stationmaster and find out if anybody sent Danforth a wire yesterday. He had to get word of it some way."

The stationmaster pushed up the shade which covered his eyes. "Danforth? Danforth? Seems to me I remember that name. Just a minute."

He riffled through a stack of papers, then pulled one out. "Here it is. I remember now. Brant Lawton came in and sent it. It was about half an hour after the robbery. I know, because I just had got it sent when John Lane got over here with the serial numbers of those bills."

Dolph glanced at the message, then handed it to the captain.

It read: "Have horses ready for your selection. Better bunch than anticipated. Lawton."

The Ranger looked directly at Dolph. He didn't have to speak, for his eyes said all there was to say.

The three lawmen eased down to the sheriff's office and waited inside, watching Lew Matlock's livery through the streaked window. Tommy was silent for a long time, nervously toying with a cartridge in his gunbelt. Presently he spoke.

"Dolph, I hope you're not disappointed about this—about me joining the Rangers, I mean."

Dolph looked at him and smiled a little. "I won't say that I'm in favor of it, Tommy. But I'm through telling you what to do. If this is what you want, I'm not going to stand in your way."

Confidence came into the boy's voice. "Thanks, Dolph. I'm glad you see it like that."

The Ranger captain pointed toward the window. "There he comes. He's got him a buckboard."

Dolph watched while the stranger paid Matlock. The livery man was pointing in a westerly direction. Then the man climbed into the buckboard and headed out in the direction Matlock had shown him.

As soon as Danforth had gotten a safe distance

away, Dolph rushed down the street to Matlock's, Tommy and Barnhart behind him.

"That man who rented the buckboard, Lew," Dolph said quickly. "Where was he going?"

Matlock pushed back his greasy hat and wiped the sweat from his forehead. "He said he was a horse buyer, and he asked me how to get out to Brant Lawton's place." The old man's eyes fell upon Tommy, and upon Tommy's badge. "Tommy," he exploded with a broad grin. "You, a Ranger? Well now, if that don't beat all. When did you—"

Dolph broke in. "We haven't got time to explain it right now, Lew. Tell you all about it when we get back in."

In the corral Dolph flicked a big loop into a milling bunch of horses and hauled out a sorrel he liked to ride.

Captain Barnhart watched him seriously. "We're sure liable to need a full posse," he said, "if we get in any kind of tight at all. But we can't afford to take one. It'll be hard enough for just the three of us to follow Danforth to Chasteen's camp without being spotted."

Dolph nodded gravely. "You're right. A full posse couldn't slip up on them. But three of us might. We'll just have to take our chances without any help."

Tommy was studiously rubbing his jaw. "Look," he frowned, "maybe it's not my place to be making suggestions, but it seems to me we *could* have a posse. We could have it give us a long head start, then trail us. It wouldn't be any trouble at all for us to leave a trail old George Castleberry could follow. Why, George can track a cat over bare rock."

Dolph began to grin slowly, remembering what Tommy had said about George Castleberry and Andy Biederman not many days before.

Tommy went on enthusiastically, "We could get George and Andy Biederman and a few more of those old boys to trail after us. Then if we got into a jackpot over our heads, we could at least hold the fort till they got there."

A pride began to glow in Dolph. "Tommy, I hate to say it, but it looks like you've got the makings of a lawman."

It didn't take Dolph long to find the men he wanted and quietly spread the word. "You all just slip out in about three hours, one at a time, and meet George where the Long L trail forks off," he told Andy. "Be prepared to stay out a couple of days. We're bringing in Chasteen's bunch this time, or Twin Wells is fixing to get a new sheriff."

There was no real need in trailing Danforth to the Long L, Dolph knew. He was bound to go there any way. The important thing was to watch where he went after he left the Long L.

Under a furnace-like sun, the sheriff and the two Rangers rode south of the wagon trail that Danforth followed to Lawton's ranch. There was always the possibility that Lawton might send somebody back to be sure Danforth wasn't being trailed. The three men rode in silence across the brushy flatland and into the broken, brush-studded hills east of the Long L. They stayed within the protection of the brush as much as they could, their eyes warily scanning the terrain around them.

A tall, rocky hill topped by scrub cedar gave a good view of the Lawton headquarters. The three riders climbed to the top of it. Dolph reached int his saddlebags and took out an old folding spyglass that he had bought somewhere a long time ago. The captain looked at it and grinned.

"Pity I didn't think of that."

Dolph settled on his belly on the sun-baked ground and trained the spyglass upon the ranch headquarters. He could see Danforth's rented buckboard standing near the main building. Out in a corral someone was saddling a horse. Dolph blinked his eye and rubbed it, trying to see a little better. When a man finally mounted and rode out the open gate, Dolph recognized Brant Lawton by the way he sat his saddle.

Lawton pointed east, along the wagon road to town, and said something to one of his men standing nearby. Then he pulled the horse around and headed southeast in an easy trot. Danforth followed him in the buckboard.

The cowhand to whom Lawton had spoken rode eastward. Checking to be sure no one had been trailing Danforth, Dolph knew.

Dolph watched until he knew for certain the course Danforth and Lawton were taking. Then he stiffly climbed to his feet and headed back for his horse.

"We'll skirt along the south side of this range of hills," he said. "They'll be going out through a gap down yonder. We can trail them on from there." He indicated with a wave of his hand.

They were safely hidden in a long, brushy draw when the buckboard and the horseman emerged through the gap five hundred yards away.

Dolph's biggest fear was that Lawton's horse or the buckboard team might scent the lawmen's horses and

nicker. But luckily the wind was out of the west. As
long as it remained that way, there was little chance
the other horses would catch their scent.

"All my life I've cussed the west wind because it
never did anything but blow the rain away," Dolph
commented. "But this time I hope it holds up."

The terrain ahead of them became rockier and
rougher as they worked along. Worriedly Dolph
paused and looked back at the shallow tracks the
horses were leaving, when they left any tracks at all.

"George would have to be part Indian to follow
us if this gets much worse."

Tommy said confidently, "Don't you worry.
George'll make it."

Occasionally, when the ground got too hard, Dolph
would purposefully have Tommy ride around the
long way, seeking out softer ground which would
leave a good track. They broke down branches of
bushes and laid them on the ground to point their
course.

Only once in a while did they actually have to pick
up the tracks of the buckboard. Most of the time
when he was in doubt that they were heading in the
right direction, Dolph could climb up on a point
afoot and search out the two men with his spyglass.

Even rougher country lay ahead. Dolph wondered
how the buckboard would ever make it. But Bran
Lawton seemed to know where to find the easiest going. Sometimes he had to skirt far around a line of
hills or through a water-carved canyon. But he always unerringly found the way.

Once the buckboard got jammed up in a pile of
rocks. Through the glass Dolph watched Lawton tie
on with a rope and with his horse help the buckboard team pull out.

Tommy was puzzled. "Why the dickens did they bring along a buckboard, anyway? Easiest thing for them to do would've been to take a packhorse and ride."

Captain Barnhart grinned. "Didn't you see the soft padding in the seat of the lawyer's pants? That's why they didn't take horses. I'll bet he's even got him a pillow in that buckboard seat."

With the sun sinking low, the lawmen found themselves in a broken country where tall sotol stalks stood starkly against the ragged skyline like a thousand Comanche lances, and the thick-trunked dagger plants in the distance took on the grim look of waiting men. There were a hundred places where a man, a horse, even a wagon could drop out of sight and remain hidden from searching eyes.

A prescient tingle began working up the back of Dolph's neck. He glanced at the two men flanking him and saw in their tense faces that they felt it too. They could see no more than they had seen all day. Yet somehow they knew they didn't have much farther to go. It was in the vague tension that lay over the silent land like the shimmering heat waves that were fading with the setting sun.

"Can't be much further," grunted Captain Barnhart. "They haven't got any camp gear in that buckboard. So they're expecting to get where they're going by dark."

Dusk settled quickly after the sun disappeared behind the hills.

Tommy's horse struck a stone with a hind foot and sent it clattering down a slope. Dolph whirled in the saddle, needles driving into him.

"Easy. Take it easy. Sound carries a far piece at this time of day."

He drew up and listened. Straining, he could hear the grating of the iron buckboard rims on rock far ahead. He looked at the captain. The Ranger nodded and they moved on. But they were moving more slowly now, stopping every few hundred yards to listen. Each time they could still hear the rattle of the tires.

Then there came a time when they couldn't. Darkness had dropped down upon them. The moon rising yonder was only a dull sliver that would provide little light.

Dolph eased forward to listen, leaving his horse behind. He came back shaking his head. "Tommy," he whispered, "you go listen. You ought to have better ears than either one of us."

In a moment Tommy was back. Excitement tingled in his voice. "I don't hear anything. I'd bet they got to where they were going."

Captain Barnhart said, "Then we'd better go on afoot. We can lead the horses. Less noise that way."

They started on afoot. Dolph became conscious of a faint tinkling of his spurs. He stopped long enough to shove a twig into the shank of each spur, to bind the rowel. Tommy watched him and did the same. Captain Barnhart had taken off his spurs when he had dismounted, and had hung them over the saddle horn.

The lawmen worked ahead slowly, carefully testing each forward step for treacherous rocks that might roll and slide and send their sudden clatter hammering through the night. Every so often there was a quick strike of boot or hoof against rock, and rock against rock. Dolph's hands broke with cold sweat.

"No use," he said softly. "We've got to leave these horses behind. They'll give us away."

They tied their mounts at the foot of a thorny hill. Dolph looked overhead at the stars which stood out like brilliant diamonds against a pitch-black sky. He picked out the Big Dipper and the North Star, and thought he could find this spot again in the darkness. Then he moved on, Tommy and the Ranger beside him.

A quarter-hour later they painstakingly worked up the stony side of a hill and squatted at the top to look down upon the other side. Dolph's hands burned from sudden biting contact with a thorny bush of some kind.

Below him he saw the reddish glow of a small campfire, apparently built in a hole to keep from showing any more than it had to. The outlaws had picked out a small hollow between hills for their camp. A searching party would have had one chance in a hundred of lucking onto it. Fact of the matter, Dolph was sure one or two must have passed plenty close.

"Three men, maybe four, by that campfire," Captain Barnhart muttered, hunkered low beside Dolph. "The rest are probably close by. It's just too dark to see them."

The buckboard showed dimly when an occasional flame licked upward above the top of the hole. The team had been unhitched.

"We going to jump them now?" Tommy breathed in excitement.

"No," whispered the captain. "No use in having

that bunch on our hands all night. We'll wait till just before daylight. They'll all be asleep. We can slip in and take them then before they know what's up. Till then, we'd just as well flop down here and get us some rest."

Weariness had worn through every fiber of Dolph's body. He stretched out on the rocky ground. In a few minutes he was asleep.

He awoke to the gentle pressure of a hand on his shoulder.

"Sunup pretty soon, Dolph," Tommy whispered in his ear. He glanced around and saw the captain sitting up in the near darkness.

Dolph managed to shake loose the ragged edges of sleep. He glanced at the east and saw color amid the fading stars.

Tommy's eyes were pinched, and his face was drawn. "Didn't you sleep at all?" Dolph queried anxiously.

Tommy shook his head grimly. "No; and I don't see how you all could do it, either, knowing what's coming up."

Dolph glanced at Captain Barnhart and caught a touch of a grin hovering around his trimmed mustache. Dolph's face twisted to the sour taste in his mouth. He pointed with his chin to the bottom of the hill.

"Coffeepot's down there," he said. "Let's go get it."

Tommy touched his arm and pointed back to the left. "I got their horses spotted. They're right down yonder, just around the edge of this hill. They got them on a picket line, like cavalry."

Dolph frowned. "See anybody watching them?"

Tommy shook his head. "No. There might be somebody, but I couldn't see anyone in the dark."

Stealthily they began to work their way down the hill, guns in their hands. Dolph took his time, testing every footing before he put his weight down. The fire had died out, and there was no light from it. The moon had paled leaving only the barest of illumination from the coming dawn to show the men their way.

An old dread began to tighten in Dolph, a dread of the gun he gripped in his sweaty hand. In his mind roared the deadly gunfire of another day. He tried desperately to shut his mind to the awful memory of a wild kid who had died in pain and terror. But the picture was there to stay, burned deep as the stamp of a hot branding iron. He found himself trembling, and not from fear. He glanced at Tommy and wished the boy was not here. This was the thing from which Dolph had tried so hard to shield him.

Then they were at the bottom of the hill. Dolph paused to catch a deep breath and give his thumping heart a chance to settle. He counted the still figures scattered on blankets on the ground. He held up seven fingers for the captain to see. Chasteen and four men had held up the bank. Lawton and Danforth made it seven.

Captain Barnhart nodded in satisfaction. He pointed the muzzle of his gun straight up in the air and squeezed the trigger.

In the instant the shot exploded and sent its sharp echoes rocketing out among the hills, the outlaws started flinging their blankets aside. In the same instant Barnhart's voice bawled with the thunder of a cannon:

"Hands up! Don't any man move!"

Caught by surprise, the outlaws stared, sleepy-eyed, their mouths open in shock. Their muddled minds hadn't fully grasped the situation.

"Now get up," Dolph ordered. "Get over here together, all of you."

Clayton Chasteen stood still and silent, his heavy face sullen. There once had been a careless charm about him, an easy-going attitude that long since had dropped away. A burning intensity had gradually taken its place, an intensity born of a growing greed and an ever-increasing callousness.

Now a three-day growth of beard bristled on his face. His clothes were crumpled from sleeping in them. His eyes dwelt heavily on Dolph, eyes that glowed in hatred.

Dolph's hand tightened on his gun. Hatred burned in him. He felt a momentary compulsion to pull the trigger, to blow Chasteen apart—for Lila's sake, he told himself. For Lila's sake.

But he eased the pressure on the trigger and felt a shudder work through him. No, he couldn't do it. He had sworn to, but now he had the chance, and he couldn't bring himself to do it.

Chasteen's eyes bored at him. "You ought've pulled that trigger, Dolph. Some day you'll wish you had."

Dolph swallowed bitterly. "Go see about those horses, Tommy," he said.

Tommy turned. A second later Dolph heard him shout, "Dolph, look out!"

Dolph whirled, and a rock slipped under his foot. As he fell, he caught a glimpse of a figure in the darkness swinging a gun toward him. Another gun boomed—Tommy's—and the man slumped, his pistol hitting the rocky ground with a clatter.

A ragged groan tore from his throat, and the fallen outlaw cried in agony, "Tommy, Tommy!"

Dolph stiffened at the voice. He heard something like a whimper burst from Tommy. The boy flung his gun aside and went running, tripping, getting up to run again, until he had fallen to his knees beside the man on the ground.

"Pete," Tommy cried. *"Pete!"*

He looked at Dolph then, his chin quivering, his voice starting to break. "Dolph," he sobbed, "I've killed Pete. He was my friend, and I've killed him."

Dolph's throat swelled. An emptiness ached in him. Gently he placed his hand on his kid brother's shoulder. But he knew that right now he couldn't really touch the boy. For this, there was no sympathy deep enough. Dolph knew. He'd been there.

Tommy's thin shoulders heaved as he knelt over the silent body of the boy who had played with him, walked with him, ridden with him since the days of their boyhood. After a long while Tommy looked up, his eyes blurred. "Dolph," he begged, "what'll I ever do?"

Dolph's eyes hardened, and his gaze set atop the stony hill, where cactus stalks stood stately and tall against the swelling light of dawn.

"You'll just have to learn to live with it," he said, "like I did."

With gentleness he pulled the boy up to a stand. "You better go pick up your gun, Tommy, and get those horses like you started to."

Tommy looked toward the gun, and a shudder passed through his body. "I don't want it, Dolph. I don't ever want to touch a gun again."

His voice was like steel.

But Dolph's voice was hard, too. "You've got to, Tommy. We've gone too deep to stop now. Go get your gun."

Shoulders slumped, Tommy walked like a drunken man. He knelt and picked up the gun. He held it a moment as if it were a snake, then dropped it into his holster. He turned mechanically and walked out toward the picket line.

Dolph knew he should be helping Barnhart watch the Chasteen bunch. But he couldn't tear his eyes from the tragic figure of his brother.

He heard the shot and whirled just as Captain Barnhart grabbed at his shoulder and sank to his knees. In a flash Dolph picked the outlaw who had done the shooting and fired at him. The men suddenly were scattering like quail. Dolph realized with a sagging heart that some of them certainly had managed to grab up guns as they fled in confusion. Dolph fired into the fleeing men and heard one yelp in pain. He saw the pudgy Danforth make a grab for his big leather grip. Dolph directed a bullet at him, and the lawyer lit out with empty hands.

"Tommy," Dolph yelled, "get hold of those horses, quick. We can't let Chasteen's bunch get mounted!"

But Tommy was too slow. Dolph's heart sank as he heard the sudden clatter of frightened hoofs. Someone had cut the picket line.

He dropped to his knees beside Barnhart. The Ranger's teeth were gritted in pain. His leathery face had drained from shock. A steady trickle of blood sopped his shirt beneath a bluish wound high in his left shoulder.

"We've got to get out of this hole," Dolph said quickly. "If they get above us and go to shooting we're done."

He didn't know what made him think of the money then. He knew with a dead certainty that Chasteen wouldn't go far without the money. Dolph grabbed up the lawyer's leather grip and spotted two bulging pairs of saddlebags. These he flung over his wide shoulder. Then he helped the wounded Ranger to his feet and supported him as they moved on toward Tommy.

Pride was stiff in Captain Barnhart. "Damn it, do you think I never got shot at before? I can make it."

Tommy grabbed hold and helped Dolph take Barnhart up the hill. The boy's face was set in pain, his eyes empty.

On top of the hill Dolph paused to look around him in quick desperation. A bullet searched for him from below. On another side he caught a quick flash of a blue shirt. The outlaws were moving to surround them. For a moment Dolph considered trying to get to the horses they had left tied the night before, but he knew they couldn't make it with the wounded Barnhart.

Another bullet searched for him, and a third. He realized grimly that they were trapped here atop this hill.

But it was a good place to make a stand, if it came to that. The hilltop was not large, and a rain-cut watercourse on its crest was deep enough to give protection against enemy guns.

Barnhart's eyes were glazed in pain.

"They got away with their horses, didn't they?" he asked weakly as Dolph tore a hole in his shirt. Dolph nodded. The Ranger said, "Then we've lost them."

Dolph shook his head. "I don't think so. We've got the money. They're not apt to leave here without it. We'll just have to hold out till George Castleberry and his bunch get here."

Barnhart's face was a deathly white. "And if Castleberry doesn't find us?"

"He's got to!" Dolph's fists doubled.

Sunrise came, and the sun started its steady climb above the dry, thorny hills. With the expanding heat of a growing new day, Dolph began to realize that he had overlooked one vital point in his haste. That was water.

They could get along without food, for a while. But they couldn't do long without water, especially the wounded Ranger who lay under the lacy shade of a stunted bush, the fever rising in him.

They had left their canteens tied to their saddles, and Dolph knew there was no chance ever of reaching them. But no doubt there was water in the outlaw camp.

His eyes dwelt a long time upon the two men with him—the old, experienced Ranger who lay wounded and helpless, and the young, green kid who had been wounded just as badly in his own way, and who was also near helplessness as he fought a grim, fruitless battle within himself.

Grimly Dolph studied the bags of money. What if he tried to reach the outlaw camp for water, and Chasteen climbed the hill while he was gone? Barnhart couldn't fight. And Dolph felt a strong conviction that Tommy no longer had the will to do it.

But there was little choice between the money and Barnhart's desperate need of water. Dolph quietly told Tommy where he was going. The boy heard but he made no sign. He maintained a glassy stare at nothing, far off in the distance. Worriedly Dolph went on and left him.

It wasn't far down to Chasteen's camp, as distance goes. But it was a long way for a wary man moving in a low crouch, scuttling from protection of one bush to another. In a few minutes Dolph made it. His gaze fell upon a pair of canteens hanging from the buckboard. He eased over and pulled the first one off. It was full. A glad grin touched his face, and he reached for the other.

A bullet whined by his face and ricocheted off the rocky hillside. Dolph jerked backward, leaving the second canteen. He fired once over his shoulder at the unseen gunman and struck out in a run. He felt a bullet rip into the canteen, almost tearing it loose from his grasp. His heart sickened as the water spouted out in a finger-thick stream.

Dolph finally gained the top of the hill, the gunman still firing intermittently at him. He knelt beside Barnhart, his heart hammering from the hard, fast climb. He wiped the sweat from his face onto his sleeve. Then he tilted the punctured canteen to the captain's lips. His heart sank. There was hardly a good swallow left in it for the wounded man.

It seemed forever before the sun reached the midpoint and began to slope downward again.

The heat was thick, and a swimming heat haze blurred the distant hills. Hunger gnawed at Dolph's stomach, and thirst swelled his tongue.

Captain Barnhart had passed into a dreamy subconsciousness. In town, with a doctor to take care of it immediately, his wound might not have kept Barnhart out of the saddle long. But out here in the sun, without care, without water, it was something else. There was a big chance now that Barnhart would never get off this hill.

Tommy had gotten hold of himself somehow. The haunted hollowness was still in his eyes, but he was doing what little had to be done, and most of it on his own initiative.

Yet, when Dolph asked him to check his gun, Tommy shrank away from it.

It was sometime early in the afternoon that Clayton came forth with his proposition. He came a-horse-back, reining in at the foot of the hill. His hand was up in the sign of peace.

"Listen, Dolph," Chasteen called, "it looks like we got a trade to make. You need water, and we want that money. Now we got plenty of water. We'll let you have it if you'll give us those bags."

Dolph thought for a long time before he gave his answer. He saw the quick anger strike Chasteen. Then the outlaw shrugged. "It's your choice, Dolph. You're never getting down off that hill as long as you've got that money."

Dolph watched him pull the horse around and ride away. He licked his cracked lips and realized how desperately dry he was.

*George,* he murmured, *where are you?*

It was watching the captain that did it. Dolph finally could stand it no more. It was one thing for a lawman to die a quick death in the line of duty. He might expect that at any time. It was quite another for him to lie in prolonged agony just for two pairs of saddlebags and a leather grip full of greenbacks.

Resignedly Dolph got to his feet. He picked up the

saddlebags and flung them across his shoulder. He took hold of the leather grip.

Tommy was watching him woodenly. "You think they'll really make a trade?"

Dolph shrugged. "Can't tell. But we've got to take the chance." He glanced at the boy's gun, lying on the ground. "Better pick it up, Tommy. You're going to have to cover me, in case there's a trick."

Tommy picked it up again, his face twisted in loathing. "Dolph," he grated, "if it comes to shooting . . . I'm afraid I can't."

Dolph's mouth was hard. "You'll have to!"

He worked his way down the hillside, the heat of the sunbaked rocks blistering through the soles of his boots. He paused at the bottom, where the horses had been picketed, and looked across at Clayton Chasteen and his men. They stood silently in a rough line, watching him. Dolph waited only a moment, then walked toward them. He watched only Chasteen as he narrowed the distance between them. The black stubble of beard on Chasteen's face was caked with dirt and the sweat that had trickled through it. His eyes were reddened wickedly by the heat of sun and wind, and the constant irritation of dust. His shirt was starched in dirty wrinkles from his sweat.

Grudgingly Dolph cast down the saddlebags and the grip. "You don't really think we could let you go, do you, Dolph? We got our money again. You think we'd let you out to bring a posse in here and trap us before we could get out?"

Cold fear tightened in the pit of Dolph's stomach. He let the canteens ease to the ground. His hand passed near the gun on his hip, but he knew better than to try to reach for it.

*Tommy!* he thought desperately.

"You made a deal, Clayton," he pointed out, his voice even. "Haven't you got any honor left at all?"

Then the real hatred began to worm into Chasteen's dirty face. His eyes narrowed briefly, and the corners of his mouth pulled down. "Honor? You're talking to me about honor, you night-crawling, wife-stealing . . ."

The hand with the gun lashed out. Dolph swayed back, pain exploding where the gun had struck him high on the cheekbone. An instant flash of fury made him drop his hand. But he caught it and raised it again. There was ice in his stomach, and death looked at him from the hate-filled eyes of Clayton Chasteen, and from the awesome bore of Chasteen's gun.

"Clayton," Dolph said quickly, hoping for time, "I didn't steal Lila from you—you drove her away. You made her so miserable she couldn't stand to be around you anymore. After that you had no right to her."

Chasteen's voice was like the cracking of a whip. "She's still my wife. Nobody takes anything that belongs to me."

Chasteen's hand tightened convulsively on the gun. Then he relaxed it momentarily, a twisted grin crossing his stubbled face. "I taught her the other night. Now I'm fixing to teach you, Dolph Noble."

Dolph's heart bobbed up as Chasteen's gun suddenly steadied.

The slap of a .45 echoed across the hills and bounded back like a clap of thunder. Chasteen buckled, his eyes sightless before he crumpled in a heap on the rocky ground.

Dolph glanced at him only a split second, long enough to know he was hit. Then he jerked his own gun and put a bullet through the outlaw at Chasteen's left before the man could free his holster. With one quick step forward, Dolph swung the gun barrel upward and down across the temple of the other man. He whirled to face the rest of the outlaws. The sudden, sharp turn of events had caught them up in panic. Only one man had drawn his gun. Dolph leveled a shot at him and saw the outlaw drop like a sack of grain.

There was no fight left in those who remained. Their wits had shattered in the brief span of seconds when death had thundered down among them. They stood wide-eyed, staring into the smoking muzzle of Dolph's gun, and wincing against the biting smell of gunpowder that drifted among them and lifted lazily upward into the brassy sky.

Tommy Noble eased down the hillside to stand by Dolph. His young face was drained white. He looked at Chasteen, then quickly turned away. Dolph thought the boy was going to be sick. But Tommy got hold of himself.

"That was a real shot, Tommy," Dolph said quietly. "I don't think I could ever have done it at that distance."

Tommy's voice wavered. "I wedged the gun between two rocks. It had to hit him." Desperately he added, "But I didn't really want to kill him, Dolph, I *had* to, that's all."

Dolph nodded, his voice just above a whisper. "I know, Tommy. That's how it is when you're a lawman. Sometimes you've got to do things you'd never do if the choice was your own."

Tommy pondered that for a long time, his face knitted. Then, without a word, he took the Ranger badge off his shirt and dropped it on the ground.

Most desperate of the captured men was the lawyer Danforth.

"Sheriff," he pleaded in a wild, cracking voice, "this is all a terrible mistake. I don't belong here. I was kidnapped, dragged here. Look," he begged, his hands shaking, "there are thousands of dollars in that grip. They're yours, if you'll just give me a horse and let me get out of here."

Brant Lawton's face twisted in disgust. "Shut up," he roared at the quavering lawyer. "You took your chances like the rest of us, and you lost. Now you'll at least stand up to it like a man."

But Danforth couldn't. He collapsed to his knees and sat there in helpless desperation, his plump body trembling.

Less than half an hour later George Castleberry came riding up with Andy Biederman and nearly a dozen men. His old eyes took in the whole story in a three-second sweep of the hill.

"Got so it was easier to trail a hawk's shadow across a lake of water than it was to keep up with you," he said. "It was the shots that brought us on in. How bad hurt's the Ranger?"

"Bad enough," Dolph said. "But I think he'll make it now. We'll have to haul him in on the buckboard."

They buried the dead beneath a tall mound of rocks. Then the surviving outlaws were put on horseback. Danforth raised some Cain about it, but it did him no good. All the way across the rough country and back to town, he rode in the rear, just in front of the last posseman, bouncing miserably in the saddle.

Tommy Noble, when the posse arrived, walked off a little way by himself. He pulled the gun out of his holster and hurled it as far as he could across the rocky ground.

A bleak misery in him, Dolph Noble stood on the railroad station platform and looked far down the track to where it curved back behind the distant hill. He could see the gray smoke begin to rise there.

He turned back to Lila Chasteen, who sat stiffly on a platform bench. Her black formal traveling dress looked hot and uncomfortable, but good manners took little heed of a woman's comfort.

"I'm going to miss you, Lila," he said.

She smiled at him, a quick smile that failed to cover up the sadness misting her dark blue eyes. "Maybe not too much, Dolph. You won't have time, what with the preparations for Tommy's and Susan's wedding. I'm going to hate to miss it. It will be the biggest Twin Wells ever had." Then, in all seriousness, she asked, "What were you and John Lane arguing about? Whatever it was, he walked away awfully disappointed."

Frowning, Dolph studied the splintered planks of the platform. "He was wanting me to hurry up and file for sheriff again. The deadline is today."

Her eyes looked levelly at him. "And you told him no?"

"I told him I'd had the office long enough. I told him that after all that's happened, I owed it to you, and to myself, to turn the job over to somebody else."

She said pointedly, "But there is no one else, is there? No one but Rance Ostrander."

Dolph's fist tightened. "You're right. He's the only one who's filed."

"Dolph," she said evenly, "you know he has to be beaten. A sheriff like him could ruin this town. You could beat him, easily." Her voice lowered. "You've been a lawman so long now, Dolph, that you'll never really be anything else the rest of your life, no matter how hard you try. So why don't you admit it to yourself?"

Dolph touched her arm. He told himself that he hadn't really wanted to run for office again, that he had wanted to quit. Yet somehow her words brought him relief.

"You're asking me to file?"

She nodded. "Yes, Dolph."

The train roared into the little station and stopped for its brief moment to load and unload mail and passengers. His big hand still gripping Lila's slender arm, and his heart beginning to beat faster, he watched her trunk being loaded onto the baggage car.

Desperately Dolph tried to frame the words he wanted to say. "Lila," he managed finally, "when you think enough time's passed to be right and proper, you can send me word. I'll be there on the first train, if you still want me."

She turned to him and melted against him, her warm cheek flat against his broad chest. "I'll want you, Dolph."

Dolph stood alone on the station platform and watched until the train was only a speck on the horizon, its trail of smoke disappearing into the summer sky. A few months—that wouldn't be so long.

At last he looked back over his shoulder toward the lowering sun. The day would soon be over. If he was going to file, he'd better be getting it done.

He looked down at the silver star on his shirt. He polished it with his sleeve, an eager smile beginning to flicker on his face. If it was a campaign they wanted, he'd give them one. He turned then, and headed back toward the sheriff's office in a quick, sure stride.